"Absolutely delicious! This is the triple cream of the crop: a charming heroine, a deceptively cozy little town, and a clever cast of characters. This is more than a fresh and original mystery— Aames's compassion for family and friends shines through, bringing intelligence and depth to this warm and richly rewarding adventure."

—Hank Phillippi Ryan, Agatha Award–winning author
of *The Other Woman*

"The charm of the story is greatly enhanced by a very rich cast of characters." —*Booklist*

"Avery Aames delivers another deliciously fast-paced, twisty mystery filled with lovable, quirky characters and Charlotte's delightful attempts at amateur sleuthing. Come sample what Fromagerie Bessette has to offer. I guarantee you'll be back for more."

—Julie Hyzy, *New York Times* bestselling author of the
White House Chef Mysteries and the Manor House Mysteries

"Fans of Aames's *The Long Quiche Goodbye* will be just as pleased with the latest mystery . . . Settle in with a nice cheese, a glass of wine, and enjoy *Lost and Fondue*."

—*Lesa's Book Critiques*

The Long Quiche Goodbye

Agatha Award Winner for Best First Novel

"Avery Aames's delightful debut novel . . . is a lovely Tour de Fromage. It's not just Gouda, it's great!"

—Lorna Barrett, *New York Times* bestselling author

"A delicious read. Charlotte Bessette is a winning new sleuth, and her gorgeously drawn world is one you'll want to revisit again and again. More please."

—Cleo Coyle, *New York Times* bestselling author
of the Coffeehouse Mysteries

Berkley Prime Crime titles by Avery Aames

THE LONG QUICHE GOODBYE
LOST AND FONDUE
CLOBBERED BY CAMEMBERT
TO BRIE OR NOT TO BRIE
DAYS OF WINE AND ROQUEFORT

Days of Wine
and Roquefort

AVERY AAMES

BERKLEY PRIME CRIME, NEW YORK

THE BERKLEY PUBLISHING GROUP
Published by the Penguin Group
Penguin Group (USA) LLC
375 Hudson Street, New York, New York 10014

USA • Canada • UK • Ireland • Australia • New Zealand • India • South Africa • China

penguin.com

A Penguin Random House Company

DAYS OF WINE AND ROQUEFORT

A Berkley Prime Crime Book / published by arrangement with the author

Berkley Prime Crime Books are published by The Berkley Publishing Group.
BERKLEY® PRIME CRIME and the PRIME CRIME logo are trademarks
of Penguin Group (USA) LLC.

For information, address: The Berkley Publishing Group,
a division of Penguin Group (USA) LLC,
375 Hudson Street, New York, New York 10014.

ISBN: 978-0-425-25555-1

PUBLISHING HISTORY
Berkley Prime Crime mass-market edition / February 2014

PRINTED IN THE UNITED STATES OF AMERICA

10 9 8 7 6 5 4 3 2 1

Cover illustration by Teresa Fasolino.
Cover design by Jason Gill.
Interior design by Laura K. Corless.

To every single person in my family.
You fill my heart with joy.

ACKNOWLEDGMENTS

Your success and happiness lies in you. Resolve to keep happy, and your joy and you shall form an invincible host against difficulties.

—HELEN KELLER

First and foremost, thank you to my family and friends for loving me and understanding the hours and focus it takes for me to write a book. I'm nuts, yes, but you all knew that. Thank you to my sweet lifelong friends, Jori and Carol, for your support. Thanks to my talented author friends, Krista Davis, Janet Bolin, Kate Carlisle, and Hannah Dennison, for your insight and words of wisdom. Thanks to my brainstormers at PlotHatchers. Thanks to my blog mates on Mystery Lovers' Kitchen and Killer Characters. And thanks to the Sisters in Crime Guppies, a superb online writers' group.

Thanks to those who have helped make the Cheese Shop Mysteries a success: my fabulous editor, Kate Seaver; Katherine Pelz; Marianne Grace; Kayleigh Clark; and my cover artist, Teresa Fasolino. I am so blessed.

Thank you to my business team. You know who you are!

Thank you librarians, teachers, fans, and readers for sharing the world of a cheese shop owner in a quaint, fictional town in Ohio with your friends.

And last but not least, thanks to my cheese consultant Marcella Wright and my wine consultant Keith Mabry. I love research; you guys make it that much more fun!

Anything worth having is worth suffering for, isn't it?
— Days of Wine and Roses, J. P. Miller

CHAPTER

"Get a move on, Charlotte Bessette," I muttered. Time and I were not fast friends. On any given day, I felt like I was behind. Rags, my sweet Ragdoll cat, twitched his tail and meowed, the little taskmaster. When my cousin Matthew and his twins moved out a few weeks ago, I made a pact with myself to refurbish each of the rooms in my Victorian home, one at a time, after work at Fromagerie Bessette and on weekends. I had a to-do list so long that it would make an obsessive person nuts. Me? Okay, I was nuts.

Seeing as many tasks were going to be messy, I had decided to convert my rarely used garage into a workshop. But before tackling the job, I needed sustenance. I stood in my kitchen preparing an appetizer that was fast becoming one of my favorites: Charlotte's Nirvana. To make the appetizer, I chose a sliver of an heirloom tomato, a hearty slice of San Joaquin Gold, which was a buttery, Cheddar-like cheese, and a portion of prosciutto. I stacked the trio on top of sourdough slathered with homemade pesto and cut it into bite-sized pieces. I popped one into my mouth, set the rest on a platter, covered them with a checkered napkin, poured a glass of water, and with Rags trailing me, traipsed to the garage . . . workshop.

The space teemed with books and boxes filled with discarded clothing bound for the homeless shelter. My mountain bike and cross-country skis—neither used in well over a year—hung on the wall. A sizable wine cooler that contained nearly sixty bottles of wine, all recommended by my savvy cousin, stood in the far corner and hummed with energy. I set the snack on a red metal cart that held my tools, then pushed everything from the center of the garage to the sides and laid out a tarp. Cool air whistled through the opened windows and the pedestrian door to the garage, but I was too revved up to care.

I moved the Tiffany desk lamp, Chippendale side tables, and antique desk from the office to the workshop with a dolly. Matthew had promised to help me repaint the office; meanwhile, I intended to repair the furniture. Rags paraded beside me. He tilted his chin with curiosity. I said, "Relax, buddy, I'm not going anywhere."

The secretary desk was first on my makeover agenda. My great-grandfather on my mother's side had purchased the desk in the early 1900s. Sometime between then and now, someone had given the desk a coat or two of murky brown paint—why was beyond me.

Intent on restoring the desk to its original beauty, I set a can of stripper and a stack of sanding paper on the tarp. Next, I donned a pair of gauntlet gloves to keep my hands from becoming shoe leather, and I strapped on a pair of goggles. Using a power screwdriver, I disassembled the desk. I placed the organizer cubby, carved legs, and dovetail drawers on the tarp, and then eyed the desktop.

"I'll sand the belly first," I said to Rags. He mewed his assent.

Carefully balancing the desktop against my legs, I flipped it on its edge and lowered it to the tarp. As it landed, dust poofed into the air. When the dust settled, I spied a hidden compartment on the underside of the desk. I pushed up my goggles and wiggled open the drawer, expecting to find nothing more than a nest of spiders. Excitement rushed through me when I caught sight of a stack of letters tied with gold ribbon. Whose were they?

The single overhead garage light was not enough illumination to do the letters justice. I plugged in the Tiffany desk lamp and switched it on.

Rags nuzzled his head beneath the hem of my tattered jeans and purred: *Tell me. What did I help you discover?*

I removed my gloves and lifted the stack of letters. I plucked the topmost and unfolded it, mindful that the stationery was delicate. My heart snagged in my chest as I scanned the words: *missing you . . . adore you . . . be together soon.*

Rags yowled.

"It's a love letter from my father to my mother," I explained. "When Dad had to go to an education convention." As a school principal, my father had traveled often to keep up with the trends. He had given my mother the same assurances that Jordan, the love of my life, had given me weeks ago. Jordan was involved in a WITSEC trial in New York, giving his testimony to put criminals away, and he might be away for a long time, but he promised we would be together soon.

Not soon enough.

Rags flicked me with his bushy tail.

"You're right. If I take the time to read all the letters, I'll fall behind on my project, not to mention I'll wind up a mess of tears."

Reluctantly, I inserted the love letter back into the stack with the others, but I didn't return the packet to the drawer. I grabbed a pair of Tupperware boxes, emptied them of nails and screws, dusted them with a clean rag, and deposited the letters into them. I sealed the containers and set them high on the shelves that held the rest of my tools and rags. I would read the letters another day, when I was stronger and not aching with loneliness.

"It's back to work we go," I sang while lifting Rags with both hands, my thumbs tucked beneath his forearms. I kissed

him on his nose and mismatched ears. Then I hooked him
over my shoulders. He loved being carried like a rag doll, as
many of his breed did, hence the name. He chugged with
contentment.

Better a cat's love than no love, I mused.

For a half hour, I applied stripping fluid with a paintbrush,
scraping occasionally with a curved-edge scraper when nec-
essary. The spindles would be the hardest to clean. I shaped
a wooden dowel into a sharp tool to work the grooves. I had
purchased a sanding cord for the tightest turnings. When my
fingers ached from cleaning the main body of the desk, I
took a break. I plucked an appetizer from the plate atop the
tool cart and downed it in one bite. After savoring the salty
goodness, I quickly ate a second. Heaven. Rags begged for a
taste of cheese. I obliged, although I never let him have more
than a fingernail-sized portion. Then I re-covered the platter
with the napkin, hoisted the sander, and returned to work.

I was lost in a world of my own when I felt Rags grumble.
Glancing up, I noticed the silhouette of a man on the shelving; his arm was raised. I whirled around, brandishing the
sander like a shield. Rags leaped to the floor.

"Whoa, cuz." Matthew backed up, arms raised, a goofy
grin on his handsome face. "It's just me bearing gifts."
He offered the bottle of wine he carried. "Bozzuto chenin
blanc." Bozzuto was a local winery north of the town of
Providence. "It's a lively wine, offering fine concentration
and balance."

"Sounds delish."

"And the sweetness of the wine won't be overcome by the
pungent flavor of any cheese."

I took the wine, admired the artistic label, and set the
bottle on a side table. "To what do I owe—" I glanced at
my watch. Nearly seven thirty. "Oh my. Time got away
from me."

"You and your projects." Matthew grinned as he ran his
fingers through his tawny hair, which was in dire need of a
trim.

"Is she here?"

"Right outside." He leaned out of the garage and beckoned.

Seconds later, Noelle Adams entered. "Hello, Charlotte."

I had met Noelle last month at Matthew's wedding. Willowy, with classic features, she reminded me of a French movie star, the kind that could make the hardest-hearted man swoon. She was certainly working her charms on my Ragdoll cat. He rubbed Noelle's calfskin boots with fervor.

"Hi, Noelle." I fingered the scarf I had tied around my head to prevent sawdust from sticking to my hair. "Sorry about the mess."

"Forget it. Matthew warned me. And don't fuss. You look great."

"Yeah, right."

"You do. Fresh and natural, the all-American girl. Don't forget, I know what you look like in a fabulous gown." Noelle hoisted the strap of her purse higher on her shoulder and bent to scratch Rags's ears. "Hello, gorgeous. Marry me?" Rags rumbled with motorboat intensity, the traitor. After a second, Noelle stood and tugged at the ecru wool serape she had draped dramatically over her shoulders. "What a great place you have, Charlotte." Even her voice was deeply sensual, like fine wine rolling over the tongue. "It's so nice of you to let me stay with you."

A contemporary of Matthew's, Noelle used to be a sommelier that offered her expertise to famous restaurants in Cleveland, Chicago, and New York. Recently, she had been hired by the local Shelton Nelson Winery to help them create buzz about their business. I had offered her the guest room because the inns were full up with pre-Thanksgiving events in town, and Matthew's place was jammed with the twins, the dog, and mounds of unpacked boxes. The cottage Noelle had rented wouldn't be ready for a couple of weeks.

"Matthew said you were tweaking a few things around the house." Noelle's eyes sparkled with amusement. "Perhaps I could help. I see you mean business." She lifted the pencil-sharp dowel and sanding cord. "I've done some refinishing before. My paps was a master builder."

"You don't have to—"

"But I'd love to. I'm willing to work for my bed and board, and it'll help me stay grounded. You know what they say about busy hands." Noelle smiled with warmth that would melt icebergs. "I feel like my feet haven't touched earth for days. I've been flying around the Northeast meeting all my former contacts in person to tell them about the career change."

To snag her, the Shelton Nelson Winery must have offered her the stars.

"However, I should unpack and change before tackling this project." Noelle fingered her sheath. "These aren't exactly my furniture-stripping togs."

"I'd help, too," Matthew said, "but I've got to split. PTA meeting. I put her suitcases in the kitchen." He kissed Noelle and me good-bye.

I led Noelle back to the house, hoisted her two small suitcases, and guided her up the winding mahogany staircase. The wood creaked beneath our weight. I sighed. The steps, too, were on my to-do list.

"Love the chandelier," she said about the grape motif fixture hanging in the foyer.

I adored everything about my home, from the Necco candy–style tiles surrounding the dormer windows on the exterior to the bay windows, quaint kitchen, and built-in shelves inside. I swung back the door to the guest room. "This will be your room."

"Mm-m-m." Noelle inhaled. "It smells good in here."

My throat clogged with emotion. Even though I had turned the twins' bedroom into an adult space, and I had decorated for Thanksgiving with gourds, colorful fall foliage, and homemade pumpkin-scented candles, I could detect the girls' youthful fragrance.

"The room is so pretty and quaint," Noelle continued. I had added a patchwork quilt, lace runners, brocade drapes, and a gold-based lamp with gold shade, which sat on a turn-of-the-century writing desk. "It's just like"—she hesitated—

"when I was a girl growing up in Cleveland. I . . ." She let the sentence hang. I didn't press.

I set Noelle's overnight-style suitcase on the bed and the other on a luggage rack, and then opened the doors to the closets. "Make yourself at home. There are lots of hangers. And the drawers in the bureau are empty."

"I only brought the basics—movers are hauling the rest." She placed her cell phone and a bright pink iMac computer on the desk, and emptied her overnighter onto the bed. As the contents spilled out, she giggled. "Who am I kidding? Maybe I did bring all of my worldly goods." The items were varied—a chic leather briefcase, a silver corkscrew with a sweetheart handle that had been given as a table favor at Matthew's wedding, a book of wine references, two personal leather-bound booklets, a Montblanc pen, a Nikon camera with multiple lenses, and toiletries.

"Are you nervous about starting the job?" I asked as Noelle unzipped her other suitcase and removed clothes draped in plastic dry cleaner bags.

"Absolutely. I want to make a good impression."

I didn't think she would have to work too hard. Miss America would have a tough time competing with her.

"So much is at stake." Noelle pressed her lips together; her face clouded over.

"What exactly will you be doing for Shelton Nelson?"

"Hmmm?" She looked in my direction. "My job. Right. He wants me to get the word out about his white Burgundies. An interview piece in *Wine Spectator* wouldn't hurt."

"Can you do that?"

"I'm sure going to try. White Burgundies are unusual to find in this climate, but Shelton's done a lot of prep work to the soil, and he keeps the vineyards heated to prevent frost. He also ships in grapes from a few California vineyards. No shortcuts for him, he says." Her mouth quirked up. "If I can get some of my former clients to start touting the Burgundies, word of mouth plus a dose of passion will sell them to the general public." She removed elegant suits from her suitcase and hung each carefully in the closet. "I'll be hosting an auction to start the buzz. Among my other duties, I'll be guiding personal tours for collectors and throwing some fabulous multicourse dinners."

According to Matthew, Noelle was at the top of her game as a sommelier, yet she had wanted a change of pace. She had met Shelton Nelson a few months back at a tasting of his wines, and suitably impressed, had fashioned the job for herself. She had asked Matthew to tell Shelton that he would be an idiot not to hire her.

"I have to admit, I'm a little wary about being accepted by Shelton's daughter and the manager of the winery," Noelle said. "Both have been, how can I put it nicely, a little stand-offish."

"Change isn't easy."

"You can say that again, sister."

After she stowed her toiletries in the adjoining bathroom, I said, "Let's get something to eat before we do anything in the workshop. I'll throw together a fall salad with toasted pumpkin seeds and some local chèvre. Do you like cheese?"

"Adore it. All kinds. I'm most fond of triple creams. They're sinful." Noelle dressed in jeans and a long-sleeved tee shirt that said: *Life is too short to drink bad wine!* and we retreated to the kitchen. "By the way, I've heard great things about Fromagerie Bessette. The locals call it The Cheese Shop, right? I can't wait to visit and inhale the aromas."

"We'll go first thing in the morning."

Over our light dinner, I listed all the fun things to do in and around Providence in November, like hiking along Kindred Creek, taking an Amish tour, or visiting the nearby city of Columbus to see the Ohio Historical Center and the Center of Science and Industry.

"Locally, there's also the Providence Playhouse," I said. "Usually the theater puts on an eclectic array of productions, but right now, my grandmother is directing a Thanksgiving Extravaganza. Matthew's twins and their schoolmates will be reenacting the first Thanksgiving. And then there's the

Thanksgiving Parade. You'll see people decorating the streets around the Village Green for the next few weeks."

"Sounds fun." Noelle promised to attend both.

An hour later, I made a dessert platter of crisp apples and slices of Roquefort, grabbed two Riedel wine tumblers and the bottle of chenin blanc that Matthew had brought, and we returned to my makeshift workshop.

"This cheese is deliciously smoky." Noelle licked remnants off her fingertips. "Cow's milk?"

"Sheep, aged in the Combalou Caves of Roquefort-sur-Soulzon."

"There's some European law, isn't there, about Roquefort cheese only coming from Roquefort?"

"Yep. It's called protected designation of origin," I said. "The laws about importing the cheese are strict, as well. The U.S. doesn't get nearly as much Roquefort as I would like. And the tariffs? Don't get me started."

Noelle laughed.

"It's best if eaten between April and October," I added. "After a five-month ripening period."

"So we're eating it a month late? It's still excellent, in my humble opinion." She downed another piece then wiped her hands on a cocktail napkin and eyed the secretary desk. "Tell me what to do, boss."

I pointed out the various boxes on the shelves and what they held: sandpaper, tools, paintbrushes, and rags. I mentioned that she should bypass the two Tupperware containers because they held my parents' love letters. I told her about finding them in the secret drawer.

"How romantic." Noelle's eyes grew misty. "I can't imagine finding a treasure like that after all these years."

Together we stripped the desk's legs. We held them over a drip pan while daubing them with paint remover, making sure junk didn't collect beneath the T-joint in the hollow of the leg. The buildup of paint wasn't as bad as I had expected. In less than an hour, the grain of the wood peeked through.

When we took our first break, Noelle picked up the

wooden dowel I had carved into a digging tool. "I remember
how my paps and I would sit on the stoop and whittle."

"Paps. Is that what you called your father?"

"No, my grandfather. My parents were . . ." She pursed
her lips. "Hmm, how to describe my parents?" Her last word
popped with sarcasm. "They weren't really there for me
and then—" She swallowed hard. "I'm not sure if Matthew
told you, but I was orphaned at the age of seven."

He hadn't, but I wouldn't have expected him to. "I'm an
orphan, as well. My parents died in a car crash." My throat
grew thick. "I was raised by my grandparents. They are salt
of the earth."

"You were lucky. I ended up in a Catholic dump after
Paps died of cancer." She swizzled the wooden dowel between her fingers. "The place wasn't all bad. I learned an
incredible work ethic from the nuns."

"How's that?"

"I hate pain. It only took a couple of penitence sessions on
my knees and extra duty scrubbing the bathrooms to get me
in line." She twitched her nose. "I don't think I'll ever erase
the scent of Lysol from my memory bank."

"How did you become involved in the world of wine?"

"When I left the orphanage at the ripe old age of eighteen,
I took up bartending. A patron at the restaurant offered me
the job of a lifetime to become a wine sales rep." She raised
an eyebrow. "There were strings, of course, and not being the
kind of gal who wanted to go down the dating-a-married-man
path, I quit, but not before I became an apprentice sommelier.
Turns out I have a great nose. Matthew was my mentor." She
pressed her palm to her heart. "I'm so happy for him and
Meredith. Wow. I can only hope to find their kind of love."

"Tell me about the dinners you'll be throwing at the winery," I said.

"We'll set them in Shelton's private tasting room. Have
you seen it?"

I hadn't, but I had heard about it. Like the cellar at Fromagerie Bessette, it was belowground, with nooks and cran-

nies, and a fabulous dining table made of preserved redwood that Shelton had picked up in California.

"We'll feature the wines from his famous private collection."

"Why did you decide to make a career change?"

Noelle contemplated the question then said, "I wanted a fresh new start. Away from Cleveland."

"Why not in New York or another big city?"

"Bigger isn't always better." Noelle's mouth screwed up like she wanted to say more, but she didn't.

* * *

The next morning I woke to the aroma of fresh coffee. Though I was an early riser, Noelle had beaten me to the kitchen. Rags lay nestled in her lap at the kitchen table when I entered.

"He's going to leave hair on your beautiful suit," I said. The woman had exquisite clothes.

"I don't mind. I can use the love."

Rags nuzzled her, his eyes so dreamy he appeared to have been drugged with a love potion.

"I've eaten," Noelle added. "So has Rags, which means we're ready when you are."

I had offered her a walking tour of Providence, followed by a visit to Fromagerie Bessette. She had a couple of days to sightsee before taking on her new job. I put together a quick piece of toast topped with fig jam and Rush Creek Reserve, a pasty raw cow's milk cheese, and I downed it in four bites. Divine.

A short while later, we left Noelle's BMW parked in the driveway and set off with Rags on a leash. He was one of the few cats I knew that had taken to one. Because he was a rescue cat, I think he felt safer and somehow protected.

No season thrilled me more than autumn in Providence. Spring was beautiful, with all the hope of new growth, but autumn stirred something deep inside me. The sky was a brilliant blue. Most of the leaves had turned gold or crimson.

Plumes of warm breath clouded the crisp air as I pointed out the Village Green, the Congregational Church, Timothy O'Shea's Irish Pub, and some of my favorite shops. Although Noelle had visited Providence on previous occasions, a refresher tour never hurt.

"It's so charming," Noelle said. "I love all the people walking around, and it's not even eight A.M."

"We have lots of strollers. Many of them congregate at our local coffee bistro, Café au Lait, or the Country Kitchen, a diner known for its homey comfort food."

"I'm game for either . . . both." She laughed. "And the decorations are so festive."

"Our town council, mainly my grandmother, loves the Thanksgiving holiday."

For the past week, local volunteers had been decorating for the Thanksgiving holiday, hanging *We Love Providence* banners at intersections and attaching gold and burnt orange flags to the lampposts. Soon parade stands would appear. There wouldn't be any floats in the parade, but nearly every farmer would arrive in a festooned carriage. The high school band, heavy on the brass, would march. Shops would line the sidewalks with their goods for inspection by the multitude of tourists. And my grandmother, our eloquent mayor, would give a rousing speech that would remind each of us how thankful we should be.

We purchased a couple cups of coffee from the diner and proceeded to the shop. When we entered, I spied Matthew polishing the wine bar in the annex. My assistant Rebecca, a young Amish woman who had left the fold years ago, moved about the kitchen at the rear of the shop fixing the morning's allotment of Roquefort Bosc pear quiches. In addition to cheeses, we offered a few seasonal savory delights. The Roquefort's pungency was a perfect complement for the firm, sugary fruit.

Noelle's eyes widened with delight. "Look at your beautiful display window."

"We get into the spirit for a number of holidays."

Our grandfather, who had given the shop to Matthew and

me, said appealing displays drew customers. In the front window, I had set out huge waxed wheels of Edam, each topped with a fluted vase and filled with orange-tinted silk orchids and berry branches. At the base of the vases, I had scattered pinecones and small apples. A variety of baskets held crackers and accoutrements like jams and dried fruits. The idea was that we would build similar baskets for customers, adding three cheeses to each. My suggestions for this week included three distinctly different cheeses: the ever-popular Pistol Point Cheddar from Oregon, a Salemville Amish Gorgonzola in the pretty blue box, and Snofrisk goat cheese, a tart, cream cheese–like delicacy. Of course, customers could ask for their favorites instead.

The telephone rang. I headed to answer. Before I reached the phone, the ringing stopped.

Seconds later, Rebecca raced toward me while flagging me down with pot holders. "Charlotte, phone! Hurry." She swatted me with the pot holders. Flour dusted the air. "It's *him*. He's on hold."

Him, as in Jordan?

Eager to talk to him, I shoved my cup of coffee into Rebecca's hand and sprinted to the office. Rags galloped to keep pace. I swooped up the telephone. "Hello?"

Jordan said, "Good morning, sweetheart." We had spoken a mere three times since he had left town. I couldn't contact him. He needed to call me on a secure telephone, probably one of those disposable kinds that had to be tossed after one conversation. "I miss you."

My soul wrenched with longing, but I forced myself to sound happy-go-lucky. "Ditto." Rags leaped onto the desk chair and craned his neck to listen in on the conversation. He adored Jordan. I bent and placed the receiver between our ears. Rags cooed his appreciation. "How's it going?"

"Slow," Jordan said. The attorneys forbade him from revealing any particulars of the case. For his safety. And probably for mine. Jordan said if word got out that I was his fiancée, I could be in jeopardy. The men he was trying to put away with his testimony were dangerous. They wouldn't hesitate to take me hostage. They could use my capture to coerce Jordan. The thought sent shivers down my spine. "I can't talk any longer today. Will you make sure my sister is okay?" His sister owned a pottery store in town and was also overseeing his farm.

"You know I will. Jordan—"

"Where are you?" a man yelled from the shop.

"Charlotte!" Rebecca screamed.

The front door slammed with a crack. Had Jordan's foes found me?

I bid Jordan a hasty good-bye, grabbed a pair of scissors off the desk, and bolted from the office.

A man appeared at the junction to the shop and the hallway leading to the office. He was a fury of red—red face, red hair, and red parka—and looked like he would burst into flames if I struck a match. "I know she's here."

"She, who?" I sputtered.

"Noelle!" he brayed. "I know you're here."

"Charlotte, do something." Rebecca hovered behind the man, oven mitts crisscrossing her chest.

What could I do? A pair of scissors was no match for this enraged bull. I snagged a slender tube of Genoa salami from the S-curve holder on the tasting counter and instantly felt like an imbecile. Perhaps the Three Stooges could pull off a salami fight. Not I.

"Noelle," the man yelled again.

The door in the kitchen that led to the wine and cheese cellar burst open, and Noelle emerged carrying a wheel of cheese and a bottle of white wine. "Boyd." Her face registered shock.

"How could you leave me?" Boyd walloped his chest with his knuckles.

"I didn't leave *you*." Noelle's nostrils flared. Her shock morphed into fury. "We split up months ago. I left Cleveland."

"I asked you to marry me."

"I never said yes."

"I want you to come back. I've changed."

"I haven't."

The barb struck home; the man flinched, but he quickly regrouped and moved toward her. "This is a small town."

"So?"

"You're not a small-town girl."

"Boyd . . ." Noelle set the cheese on the counter and gripped the wine bottle by the throat. I was impressed with her response. A whack with a wine bottle would have a ton more impact than a cylinder of salami. "You should go."

"What've you got up your sleeve?" he snarled.

"I'm warning you." She shot a finger at him with her left hand while raising the bottle over her shoulder with her right. "Stop harassing me. Get out of town, or else."

CHAPTER

2

Needless to say, Noelle's ex was not happy about her mandate. He stomped out of the shop and practically threw himself into the driver's seat of a metallic green Chevy Malibu parked in front of the diner. He sat there awhile, his fingers strangling the steering wheel, his smoldering gaze fixed on Fromagerie Bessette, but ultimately he started his engine and sped off.

An hour later, Noelle, who was perched on a stool behind the cheese counter, yawned. Who could blame her? She had been observing Rebecca and me tending to dozens of customers at The Cheese Shop. We had sliced and wrapped more than fifty pounds of cheese. If she had been a gossip hound, she might have found the chatter interesting.

"If you don't mind, I think I'll browse the stores," she said. She added that she wanted to commemorate her big career decision by buying mementos.

I mentioned the ex-boyfriend, but she assured me she knew Boyd well enough to know that he was gone for good.

At the end of the day when I arrived home, I was surprised to find Noelle had arrived before me. For a tall woman, she looked petite sitting cross-legged on the bed, her back to the entrance, her right arm moving as if she were scribbling notes on something. Her computer sat propped on the bed in front of her. A shopping bag nestled beside the desk. Only the reading lamp on the desk was illuminated.

I rapped on the opened door. "Hi. What are you writing?"

"Oh, nothing. Journals, notes, the usual." She closed the computer and, like a yoga pro, twisted at the waist as she set two leather-bound books and a pen on the bedspread. "Did you have a good day?"

"Fruitful. Plenty of customers, lots of sales. I wasn't expecting to see you until much later." She had made plans to have dinner at Matthew's house. "Have you eaten?"

"Grilled pork chops smothered in onions, roasted potatoes topped with Roquefort, and a crisp autumn salad. Delicious. But the twins have exams tomorrow," she explained, "so I left before dessert. They miss you by the way."

A lump formed in my throat. I missed them, too. I missed drilling them on multiplication tables and teaching them new recipes and reading in the attic and . . .

Buck up, Charlotte.

"That French Briard is something else," Noelle said.

"Isn't he?" I adored the way Rocket begged for treats and how, on our walks, he would bop his head against my thigh so I would take his favored route. But life marched on, like troops to war. He was the twins' dog; he belonged with them. I blinked back tears.

"What are you going to eat?" she asked.

"I'm skipping dinner and going right for dessert. I made a batch of Roquefort honey ice cream last week that will be perfect served with some honeyed pears and raisins. Add a glass of sauterne and I'll be good to go. What did you buy at the shops?" I indicated the gift bag.

"Oodles of goodies. Some hand-embroidered kitchen towels, decorative wine stoppers, and yarn. I was thinking of taking up crocheting."

"Good luck. I can't figure it out for the life of me, though

the shop owner next door to Fromagerie Bessette is a whiz."
I stepped a little closer. "Hey, have you been crying?" Streaks
of mascara trailed down Noelle's face. I hoped my tears
weren't catching. "Are you okay?"

"Fine." She swiped a forefinger across each cheek. "I'm a
little overwhelmed."

"No more Boyd encounters?"

"I told you. Don't worry about him. He's harmless."

Her innocent dismissal made me shudder. Boyfriends
weren't always harmless. I knew from personal experience.
"Want to join me for ice cream?"

"I'll pass. I've got to hit the hay. Tomorrow's the tour. The
day after that, it's down to business." Noelle slid off the bed
and toted the computer and journals to the desk. As she pulled
a shiny blue thumb drive from the USB port of the computer and hit enter to trigger the screen saver, the topmost
journal flipped opened.

Inside the journal were glossy squares that she had pasted
on the pages like scrapbook art. Intrigued, I moved closer.
"What are those?"

Noelle glanced from me to the opened book. "Wine labels. I'm a collecting fiend. Do you know how hard they are
to remove from bottles? Labels from old bottles are the easi-
est; modern labels have better glue. I adore the intricacies."
She stretched her arms over her head, yawned, and then
slapped the book closed. "You're coming with Matthew and
me to the winery, right? You promised."

I nodded. I hadn't visited the Shelton Nelson Winery in
ages. I looked forward to the tour.

* * *

"Welcome, ladies." With his leathery skin and guy-who's-
sat-in-a-saddle-all-his-life gait, Shelton Nelson reminded me
of old-time westerns. *Happy trails, to you.* He unbuttoned
his sheepskin jacket, then removed his cowboy hat and ruf-
fled his dirty blond hair. "This way." He led Noelle, Matthew, and me around the rustic winery's visitor room.
Afternoon sun blazed through the west-facing windows. A

few tourists tagged behind us, ears craned to glean some juicy tidbit of the vineyard's history.

"I started with a modest twelve acres," Shelton said. He hitched a thumb toward the first of a series of chronological photographs—this one of a small, lush plot of land with a modest home at the top of the bluff. "I thought I only wanted a retreat from my law practice in Cleveland, but then my passion grew and so did my holdings."

If Noelle hadn't divulged on the drive over that Shelton had been a litigation lawyer, I never would have guessed. He didn't seem to have the flair or doggedness, though she claimed he had been very good at it. He had won a number of hefty environmental class action lawsuits and made millions from them.

"Now, I own over five hundred acres," he went on. The next photograph depicted the growth of the estate. "Half of the acres are planted. We grow four different grapes. Only the finest, mind you. And we take no shortcuts. Making fine wine takes time."

Like a good cheese, I mused.

"I care more about the process of making wine and preserving the land than about how the wine tastes."

"Ha! Don't let him fool you," Noelle said. "His wines appear in many of the top restaurants in the U.S. He cares about taste."

"We make them without SO2," Shelton said.

"That means no sulfur dioxide," Noelle translated. "They're all natural."

"Shelton only uses horses to till the soil," Matthew added. "He believes that tractors smother the roots."

"It's all about the roots and how they search"—Shelton demonstrated by twisting his hand downward—"digging deep, as if they are on—"

"A quest," Noelle said.

"Exactly, darlin'. A quest to drink in the earth's flavor." Shelton paused in front of a landscape oil painting that could have hung in the Louvre. Blue skies and fluffy white clouds set the backdrop for deep green rolling hills tinged with the first golds of autumn. "*Home Sweet Home* is my flagship vineyard."

The door to the visitors' gallery swept open. A young woman, whom I recognized as Liberty Nelson, with heavily lined oval eyes and a catlike gait, strode in. Dust clung to her black denim outfit and riding boots. While removing her cowboy hat and shaking out her sleek black hair, she said, "*Home Sweet Home* produces our best grape."

A bookish-faced man with longish hair followed her inside while saying, "We have two other fine vineyards: *Sweet Darlin'* and *The Good Life*."

"But *Home Sweet Home* is our best, Harold," Liberty countered while shooting him a feral look that would have made the most stalwart man cringe. Harold didn't appear very stalwart. In fact, he looked emaciated. His tweed jacket and slacks hung on him as if he had lost quite a bit of weight. "By the way, Daddy." Liberty crossed to her father and pecked his cheek. "The workmen are doing a good job. I made the rounds."

"You mean, *we* made the rounds," Harold said. "Liberty insisted on riding the mare." His ropy neck muscles ticked with tension. It appeared he didn't like Shelton Nelson's daughter.

Missing the clash or choosing to ignore it, Shelton looped an arm around his daughter's back. "Noelle, you remember my daughter."

"Yes, we met on a previous visit. You're getting married soon. Congratulations." Noelle thrust a hand in Liberty's direction first. A wise decision. I suspected Liberty had her father wrapped around her little finger.

Liberty didn't reciprocate. Instead, she assessed Noelle, who had dressed in a chic silk sweater and matching skirt, pearl stud earrings, and a simple pearl necklace. Self-consciously, Noelle's hand moved to the collar of her sweater and then her throat.

Shelton continued, "And this is Harold Warfield, the vineyard's manager."

"Overseer," Harold said.

"I don't pay more for the title," Shelton joked.

Harold grinned. I was pretty sure he liked his boss. "We met, too, Miss Adams." He extended his hand to Noelle. His grasp appeared weak, not an I'll-show-you-who-is-in-power grip. In fact, he didn't seem to want to touch her. Was he a germaphobe? Perhaps an illness had caused the apparent weight loss. "Welcome," he said, though his tone held an edge, whether for Liberty or Noelle, I wasn't sure. "Matthew, good to see you. And you're Charlotte." He acknowledged me. "I've heard so much about Fromagerie Bessette. Sorry I haven't stopped in. My wife keeps me on a strict diet."

Aha. That explained the weight loss. I had met his wife on a number of occasions. She was nice, although somewhat timid. I remembered her saying that her husband and his college buddies were real foodies. She adored double-cream cheeses. The *men*, as she called them, preferred hard cheeses like Parmigiano.

"You shouldn't pass up the opportunity for a visit, Harold," Shelton said. "Charlotte and Matthew have done wonders with the place. There's a fabulous cheese counter, all the trimmings, and a wine annex that will knock your socks off. When you go, see if Matthew will give you a tour of the cellar, although"—he winked—"his cellar doesn't hold a candle to mine."

Matthew chuckled. "Not many can."

"Charlotte," Shelton continued. "I swear that Golden Glen Creamery River Cheddar with the pineapple finish you offer is going to be the death of me. I buy a pound every time I stop in the shop and devour it inside of two days."

In my head I heard my grandmother's voice whisper: *Everything in moderation*, but I kept mum. Shelton Nelson was probably stretching the truth. He didn't look like a glutton, unless he overindulged by taking in too much sun and fun. "Now, how about that tour?" he said.

"Mr. Nelson, wait." A striking dark-haired man, with a prominent widow's peak and a cocky swagger, burst into the room and jogged to Shelton. He pulled a tape recorder from the inside pocket of his natty plaid blazer and, in a British accent that bordered on Cockney, said, "Could you spare a moment? Ashley Yeats, *The Brit Speaks*." He tapped the butt of his pen against his lapel. "I would like to do an article on the winery." He paused. "That's not entirely truthful. I want to do a piece on you, actually. *From Sic 'em Lawyer to Kick 'em Winemaker*." He swept the air to display the imaginary title. "Catchy, don't you think? But I haven't been able to get through to you for approval. Your girl"—he paused—"your *assistant* is like the bloody Wall of Jericho. I think I need a trumpet."

Shelton cast an indulgent glance at his daughter. "My daughter can be stubborn."

"Oh, it's you?" The journalist offered Liberty a smirk. "Beg our apologies."

I didn't believe he was sorry in the least. Neither did Liberty, it appeared. She puckered her mouth like she had downed a handful of sour grapes.

"What's your name again, son?" Shelton said.

"Yeats. Ashley Yeats. Call me Ashley. *The Brit Speaks*. I heard about your renowned wine collection. I thought I'd come to town to check you out."

"When did you arrive?"

"Yesterday. I'm getting used to the time change." Ashley pocketed the recorder and whipped out a leather business card holder. Like a deft card dealer, he offered a white linen card to Shelton and Harold but shunned Liberty, who arched her back and wrinkled her nose with displeasure. To Noelle he said, "You're the new hire, aren't you? Sommelier extraordinaire. What was that wine you touted a month or so ago in *Bon Appétit*?" He twirled the pen in his fingers. "Testa Winery Meritage, wasn't that it? I believe you wrote, 'It opens with notes of blackberry and anise. With a little more air, you'll detect hints of crème brûlée.'" He added, "Great legs," though I didn't think he was referring to the wine. His eyes grazed Noelle from her calves to her face. "After interviewing Mr. Nelson, I would love to get your take on the health of the wine industry."

"We'll see." Noelle sounded tense.

Ashley held out a business card. Noelle didn't reach for it. Did she know the guy? I glanced at Matthew for corroboration. His forehead was pinched with tension.

The journalist turned back to Shelton. "So what do you say, Mr. Nelson?"

"I like you, son. You've got chutzpah. Sure, I'll give you an interview right after I show these nice folks around the spread. And call me Shelton."

"Daddy, no," Liberty said.

"No secrets here, darlin'. If I've told you once . . ."

". . . we are an open book," Liberty finished through tight teeth.

"Can I come along?" Ashley said. Cheeky didn't even begin to describe him.

"No, you may not," Liberty hissed. I was surprised she didn't stamp her foot. A pampered girl like her could probably drum up megawatt tears at the drop of a hat.

"In a while, son," Shelton offered. "In a while."

* * *

Single file, we followed Shelton out of the visitors' gallery and into the primary winery structure. In less than ten minutes, I realized the Shelton Nelson Winery rivaled many of the U.S. wineries that Matthew and I had visited on one of our cheese-and-wine-tasting ventures. In a word, SNW, as the locals called it, was spectacular. The facility, with two cellars—one strictly for oak casks and the other fitted with state-of-the-art stainless steel vats—was enormous. The tasting room was set up with an L-shaped bar, the far side for sampling red wines and the nearer portion for sampling whites. Shelves along the walls were filled with beautiful stemware, each glass etched with the SNW logo. Rotating book stands crammed with literature about the vineyard, the history of the grape, and wine-related cookbooks stood in the center of the room.

"This is Harold's office," Shelton said, indicating like a tour guide.

Harold's office was organized to perfection, with every file folder and earnings or growing chart in a tidy pile, and yet artwork that hung on the walls—a couple of Jackson Pollock–style oil paintings—hinted at a chaotic alter ego. Liberty's office of beige-on-beige was elegant yet forced. Something about the young woman cried out for personal expression. Shelton's offices were decorated with plush furniture and handsome antiques. His desk was super-neat with all the corners of the blotter, photographs, and boxed pen set squared. Beyond his desk stood a legal-length table that held plans for expanding the winery and printouts of inventory. On the walls hung photo ops of Shelton with Ohio's famous and infamous. His grin was infectious.

"What's in there?" Noelle pointed to the room that lay beyond a glass wall.

"A recording room. Daddy likes to do his own commercials." Liberty intoned, à la Shelton: "Shelton Nelson Winery. The finest flavors this side of the Mississippi."

Whenever I made the rounds of farms, I often listened to the radio. I had heard the commercials.

Shelton beamed like a proud papa. "Liberty had a hand in designing everything."

"If he doesn't watch out," Liberty teased, "I'll take over, too."

"Look at this." Shelton crossed to a mahogany credenza and picked up a vase painted with a depiction of the vineyard. He held it out for inspection. A date was scrawled at the bottom. "My ex-wife had this commissioned the day we signed the deed."

"It's exquisite," Noelle said.

Shelton set the vase down and said, "Psst. Let's have a little look-see, shall we?" Like a kid on a secret mission, he beckoned us with a finger and guided us outside the facility. Matthew and Noelle trailed him, then I followed. Liberty and Harold took up the rear. We went around a corner, down a dirt path, and beneath an arbor of leafless grape vines.

"Where are you taking us?" Noelle asked.

"My hideout, darlin'. Careful, the path is a little slippery with the recent rain."

"I love hideouts," Noelle said. "When I lived in the orphanage, I had all sorts of hiding places. I tried to keep the nuns on their toes."

Shelton chortled. "Were your hideouts well stocked with rare wine?"

"Hardly. I'd have been lucky with a dried piece of toast wrapped in a napkin."

When we reached a pair of ironwork-studded oak doors, Shelton rapped once and waited. He appeared perplexed, but after a moment, he chuckled. "Heh-heh. I'm fooling around. We don't need a secret knock to enter." He pulled a ring of keys from his pocket and slotted one into the lock on the door. After giving it a twist, he pressed the door open. It groaned with resistance. "Welcome to my lair. Drink in the scent as you enter."

Though double in size to the cellar beneath Fromagerie Bessette, Shelton's cellar was similarly decorated. Paintings of the Providence countryside adorned the walls; alcoves were lit with warm amber sconces.

As we passed beneath brick-and-mortar archways, Shelton said, "And now, the pièce de résistance. Voilà and welcome."

We entered a huge cave. My breath caught in my chest. It was spectacular. Massive hurricane candles decorated a long dining table. Rows and rows of wood-hewn cubbies holding bottles of wine filled me with awe.

Matthew wandered away for a moment then raced back and squeezed my hand. "You've got to see this."

Shelton heard him. "My mini-fortune? Yes, come see." He led us to an area protected by a heavy wrought iron gate with a latch handle and spear tops. The gate reminded me of something I had seen in an old church.

Noelle said, "I absolutely love this French motif." She caressed the floral scrolling. "If I recall, you said it was mid-nineteenth century, purchased from an old winery in Bordeaux."

"Purchased is a nice term. I'm pretty sure I stole it." Shelton laughed.

"The owner was desperate to sell," Harold said. "The economy had hit him hard."

Ticking off his fingertips, Shelton said, "If you look carefully beyond the gate, you'll see a couple of 1966 Pétrus . . ."

"Pétrus is from the sub-appellation Pomerol," Matthew whispered to me while rubbing his fingers together to mime *pricey*. Over the past few years, Matthew had taken great pride in educating me about wines while I tutored him about cheese. Pomerol, as an appellation, was as prestigious, if not more so than Pauillac. Basically, if Pauillac was Beverly Hills, then Pomerol would be the Bel Air of Bordeaux.

". . . a 1978 Château Lafite Rothschild," Shelton continued. "I have dozens more from Pauillac. In addition, I have Château d'Yquem and Château Haut-Brion Blanc."

I said, "The latter is from the southwest region of France, isn't it? That's home to five first growth wines." First growth, or *Premier cru classé*, referred to a classification of prestigious wines from the Bordeaux region that dated back to 1855.

"Actually," Shelton said, "Château Haut-Brion is in Pessac Leognan, which was originally part of Graves. Pessac would be a sub-appellation of Graves like Pauillac is a sub-appellation of the Medoc. Haut-Brion is the only classified *red* not grown in the Medoc."

Okay, so maybe I hadn't learned every fact perfectly. Rats. I wished I hadn't opened my big mouth. I hated sounding stupid. I could hear my grandmother's admonition: *If one is not certain of a fact, it is better to remain quiet and appear brilliant*. When would I learn?

"The Blanc, which I have," Shelton said, "is a dry white wine."

"Excellent in virtually any year," Liberty added.

"Noelle." Shelton snapped his fingers. "Perhaps we'll throw in a collection of six magnums of the Château d'Yquem for the auction. They're worth a pretty penny. In addition to the wine, we'll include a dinner at the winery. What do you think?"

"Magnanimous," Noelle said.

He chuckled. "Magnanimous . . . magnum. You're making fun."

"I'm impressed, Shelton." Noelle smiled. "There's a difference." She moved forward, strumming her fingers along the gate as if it were a harp. "How many bottles are in the cellar? Three thousand?"

"Good eye. Three thousand eighteen at last count, with room for up to five thousand."

Noelle cleared her throat. "Do you keep a register of all of them?"

"I do. Care to hold the Pétrus?" Shelton removed a single brass key that had to be four inches long from the pocket of his trousers.

"What the heck is that?" Matthew said.

Shelton chuckled. "Don't be intimidated, Matthew. I merely want people to gawk when I take it out to open the giant lock on these babies."

I was definitely gawking. It resembled a jailer's key from medieval days. Shelton slotted it into the gigantic keyhole. The gates groaned open.

"This way." Shelton entered and we followed. He pulled a bottle of Pétrus from a cubbyhole and handed it to Noelle.

"I don't see a speck of dust," she said. "Do you polish the bottles on a daily basis?"

"We have a good ventilation system," Shelton said.

Noelle cradled the Pétrus in her hands then handed it off to Matthew, who returned the bottle to its cubby.

"Notice the jeroboams of the finest champagne," Shelton said.

According to my brief education, a jeroboam held the liquid equivalent of four bottles of wine. There had to be at least twenty.

"I also have a number of bottles of Opus One," Shelton went on.

Matthew said, "Have you got any Schrader?"

"I do."

"Fabulous, isn't it? With rich, opulent notes of plum and spice."

"I also have a single bottle of Screaming Eagle."

"You don't." Matthew turned to me. "At an auction in 2008, a collection of six magnums of Screaming Eagle sold for five hundred thousand dollars. How did you get one, Shelton?"

"I have an influential friend in the Silicon Valley."

Noelle faked a yawn and whispered in my ear, "It's like watching boys on a playground saying, 'Show me yours, I'll show you mine.'"

I suppressed a smile.

"The Schraders' divorce is a curious story," Shelton said. "It resulted in two vineyards."

"Mr. Schrader limits production so he can boost his price," Harold said.

"That's exactly what Daddy's doing with our white Burgundies from *Home Sweet Home*." Liberty raised a finger. "Because they're as good as any from France."

Shelton shrugged. "Pshaw. They're not nearly as good as a Château d'Yquem." At least he had an ounce of humility.

Matthew cupped his hand and whispered, "With proper care, a Chateau d'Yquem can keep for a century or more."

"Wow," I said.

Shelton clapped his hands once. "To wow you properly, come to the winery next Friday, and we'll have a special dinner and tasting for twelve. You'll arrange everything for that, too, won't you, Noelle?"

"The dinner is on my agenda."

"Work with Charlotte on a menu. I hear she's a fabulous cook."

I felt my cheeks warm.

"I insist there be a cheese plate for dessert." Shelton pointed at me. "I'll trust your judgment on that, young lady. Include that Tuscan Tartufo, would you?" He tapped Noelle. "If you haven't tasted it, you absolutely must. Hints of mushroom. Almost heady when served with a glass of champagne."

Noelle scanned the area. "Um, Shelton, I apologize, but I need to find the loo."

"Let me show you the less clandestine route." Shelton led Noelle to a wall of gilded books, pressed a handle, and the wall opened up to a secret passage. "Up the corridor, to the right of my office."

"You dog." She punched his arm. "There's an inside entrance back to the main building?"

"It's very hush-hush." He nudged her to get a move on and then glimpsed his watch. "I'm sorry, everyone. We've got to wrap this up. I've got an appointment. I nearly forgot."

Minutes later, we reentered the corridor by Shelton's office. He gave us directions back to the visitors' wing and bid us a hasty good-bye.

As we waited for Noelle to rejoin us, Liberty cornered her father. "Daddy, a word." She herded him into his office. The door closed with a thud.

An instant later, Noelle appeared. "What's going on?" she asked.

"No clue," Matthew replied. "Let's—"

"No," Liberty shouted from behind the closed door. A fist pounded wood. Shelton's or hers, I couldn't be sure. "Daddy, you're not getting it."

He shushed her.

Though both lowered their voices, a few words filtered out.

Liberty said, ". . . lover . . . phony . . . financial mess."

"Can you make out what they're saying?" Noelle whispered.

"Sort of." My grandmother said I had the ears of an elephant. I listened harder.

Shelton responded with a string of words and, ". . . charted for disaster."

Somebody slammed something.

Shelton growled. ". . . always about money for you."

Liberty: ". . . label would you put on it?"

Shelton: ". . . nose . . . your mother."

Liberty: ". . . out of it."

Shelton: ". . . my business, not yours."

Liberty, loudly: "Yes, it is."

"Only when I die." They must have drawn near the door because the conversation started to link together.

Liberty said, "Noelle—"

"—is here to stay," Shelton finished. "Live with it."

"You're blind, Daddy."

Something ceramic crashed within the office. Seconds later, the door whipped open.

Liberty stomped past us without so much as a glance and strode down the hall. She disappeared in the direction of the tasting room.

Worried about Shelton, I peered into the office. He balanced on one knee as he picked up the pieces of the vase his ex-wife had commissioned.

Noelle covered her mouth with her fingertips. "They were arguing about me."

"C'mon," I tugged her elbow. "Handling family dramas is not in your job description."

Moments later, as I climbed into Matthew's Jeep, movement caught my eye.

Ashley Yeats was sneaking toward the secret entrance to Shelton's hideout. How had he figured out where it was? Had he followed us even though Liberty had told him he wasn't invited? Would he skip the interview with Shelton for a covert peek inside? I pitied the sap when Liberty caught him snooping. And she would. She was on the warpath. I was only sad that I couldn't stick around and watch.

CHAPTER

3

For the remainder of the afternoon, I kept busy at The Cheese Shop. There was plenty to do on a daily basis: inventory, refacing cheeses, sweeping floors, cleaning up displays, Internet PR, and so much more. On certain unglamorous days, like today, I could barely breathe. I dreamed of returning home and tuning out work by tinkering on the secretary desk—maybe even taking a private moment to read more of my parents' love letters. How I wished I had known my folks better. My grandparents had been wonderful caretakers, but what I wouldn't have given to have special memories with my parents carved in my mind: vacations, games, stories that were repeated year after year.

At six P.M., Noelle and I tucked into the renovation project with a vengeance. We sanded the top of the secretary desk for an hour. As I had hoped, the original wood was stunning.

At seven, I rose from the tarp to stretch my legs and back, then turned up the sound on the radio that I had brought out to serenade us. The rock group O.A.R., whose initials stood for Of a Revolution, was singing its popular single, "Heaven."

While at Ohio State University, I became a fan of the emerging rock group. They played the frat and sorority parties and became a cult hit. I knew the words to all of their songs.

"Are you certain you don't want to go to the theater with me?" I asked.

"I'm sure." Balanced on her knees, Noelle examined the screw attachment on the legs, which were still unattached. "I want to get this baby on its feet."

"I told you—"

"I know, I know. I don't owe you a thing, but I want to do this, and the music is nice." She sang along.

I joined her. When the song ended, I said, "Hungry?"

"Absolutely." Noelle set aside the table leg and scrambled to her feet while wiping her fingers on her black jeans.

From a platter of cheese that I had brought to the garage, I slipped a morsel of Beaufort into my mouth, savoring the moist, sticky rind and flavors of alpine flowers. Noelle opted for a slice of No Woman cheese, which was made by Beecher's Handmade Cheese in Seattle. The Cheddar-style goodness was a spicy tribute to the island of Jamaica and the Bob Marley song "No Woman, No Cry."

"After I finish up," Noelle said, "I think I'll take a hike."

"At night?"

"I like exploring in the dark. It's peaceful. I've got a flashlight in the glove compartment of my BMW. I could use the break. My official job starts tomorrow. After that I'll be so busy that I won't have time to investigate." She grinned. "Hey, wipe those worry lines off your forehead. I'll be fine. Really. A girl raised in an orphanage knows how to navigate in the dark. It'll be like I'm on a quest."

Beside the cheese platter sat a couple of glasses of Mendoza Malbec, a red wine with violet aromas and raspberry and currant flavors. Noelle picked up a glass and swirled the wine while assessing it at an angle. "Great legs."

"That's what that journalist said about you earlier," I teased.

"Ew, ick, bad memory." Noelle wrinkled her nose. "That put me off taking another sip. Probably better to keep a clear head. Instead, if it's okay with you, I'll throw together a grilled cheese." She took another bite of the No Woman cheese. "Mmm, how I love the aromas of allspice and cloves."

"Have at it," I said.

In less than five minutes, I showered and dressed in a sweater and comfy trousers. As I was exiting through the kitchen, I found Noelle crouched beside Rags in his wicker bed. She cooed a lullaby to him.

"You're getting spoiled, Ragsie," I said.

He gave me a look that said, *I deserve it*, and he was right. He did. He missed the twins and Rocket as much as I did.

* * *

When I arrived at the Providence Playhouse, the place was buzzing with energy. A dress rehearsal always generated excitement. While crewmen strung twinkling lights around the backdrop of the *Mayflower* and Plymouth Rock, my good pal Delilah—owner of the Country Kitchen Diner and current director of the Thanksgiving Extravaganza—was positioning twenty-plus children, each dressed in either a Pilgrim or a Wampanoag Indian costume, at specific places onstage.

When she was done, Delilah brushed her long, dark curls over her shoulders and planted her hands on her ample hips. "Perfect. Now, stand there and don't move." Her instructions came across loud and clear.

"*Chérie. Bonsoir.*" My grandfather beckoned me to the right wing of the stage where he had set up a buffet to feed the group. Savory aromas wafted from the fixings: turkey pizza, turkey-cranberry sliders, and turkey meatballs. My grandfather was a firm believer that turkey was not only for Thanksgiving dinner.

"You look *superbe*," he said and kissed me, *la bise*—the French tradition of a peck to one cheek and then the other.

"So does your meal, Pépère. *Vous étes un chef merveilleux.*" I pinched his cheek. He enjoyed when I complimented him about being a good cook. "What have you put on the pizza?"

"Turkey, chèvre, shallots, and my special seasonings.

Simple but tasty." He patted his generous stomach, which protruded over a well-stocked tool belt. "I will eat only one slice."

"Uh-huh," I said, disbelieving. He loved to nibble and was forever trying to control his weight.

"I have promised your *grandmère*. Oh"—he tapped his head and gestured to the far end of the table—"I made a gluten-free Italian herb pizza for Clair, and Rebecca brought two pear and Roquefort quiches from the shop."

I glanced around. "Where is Rebecca?"

"She left."

"Left?"

"She has a date."

"A date?" I repeated like a parrot.

"She and her boyfriend are no longer engaged."

"What?" Did my voice do a glissando?

"They wish to make sure they are well suited, so I am told." Pépère petted my arm.

"Whose choice was it to break up?"

"I would gather it was Rebecca's decision. She seems fine with the arrangement. Young love, it is sweet, *non*?"

I nodded. "Sometimes it can be bittersweet." Poor Ipo, the former fiancé. I would bet he was heartsick. He adored Rebecca.

"Speaking of love, your *grandmère* is in love with the new theater equipment." He jutted a finger. "Look."

On the left side of the stage, my irrepressible grandmother, dressed in black turtleneck, trousers, and tennis shoes, was slinging on a Peter Pan–style flying harness. A crewman tightened the straps.

"*Attention*." Grandmère, who seemed more than frazzled—her spiky gray coif was a little hairy-scary—clapped her hands sharply. "Gather round, *mes amis*. We will have a demonstration."

The children—which included my preteen nieces who weren't really my nieces; they were cousins once removed—broke from their spots onstage, all chattering with anticipation.

"Quiet, everyone." Delilah formed a T for *time-out* with her hands. The children mimicked her. "Let's pay attention to what Mrs. Bessette is going to show us."

Grandmère, who was finally accepting that she, as mayor of our fair city as well as theater manager and full-time fundraiser, wore too many hats, had ceded her director's hat to Delilah.

"Where is the duck?" Grandmère asked.

"Thanksgiving duck, step forward," Delilah said.

Pépère said, "Do you know turkey was not served for the original Thanksgiving dinner? The feast consisted of duck and venison and probably corn, onions, and squash."

I adored how much he knew about our culture. When he and my grandmother migrated from France to the United States, they adopted everything American. The history as well as the idioms.

"Yoo-hoo, Mr. Duck," Delilah called. "Where are you?"

"Here I am." A preteen boy in a mallard costume with green head and black and white tail feathers emerged from the rear of the pack of children. Tentatively he raised his hand.

"Don't look so scared. You'll be safe in this getup," Delilah said. "Did you see all the safety latches our talented crewman secured? Now, we'll raise you up like this. Watch." She gestured to a second crewman in the wings. The guy pulled on a rope that had a sizable sandbag attached to one end, and my grandmother rose slowly off the ground. "With a push, you'll sweep to one side and return." Delilah gave Grandmère a nudge.

"Whee-e-e-e!" Grandmère crooned.

All of the children cheered except the gawky boy, who looked pea green with fear and doubt.

My niece Amy, a spitfire of a tomboy, elbowed the kid. "If you don't want to do it, I will." She had been given the role of warrior counselor to the lead Indian, Massasoit. According to her, any role would be better than a warrior counselor—no lines. Like my grandmother, Amy was a ham at heart.

Delilah said, "All right, that's all the time we have for the demonstration. Let's take a dinner break so the crew can get back to work on the stage. Remove your costumes and wash your hands. We'll rehearse in street clothes afterward."

"I must return to the set." Pépère pulled a mini power drill from his tool belt and revved it.

"Aunt Charlotte." Clair, the younger of the twins by minutes, raced to me and threw her arms around my waist. Her Pilgrim hat fell to the stage. She looked up at me with the eyes of an old soul.

I stroked her silky blond hair. "I've missed you, too."

Amy scurried to join the group hug and then whipped off her Indian headdress and said, "Clair, I saw Daddy and Meredith by the food table. They've brought ice cream for everyone."

"Yay!" Clair clapped her hands.

"Dinner first." I wagged a finger as if I had control over them.

They scampered away, giggling, and Delilah joined me. Her skin glistened with perspiration; her eyes sparkled with delight. A former Broadway actress, Delilah had returned home to Providence when New York proved too tough. She took over her father's diner and found great pleasure there, but she yearned for a creative outlet. Directing, acting, and writing local plays had turned out to be just what she had needed.

"Your houseguest stopped in to the diner at lunchtime," Delilah said. "Nice gal. Good little journal writer. I enticed her with a grilled Swiss, bacon, fig jam, and scallions sandwich."

"You could entice me with that," I joked.

"Like you would come in on your own." Her mouth turned down in a frown. "You never call, you never write. With Jordan out of town, you've turned into a hermit."

I gave her the evil eye. "I work for a living. I'm tired at night. And I made it to girls' night out this week while you didn't. What were you doing on Monday anyway?"

"Taking a class."

"In what? Anatomy?" I teased.

"As if. I attended a writing workshop in Columbus. A four-week course. My love life is dormant."

"What about—"

"We broke up."

Was something in the air? First Rebecca and her beau, and now Delilah and hers? I vowed to be extra vigilant of my relationship with Jordan, except I was certain that absence made the heart grow fonder. I missed him so much.

"We weren't in sync," Delilah went on. "The age difference was a little weird. You were right."

"Me?" I gulped. "You didn't end it because of something I said, did you?" I would hate it if I were responsible for inserting a wedge into the relationship.

"No. It's . . ." She ran her fingers down her long neck. "Another time, okay?" She tilted her head. "Have you heard from Jordan?"

"Briefly."

"I'm worried about you."

And I was worried about her, but Delilah was one of those people that kept a tight rein on her emotions. I wouldn't pry. Not tonight, anyway. "Speaking of worried, Pépère was concerned about my grandmother flying across the stage."

"She begged me." Delilah held her palms out. "What was I to do? You know your grandmother. As stubborn as an ox. It wasn't like she was on a zip line sailing across a canyon."

"Hello-o-o." Meredith, my best-best friend, a sun-kissed beauty who appeared even younger since her honeymoon with my cousin, joined us. "You two are gossiping, aren't you? Don't leave me out." The three of us had been buddies since grade school. More often than not, Meredith had been the instigator in our wild childhood escapades, though no one would suspect that now. A schoolteacher and advocate for higher education, she followed rules to the letter.

I hugged her. "We were talking about Grandmère's flying turkey demonstration."

"Duck," Delilah corrected. "Flying duck. The first Thanksgiving—"

"Didn't serve turkey," the twins proclaimed as they walked past us carrying paper plates filled with dinner. The Thanksgiving Extravaganza, if nothing else, was teaching basic history points to the students involved.

"Charlotte, *chérie*." Pépère shuffled up. "I am so sorry to bother you. I am in need of my old drill. I lent it to you for your renovation project, remember? All of the drills at the theater have run out of power."

"Run out?"

"Do not get me started on the theater's paltry funds." He scruffed his thinning white hair in frustration. "We must finish tonight. When it comes to schedules, your grandmother is a little general." He did an imitation, nailing Grandmère and her finger-wagging, shoulders-swaying behavior. Meredith, Delilah, and I stifled smiles. "Please, do you mind fetching the drill from home? And, if you have them, would you bring some D batteries?"

Amy leaped to her feet. "Can we go with you, Aunt Charlotte?"

Clair bounded to her side. "Yes, can we?"

"I want to see our old room," Amy said. "And the attic where we used to drink cocoa and read books together."

"And I want to hug Rags," Clair added.

I eyed Delilah. "Will you miss a Pilgrim and an Indian for a half hour?"

She shrugged. "I'm sure we'll cope."

"First, bus your dishes to the trash." I pointed toward a garbage bin that my grandfather had wisely stationed at the end of the buffet table.

"I'll drive." Meredith said with a wink. "And I expect an update on gossip."

* * *

On the way home, I called Noelle, just in case she was still there, to warn her about the impending invasion. She didn't answer her cell phone. Minutes later, Meredith pulled to a stop in front of my Victorian. All the lights in the house, other than the porch light, were off. A dim light glowed in the garage. Noelle's BMW was parked on the right-hand side of the driveway.

Acting like they hadn't visited the house in years, the twins bolted from Meredith's newly purchased Chevy Tahoe and up the cobblestone path to the front door.

"It's so beautiful," Clair exclaimed.

"We've missed you, House," Amy cried.

"Wait for me," Meredith called as she unlatched her seat belt and dashed after them. "Charlotte, is the door unlocked?"

"No."

"Don't worry. You get the power drill. I'll use my key, and I'll make sure the girls don't drive Rags to distraction. By the way, I love the wreath on the front door."

"It was a gift from Grandmère. She and her Do-Gooder ladies are making Thanksgiving wreaths as a theater fund-raising project."

Meredith smirked. "What doesn't she do?"

"Slow down . . . Ever. Stay away from her if she's wielding a glue gun. It means she's recruiting."

"No argument here." Meredith laughed.

I traipsed down the driveway hoping that Noelle wasn't still slaving over the desk. She had done enough. The side door was ajar. As I approached, I didn't hear anything. No scraping old paint off wood, no oldies music.

The moment I stepped inside worry spiraled up the back of my neck and into my senses. Something wasn't right. There was a smell—metallic yet marshy.

"Noelle?" I called into the gloom. I flipped on the overhead light switch and gasped. The garage had been ransacked. Cabinet doors hung open. Boxes of nails and garden supplements lay upside down, their contents spilled on the cement floor.

Someone moaned.

I spun to my right. Inches beyond the secretary desk, which stood on its feet with its legs secured, I saw her—Noelle, lying on her side, her legs and arms at an angle. The heart-shaped corkscrew from Matthew and Meredith's wedding jutted from the hollow of her throat. Her chest moved; she was breathing . . . barely.

"Oh no." I rushed to her. "Noelle."

Her mouth moved. "Ch-h-h—" The beginning of my name. Barely a whisper.

"Yes, it's me. Charlotte."

Noelle licked her lips. "Hell's . . . key."

"Hell's key?" I repeated.

Her eyes fluttered. She inhaled sharply. "Ch-h-h—"

I gripped her hand. "Stay with me, Noelle. Stay with me."

But she didn't. Couldn't. Her body shuddered and went quiet. I didn't detect a pulse. Pressing on her chest wasn't the right thing to do, not with a puncture wound to her neck. I pinched her nose together and blew into her mouth. Nothing. I tried again. She didn't revive.

Yanking my cell phone from my purse, I stabbed in 911. A woman asked me to relay information. When I ended the call, my shoulders gave way and tears flowed down my cheeks.

Suddenly, another realization hit me. Whoever had killed Noelle could be lurking nearby. Was he in the vicinity? Had he run into the house? Were the twins and Meredith in danger?

Grabbing the screwdriver that lay near Noelle, I bolted from the workshop and peered into the yard. I didn't see anyone hiding in the shadows. The kitchen door was closed. I saw silhouettes of the girls and Meredith dancing in a ring-around-the-rosy pattern in the attic. Wouldn't they have screamed if a killer had run through the house?

I raced to the kitchen door. It was unlocked. I threw it open and called, "Meredith!" She didn't respond. The good news was that Rags didn't come tearing out of the house, which meant the killer, if he had entered, had fled. Door-to-door salesmen spooked Rags. Even so, I called again, "Meredith! Bring the girls downstairs right now."

"Ooh, are there shooting stars?" Amy said, her voice tinny over the pounding of galloping footsteps.

I tore to the street. No one was running away; there wasn't

even a neighbor walking a dog. A couple of parked cars stood across from Lavender and Lace, the bed-and-breakfast next door. The night was quiet. Deathly quiet.

I sprinted back to the garage, placed the screwdriver on the desk, and crouched by Noelle's side. I pinched her wrist to feel for a pulse a second time, hoping I had been mistaken the first time around, but I hadn't been. She was dead.

"Charlotte," Meredith appeared at the side door of the garage. "What's wrong?"

I jumped to my feet and darted to her. Over her shoulder, I saw the girls twirling on the grass, gaping with their heads tilted back at the starlit sky. Rags had nestled into a comfy chair on the patio.

"Noelle . . . She's . . . She's been murdered."

Meredith slapped a hand over her mouth and peered past me. "Is that a corkscrew?" She gagged and stumbled backward. "It's our wedding favor."

A siren pierced the air. Its wail grew louder.

The girls scurried to Meredith like baby chicks. "What's going on?"

"Nothing." I herded the girls away from the crime scene, back to the center of the grass. "Look up there." I pointed. "Count the stars in the Orion constellation." When they became rapt in the activity, I said to Meredith, "Noelle was alive when I found her. The killer must have just escaped." Guilt burned inside me. If only I hadn't left her alone. If I had arrived earlier. "Did you notice anything different in the house?"

"What do you mean?"

"Was the front door unlocked as you entered?"

"No. It was secure."

"Did you spot an opened window?"

"I wasn't looking."

The killer hadn't hurt my family. That was the one silver lining to an ugly storm cloud.

"Whoever killed her was searching for something," I said and explained the state in which I had found the garage—the overturned containers. "Did you go into the girls' room?"

"No, we bypassed it. The girls wanted to see the attic first, and then you yelled, and—" She paused. "Now that you mention it, the guest room was sloppy. I peeked in as we slipped past. Things hung out of the suitcase. A drawer was open. There was a pile of clothes on a chair closet. I turned a blind eye."

The killer had to have searched Noelle's things. Where else would he have found the corkscrew? Had he—or *she*, I heard Rebecca the TV crime junkie reminding me—come up empty searching in the guest room? Was that why he—or *she*—had scoured the garage? Why had the killer used the corkscrew? What significance did it have? A hammer or screwdriver would have been so much more convenient and lethal.

"Meredith, please keep the girls away from the garage," I said. "And call Matthew."

The blare of sirens pierced the night again. Louder. Closer.

I returned to Noelle. After I had left her to go to the theater, she must have changed clothes. Now, she wore a black sweater over her jeans and lace-up hiking boots. Had she ventured out? I moved closer. Mud clung to her boots. That must have been the marshy smell I detected when I first entered. Had she gone to Kindred Creek for her hike? Had someone seen her and tailed her to my house? Her ex-boyfriend, perhaps. She could have been wrong about him. He could have returned to Providence. What could he have been searching for? Noelle's last words were *hell's key*. What had she been trying to tell me?

CHAPTER

"We don't want to leave you, Aunt Charlotte." Amy threw her arms around my waist.

My nieces, Meredith, and I stood on the patio outside the kitchen. The cool night air cut through my trousers; sorrow pierced my heart. I tucked a strand of Amy's hair behind her ear. "I know, sweetheart, but it's time to go. This is adult stuff."

"Please don't make us." Clair held her hands in prayerful supplication to her chest. "You aren't safe."

Like they could do anything to protect me. I forced a smile. "Of course I am. With all these police around, I'll be fine."

Chief of police Umberto Urso and his deputies had arrived minutes ago. After I offered a quick recap of finding Noelle, they cordoned off the garage and ordered us to the patio. At the moment, they were photographing the crime scene. Occasional flashes of light flared through the garage windows. With each spark, my breath snagged in my chest.

A Ford Explorer tore into the driveway and screeched to

a halt. My cousin Matthew bolted from the SUV and dashed up the driveway. His face was flushed; his eyes, moist. Meredith hurried to him. They hugged for a lengthy moment and exchanged supportive kisses. Then Matthew jogged to his twins and crouched to meet them at eye level. He took hold of both of their hands. "Meredith is going to take you home."

"What about rehearsal?" Amy said.

So much for the twins wanting to be my bodyguard.

"Delilah and Grandmère understand." Matthew looked up at me. "They're so sorry to hear about . . ." He closed his eyes for a moment then opened them slowly. "It's all my fault. I encouraged Noelle to come here. To take the job. If she'd stayed in Cleveland or taken any of the other opportunities . . ." His voice was ragged, his words running together.

"Matthew Bessette, you cannot think that way," Meredith said, then added, "Girls, let's go."

Matthew swallowed hard. "I'm staying to see if I can help in any way."

Meredith traced a loving finger along the back of his neck and herded the girls away.

"Charlotte." Urso, a mountain of a man who looked even taller with his police hat atop his head, appeared at the door to the garage and beckoned me. The chief, who was a life-long friend, would ask for my initial reaction, although I was pretty certain he wouldn't tolerate much more than that. He didn't like when I butted into his investigations. On the other hand, Noelle had died on my property. In my garage. While working on my renovation project. Not to mention that I liked her—*had* liked her—a lot. I had envisioned inviting her to girls' night out and family dinners.

I hurried toward him.

Matthew caught up with me and whispered, "How, Charlotte? Why?"

I shook my head; I had no answers.

As we entered the garage, Urso regarded Matthew with suspicion. "Matthew, I don't think you should—"

"She was my friend, U-ey."

Urso bridled. Pals called him U-ey because of the double U in his name. He hated the nickname, but it had stuck for life.

"She was also my"—Matthew slicked his tongue beneath his lip—"my . . . my . . ."

Tears flooded his eyes. They filled mine, too. I threw my arms around him for support. Someone had died. Not any someone. Matthew's friend and close business associate.

We remained in the embrace for a very long moment. When both of us regained our composure, I pressed away from him. "Are you okay?"

"Yeah."

He was lying; his skin had turned alabaster white.

I urged him toward the wall for support. "Is there anyone we should call? She said her parents were dead. Maybe an uncle, an aunt?"

"I don't . . . know. She . . . we . . . didn't discuss family."

Urso said, "Matthew, breathe. In through your nose, out through your mouth. Charlotte"—he gestured with a thumb— "walk me through this. One more time, tell me what happened when you entered." Usually Urso liked to use formal names when conducting investigations. Matthew and I were exceptions.

I recounted my movements, step by step. I told him about seeing the items turned topsy-turvy and spotting Noelle. "She wasn't dead yet."

Urso crouched beside Noelle and pointed at the weapon. "This is a corkscrew."

"Yes, it was a wedding favor from Matthew and Mere-dith's wedding."

Matthew gasped, apparently not having seen the weapon prior to that moment.

"You kept the corkscrew in your garage?" Urso said.

"No. Mine is in the kitchen." While waiting for the police to arrive, I had checked. The favor I received at the wedding was still in its silver box nestled in a drawer. "That must be Noelle's. She attended the wedding. Do you remember meeting her? She was in for a few hours and left."

Urso grimaced. "If you recall, I was preoccupied with another situation."

How could I forget? Our fair town had been in turmoil then, too. After the last murder that had occurred in Providence, a journalist wrote that evil comes with growth, and Providence, which was burgeoning, could not escape what the rest of the world knew to be commonplace. I had wadded up the article and used it to light tinder for a fire.

"She brought the corkscrew with her," I said. "As a memento of good times and good fortunes."

"Go on." Urso rose to his full height and eyed the mess of Tupperware boxes, the nails, and the other items that had spilled onto the tarp.

I noticed stacks of my parents' love letters among the chaos. The killer had emptied out one of the Tupperware boxes. I moved to fetch them.

"Hold it," Urso said.

"U-ey." I explained what the letters were. "I've been all around this garage. Evidence of my DNA has to be everywhere. Let me collect those. They're fragile." When he didn't argue, I gathered up the stacks, showed him the Tupperware was empty of anything else, then returned the letters to the box and sealed it. Refocusing on Noelle, I said, "She was still breathing when I got here. I raced to her. She tried to say my name."

"Why didn't you mention this before?"

"I only had time to tell you the basics. I had the twins to think of." I replaced the Tupperware box on the shelf. "Noelle also whispered, 'Hell's key.' Does that mean anything to you?"

"Boyd Hellman," Matthew blurted.

"Hellman?" I said. "That's his last name?"

Urso said, "Who's that?"

"Her ex-boyfriend." Matthew stepped forward, hands balled into fists.

"I met him," I said, recalling the rage of red. "He showed up at the shop yesterday, furious that Noelle left Cleveland without telling him. She was embarrassed then angry that he had tracked her down. She ordered him to leave her alone. He stormed out of the shop. Later, when I asked her about him, she said she wasn't worried because she saw him split town in his beat-up Chevy Malibu."

"Color of the car?" Urso asked.

"Metallic green."

Matthew's eyes widened. "U-ey, I saw a car meeting the description parked near the pub about two hours ago. He might still be in town. If Noelle said, 'Hell's key,' maybe she meant that Boyd Hellman killed her."

"Was the guy abusive?" Urso jammed a hand into his trouser pocket and worked coins through his fingers, a habit he had picked up way back in seventh grade. "Was that why she left him?"

"I don't know," Matthew offered.

"They broke up a few months ago," I said.

"That had to tick him off," Urso said.

"But would he kill her with something as telltale as a wedding favor?" I asked. "That seems a little, how do you say it, 'on the nose.' He asked her to marry him. She turned him down. So he skewers her?"

"Chief Urso." Deputy O'Shea, our local barkeep's handsome nephew and new hire to the police department, rapped on the garage side door. "We're all clear in the guest room upstairs. We've confiscated a computer, cell phone, and address book. We can't tell if anything else might be missing."

Urso turned to me. "Would you know?"

"Not to the letter. Noelle had a briefcase, a couple of suitcases, notions, a Nikon camera, and gifts she bought at the shops in town."

"A gift bag is on the floor," the deputy said. "We fanned through it. Nothing of interest. We've dusted for fingerprints, too."

I sagged. My home was officially a crime scene.

Urso brushed my forearm. "Charlotte, are you okay?"

No, I wasn't. I was bummed beyond words.

"I'm worried about you staying here," Urso continued. "It's a big house. You don't have an alarm."

Barely anyone in town did; only our local society diva and some of her pals who were worried about the tourist *riffraff*—her term, not mine.

"And with Jordan out of town," Urso added.

I tilted my head. "He doesn't stay at my house when he's in town."

Urso turned crimson. "I didn't mean to pry."

"You weren't."

Delilah was right. The synchronicity of Jordan leaving town at the same moment that Matthew and the twins moved out of the house had changed the way I lived life. In a matter of weeks, I had become a homebody. I probably needed to get out and see my friends more. And yet I felt strong and clear of mind, not reclusive, and I had checked five items off my to-do list. This one with Noelle . . .

I pinched myself to remain present. "U-ey, I'm fine. Really. Besides, the killer wasn't after me."

"How can you be sure?"

I glanced at Noelle. "Because this was a personal murder, don't you think? The killer went to Noelle's room, specifically found that murder weapon, returned to the garage, and plunged it into her throat as if to ensure she wouldn't talk. He . . . or she . . . wouldn't dare come back tonight."

"Unless he wants to find what he didn't find the first time," said Matthew, who seemed steelier—steadier. "This place is a mess. He was looking for something."

The notion sent a shiver through me.

Urso removed his hat and scrubbed his hair. "Noelle . . . Miss . . ."

"Adams," I said.

"Miss Adams said, 'Hell's key.' You're sure?"

I nodded.

Matthew said, "I repeat, Noelle was cluing Charlotte in that Boyd Hellman was the killer."

Urso narrowed his gaze.

"Key means vital," Matthew continued. "Boyd was essential to something."

"Or she meant a physical key," I said. "Like a house key. Did they live together, Matthew?"

"They used to, in an apartment in Cleveland."

"Maybe she was trying to tell me to focus on the apartment. We should—"

"No," Urso snapped. "Don't do anything. This is my investigation."

Here we go. I held up my hands to appease him. "I know you will cover every angle. I was merely suggesting—"

"Charlotte." He clutched my upper arm; heat penetrated my sweater. "I don't want you to put yourself in harm's way."

"I take self-defense classes."

"Like those work."

In a flash, I wrenched free of Urso's grasp simply to prove I could.

He frowned and looked to Matthew for support.

My cousin's concerned face matched Urso's. "You should listen to U-ey. I happen to know that Meredith's self-defense classes aren't doing her much good. I can take her down in an instant."

"Jordan taught me a few extra moves." I threw a karate jab at my cousin's shoulder. He blocked it and grabbed my wrist with his other hand, restraining me in an instant. Okay, so maybe I needed to learn more moves, but to date, I had protected myself pretty darned well. On the other hand, did I want to test fate?

"Why don't I stay the night?" Matthew offered.

"No, Meredith and the girls need you."

"Charlotte," Urso said, "why don't you go to your grandparents' house?"

"Oh, for Pete's sake." I didn't mean to sound so exasperated, but both men were acting like I was a child. "I'll see if Lavender and Lace has an available room. Will that satisfy you both? Rags will be thrilled to have some playtime with Lois's precocious Shih Tzu." I didn't want to put out my grandparents, nor did I want to be fussed over.

As I started to leave the garage, a thought flew into my

mind. I slapped my thigh. "U-ey, I just remembered something. When I entered, I smelled a marshy odor. It was probably the mud on Noelle's shoes, but the mud looks dry right now, so you can't really pick up the scent."

Urso crouched beside Noelle and inspected the undersides of her shoes. "Do you know where she might have been?"

"She mentioned taking a hike. Maybe she went to Kindred Creek."

"At night?"

"I warned her that it was too dark, but she seemed set on the idea. She wanted to explore Providence before she settled into her new job. She'd called it a quest. Maybe Boyd Hellman caught sight of her on her outing and followed her back here."

Urso shook his head. "But there isn't a second set of muddy footprints. Is this guy smart enough to have removed his dirty boots?"

* * *

By the time Urso and his deputies left, I felt drained, and to be honest, no matter what kind of bravado I had put on earlier, I didn't feel like sleeping alone in my house. Humbled and shivering, I gathered up Rags and headed to Lavender and Lace. With all the comings and goings at my place, I was surprised that a crowd hadn't collected on the street by the B&B to gossip.

Guests sat on the porch having tea and scones. Lois kept space heaters turned on through the winter.

"Welcome, Charlotte." Lois passed across the front door threshold. Agatha, her Shih Tzu, scampered alongside. "I'm so glad you called."

I hadn't; Urso had, to guarantee that a room was available. Talk about a lack of trust. I said, "I don't mean to be an inconvenience."

"Nonsense, we always like company, don't you know." Lois knotted the belt of her lavender sweater, tucked a loose hair behind her ear, and then nuzzled Rags's neck. "There are lots of people in town for Thanksgiving holidays. Why, I have more grandparent guests than I can count. They're all in to see the play at the theater. However, I have a few rooms empty. I always keep at least one . . ." She paused. Had she meant to add that she kept one room ready for her husband, should he reappear? A whisper of sadness filled her eyes, but she pushed it aside. "Tea?"

"I'd love some."

I entered the great room and instantly felt calmer. A fire crackled in the fireplace. Many guests had cozied up to the fire. Others played board games or chatted at the various groupings of chairs and sofas. I settled into a corduroy chair— lavender in color, of course; Lois had a passion for purple— and seconds later Lois returned with a Haviland Rose china set and a plate of homemade raisin cinnamon scones with a side of clotted cream. Locally, Lois was famous for her scones. I set Rags on the floor, and he immediately grappled with Agatha. The dog yipped, and the two tore off toward the kitchen. "Play nice," I called.

"Don't worry about them," Lois said. "Two peas in a pod. I swear your cat is a dog." She nodded toward the scones, beaming with pride. "These are freshly made and piping hot from the oven. I'm planning to make a batch of gluten-free scones for your niece."

"How sweet of you."

"I miss seeing the girls running around the yard. All that lovely energy." After setting my tea to steep, Lois nestled into the chair opposite mine. "Now, tell me what happened. Why were the police at your house? Did you have a break-in?"

"Worse. A murder."

She shuddered. "To think what this world is coming to."

I was pleased how confidential Urso and his deputies had kept the investigation so far. In the past, when a murder occurred, within seconds the town knew and journalists showed up to cover the story. A small town grapevine could be a positive or negative thing.

In a hushed tone, I related what had happened in my garage.

Lois shook her head with dismay. "How horrid."

"Did you happen to see anyone running from the house earlier?" I said. "Man or woman?"

"I didn't, I'm sorry to say. I'll ask the other guests if they saw anything and report back. I've been busy. I served a full meal. Leg of lamb with mint jelly and all the fixings. We ended with a cheese course, as you advised me, with that scrumptiously smooth Doux de Montagne cheese, almonds, green grapes, and a drizzle of honey. Everyone raved."

My stomach grumbled in protest. I hadn't eaten at the theater, and my appetite had been squelched after finding Noelle. Until now. I picked up a scone and bit into it. Melt-in-your-mouth tender.

"Dear girl, you look spent. Put down the scone. I'll fix you a plate of real supper, and then let's get you settled in your room. You didn't bring a suitcase." She rose. "It matters not. Guests can sleep in the raw, if it suits their fancy."

A short while later, Lois, carrying a supper tray, beckoned me to follow her.

I gathered up Rags. As we trudged upstairs, the notion that the killer had disappeared mighty fast dawned on me. Was he a guest at the inn? "Lois, do you have a guest named Boyd Hellman registered here?"

"No. Why, dear? Is he the killer?"

"No. I was . . . Never mind." I clutched Rags closer to my chest, unwilling to reveal all of the facts of the case to Lois. Urso would have my hide.

As Lois used a key to open the door of my room, I reflected again on Noelle's last words: *hell's key.* A key was an island, an inset in an atlas, a list of answers to a test, a code breaker, and so much more. What had she meant? Why couldn't I have saved her?

CHAPTER

I slept fitfully, dreaming or *nightmaring*—if that was a word—about Noelle fighting off her killer. At dawn, I startled awake. Had Noelle struggled? Why did it matter? How could I find out? I scooped up Rags and slipped out of the B&B vowing to repay Lois for her hospitality with a cheese basket filled with Brie, Camembert, and Fromager d'Affinois. She liked creamy cheeses.

When I reached home, I sprinted down the driveway, set Rags on the grass to explore, and headed to the garage. Crime scene tape crisscrossed the side door, but that didn't stop me from clicking on the garage door opener and entering. It was my property.

Crisp air swirled around me and the tarp crackled beneath my feet as I tiptoed toward where Noelle had lain. I stopped beside the secretary desk and ran my hand along its smooth bare wood. I begged the desk to tell me about the tragedy, but it revealed no secrets. A raw feeling gripped my insides. Noelle had been selfless. Who had ended her life so young? Why? She had dedicated her last hours on earth to helping me get one step closer to completing my renovations. She hadn't known me well, nor I her, and yet I felt that we could have become fast friends. I owed her a speedy answer to the question.

Even though I knew Urso and his men had reviewed every inch of the scene, I searched for telltale signs of the killer's identity. I was no forensic expert, but thanks to Rebecca's insistence, I had watched plenty of crime shows on TV. I saw no footprints. No fibers. No stray hairs. Last night, other than seeing the boxes of nails and other garage items turned inside out, I hadn't noticed signs of a struggle. Had Noelle and her killer been discussing something? Had the attack come as a surprise? Her clothes hadn't been torn. I hadn't noticed scratches on her face. Had she known her killer? If only she had written a message, something like *Hellman was here*.

If wishes were horses . . .

I heard a swoosh behind me, then a huge clatter. I swung around, my pulse pounding and relaxed instantly. Rags, the sneaky devil, had followed me in. His vigorous tail had caught the cord of the sander and pulled the thing to the ground. Dust rose up as Rags disentangled himself and bolted toward me, eyes blazing with fear. He sprang into my arms. I scruffed his ears and said, "Yeah, you're right. Let's leave this horrible place."

Before exiting, I tried to commit everything I saw to memory. Perhaps the fresh memory would trigger a past one.

Over the course of the next half hour, I fed Rags, took a shower, donned the most colorful clothes in my wardrobe for an emotional boost, and downed a single cup of coffee. I couldn't eat. The image of Noelle lying dead curdled my stomach.

When I arrived at The Cheese Shop, I had a craving to do something normal or at least semi-normal or I wouldn't function. In *Culture Magazine*, a publication dedicated to all things cheese, I had read about a way to infuse humor into a cheese shop. I would insert flags with eclectic sayings on them into wedges of cheese in the display case—sayings like

Don't be blue; eat blue. Or *This is the cheese you'd ditch your boyfriend for.*

Grabbing toothpicks, construction paper, and scissors, I set to work.

An hour later, Rebecca entered, her face pinched with concern.

"I heard what happened," she said. "I'm so sorry. Why didn't you call me?"

"I didn't want to stir the gossip mill."

"Then you shouldn't have stayed the night at Lavender and Lace." She planted her hands on her narrow hips. "At two A.M., Lois was online chatting up everyone. She's such a gossip. So, who do you think killed Noelle?"

I held up my hands. "No. I don't want to speculate." Though, of course, I was rehashing the event in my head.

"If you don't, who will?"

"Chief Urso is on top of this. Let's you and I keep our noses out of it."

"But—"

"No." I pointed to the Chiriboga Blue, a German cheese made in the French Roquefort tradition, and the Bayley Hazen Blue, which was Jasper Hill's delectable flagship cheese, crumblier than most blues but developed to hold up under challenging retail conditions. "Set those two at the front of the display case so everyone can read the sayings on the flags."

Rebecca scanned the tags I had inserted and sniggered. "These are cute. Can I write a few?"

"Sure."

"By the way, I heard that Noelle said something to you before she died."

"Who told you—" I peeked into the wine annex. Had Matthew participated in the social networking hullabaloo? Only he, Urso, and I knew what Noelle had said—and possibly the deputies. Shoot, shoot, shoot. Keeping those words secret might have been important to the investigation. "Go to work," I ordered.

Rebecca saluted while mumbling, "Spoilsport," under her breath. Real adult.

By ten A.M., customers were laughing and calling to friends on the street to come inside and read the cheese tags. Laughter was the best medicine, my grandfather often reminded me, and hearing my customers' chuckles helped keep the bad memories from the night before at bay. Laughter also increased sales. By eleven A.M., Fromagerie Bessette had sold out of all blue cheese.

At noon, Matthew sidled up to me. "Hungry? Want to grab some lunch?"

"A quick bite in the office," I said. "I don't want to leave Rebecca out here alone. We are busy-busy with Thanksgiving Day gift baskets and weekend parties."

"Where are Bozz and Tyanne?"

I explained. Bozz, a part-timer, had called to cancel his work shift. He was a first-year college student and was bogged down with midterms. Our other part-timer, Tyanne, was also the town's premier wedding planner. Currently she was busy prepping Liberty Nelson's wedding.

"Okay, we'll eat fast. Grab two of those sandwiches." In addition to daily quiches, we offered gourmet sandwiches, but once they sold out, we didn't make more. Matthew pointed at the Mortadella and Scharfe Maxx Swiss cheese torpedoes layered with peppers and red onions. "I'll fetch a couple of sparkling waters, unless, of course, you want to try the Plavac Mali from Croatia."

"Never heard of it."

"It's what a pinot and cab franc would taste like if they had a lovechild. Zinfandel is one of the two parent varietals of Plavac. I'm offering it at this afternoon's tasting."

"You're on. But just a smidgen." I signaled a thimbleful. Drinking wine midday made me crave a long winter's nap.

When I settled into the chair at my desk, Rags hopped into my lap. He kneaded my thighs with his claws and meowed like the dickens. Last night, he had acted like nothing was wrong, but I sensed something more today. Perhaps his trek into the garage had disturbed him on a deeper level. If only he could talk. Would I have to hire a cat whisperer to determine the problem? I pulled a treat out of the lower desk drawer and waved it under his nose. He slurped it into his mouth and begged for more.

"What's his problem?" Matthew said as he shuffled into the office.

I arched a brow.

"Never mind," Matthew said. "Stupid question. He's a sensitive soul. He knows Noelle is dead." He handed me a Riedel "O" Series glass containing a small portion of ruby red wine and raised his own glass. "À votre santé."

"À la votre."

Matthew sat in the chocolate brown director's chair that I had picked up at a garage sale. In silence, we bit into our sandwiches. The combination of the salami, cheese, and peppers made me swoon. Scharfe Maxx, a robust Swiss cheese made near Lake Constance in north Switzerland, was one of my favorites. Homemade rennet was key to its extraordinary complexity. I adored the lingering flavor of mushrooms.

After finishing half of his sandwich, Matthew wiped his mouth with a napkin and said, "Do you think Urso is going to track down Boyd Hellman?"

"Of course he will. Don't worry."

Matthew set his sandwich on the desk and slumped forward in his chair, elbows perched on his knees, head cradled in his hands.

"What aren't you telling me, Matthew?" I asked.

"Nothing."

"Were you involved with Noelle?"

"No!"

Rags startled and hurtled to his feet. He padded in a circle in my lap.

"Shh," I cooed. "Lie down." He obeyed.

"Noelle was . . ." Matthew's voice drifted away.

"She was what?"

Matthew didn't answer at first and then in a whisper, he said, "She was the first assistant sommelier I ever had. We became good friends."

"How good? You don't know whether she had any other family."

"And you didn't know anything about Jordan for a long time."

"Touché."

Matthew shrugged. "Noelle was very private."

"Did you know Boyd Hellman? Had you met him?"

"I'd already relocated here when she got involved with him. For the second time. She broke it off the first time because . . ." Matthew sighed. "They were teens. Boyd did something stupid. He participated in a couple of petty thefts. No arrests. Kid stuff. But Noelle couldn't stand it. She kicked him out. He reentered her life a few years ago and somehow convinced her he had changed. He claimed he was an up-standing guy. Salt of the earth." Matthew shook his head. "I urged her to keep away from him, but sometimes smart peo-ple make dumb decisions. If only I . . . I want to make sure that U-ey is doing all he can."

"He will. He's good and diligent. We're so lucky to have him."

"Yeah, but without your help in the past—"

"He'll get this done. Promise."

Matthew laced his fingers behind his neck and gazed up at the ceiling. "Noelle said, 'Hell's key.' Why?"

"About that. Did you mention those words to others?"

"No."

"Huh. Rebecca heard it from someone. I guess one of the deputies must have leaked it."

Matthew nodded. "I can't get the words out of my head. She had to be accusing Boyd of murder."

"Not necessarily." I reiterated all the synonyms of the word *key* that had popped into my head when I had entered my room at the bed-and-breakfast last night.

"It's used in music, too," Matthew said.

"Was Noelle a musician? I heard her sing along with O.A.R. last night. She had a nice voice."

"I don't think so. I don't know." Matthew leaped to his

feet. Rags jolted and hissed at Matthew, who growled back. "Man, this is so frustrating."

"Tell me about it." I nuzzled Rags behind the ears to calm him. "I feel guilty for letting Noelle stay home while I went out."

"It's not your fault. She wasn't the kind of person you could tell what to do. She had a mind of her own. She was like a Mustang. Stubborn and wild. That was the thing that won Shelton over. That's why he hired her. He liked her spirit."

And it was probably the thing that Boyd Hellman hated about her.

Matthew wrapped up the other half of his sandwich. "I'm going to store this in the fridge and head to the cellar. Need anything from down there?"

"More blue cheese."

"Anything in particular?"

"Chiriboga. Bayley Hazen Blue. Any we have, please. We ran out of all of them at the cheese counter. I haven't had time to send Rebecca down to restock."

"Thanks for listening," he said as he slipped out of the office.

I didn't quite know what I had listened to, but I said, "Sure thing."

When I returned to the shop, the place was empty of customers. I found Rebecca bent over, tweaking the display in the window. I tapped her back.

She swooped to a stand. "Sheesh, you startled me." She flipped her ponytail over her shoulder and tugged on the hem of her sweater, which had crept up beneath her apron.

"What are you doing?" I asked.

"I thought the display could use more of the fun descriptions you've been adding to the cheeses. So . . ." She held up two toothpick flags and read: "*For a quick pick-me-up, try Beehive Cheese Co.'s Barely Buzzed.*" She giggled. "Or listen to this one. *Want something smokin' sexy in your home on Thanksgiving? Try Three Ring Farm's Up In Smoke.*"

"Smokin' sexy?"

"I really like that one. I was browsing the Victoria's Secret online catalogue last night, and—"

"I got it, I got it." I clapped her shoulder. "You're doing great."

She beamed.

I started to turn and paused. Out on the street, a red-headed male pedestrian in a red plaid coat caught my eye. Did Boyd Hellman own any other color of clothing? Hands jammed into his pockets, he peered into the Country Kitchen's windows. He wasn't standing near the menu that hung beside the door. What was he staring at? Or who? I nudged Rebecca. "Did you see Chief Urso go into the diner?"

"No, but I haven't been keeping a lookout. Why?"

"Boyd Hellman has surfaced." Noelle had sounded certain that he left town. Did she make a fatal error? I hurried toward the rear of the shop to call Urso and give him a heads-up when the front door chimes jingled.

I paused when I saw Deputy O'Shea enter the shop. He removed his hat.

"Hello, Deputy," Rebecca said loudly enough for her deceased Amish grandmother to hear. "Isn't it horrible what happened last night?" She slipped her arm through his and batted her eyelashes. If only she wouldn't watch so many TV crime shows and old movies, I mused. Only last week she admitted that the wily, manipulative Barbara Stanwyck in *Double Indemnity* was her new idol. "Care to enlighten me about the facts of the murder investigation?" she asked.

As obvious as it was that Deputy O'Shea was enthralled by Rebecca—he looked like a hangdog pup the way his eyes were lapping up her pretty face—he said, "No, ma'am."

"I'm not a ma'am; I'm a *miss*. And really? You don't have any leads? Nothing at all?"

"Nope." Obviously Urso had taught his deputy the fine art of shutting down. "I came in to buy a wedge of that Huntsman cheese. I like it for lunch with apples."

"You should," I said. Huntsman was a fascinating cheese made with layers of English Double Gloucester and Stilton—

England's answer to blue cheese. The orange and blue-white combination looked beautiful on a cheese platter.

"Since you're acting as stoic as Zeno"—Rebecca fluttered her eyelids some more and squeezed his arm brazenly—"shall I tell you something instead? Something really, really secret?"

O'Shea tensed his chiseled jaw.

"Your main suspect is standing right there." Rebecca pointed out the window. "If you hurry, you might catch him." She nudged the deputy.

Like a cartoon character, the deputy did a double take and then dashed outside. Rebecca burst into giggles. At the same time Sylvie, Matthew's ex-wife, entered. Though the woman owned Under Wraps, a classy women's clothing boutique and spa, she had no taste in clothes. She sashayed in wearing a gaudy getup that only she would think was chic: a heavily beaded fringed shirt and leather pants tucked into cowboy boots, her ice white hair drawn into a topknot. She probably thought she looked like a hip rocker. At forty-plus, she simply came across as a woman trying too hard. Perhaps she had purchased the outfit for Halloween and felt compelled to squeeze another wearing out of it.

I retreated behind the cheese counter. Though Sylvie had simmered down since Matthew and Meredith married, I didn't care to buddy up to her. Too often, she invaded my personal space and gave me uncalled-for wardrobe tips.

She followed me to the counter and surveyed the wares. "Did you see him?" she cooed in her British accent.

"Him who?" I rearranged a few items and twisted the humorous flags toward the cash register so customers could catch a better view.

"Ashley Yeats, the journalist." Sylvie twirled a loose strand of hair at the nape of her long neck. "He's so charmingly British."

And soaked in snake oil, I thought. Doing my best to heed my grandmother's warning to say nothing if I couldn't say something nice, I kept my opinion to myself. I wasn't always so self-controlled.

"I'm thinking he's an Eton man," Sylvie continued. "And Eton, I'll have you know, is traditionally considered the chief nurse of England's statesmen."

Ashley Yeats was far from a statesman. I recalled him tiptoeing toward Shelton Nelson's private cellar yesterday. What had he been after? What was his angle?

The front door opened and Prudence Hart, a descendant of original settlers in Providence, marched into the store. When didn't she march? She wore a pale blue skirt and blazer that washed out her already sallow skin. Her ultra-thin face looked in dire need of moisturizer and a smile.

"Good morning, Prudence," I said. She could be sour; I wouldn't be.

Per usual—which wasn't often because Prudence was not a Cheese Shop regular—she didn't respond. She normally entered when she wanted to stir up trouble. She headed for Sylvie. I braced myself.

"Sylvie." Rebecca pulled a round of Bonne Bouche, the flagship of the Vermont Creamery, from the cheese case. "How about a sliver of your favorite?" In French, *bonne bouche* meant tasty morsel.

"I don't have a favorite," she sniffed.

"Sure you do," Rebecca said like an expert salesman. "This one. It's creamy white and tart."

"Like you," Prudence said, coming to a decisive halt beside Sylvie.

Sylvie said, "Why you—"

Prudence cut her off with a hand wave. "Have you seen them?" Her voice rose an entire octave. An opera diva couldn't have sung the final note of an aria with more confidence.

"*Them* who?" Sylvie huffed, the nearness of her archenemy turning her into an instant shrew. Prudence owned the other women's boutique in town—sans spa. The two were forever trying to undercut the other's business.

"The new shop owners," Prudence said. "There are at least ten who have taken over preexisting business concerns since the first of the month. The movie theater and the ice cream parlor, to name two. Providence is under siege. Soon it will turn itself into a huge town of commerce."

"Fiddle-dee-dee. You're imagining things," Sylvie said. "Providence is growing at the same pace as always. Two move out, two move in. Big deal."

"But there were ten getting business licenses today at the precinct. Ten. Some for new businesses." Prudence wiggled her glossy fingernails. "If I had a mind, I'd buy out all of them and start this town over. Get some structure."

"Tosh."

"Prudence," I cut in, determined to break up a fight before it began. "Are you enjoying all the parade fixings? I noticed there is a parade stand right near your shop." La Chic Boutique stood next to the Country Kitchen, catty-corner to The Cheese Shop. "That will draw in a number of customers, I'll wager."

She threw me a caustic look.

I wouldn't be deterred. "How about some cheese, Prudence? A slice of Iberico. It's a combination cow, sheep, and goat cheese and the most popular cheese in Spain."

"No, thank you. I only eat American."

"Well, then, how about a taste of Stravecchio from the Antigo Cheese Company? They're based in Wisconsin. The cheese tastes like Parmesan." More customers were entering. I didn't want the two enemies to scare them away. I wanted happy feelings radiating throughout the shop. I wanted laughter and goodwill. A girl could dream.

"I said no, Charlotte. Back to the new owners—"

"Don't be such a blowhard," Sylvie said.

"A wh-wh-wh . . . ?" Prudence sputtered. "What did you call me?"

Sylvie toyed with the beaded fringe of her shirt as if trying to keep herself in check, but typical Sylvie, she couldn't. "Blowhard," she said.

I flinched. Granted, there were no canapés for the two to hurl at each other—a long story—but there were plenty of accoutrements sitting on the display barrels and shelves around the shop that would serve as ammunition.

Sylvie smirked. "You brag about having money and you brag about your plans to invest, but you never spend a dime. Hence, you're a blowhard."

"Sylvie, how about a taste of Tartufello?" I said, trying hard to distract her. "It's an herbaceous semi-firm raw cow's milk cheese with black truffles. Remember how you swooned over it last month at Matthew's wedding?"

"Nonsense, I would never swoon over a cheese. "

I persisted. "Yes, you did." I skimmed slivers from a wedge of the cheese and offered a piece to her and another to Prudence.

Neither woman budged. Like gunslingers standing in the middle of an old-time dusty street, their hands fell to their pocketbooks as if they were holsters. Did each of them carry a concealed weapon? Craving normalcy in the shop, I skirted around the counter and said, "That's it, you two. Out, now." I sliced the air with my hand. A magic wand couldn't have had better effect.

As Sylvie and Prudence exited, with Sylvie launching the final verbal bomb by insisting that Prudence needed intense therapy, Shelton Nelson hurried into the shop, followed by his daughter Liberty.

Shelton, whose face was ash white, jogged to me. "Charlotte, we need to see Matthew. A.S.A.P."

CHAPTER

6

A cold blast of air swept into the shop behind Shelton and Liberty. I shivered and wrapped my arms around my core. "Matthew's in the cellar, Shelton. What's wrong?"

"Let's go, Daddy." Without an invitation, Liberty prodded her father toward the kitchen at the rear of the shop. "Matthew will know what to do."

Their footsteps thudded on the cellar stairs as they descended.

So much for asking for an invitation.

Rebecca hurried to me. "That Liberty Nelson. I don't like her. I never have. She's snooty and dismissive and always acting high and mighty with her pert little nose in the air. I know we're supposed to be nice to all the customers, and I am, but it's difficult sometimes."

I couldn't fault Rebecca. Being nice to someone and liking them were two entirely different things. Take Prudence or Sylvie, for instance. *Take them, please.* The two were still arguing on the sidewalk. Though I was a fixer by nature, I couldn't fix everyone, so I decided to let Prudence and Sylvie go toe-to-toe without any more interference from me. Maybe they would resort to fisticuffs, and Ashley Yeats would come along and take a picture and plaster it in the papers, and . . .

Yes, a girl could dream.

"Did you see what Liberty was wearing?" Rebecca went on. "The angora sweater and the furry collared vest and that black hair of hers hanging like curtains around her face? She always dresses like that. Slinky and feline. If I didn't know better, I'd say she had cat ancestors."

"Rags would take offense at your analogy."

Rebecca giggled. "I saw a sign in the window of Tailwaggers"—Tailwaggers was the pet shop on the north side of town—"that said: *Women and cats are queens and princesses. Men and dogs should get used to it.* But back to that Liberty. You need to go downstairs so you can listen in. You don't want her wrangling Matthew into a nefarious scheme."

I swear the words Rebecca used came straight from television crime shows. "We don't know that they went downstairs to wrangle him into anything."

"Please see what's going on," Rebecca begged. "There was a woman murdered in your garage last night, a woman who was supposed to start work today for Shelton Nelson. Something's afoot."

I had to admit that curiosity was brewing inside me. Shelton Nelson seemed the kind of guy who would never be thrown off his game. Did he know something about Noelle's murder? "I guess I could go down saying I need the blue cheese that I'd asked Matthew to fetch."

"Yes, yes, yes." Rebecca nudged me. "Listen in and get the scoop."

The reassuring musky scent of ripening cheeses met me as I opened the cellar door, but as I descended the staircase, a chill gripped me. The temperature in the cellar stayed at a cool fifty-eight degrees. I wished I had grabbed a shawl. Shivering, I stopped three stairs shy of the lower level and peered around the corner. Matthew, Shelton, and Liberty were sitting at the mosaic table in the alcove.

". . . and then Chief Urso asked me about my alibi for last night," Shelton said.

So Shelton Nelson was a suspect? Wow. What about Liberty? She was quivering like a cat eager to find refuge from a storm.

"Don't worry," Matthew said. "I imagine Urso will question everyone who knew Noelle at some point. Do you have an alibi?"

"I was at home working out," Shelton said. "Every evening, I ride my stationary bike and walk at least five miles on the treadmill. It's a ritual. Then I shower and read until bedtime."

"Any witnesses?"

"The housekeeper was there the whole time, but she's Danish and doesn't speak very good English. Not to mention she's as deaf as a tombstone."

Bad choice of words, I thought.

"I was home, too," Liberty said. "In my room. I heard Daddy singing in the shower." Her cheeks blushed a soft pink. "His room abuts mine," she added quickly as if the notion that she knew her father was in the shower was a little odd. "I was reading Jane Austen for the umpteenth time. I adore Mr. Darcy."

"Did you tell Chief Urso, Liberty?" Matthew asked.

"I wasn't around this morning when the chief arrived. My fiancé and I had to meet with Tyanne. She's our wedding planner." Her face flushed a deeper red. "We were going over last-minute details, the cake and the flowers, and well, you know, Matthew. You just went through it. There's so much to think about."

"So you haven't gone to the precinct to tell the chief?" Matthew said.

"Not yet. Daddy wanted . . ." Liberty raked the collar of her furry vest with her fingernails. "Daddy wanted to talk to you first."

I took the last few steps of the stairs loudly so my appearance wouldn't be a surprise. "Hi, sorry to intrude. I need to fetch some blue cheese right away."

"Gosh, I apologize," Matthew said. "I meant to—"

"No worries."

"Charlotte." Like a gentleman, Shelton rose partway. "Sit, please. For a minute. I'm so . . . Noelle . . . I can't believe . . . in your house."

"My garage." I perched on the front of the chair opposite him.

"Noelle was"—his voice broke—"a special woman. An expert in her field. With her qualifications and background, she brought so much to the table. It's such a loss."

"Daddy had high hopes for her." Liberty whisked a tissue from her huge tote bag and dabbed her eyes, which looked pretty darned dry. Left unsaid was that she didn't have the same high hopes.

I thought of how she and her father had argued after we toured the vineyard. Noelle believed they were fighting about her. Was I wrong to think that Boyd Hellman had killed Noelle? Was Liberty or Shelton capable of such an act?

Liberty put her hand over her father's and squeezed.

Shelton pressed back then removed his hand. "Chief Urso said you found her, Charlotte." His chin trembled. "He said she spoke to you. What was it she said? Something like *hell's key*?"

Aha. Urso was the one leaking the words Noelle uttered. Why would he reveal that much unless he hoped to judge suspects by watching their reactions?

"It sounds religious to me," Liberty said.

"Religious?" Shelton scoffed. "Everything sounds religious to you, now that you're marrying that—"

"Daddy," Liberty cautioned.

"God-fearing man."

"We all should be half the human being he is."

"You know, darlin', speaking of religion"—Shelton folded his hands in front of him—"wasn't Noelle raised in a Catholic orphanage? Maybe her last breath was about needing some spiritual key to avoid going to hell."

"You could be right, Daddy."

"Interesting," Matthew said.

Personally, I thought the theory was a stretch.

"I'm going to mention that to Chief Urso," Shelton said.

Liberty huffed. "Like he'll listen. He's so bullheaded."

"Now, darlin'."

"You said so yourself. The chief—"

Shelton tapped a firm finger on the table. "Let's keep those thoughts to ourselves."

Liberty flicked her hair off her shoulders. "I'll bet that horrible Harold Warfield sicced Chief Urso on you, Daddy."

"Harold?" Matthew said. "Why would he do that?"

"He's mad that Daddy hired Noelle. He told me so when we toured the vineyards."

Harold clearly didn't like Liberty. I doubt he would have revealed anything so intimate. I tried to recall his introduction to Noelle—or rather, reintroduction. She said they had met before. He was polite yet distant. I said, "What exactly did he say, Liberty?"

She sat taller in her chair. "He said she was gunning for his job." Her eyes blinked rapidly; she was lying. "He said that if he had the chance, he'd wring her scrawny neck."

Except Noelle hadn't been strangled. She had been skewered.

* * *

After locating a dozen wheels of the last of our blue cheese stock, Rogue River Blue, a scrumptious blue cheese that was aged in caves that had been crafted to emulate the ancient caves in Roquefort, I returned upstairs, set the cheese in the kitchen, and went to the office to make an immediate reorder of cheeses we needed. Luckily, no early snowfall was in the forecast that might delay deliveries.

Rebecca followed me. "Well?"

"Shouldn't you be attending to customers?" Before heading to the office, I had counted at least a dozen roaming the shop.

"Your grandfather came in for a snack. Afterward, he asked if he could tend the counter. You know how he loves to help out."

I slipped into the office. Rags, who lazed on the desk chair, lifted his head and perked his ears.

Rebecca shut the door. "Come on, spill."

I recounted what I had heard in the cellar, ending with Liberty's alibi.

"She loves Fitzwilliam Darcy?" Rebecca squeaked, totally off topic. "How could she? I mean, he's so rude and obnoxious." When Rebecca left her Amish community, she decided to educate herself. Following my grandmother's recommendations, she had read many classic plays. Now, she was blasting through classic novels denied her when she was a girl: *Little Women*, *Gone with the Wind*, *Pride and Prejudice*.

I tilted my head. "Um, have you read the whole book?"

"I'm halfway through."

"Finish it and then we'll talk about the fabulous Mr. Darcy."

"Fabulous, *shmabulous*."

"Back to Shelton Nelson," I said. "He acted bereft." That was the only word for it. Trembling chin, white knuckles, a break in his voice.

"And he knew Noelle spoke to you?"

"Urso must have revealed that to him."

"You've got to be kidding. Ultra-secret Urso? Ha!"

I scooped up Rags and slumped in the chair, blown away by the last twenty-four hours. Rags must have sensed my melancholy. He stood on his hind legs and climbed up my chest with his forepaws, seeking a kiss. I obliged. Then I sought a kiss of my own. A different kiss. I kept a stash of Hershey's Kisses—my mother's favorite candy—in a desk drawer. I unwrapped the silver foil and plopped the morsel into my mouth. Delish.

Rebecca stomped to the desk. "Charlotte, what's wrong? You're keeping something from me."

"No, I'm not."

She folded her arms and tapped her foot, a set of moves she had learned all too well from my grandmother.

"What if . . . ?" My voice trailed off.

"What if what?"

"Nothing."

"Out with it."

"What if Noelle was saying *Shel's key*, not *hell's key*. Noelle only uttered the first blend of my name: *Ch*. That sounds like *Sh*. Add that to hell, it becomes *Shel's key*."

Rebecca shot up a finger. "You could be right. She was dying. People in pain aren't always able to say exactly what they mean." Her mouth tightened, making me wonder what she had witnessed as a girl. Her mother had died young.

"But I still don't know what she meant."

"What if"—Rebecca inhaled; her eyes blazed with intensity—"Noelle was saying that Shelton was key to knowing the truth about who murdered her, namely, Liberty."

"Liberty?"

"You said Liberty's alibi was hearing her father singing. Doesn't that seem strange?"

"People sing."

"You're not following me. Doesn't it seem odd that the whole case could rest on testimony like that?"

"What case?"

"Think like an attorney." Rebecca tapped her head. "You've got a daughter as the sole witness for a father. Remember that movie *Legally Blonde*? Remember how the daughter's alibi about taking a shower with recently permed hair blew the case wide open? Spoiler alert: she was the killer." In addition to being an avid reader and television viewer, Rebecca had plowed through *AFI's 100 Years . . . 100 Movies* and *AFI's 100 Years . . . 100 Laughs*. Now, she was intent on watching the complete bodies of work of her favorite female stars: Barbara Stanwyck, Meryl Streep, and Reese Witherspoon—an eclectic mix to say the least.

"If only cracking the case were as easy as proving Liberty's alibi was false," I said. "What's her motive? Why would she kill Noelle?"

Rebecca paced in front of the desk. "Jealousy."

"I would buy jealousy if Noelle was hitting on Liberty's fiancé, or if Liberty had wanted Noelle's job, but she didn't."

Unless that was what Liberty and Shelton's argument had been about.

"If you ask me, Liberty is a daddy's girl," Rebecca said. "She doesn't want to share him with anybody. Did you see her when she came in? What was that fanning thing she was doing to move Shelton to the cellar?" She mimed Liberty's fingers crawling up her father's back.

I recalled Liberty doting on him downstairs, too. She had placed her hand on his. But that didn't mean anything. Lots of daughters held their fathers' hands. "She's getting married."

"Fine, so she's betrothed. So what?" Rebecca perched on the corner of the desk. Rags eyeballed her. She hissed, "Cool it, buddy boy. I live here, too."

Rags grumbled and hunkered down.

Rebecca smirked, the victor. "What if Liberty was afraid her father might abandon her for another woman?"

"You mean Noelle."

"She was beautiful."

"And his junior by a ton of years."

"Fifteen, tops. That's not so far apart." Rebecca flicked her hand. "Let me remind you that Delilah's beau is at least twenty years older."

"They broke up."

"No!" She patted her chest.

"Staying on point, Liberty and her father did have an argument, right after Shelton gave us a tour of his private cellar. I couldn't catch everything, but I heard Liberty say the words *lover*, *phony*, and *charted for disaster*."

"That sounds like Liberty was talking about a doomed love affair."

I couldn't dispute that. "At the end of the disagreement, they neared the door, and I heard every word."

Rebecca did an arm-pump.

"Liberty was protesting something. She said, 'Noelle,' but Shelton cut her off, saying Noelle 'is here to stay.'"

"That confirms it." Rebecca hopped to her feet and began to pace. "Noelle was his lover, and Liberty was jealous."

Forgive me if I wasn't one hundred percent sold, yet

adrenaline took hold. I rose, set Rags on the chair, and paced alongside Rebecca. "If Shelton and Noelle were in a relationship, that could have angered Boyd Hellman."

"You know, Deputy O'Shea might be grilling Noelle's ex this instant." She jabbed a finger at the door. "When he's done, I might be able to ply him for information."

Matthew rapped on the door and opened it. He poked his head inside. "Am I interrupting?"

"Not at all. C'mon in." Rebecca pulled him by the shoulder. "The more heads the better. We're theorizing."

"About Noelle's murder?" he asked.

"Yes." Rebecca brought him up to date with our speculations.

When she concluded, Matthew said, "Do you think Urso has something on Shelton? Is that why he questioned him at the precinct?"

I said, "Shelton was Noelle's employer, however briefly, but rest assured, if Urso has something concrete, he'll—" I paused and searched my cousin's face. "You look worried for Shelton. Why?"

"SNW was one of my first accounts in Providence. Shelton and I have been friends for longer than that. He sold his wines at the restaurant where Noelle and I worked."

"And he knows that you're friends with U-ey." Rebecca jabbed his chest with her finger. "He might be playing you so you'll be his buffer."

Matthew's mouth fell open. "You don't really think he killed Noelle, do you?"

"My money is on Liberty," Rebecca said.

Not willing to rule out a soul, I said, "Can you think of any reason Shelton might have wanted Noelle dead?"

Matthew shook his head emphatically. "Absolutely not."

"Were they lovers?" Rebecca asked.

"What?" Matthew's voice thinned. "No. At least I don't think so. She hadn't visited town more than three times."

"Haven't you ever heard of love at first sight?" Rebecca said.

I fell hard for Jordan the moment I met him.

Matthew swiped a hand down his face then massaged the back of his neck. "Okay, what if they were? He's single; she's single." He bit his lip. "*Was*. She was single. When I introduced them, he was over the moon because she knew so much about wine. He called her his guardian angel."

I wanted to be gentle with Matthew, but other than Boyd Hellman, Matthew was the one person who knew the most about Noelle. "You said she fashioned the job for herself and asked you to pitch her to Shelton."

"That's right."

"Didn't her wish to move to a small town seem odd?" I reiterated what Boyd had yelled at Noelle. "He said she was not a small-town girl. He thought she had something up her sleeve. Why would he say that?"

"I don't know." Matthew sighed. "Noelle told me that she hoped the switch might add a layer to her résumé and boost her career to another level. Sommeliers can get stuck doing the same thing. Sometimes you have to take a step sideways to get on the right path."

Her death had ended that prospect.

After a respectful moment of silence, I explained Rebecca's theory that Liberty, being a daddy's girl, might have killed Noelle out of jealousy. "What do you think?"

Matthew worked his teeth back and forth.

"Wait a sec." Rebecca slashed the air. "How about a different theory? Charlotte, you heard Liberty argue that the winery was 'charted for disaster.' Matthew, do you know of any financial problems at the place?"

Matthew eyed me. "You heard what they were saying? I couldn't pick up a word."

"Good ears." I tapped my left one. "After my folks died, Grandmère and Pépère whispered for months. I trained myself to listen well." I repeated what I'd heard at the winery.

Rebecca said, "I'll bet Noelle asked for a large paycheck. Maybe large enough to break the bank."

I concurred. "Maybe Liberty demanded her father fire Noelle so they could remain solvent. Liberty said to Shelton that it was 'always about money.'"

Matthew waved away the thought. "Noelle had a contract. If Shelton had wanted out, he could have paid her off with a minor penalty. I had the same kinds of contracts for all my full hires back at the restaurant. If business went down the tubes—" He paused.

"What?" Rebecca and I said in unison.

"While we were touring the winery, I spotted some financial breakdowns on Shelton's desk. I only caught a glimpse, mind you, but they appeared bleak. No futures. Little demand. You've got good ears. I have fast eyes."

I edged toward my cousin. "Were they recent?"

"I can't be sure."

"Is his product bad?"

"No, it's good. Excellent, in fact. The winery makes delicious wines. Not plentiful, mind you. Only two hundred barrels, which tips the price upward. Vineyards all over the world do this."

Rebecca pivoted. "Charlotte, maybe you were right."

"I was?"

"You said earlier that *hell's key* might have been *Shel's key*." She recapped my earlier theory. "Maybe Noelle saw Shelton lock up financial information in a desk or a safe that required a key—"

"Hold it." Matthew raised his hands. "What if the winery was struggling, and Liberty thought Noelle, the new kid on the block, was spurring her father to sell?"

I nodded in agreement. "What if Liberty killed Noelle to prevent the sale?"

"*Shel's key* could mean that Shelton knew the truth," Rebecca said. "He was the key witness."

Matthew smacked his hands together. "We're going to get to the bottom of this, no matter what."

Rebecca patted him on the shoulder. "Welcome, Matthew."

"To what?"

"The Snoop Club."

CHAPTER

That evening, as I was closing up shop, Meredith called and demanded my presence at her house for a game of Bunco, a dice game that had been popular in the United States since the Gold Rush. She promised it would be an evening of fun, food, and laughter. She said she wouldn't take no for an answer.

When Rags and I entered Meredith's baby blue Victorian, Rocket, the Briard that had doubled in size since Sylvie had gifted him to the twins, danced around us and whimpered with joy. I set Rags on the floor with a strict order to both animals to be good. The two romped away like bosom buddies—Rags scampering in and out beneath Rocket's legs like the dog was a moving bridge.

"She's here!" Amy and Clair chirped as they scampered toward me.

"Aunt Charlotte." Amy clutched my hand. "Meredith wants you to come to the kitchen. Delilah is making stew, and Meredith is fixing an autumn salad with pears, cranberries, and Cowgirl Creamery Pierce Point."

"What is that?" Clair said.

I petted her shoulder. "That's their fall/winter cheese. Its rind is washed with Muscato, a sparkling Italian wine, and then dredged in dried herbs."

"Will I like it?"

I tweaked her nose. "Yes."

"And Grandmère is baking gluten-free cookies," Amy added. "Chocolate cherry mascarpone bars."

"Sounds yummy." Following the girls, I traipsed down the hall drinking in the rich scent of bacon and onions simmering in red wine.

"Pépère is working on a project," Amy said.

"What kind of project?"

"He's renovating the plumbing beneath the sink. We're a little worried."

"For heaven's sake, why?" I asked. My grandfather was adept with every tool.

"Daddy's helping out." Amy winked.

I laughed. Matthew was proficient with a corkscrew but not much else. "Pépère isn't letting him take the lead, is he?"

"No."

"Then relax. They're having a guy's bonding time. Go play with the animals."

Amy and Clair thundered upstairs. In minutes, youthful squealing joined yipping and meowing.

When I entered the kitchen, my grandmother drew me into her arms. "*Bonsoir, chérie.*"

"*Bonsoir,* Grandmère." I pecked both of her cheeks.

She held me at arm's length. "How are you managing?"

I treasured her concern, but I didn't want her to worry. "I'm fine."

"*C'est tragique.* Noelle was a lovely girl, *non*?"

"*Oui.*"

She widened an eye. "And you? Did you sleep at all last night?"

"I stayed at Lois's Lavender and Lace."

"What about tonight?"

"I'll sleep at home, in my own bed."

"But the killer—"

I broke free. "I'll be fine. Promise."

"Hi, Charlotte," Meredith said. "Welcome to girls' night out. But boys are allowed." She strolled to me and handed me a glass of red wine. "For you. Matthew tells me this is terrific. It's a pinot noir from the Evening Land Vineyards in Oregon. It's fresh and light with cherry and pepper overtones."

"Pepper?" I wrinkled my nose.

"Don't mock it." Matthew peered up from where he sat on the floor near the sink. Pépère was doing the work; Matthew was providing the tools on demand. "It's good with hearty dishes like stew."

"And that's what we're having. Beef bourguignon." Delilah, who was standing at the stove, pointed to a cast-iron pot. "It's Julia Childs's recipe, but I've tweaked it. She never added enough bacon for my taste."

I took a sip of the wine and definitely detected the flavors.

"Have a bite of the Nuvola cheese your grandfather brought," Meredith added. "The wine goes great with it, too."

Nuvola di Pecora—the name meant sheep's milk cloud— had a snowy crust and ivory interior, rich with the aroma of damp caves. A gal who taught cheese appreciation classes in San Francisco had introduced my grandfather and me to the cheese.

I slipped a morsel of Nuvola into my mouth and savored the mild mushroom flavor. "Thank you, Pépère."

"For the cheese?"

"For installing new locks on my doors." After working a short stint at The Cheese Shop earlier, he had switched out all the locks on my house.

"*De rien.* I like to be busy."

"Ladies." Grandmère clapped her hands. "Let's move to the dining room for our dinner and dice. We have five players, so one will have to be a ghost partner." She traced a finger along the back of Pépère's neck. "*Mon ami*, when you and Matthew are ready to eat . . ." She made a grand gesture to the two places she had set at the knotty pine table in the kitchen nook. "Serve yourselves. Charlotte, do you know where Rebecca is?"

"She'll be along. She wanted to swing by her house and get a jacket." The air had cooled to a brisk forty with promise of more rain in the forecast. As the women shuffled out, Matthew beckoned me.

I crouched beside him and patted his back. "How's it going, Mr. Plumber?"

"Fine. Listen, after today's wine tasting, I went to have a chat with Urso."

"About?"

"What you and Rebecca and I spoke about—Shelton's finances."

Uh-oh. Urso would not appreciate knowing that I was encouraging others in our fair town to, um, theorize. "What did he say?"

"He's being tight-lipped."

Big surprise.

I said, "Did you also raise the theory that Liberty might have been jealous about her father having a relationship with Noelle?"

"No. I still don't agree Shelton and Noelle were involved."

Pépère glanced over his shoulder. "I believe they were."

"You do?" I said.

"*Oui*." He asked Matthew for a wrench and hunkered beneath the sink, his voice echoing as he spoke toward the pipes. "I saw Noelle and Shelton together on one such occasion. A month or so ago."

"She was in town?" Matthew said. "She didn't call me."

Pépère nodded. "I believe they were having *une liaison amoureuse*."

"Where did you see them?" I asked.

"At the park. And again at the Country Kitchen diner. *Ils ont regardé intime*."

"You think everyone looks intimate, Pépère." Matthew buffed our grandfather's lower back then eyed me. "He's become the town crier. Mr. Jones is having *une liaison* with Mrs. Smith. Mr. Doe is playing footsie with Mrs. White.

Why, Prudence Hart and my ex-wife have nothing on you, Pépère, when it comes to gossip."

Pépère scuttled backward and sat on his haunches. "You chide, but it is so. I know of what I speak. I see with my eyes. At the diner, they were sitting at a corner booth. Their faces were close together." He indicated with his fingertips. "Their eyes were lit with *amour*." He laid a hand on his chest. "I am sorry."

"For what?" Matthew said.

"If I have upset you."

"You have a right to your opinion, you romantic fool. Now, back to work." Although my cousin sounded jovial, when he returned his attention to the toolbox, he was grinding his teeth. He had to be wondering the same thing I was wondering. If Noelle and he had been such close friends, why hadn't she told him she was in town? Why had she kept her relationship with Shelton a secret from him?

* * *

Rebecca whisked through the front door of Meredith's home, a winter scarf riding the wind behind her. "Sorry I'm late," she said, out of breath. "I got distracted. I turned on the TV for a minute, and the next thing I knew I was hooked on a show. Have you ever seen *Homeland*? It's all about conspiracy and lies. I think it's in its second or third season. I can't keep count of all these shows." She removed her scarf and coat and set them on the back of a chair in the dining room. "Anyway, I've started watching reruns of the first season, and the show is addictive." She pointed at the kitchen door. "I'm going to grab some dinner, okay?" She didn't wait for a response.

"Speaking of addictions," Grandmère said, setting out the Bunco tally sheets, dice, and a bell, "I have chosen a drama for our winter play. *Days of Wine and Roses*. I am casting over the next few weeks."

"I've seen the movie," Delilah said. "Jack Lemmon and Lee Remick starred in it. Both were nominated for Academy Awards."

"First it was a teleplay," Grandmère said. "The author got the title from an 1896 poem." She shut her eyes and recited: "*They are not long, the days of wine and roses: out of a misty dream our path emerges for a while, then closes within a dream.*"

"You don't normally put on a drama unless it has a wicked twist to it," I said. "Why are you doing this one?"

"I have been thinking lately of the difficulty of not being able to change one's past." Often, my grandmother alluded to a painful past that she could not escape. I hoped one day she would share the details.

Delilah said, "That's the theme of this play. The leading man changes his path in life, but the leading woman cannot. It breaks his heart."

I flashed on Noelle. Her face had clouded over when we were chatting that first night. She said so much was *at stake*. Had she hoped for more than a boost to her career when she came to work for Shelton Nelson? Had she banked on changing her life's path by marrying him? The use of a heart-shaped corkscrew as the murder weapon felt significant.

"Charlotte, you're up first," Delilah said. "Come on, partner."

We sat at the table opposite each other. Rebecca was learning the game and would occasionally sit in for one of us. Otherwise, she would circle the table and observe.

I grabbed the dice and shook. Of the three, two showed single pips. Spots on the die were called pips, a British term. Because we were playing the first round, only dice showing one pip counted. "Two points."

"It's a start," Delilah said. "Meredith, your turn."

Meredith shook the dice and said, "Two, as well." She pushed the dice to Delilah.

"Your mind, it is wandering, *chérie*." Grandmère petted my hand. "Are you thinking about Jordan?"

I loved how she said his name, with a soft J and the accent on the second syllable. "I was thinking of your play and how difficult relationships can be."

"Especially long-distance ones," Meredith inserted.

"Didn't you talk to Jordan recently?" Grandmère said.

"Yes, but it isn't enough, not with all that has transpired since then."

"Why can he not call *tous les jours*?"

"He can't risk using his cell phone every day," I said. "As it is now, he uses a disposable telephone."

Grandmère grumbled. I knew she worried about me, and she was concerned that whatever Jordan was involved in might follow him back to Providence, but Jordan assured me, once the trial was over, he would be a man who could roam freely, and I would never have to look over my shoulder. He wanted to show me the world. We planned to taste every cuisine and swim in every lake or ocean.

"Five," Delilah said. She had shaken three sixes, which would have been Bunco if we were in round six, but we were still playing the first round. At least three of a kind, difficult to roll, earned five points. She pushed the dice to my grandmother.

Grandmère shook and scored one point for one pip, then passed the dice to me. "Round two. Seize the moment, *chérie*."

Her words shot me back to the night Noelle died. Someone had seized the moment. Noelle had been new to town. Who else but someone who had known her could have killed her? Had Liberty killed Noelle out of jealousy, or was Boyd Hellman the culprit? What if Boyd had found out about Shelton and Noelle? Boyd could have waited for me to leave for the theater that night and then pounced. On the other hand, if he loved Noelle, wouldn't he have killed Shelton? And Noelle had mud on her boots. Where had she gone?

Footsteps pounded the upstairs hall overhead. I startled.

Grandmère clutched my forearm. "*Chérie*, it is only the animals and the twins."

Amy and Clair shrieked with laughter. Rocket barked.

"I know," I said. "I'm a little on edge." I shook the dice. "Four points."

The door to the kitchen swung open. Rebecca entered with a plate of food. "Wait a second," she said.

"That's the right count," I said.

"I can see that." Rebecca indicated with her index finger. "Two dice show twos and one die shows three. We're in the second round, so only twos count. Four points." She scooted an extra chair between Meredith and me, sat down, and balanced her meal on her knees. "But that wasn't why I said *wait*. I arrived late, so before we play any more, tell me if you discussed the murder, because I have another suspect in mind."

Delilah cut me a look. I glowered at her. Did she expect me to be the one to enforce the rules of Bunco night? I wasn't the one who had set them.

Meredith clicked her tongue. "Sorry, Rebecca, but there's no talking business during Bunco."

"But this isn't business," Rebecca said. "It's life."

"Or death," my grandmother whispered.

"Ladies," Meredith said.

Grandmère spanked the table. "I am sorry, Meredith, but this is a dire situation. If our illustrious police cannot solve the crime, then we must do so. Our town needs to heal. Go on, Rebecca. Who do you suspect?"

"Harold Warfield," Rebecca said.

Meredith sat straighter. "Why him?"

Rebecca placed her meal on the table and bounded to her feet, obviously delighted that she had captured Meredith's attention. "On my way home, I was thinking about what Liberty Nelson said, that Noelle was gunning for Harold's job."

"She said that?" Meredith asked.

"She said those very words to Charlotte in the cellar below The Cheese Shop."

Meredith gawked. "She did?"

I nodded.

Rebecca edged closer to the table. "You don't like Harold, do you, Meredith?"

Meredith gnawed her lower lip. "I barely know the man."

"But . . ." Rebecca wiggled her fingers, luring Meredith to confess more.

"Okay, he's sort of cagey, that's all."

"Cagey, how?"

Meredith drummed her fingertips on the tabletop. The Bunco dice jiggled. "I bumped into him at the pet store. I happen to know he owns cats, but he was buying a dog collar."

Delilah said, "I think his sister in Georgia owns a dog."

"Or maybe he acquired a dog," I offered. "Our local pet rescuer can be very persuasive."

"No, it's more than that," Meredith said. "When he saw me staring, he dropped the leash and hurried out."

"That doesn't make him guilty of anything," I said.

"I know. It's just . . ." Meredith flicked her hand. "Nothing. Back to the game."

"Not so fast." Rebecca turned to me. "Charlotte, right before closing, Harold's mousey wife came into the shop. You had already left. That's what made me think about him. He didn't enter. He never does. He remained outside on the sidewalk."

"His wife has him on a strict diet," I said.

"Coming into the store and smelling the fabulous aromas won't put on weight," Rebecca countered.

"Maybe he has no self-control," Delilah said.

Grandmère pointed at Rebecca. "It is not that he waited outside, is it, *mon amie*? It is what he was doing while he waited that drew your eye."

"Yes, exactly." Rebecca clapped. "Harold stood outside tapping messages via his cell phone. He looked really suspicious. I tiptoed to the window and caught sight of what he was doing. He was texting pictures to someone."

"That's harmless," I said. "I text pictures."

"Sexy pictures. Of him wearing"—she bit her lip—"leather. What if he's having an affair? What if he's got a lover?"

"A lover who owns a dog," Meredith chimed in.

"How would that have anything to do with Noelle?" I asked. "You can't believe she was his lover." The very thought gave me the willies.

"No," Rebecca said. "Of course not. But what if Noelle knew about the lover and took compromising photos?"

"Why would she do that?" I said.

"Because we have our theories mixed up. Noelle wasn't gunning for Harold's job; Harold was gunning for Noelle's. She took compromising photos of him to get him to back off. He demanded those photos, and when she didn't hand them over, he killed her. Then he searched her things, found the photographs, and fled."

Judging by the bagginess of his clothes, Harold had lost a lot of weight. Was he getting in shape to impress another woman? Was he sending her messages via his cell phone? Noelle had an expensive Nikon camera. Had she gone out that night and taken pictures of Harold and his lover? And then blackmailed him?

"No." I shook my head. "I only knew her for a short time, but blackmail doesn't sound like something Noelle would have done, and it doesn't explain why she would have said *hell's key.*"

"Okay, what if"—Rebecca held up a finger—"*hell* was a slurred version of *Harold*?"

"Oh no!" Matthew yelled like the house was falling down.

CHAPTER

8

Everyone bolted from the Bunco table and, bumping shoulders, dashed into the kitchen. We halted as a pack. Delilah giggled; so did I. Meredith and Grandmère gasped. Water was spraying everywhere. On the ceiling, the floor, and the window above the sink. Matthew tried in vain to snare the loose hose.

My grandfather scuttled through the opened door leading to the backyard and said, *"Dieu m'aider.* Matthew, I leave you for one minute to empty the trash, and this is what happens?"

"I thought I could . . . I . . ." Matthew sputtered. "Aw, heck. I didn't think."

"Sometimes that is all it takes," Pépère said. "One lapse in judgment and an accident happens."

"Don't worry. It's only water." I fetched a pile of towels from the pantry. "Everyone, grab one."

While all of us, including Matthew, who was soaked to the skin, mopped the kitchen floor, Pépère managed to wrestle the wayward plumbing tube into submission. Soon the water was capped off, and the sink was working as it should.

"Renovations are a pain," Meredith groused as she returned to the pantry for more towels.

"Speaking of renovations," Delilah said, "I heard Noelle was helping you with some."

"We refinished the secretary desk—or at least it's standing on its feet ready for its final finish. She did beautiful work. She . . ." I sighed. "I can't believe she's dead. If only I'd arrived sooner."

"Girlfriend, you can't berate yourself. You are not omniscient." Delilah clutched my hand. "By the way, why didn't you tell me what Noelle said to you?"

"I didn't think Urso would want me to."

"Point taken. But now it's out. So talk. She said, 'Hell's key'?"

I nodded. "She spoke so softly I thought I'd imagined it."

"Rebecca might be right. *Hell* could be a slurred version of *Harold*, but what if each word stood alone?"

"What do you mean?"

"Maybe each was its own phrase, its own sentence. Noelle said the word *hell's* and more of that sentence was to follow, but she couldn't get it out. The same happened with the word *key*."

I related the many variations of *hell's key* that Matthew, Rebecca, and I had come up with.

Delilah wadded up her wet towel and tossed it onto the heap accumulating by the kitchen door. "You know, that boyfriend of Noelle's, the one who has been hanging around the diner? His last name is Hellman."

"Urso has Boyd in his sights."

"Good, because he's a little . . . Wait." Delilah whacked my upper arm. "Do you need a key to open the desk you've been overhauling?"

"No."

"Maybe Noelle thought you did. Maybe she was steering

you to look in a drawer. Maybe she put something important in one of them for safekeeping, assuming only you had the key."

"Like a set of compromising photographs or a digital card from inside her camera?"

"Exactly."

I wondered if Urso or his deputies had found Noelle's camera in her BMW.

"Did you rummage through the desk?" Delilah said.

I didn't, but I couldn't imagine, given the chaotic state of my garage after the murder, that the killer hadn't gone through it. On the other hand, perhaps he didn't notice the secret drawer.

* * *

Eager to find out, I bid Delilah and my family a hasty good-bye. As I raced home in my Escort, Rags curled into me with worry. He knew I was impetuous, but he had never seen me this obsessed. I assured him I was obeying all the laws of the road. I wasn't.

The moment I pulled into the driveway and exited the car, something didn't feel right. I didn't smell anything weird, and I didn't see anyone—no unrecognizable vehicles on the street, no figures running in the shadows—but something was wrong. My skin prickled with fear.

"Do you sense it, Ragsie?" I whispered.

His ears perked and his eyes widened, but he didn't utter a sound. His silence made me feel a teensy bit better. I assured myself that I was imagining things; however, while I had every right to be edgy, I didn't like when I was that way. I preferred Confident, You-Can-Handle-Anything Charlotte, the Charlotte who didn't see the worst in everyone and everything, the Charlotte with unwavering hope and courage. Where was my Wonder Woman persona when I needed it?

Sprinting to the workshop, I talked myself through the unease. I did a pretty good job convincing myself that all was right with the world until I reached the side door. It had been jimmied open. I listened for movement inside. Hearing none,

I opened the door and switched on the light. My stomach clenched.

Someone had rummaged through my things again. Cans of paint and wood stain sat on the floor, not on the tarp. Paintbrushes and wood dowels were strewn helter-skelter, like someone had played Pick Up Sticks with them. I snatched a screwdriver from the scattered tools and spun right and left in one-hundred-and-eighty-degree arcs. A kid in a street fight couldn't have looked scrappier.

After the frightened herd of elephants in my chest stopped using my ribs as their stomping ground, I set aside the screwdriver and inspected the drawers of the desk, first the left and then the right. All were bare. I perched on my knees and craned my neck to look at the underside. The secret drawer was intact. I pawed it open and peered inside. It was also empty. Had Noelle put something there for safekeeping, expecting me to find it? Had the killer returned and discovered whatever he—or she—had been after? If so, the killer was done with me, right? I was safe. On the other hand, I still felt anxious. I should call the police and have them look around.

I pulled my cell phone from my purse and started to dial, but I paused when I caught sight of the Tupperware boxes that held my parents' love letters. Seeing them made me think of Noelle sitting on the guest bed, her back to the door while scribbling notes in her journals. Diaries often needed keys. Did hers? Did she write something incriminating in them, something that a killer needed to keep secret?

Urso's deputy said he confiscated Noelle's computer, cell phone, and address book. He didn't mentioned taking her journals. Did the killer steal the books, or did Urso's staff miss seeing them? If the latter, Noelle's journals could still be there. I remembered her bragging to Shelton and the rest of us that she learned the art of hiding things when she lived at the orphanage. I hadn't searched Noelle's things—not last night before fleeing to the bed-and-breakfast and not this morning after returning to change clothes.

Breaking speed records, I dashed to the house. The door was secure; the lock hadn't been jimmied. I entered using my new key, Rags followed, and we both paused to listen for an intruder. I didn't pick up any errant sound. Rags didn't seem to, either.

Even so, I dialed 911 as I took the stairs, two at a time, to the second floor.

While waiting for someone to answer at the precinct, I bolted to the writing desk in the guest room, switched on the lamp, and surveyed the room. I tried to think like Noelle. If I were going to hide something from nuns, where would I put it?

In plain sight.

As a cozy touch, I had inserted envelopes and stationery in the cubbies at the back of the desk. I fanned through the paper and found a wine reference guide and one of Noelle's journals, one with *Dear Diary* etched in gold on the front. It was keyless. Even so, sensing I might discover something of importance in Noelle's writing, I shuffled through the pages. Each was dated and contained a handwritten sentence that appeared to have been copied straight from a positive-thinking book, with quotes from Albert Einstein, Winston Churchill, Oprah Winfrey.

And on and on.

In addition, Noelle had written messages around the pages, starting at the bottom and routing to the top, reminding her to change her attitude, to see things differently, and to trust herself. There were no tawdry, sexy revelations about a relationship with Shelton, nor were there any comments about the breakup between Boyd and her. And there were no references to any key.

When I reached the end of the diary, I noticed frayed remainders of paper near the binding. Were pages missing? I checked the date. Entries ended the day before she arrived in Providence. Had Noelle or the killer torn them out?

Hoping that Noelle had stashed the missing diary pages in her other journal, I searched for it under the pile of clothes by the closet door, on the shelf above the hanging clothes, in the bureau drawers, and beneath the bed. I emptied the bag filled with gifts that Noelle had bought onto the quilt and

fingered through the embroidered kitchen towel, decorative
wine stoppers, yarn, and crochet hooks. The journal was not
among them. I rummaged through the lining of her suitcase
but paused halfway through my search when I realized her
chic leather briefcase was missing. Did the killer steal it?
Were the missing pages tucked inside? Was my search for
naught?

I didn't remember Urso's deputy mentioning a briefcase.
Urso. I glanced at my cell phone. Why wasn't anyone answering? So much for a quick emergency response. Feeling
that I wasn't in immediate danger any longer, I hung up and
shoved the phone into my purse.

I perched on the edge of the bed, the pluck drained out of
me, and leaned forward on my elbows to rest my forehead in
my hands. Something pointy jabbed the backs of my knees.
I shrugged off my purse, scooted from the bed, lifted the
hem of the quilt, and spied the corner of a book poking from
between the mattresses.

Excitement coursed through me as I tugged Noelle's other
journal free. Revitalized, I flipped through it. Wine labels
were affixed to page after page. As in her diary, Noelle had
sketched memos around the edges of the pages. None of the
ink touched the wine labels. She noted the flavors and the
aromas and whether the wine was a varietal or blend of
grapes. She added opinions like *yummy, flat, good value,* and
pure perfection.

When I reached the end of the journal, I was surprised—
though not shocked—to find pages missing. I searched between the mattresses for them but didn't find them. Someone
had torn them out. Why? It wasn't like the labels were original works of art. Some were beautiful, others ordinary. On
the remnants of the first missing page, Noelle had scrawled
words about the nose and aromas, and she had written the
word *short.* Squeezed onto the paper, in the crease of the
binding, was a doodle of a stick figure, its head looped by a
noose. What did it mean?

I heard something skulking outside the room. I dropped
the journal and leaped to my feet, ready to defend myself

with my fists. Rags burst into the room. Yowling. He skittered across my feet and did a cha-cha behind my ankles. I gathered him up and set him in my lap. His heart revved like a motorboat. "What happened, fella?"

He squalled some more.

"Are you scared or hungry?"

This time he offered a plaintive meow. *Hungry.*

"How is that possible? I know the twins fed you at their house."

He mewed louder. I could decipher that meaning, too: *Starved.*

"Okay, fine. Let me change into my pajamas and then we'll both get dessert."

I gathered both journals and headed to my bedroom wondering if I should show the journals first to Matthew or to Urso. As a former sommelier, Matthew might make sense of Noelle's notes. He might even understand the progression— if there was a progression—of wine labels and which were missing. On the other hand, Urso was in charge of the investigation. Would he consider Noelle's journals valuable?

I set Rags on the bed and placed the journals beside him. Like a good watch cat, he laid his forepaws over the books, reminding me of a fat cat that I had seen in an Internet video that actually growled like a lion at anyone approaching its treasure. While I fetched a pair of Victoria's Secret pajamas, I heard the ticking of the clock on the nightstand beside the bed. Could the ticks be any louder? All at once, I felt alone and extremely vulnerable.

I glanced at Rags. He raised his chin, ears perked.

"C'mere, fella." I tossed the pajamas on the bed and swooped my sweet cat into my arms. He purred into my neck. I strolled to the window to look at the crescent moon. The notion that Jordan, no matter how far away, could see the same crescent moon filled me with comfort.

The lyrics of "Somewhere Out There," a song from my childhood, came to me, and I sang out loud. I was no Linda Ronstadt, but Rags licked my chin in appreciation. I scratched his ears in thanks.

Across the yard, beyond the driveway, I spotted Lois on the porch to Lavender and Lace, scurrying from guest to guest while pouring tea and chatting. Life without her wayward husband seemed to agree with her. She smiled more; she stayed up later.

Suddenly, Lois looked to her right. A hunched woman in a pitch-black cloak bustled up the steps. She reminded me of the wicked witch in *Snow White and the Seven Dwarfs*. With no preamble, Lois beat a path to the woman, grabbed her by the arm, and whisked her inside.

What was up with that?

At first, I thought the woman might be Lois's sister returning to town, but I rejected the idea because this woman was much taller and leggier. Whoever she was, she was acting very secretive. Had Lois agreed to hide her from view? The notion made me think of Shelton Nelson and Noelle Adams. If they had engaged in an amorous relationship, as my grandfather had intimated, would Lois have known?

CHAPTER

Clutching Rags to my chest, I dashed to Lavender and Lace. He protested like I was taking him to the vet for a shot. Poor guy had no sense of night and day sometimes. The glow of streetlamps didn't help.

"Shh, buddy." I sprinted up the front steps of the inn, my clomping feet alarming a few of the guests on the patio. "Sorry," I muttered as I tore into the bed-and-breakfast. "I'm looking for Lois."

A pair of guests pointed toward the staircase.

Lois's Shih Tzu stormed me in the foyer and galloped around my ankles, yipping so loudly I thought her teensy head might bobble off.

"It's me, Agatha. Hush." I set Rags down. The two sniffed cautiously and then scampered away, Rags's hunger and his imaginary worry about some vet poking him with a needle diverted. "Lois?" I called, heading upstairs. Just as I reached the landing, I spotted Lois shuttling the cloaked woman into a room.

Lois spied me, whipped the guest room door shut, and

mouthed something against the door. I couldn't make out the words. Then she turned toward me, clutching the knot of her purple shawl into her fist. "Charlotte, what a surprise. I was checking that all the beds have been turned down."

Liar, liar, pants on fire.

"Would you like to stay another night, dear?"

"No, Lois, thank you." Not and have all the tidbits of our conversation go online like Rebecca claimed they had last night. "I have a question."

"Certainly. Follow me." Hooking a pinky, she beckoned me downstairs. "What did you wish to ask me?"

As I reached the landing, I peeked over my shoulder. Who was the woman? Why the need for secrecy?

"Join me for tea and a little bite of cheese. I've set out tasty platters for the guests to enjoy. All recommendations by your Rebecca. She turned me on to some rather tasty ones. That Twig Farm Goat Tomme is unique looking. The exterior is so hard and gray."

"Best if served with something like fig jam."

"That's what Rebecca said. Such a sweet girl. And she recommended the Weybridge from the Scholten Family Farm. She knows how I love a creamy cow's milk cheese. Oh, and she sold me a beautiful lazy Susan and showed me how to adorn the cheeses with flowers, nuts, raisins, and dried figs. I purchased some glitzy knives, too. You should hear the guests rave."

"I'm thrilled to hear it. Now, if you could answer my question."

Lois lengthened her neck.

"Don't worry," I assured her. "I'm not going to grill you about your secret houseguest."

"My what?"

Yeah, right. "I want to ask about Noelle Adams, the woman who was murdered in my workshop. I wondered—"

"Watch out." Lois blocked my descent.

At the same instant, Agatha and Rags rounded the corner and tore up the stairs, with Agatha leading the charge.

"Those two," Lois said. "Boundless energy. Now, what

was it you wanted to know about Noelle . . . Miss Adams?"

We proceeded to the foyer and paused in the center.

"I wondered if you ever saw her around town with Shelton Nelson."

Lois turned and met my gaze. "He hired her, isn't that so?"

"Yes, but did you see them together, you know . . ." I twirled a hand in the air.

"Dining?"

"Yes, dining and possibly looking like they might be, um . . . amorous? Looking closer than employee and employer should."

"You want to know if they were involved." Lois's mouth drew tight. "Why would you think I would be privy to that information?"

"You know so many people. You have so many guests. I thought you might have heard or seen something pertinent."

Lois folded her hands in front of her. "Shelton keeps to himself. He doesn't socialize much, and he doesn't gallivant around town, don't you know. Ever since his wife left . . ." She paused. "You knew about that, didn't you?"

"She left, as in, walked out?"

"Exactly. Like Sylvie did to Matthew. She ran off to the next county when Liberty was six. She has visited once or twice since then, but she has never inserted herself back into Liberty's life." Lois clucked her tongue. "It's such a shame. A mother's departure marks a child for life. The child feels abandoned and loses self-worth. I hear it on all the talk shows."

"You watch television?" I had never seen a TV switched on in the B&B.

She offered a sly grin. "When I get the time. That psychological mumbo jumbo is so relevant. Anyway, after the wife left, Shelton took to being a doting parent."

Perhaps too doting, I mused, if Liberty had killed to ensure that her father remained solo.

"Shelton is a fine man. He lodges family here whenever they come in from out of town. He puts up employees, too."

"Did Noelle Adams stay here?"

"One time. For a night or two."

"And . . ." I said, leading the witness.

"And nothing. They did not *socialize* in the way you mean. They had a drink. They talked about wine and business. He left before dinner. She dined alone. Shelton fetched her the next morning for a tour of the vineyard and his private collection."

Interesting. I could've sworn Noelle's first visit to Shelton's cellar was with Matthew and me. She had faked it expertly. Maybe she hadn't wanted Liberty or Harold to know.

"Noelle had a marvelous time and returned flushed and excited, like a girl who had found the treasure of her life. The next day she left town. End of story. Now, his daughter Liberty . . ." Lois toyed with the curls at the nape of her neck. "She's a whole other kettle of fish."

I waited.

"She's getting married, don't you know."

Rebecca often reminded me that the art of interrogation required being patient enough that the witness, however reluctant, would willingly offer up the information. I owed it to Noelle to remain calm. I cared deeply that her murder be avenged.

"Your part-timer Tyanne is the wedding planner," she said.

"So I heard."

"She's spoiled," Lois added.

"Tyanne?"

"No, dear, Liberty Nelson. Shelton has lavished her with gifts. Too much isn't good for the soul, if you know what I mean, but I can't blame him. With his wife in absentia, he felt the burden—the *responsibility*—to provide all the love, even if it meant with fistfuls of dollars. Liberty is marrying a nice boy. A religious boy. She has been quite vocal about how she intends to change her ways for him."

"What do you mean by *change her ways*?" I asked.

"She can be rambunctious. Too much partying. All through her young years . . . Liberty was willful. She dressed a little risqué. She partied hearty, as they say. And she lied to Shelton all the time."

What teen didn't? As a freshman, I had lied about going out with girlfriends to the mall but ended up at a big bash. Grandmère had caught me out. I was lucky she had. A friend, driving drunk, had died in a car crash after my grandmother fetched me. Life, even in a small town, wasn't always idyllic.

A pair of inn guests walked past us, bidding good night to Lois. She wished them a blissful sleep.

As they climbed the stairs, Lois opened a drawer of the foyer table. She pulled out a dust rag and wiped down the tray that her precious china sat upon. She could be quite fastidious. "You know, Charlotte, there is something I forgot to tell you about last night, if you'd like to hear. You were gone this morning before I could mention it. I noticed a Taurus idling on the street across from your house, just after you went out for the evening."

My breathing quickened. "A Taurus? You're sure?"

Lois's shoulders curled in. "Yes, I'm sure. It's what *he* drives." *He*, her errant husband. The one she hoped would return. She shoved the dust rag back in the drawer and closed it with a snap. "At first I thought it was him spying on me, don't you know, but then I realized it was a green car, not charcoal gray."

My interest perked up. Boyd Hellman's Chevy Malibu was metallic green. Working to keep my voice on an even keel, I said, "Are you sure this one was green?"

"It was dark, mind you," Lois said. "I suppose it could have been blue or red." A defense attorney would make mincemeat of her on the witness stand. "I didn't think much of it at the time. As I said, you had already headed out. And then Miss Adams left around the time I was serving dinner. When she departed, so did the car. I don't know if it returned."

Had Boyd tailed Noelle? "Did you see the driver?"

"Only from a distance. I believe it was a woman."

Rats. That ruled out Boyd Hellman. "Could it have been Liberty Nelson?"

Lois covered her mouth with the back of her hand. "Oh my. I wouldn't know for sure. My eyes aren't that good, and I wasn't about to pull out binoculars."

I smiled. Spying was okay, but blatant spying was taboo?

"I suppose it could have been someone wanting to meet with you," Lois went on. "A vendor or such, or"—she lowered her voice—"that lover boy of yours sneaking into town."

No way did Jordan resemble a woman. He had short hair and very masculine features.

"Where has he gone, by the by?"

Only a select few knew about Jordan being enrolled in the WITSEC Program. Lois was not one of my inner circle.

"If you ask me, he's very secretive," she went on. "Like he's a spy or something."

I laughed. "He's not a spy."

"He looks like one. Those movie star good looks, those alert eyes. He reminds me of"—she snapped her fingers—"that actor. The one that plays James Bond."

There had been so many actors that had portrayed the super spy I didn't ask which one she meant. "I'll tell him. He'll be pleased."

Rags screeched through the foyer and came to a gasping halt against my ankles. Agatha charged after him, yipping merrily.

"That's enough playtime." I bundled Rags into my arms, thanked Lois for her information, and asked her to call if she remembered anything else.

As I strolled home, I felt someone watching me. I glanced over my shoulder and caught sight of the cloaked woman—the hood still pulled up—peering through the break in the drapes upstairs at the B&B.

Who was she? Why was she staring at me?

Pulse thrumming, I raced home and bolted every lock in the house, including the windows in the attic, in case the woman had the inclination to break into my house and force a poisoned apple into my hands. I thought about calling Matthew or Urso but decided against it. What would I say? Someone at the B&B stared at me. *Ooh, so scary*. I thought of an old saying my grandmother used to tell me about spiders: *They're more frightened of you than you are of them*. I never believed her.

In case I needed to defend myself, I fetched the baseball bat Matthew had left in the foyer closet and placed it beside me in bed. A baseball bat could flatten a spider for sure. And I let Rags sleep on top of the covers—a no-no on any other night, but a rule I could break when I was the scaredy cat.

Eyes wide open, I gazed at the darkened ceiling, which grew grayer the longer I stared at it, and I pondered Providence's future. What could be done to make the town safer? Did other small towns have the same problems? We were not a big city like Cleveland or Chicago. The murders that had occurred in our town hadn't been accidental drive-by shootings. They were personal.

Feeling lonelier than I could remember in years, I picked up the phone and dialed Jordan's WITSEC handler. I knew he wouldn't answer. He would see my name and the call would roll into voicemail. When he had the chance, he would allow Jordan to listen to the message. I left a lengthy one of love and ended with my deepest fear, wondering if Jordan would ever return to Providence. I didn't tell him about Noelle's murder. I didn't want him to worry.

As I set the telephone back in its cradle, I heard footsteps. On the wraparound porch. Below my bedroom window.

I ordered Rags to stay put and, with adrenaline spiraling though me, grabbed the baseball bat, slipped into my tennis shoes, and sprinted downstairs ready to clock the woman in the cloak.

CHAPTER

10

Gripping the baseball bat in my left hand and resting its barrel on my right shoulder, I whipped open the door.

Rebecca, wearing a hoodie jacket, jeans, and Ugg boots, hopped from foot to foot on the porch, her face tearstained. The glimmer of the porch light made her eyes gleam like a manic cat's eyes. She raised her hands in surrender. "Don't swing."

"What are you doing here?" I slotted the baseball bat into the umbrella stand. "It's late." Worried to my teeth, I wrapped my arms around her. She wasn't merely my employee. She was the little sister that God forgot to give me. "Come inside."

"I had to talk to someone," she snuffled. "I don't mean to be a bother, but I—"

"Shh." Before closing the door, I scanned the street to see if anyone was lurking. I didn't see a soul. No metallic green Chevy Malibu. No dark sedan of any kind. And no woman in a cloak peering from a neighboring window. "Come with me." I guided Rebecca into the office, which until that moment I had forgotten was prepped for painting. Blue tape affixed plastic drop cloths to the base moldings. Tarps covered all the furniture that I hadn't moved to the garage. "Let's go to the kitchen instead," I said. "I'll make tea."

Rebecca settled onto a chair at the red oak mission table in the kitchen nook while I put up a pot of water and set tea bags into two cups. As I opened a canister of chocolate chip orange cream cheese cookies, Rags meowed. His tail rose in a question mark.

"You're right," I said. "I had promised you your own dessert before we ran next door." I fetched a treat from a porcelain cat jar on the counter and tossed it toward Rags's bed. He batted it around the floor like a toy before finally settling down to devour it.

"Why did you go to Lavender and Lace?" Rebecca said.

"It's a long story. You first."

"It's . . ." She removed her hoodie jacket, looped it over the back of the chair, and tugged down the hem of the sweater she wore beneath. "You know that Ipo and I aren't engaged anymore. Do you know why?"

"My grandfather said you wanted to make sure you were suited for each other."

"What? Me? No. It wasn't my choice. It was Ipo's. His parents have talked him into selling his honeybee farm and moving back to Hawaii."

"What?"

"They say a Hawaiian Ohioan doesn't make sense."

"Hawaiian Ohioan?"

She frowned. "I know. It's a mouthful."

"What about the course of true love?"

"His parents never liked me."

"Because you're Amish?"

"No, because he's a mama's boy, and he acts more independent when he's with me." She flicked her hair over her shoulder. "Personally, I think that's a good thing, but what do I know."

I poured steaming water into the teacups. The enticing aroma of Earl Grey tea wafted up to my nose. I took the cups, napkins, spoons, and a jar of honey to the table. "Didn't you tell me that his parents' marriage was not an approved marriage?"

"Yes. They eloped."

"Can't you and Ipo do the same?"

"He already did that, remember? And then his ex-wife dumped him here. His parents were never in favor of him staying. Some women keep men on a tight leash. His mother—" She took a sip of her tea. "Let's be blunt. She doesn't want to share him."

I thought of Liberty, who had a similar hold on her father. How did her fiancé feel about that? How had Noelle felt about it if, indeed, Noelle and Shelton had been involved? Had Noelle and Liberty fought?

Rebecca dripped honey into her cup and swirled it with her spoon. "If only there were tea leaves that could divine my future."

"You divine your own future," I said, surprised by the intensity in my tone. "You figure out what you want, and you make it happen."

"You know, back home, I never did anything bad. I didn't branch out. I didn't take risks, that is, until I left to work in Providence. Maybe I'm supposed to take chances now." She got to her feet, spread her arms, and twirled. "Maybe I'm supposed to do what Delilah did and see the world. Go to New York and London and Paris. Maybe work on a cruise ship."

"Whatever you decide, take it one day at a time."

"Is that what you're doing when it comes to Jordan?"

"Yes. One long day at a time." Doing my best not to think about Jordan, I cradled my tea between my palms and drank in the delicious scent. "I'm sorry about you and Ipo."

"It's okay. I'll survive. There are plenty of fish in the sea."

"Like that cute deputy?"

"I'm not making any hasty decisions." Rebecca settled into her chair and tapped a fingernail on the table. "Tell me about your visit with Lois."

I replayed our chat about Shelton and Liberty, her wild

years, and Lois's suspicions about Shelton's involvement with Noelle. I concluded with the mini-revelation about the car on the street. Rebecca and I agreed the driver had to have been Boyd. If Lois couldn't tell green from blue or red, she certainly couldn't have determined whether the driver was female or male.

Around midnight, not certain that I had anything concrete to share with Urso, I declared it was time for bed. My head ached; my body craved sleep. Considering the funk Rebecca was in, I didn't want her driving home. I asked her to stay the night. Neither of us wanted to crash in a room by ourselves, so we decided to camp out in my room. Rags found a spot between us on the bed and kneaded like a master baker.

Rebecca giggled as she pulled the comforter under her chin. "I've never had a slumber party."

"It's not a slumber party. It's a sleepover. The main ingredient is sleep."

"Got it."

As I was drifting off, it dawned on me that I hadn't told Rebecca about the mysterious woman in the cloak. I opened my eyes. A sliver of moonlight edged through the break in the drapes. Rebecca looked extremely peaceful. Even so, I whispered, "Are you awake?"

"Yep." She laid her hand against her mouth to stifle a yawn.

"I forgot to tell you something." I explained.

"And you thought I was her? I'm so sorry."

"No problem."

"Don't worry. I'm here to protect you." She patted the baseball bat that she had rested beside the nightstand.

I suppressed a smile. Two women, one bat, and a cat. Who would dare attack?

"Also"—Rebecca yawned—"Lois won't be able to keep the woman hidden for long. Secrets are hard to keep hush-hush."

* * *

In the morning, sleet pelted the town. An icy breeze, overly cool for November, swirled through the air and gusted into

the shop every time a customer entered. Though I had dressed
in a turtleneck and corduroy trousers and was running around
the place like a madwoman while restocking and cleaning
and serving up orders, I couldn't shake the chill. A midmorning snack of raisin quiche made with HoneyBee Goat Gouda
helped but not entirely. I had to admit that thoughts about
Noelle and a deep desire to solve the crime kept me on edge.
Was I missing something obvious? She had hidden her journals. Had she hidden a key? If so, where?

Around ten A.M., Urso ventured in to purchase his lunch.
Deputy O'Shea accompanied him. Like Urso, the deputy re-
spectfully removed his hat upon entering and tucked it beneath his arm.

After a quick "Good morning," Urso ordered his *usual*—
he was back to favoring a torpedo sandwich made with
maple-infused ham and Jarlsberg cheese, topped with a mixture of mayonnaise and maple mustard. While I wrapped his
sandwich in our special wrap and slotted it into a gold tote
bag, he moved off in the direction of the beverage display.

Deputy O'Shea didn't budge. He peered over the counter
into the kitchen—trying to catch a glimpse of Rebecca, I
presumed.

I smacked the countertop.

He startled. "Oh, sorry. I'll have a—"

"She's not here," I whispered.

"Who-o-o?" he stammered.

"Rebecca. I gave her a ten-minute breather."

"I wasn't—"

"Sure you were. She's taking a walk."

He gaped. "In this rain?"

I nodded. "Without an umbrella. We've got a few by the
door if you want to be a gentleman and take one to her."

"Chief, I'll be right back." Without waiting for an okay
from his superior, the deputy snagged an umbrella and hustled out of the shop.

Urso returned to the counter. "What's he doing?"

"Acting like a knight in shining armor." I beckoned him
to the register. "He's a nice kid, Urso."

"All of Tim's family are good people." Timothy O'Shea owned the tavern next to the Village Green. He had seven brothers and umpteen nephews—no nieces. Urso tilted his head. "Rebecca doesn't normally take midmorning breaks. What's up?"

"Ex-fiancé woes." I moved to the register. "Cash, credit, or on account?"

"The latter."

I sent Urso a monthly statement, as I did for many of my regular customers. "How's the investigation going?"

"Slowly."

"Did you happen to find Noelle's camera in her car?"

"We did. Why?"

"Anything of importance on it?"

"Nope. Not one picture."

That seemed odd. She must have taken it with her on her hike. Otherwise, wouldn't she have left it in the guest room? "Was the memory card missing?"

Urso tilted his head. "Why are you so curious?"

"Is that a yes?"

He didn't respond.

When I had gone in search of Noelle's journals, I'd put Rebecca's concerns about Harold Warfield from my mind, but now those concerns came back full force. Harold had longish hair. Perhaps Lois mistook him for a female driver. "There are rumors that Harold Warfield was having an affair. If Noelle knew and took pictures . . ." I hesitated. I couldn't see Noelle blackmailing anyone. On the other hand, Urso's non-answer confirmed that the memory card was missing. "Why else would someone have taken the memory card out of the camera?"

"I didn't say—"

"You didn't have to."

He frowned. "What would she have expected to gain? Money?"

"His job."

"Why would she want to manage a winery? She was a noted sommelier."

"She gave that up to move here. I can't imagine being a glorified party planner was her endgame. What if she was trying to say Harold's name when she said the word *hell*?"

Urso did everything he could not to roll his eyes, but he couldn't help himself. He drew in a deep breath and let his shoulders release.

I hurried to add what I had noticed when I had taken the tour of the winery with Matthew and Noelle. "Harold was extremely standoffish to Noelle. He acted like he didn't want to touch her. At first I thought he was a germaphobe, but the more I think about it, his aversion seemed more deep-seated. Maybe he found her odious because she had dirt on him. What do you know about him?"

"Nice wife, no kids, attends church, keeps to himself."

"In other words, not much."

Urso donned his hat. "Okay, you've got my interest. I'll look into it."

A feeling of pride swelled within me. Whether or not Harold was the killer, Urso was taking my ideas seriously. "Also, when you seized Noelle's things, did you happen to take her briefcase?"

"We did. There was no key inside, and it didn't require a key."

Dang.

"By the way," he continued, "you'll be glad to know I had a long chat with Boyd Hellman."

"Care to share?"

"Not at this time."

"Don't tell me you think he's innocent."

He didn't respond, but I could read his body language well enough to know that pressing him to reveal more about Boyd Hellman wouldn't work. I said, "Do you have other suspects?"

"Mine to know."

"Are you taking a good look at Liberty and Shelton Nelson?"

He tapped the floor with his foot.

Shoot. I needed to know more. I wouldn't rest until Noelle's killer was brought to justice. "What about that journalist, Ashley Yeats?" I blurted.

"What about him?"

"He arrived in town the day Noelle did." I couldn't put a finger on why the guy bugged me, but he did. "Don't you find that coincidental? And aren't you the one who told me you don't like coincidences?"

"Lots of people arrived that day. This is a tourist destination."

"But—"

"Stop, Charlotte," Urso said. "Haven't you got enough to do, running a thriving shop? There are ten customers"—he gestured to the amassing crowd—"who are ready for you to sell them something delectable."

"They aren't ready. They're browsing. C'mon, U-ey, I want to know who your suspects are." I ticked off the tips of my fingers. "You've got Boyd Hellman, Liberty and Shelton Nelson, Harold Warfield, and—"

"Hold on." Urso raised his palm. "Before I reveal anything, tell me what you know about this Ashley Yeats."

"You're getting good at this."

A twinkle returned to Urso's eyes. "Don't believe what they say. You *can* teach an old dog new tricks."

I breathed easier. He wasn't shutting me out. "You're not old. If you are, then I am, and I don't intend to be old until I'm my grandmother's age. And even she would claim she was young." I rang up the purchase and handed him his tote bag.

"Yeats," Urso repeated. "Why, other than his arrival date, do you think he could be Noelle's killer?"

"He's as phony as the day is long."

"After last month's run-in, I wouldn't call you the best judge of character."

Now, he was being spiteful. I had trusted someone, and that trust had put me in hot water. I stood a little taller—hard to do at five feet and a couple of inches when facing a bull of a man. "I saw Ashley Yeats snooping around Shelton Nelson's cellar after we took the tour."

"Reporters snoop. So?"

"When he met Noelle at the winery, he offered her his business card. She didn't take it. I got the feeling she knew him. He ogled her like she was meat."

"Men ogle. It's not appropriate, but they do. She was a beautiful woman."

"All I'm saying is I think the guy bears a look-see."

"Is that your gut instinct talking?" Urso smirked.

I fluttered a hand. "Here's another theory. Last night, when we were playing Bunco—"

"You play Bunco?" Urso sniggered.

"Enough teasing, okay?" I glowered at him. "Last night, someone suggested that Shelton Nelson was in a relationship with Noelle."

Urso let out a little moan. "Where are we living, Soap Opera City, USA? Charlotte, do your job and stop trying to do mine." He headed for the front door.

I skirted around the counter and chased after him. "Noelle came to town more often than she let on."

"Big deal."

"She kept a couple of journals. Did Deputy O'Shea confiscate them when he took her other things from the guest room?"

"He did."

"Aha! Caught you out. No, he did not." I scooched in front of Urso to block him from exiting. "I have them, and I've read through them."

Urso folded his arms across his massive chest. "Where did you find them?"

"In my house." I hated that I sounded so defensive. "There's no crime tape. There's nothing to stop me from—"

Urso held up a hand to stop my diatribe. "All I asked was where did you find them."

"In the guest room, tucked between the mattresses."

"Is there anything about this supposed relationship in them?"

"No, but there are pages missing. The dates on the remaining pages end the day before Noelle arrived. I have—"

"Hand them over." He opened his palm. "And then I want you to stay clear of this investigation."

"I can't, U-ey. I'm part of this investigation. My garage was rummaged through again. If the killer—"

"What?" Urso gripped my shoulders; worry lines etched his forehead. "Why didn't you tell me sooner?"

I explained how last night, during the plumbing fiasco, Delilah and I had come up with other theories for the meaning of *hell's key*, so I raced home to search for new clues only to find my garage invaded again. "I called 911, but I hung up when no one answered. I was pretty sure I wasn't in danger."

"Oh, for Pete's sake, you amaze me." He dropped his hands to his sides. So much for his brief, albeit sincere, concern over my well-being.

"I don't believe the intruder entered the house. For all I know, he"—or she, I mused—"found what he was after in the garage and split."

"I'll have a deputy come by and do another once-over. Until then, the journals, please. You've got them with you." He held out a hand for the evidence. "You wouldn't have left them at home if you felt they were important."

I fetched the journals from the office and returned. "Here."

Urso took them and placed them in the tote bag with his lunch.

"You'll fingerprint them?" I said.

He arched an eyebrow. "If you promise to butt out." He worked his tongue inside his cheek.

I mirrored him. He could freeze in you-know-where before I gave him my promise.

After a long standoff, he said, "Say, did I tell you? My brother is thinking of running for office."

"That's great." And it was. We had arrived at neutral territory.

"He wants me to manage his campaign."

Some emotion I couldn't identify lodged in my throat; I swallowed hard. "Would you give up being chief of police?"

"I'm not sure."

"Doesn't he live in Virginia?"

"He does."

"You'd move?"

"Life delivers curveballs all the time. I have to be ready for a changeup pitch."

I grimaced. I despised baseball metaphors, maybe because I was never allowed to play on the boy's baseball team even though, as a girl, I had a mean arm. And Urso knew it, the creep.

"See ya." He offered a single nod, then placed his hat on his head and marched out the door.

"Charlotte." Matthew passed behind the cheese counter into the annex with a box of wine balanced on his shoulder. "Meredith and I are catching a bite to eat at the diner. Want to join us?"

"Yes," I said, wishing I had thought to have Matthew view the journals before ceding them to Urso. Should I run after him and offer my cousin as an expert witness? Out the front window, I caught sight of Rebecca and Deputy O'Shea rounding the corner at Cherry Orchard Street. Heedless of the pelting rain, Urso swept up to them, moved the umbrella from O'Shea's hand to Rebecca's, and hitched a thumb at O'Shea. Seeing how miffed he was, I nixed my pursue-and-plead plan and stepped outside. From beneath the awning, I yelled, "Rebecca."

She waved. I tapped my watch then pivoted to return to the shop. Without any warning, Prudence Hart smacked into me. Water scattered off her umbrella.

"Watch it," she said.

I huffed. She had been the reckless pedestrian. Taking the high road, I said, "I like your raincoat."

"*Pfft*. This rain is going to turn our streets into rivers if it doesn't let up."

Rebecca trotted up to us. "Rivers? Nonsense. This is mild."

"Rivers, I tell you," Prudence said. "And then we'll have riverboats and gambling. You know about the gambling, don't you?"

"What gambling?" I said.

Prudence rocked onto the heels of her boots and back to her toes. "That reporter Ashley Yeats tells me there are card games going on in this town, and someone's contemplating putting up a pool hall."

The lyrics of "Ya Got Trouble" from *The Music Man* rang out in my head.

I smiled. "Prudence, I'm sure Mr. Yeats is exaggerating."

"He's a bit of a gossip, don't you think?" Rebecca closed her umbrella and gave it a little shake.

"A gossip?" Prudence snorted. "Heavens no. He's got his finger on the pulse of this town."

"Does he even have a pulse?" Rebecca teased. "I don't trust him. With that slick dark hair and those shiny teeth, he reminds me of a vampire."

Prudence threw her a harsh look. "Don't talk about him like that. Mark my words, you'll see." She flounced away in the direction of her dress shop.

"Whew!" Rebecca snickered. "What's got her in a tizzy?"

"She's smitten."

Rebecca guffawed. "Oh, please. Miss Lemon Juice, smitten with that reporter? She's at least fifteen years older than he is."

"Age has nothing to do with desire."

Again I thought of *The Music Man*. Like the leading man, who was a con artist salesman par excellence, Ashley Yeats had won over not only Prudence but also Sylvie with his charm. Who was the guy? More importantly, what was his relationship to Noelle, and what was his alibi on the night of the murder?

CHAPTER

Before I left the shop to join Matthew and Meredith at the diner, Rebecca nabbed me by the register. She urged me to talk to Matthew about Harold Warfield; her sixth sense was working overtime, she said. I told her I had my own concerns about Ashley Yeats. She made me swear I would fill her in on whatever I discovered.

As I entered the Country Kitchen, I inhaled the zesty aromas. The South of the Border special—baked chicken stuffed with jalapeños, onions, and Great Midwest Habañero Jack cheese—was making patrons clamor for orders. Tourists and parade volunteers, eager for a respite, waited in a line that curved out the door. Thankfully the nasty rain had subsided, although more inclement weather remained in the forecast.

I nestled into the booth with Matthew and Meredith and ordered the special. Minutes later, after I ate a bite of my fiery meal, I moaned with satisfaction, and then loudly enough to be heard above the roar, said to Matthew and Meredith, "Harold Warfield."

"What about him?" Matthew said.

I glanced at Meredith, who was too busy enjoying her tortilla soup showered in shredded good old-fashioned Wisconsin Cheddar to put the kibosh on discussing Noelle's murder. Maybe she realized how much solving the crime mattered to Matthew. "Rebecca swears something is different about Harold, and Urso isn't taking the notion seriously."

I laid down my fork. "That's not exactly true. U-ey said he would look into all suspects, but I think he has someone particular in mind."

"Boyd Hellman."

"Not Boyd."

"He's ruled him out?" Matthew said.

"You know U-ey. He can be evasive."

"Aren't you the one who told me we had to trust him?"

"Let's keep focused, one suspect at a time. Harold." I shifted in my seat. "Tell me what you know about him."

"He's different, I'll grant you that," Matthew said, "but different doesn't make someone a killer. He doesn't come in the shop, but I've seen him around. At Café au Lait and the bookstore."

"And the pet store," I said, eyeing Meredith. "Last night at Bunco you had suspicions about Harold."

"I had misgivings for speaking out of turn, too." Meredith blotted her mouth with a napkin. "I have to agree with Matthew. Different can be a good thing. An artist can open your eyes to a fresh perspective. A writer can open your heart to new thought. A musician can open your ears to innovative sound."

"Who are you?" I teased. "Our next junior statesman?"

"Very funny. All I'm saying is we were jumping to conclusions last night. Harold might simply be a high-strung individual. I mean, c'mon. He got nervous when I gawked at him buying the dog leash, so he and his friend—"

"A female friend?"

"A guy. Harold poked him and they tore out of the store like teens caught shoplifting."

"You didn't mention that last night."

"I didn't think it was important."

"But you think we should give him the benefit of the doubt."

"He's never stirred up rumors before."

I tilted my head, assessing my friend. "No wonder Providence Liberal Arts College hungers to have you as the dean of students. You're completely unbiased. I love that about you. They're still wooing you, I assume?"

"I have a meeting with them right after I finish this fabulous soup."

I drummed the table. "So, if you don't want to discuss Harold Warfield, let's talk about the journalist Ashley Yeats."

"Yeats?" Matthew said. "Why him?"

"He's a creep who can't be trusted," said a man sitting at the counter.

I swiveled to see who had spoken and felt my shoulders go rigid. Boyd Hellman, as flushed as the red wool of his plaid coat, aimed a finger at me. Why hadn't I seen him when I slipped into the booth? Had he heard all of our conversation? Given what we said, did he think he was no longer a suspect?

"You know Ashley Yeats?" Meredith asked.

"I know *of* him." Boyd's lip curved up in an Elvis snarl as he rotated on his stool. "The jerk called Noelle at home. A lot."

I recalled how wary Noelle had seemed of the journalist. "What did he say?"

"They only talked once. Supposedly he wanted to do an article about her career." Boyd raised his chin. "After that, she wouldn't take his calls."

Why would Noelle have dodged a journalist? Was there something tawdry in her past that Yeats had uncovered? "Can you speculate on what they discussed during that one conversation?"

"Lady"—Boyd slapped his thigh—"I don't speck-o-late, got me? Never have, never will."

I wasn't sure what he thought I meant by *speculate*, but he huffed and spun back toward the counter and yelled, "Hey, Delilah, I'm ready for chow." Delilah signaled that she saw

him and would return. For a split second, I wondered what
Noelle had seen in Boyd, but I pushed the thought from my
brain. Most women, including myself, had chosen poorly at
one time or another. Boyd was good-looking in a guy-who-
works-with-his-hands way. What was his occupation?

"Who's he?" Meredith whispered.

"Noelle's ex-boyfriend," Matthew said, keeping his voice
low, then added, "Do you really think Urso has ruled him out
as a suspect?"

"I didn't say that." I told them about my latest encounter
with Urso at Fromagerie Bessette and how I wished I had
kept the journals and not handed them over.

"She had more than one?" Matthew said.

"Two. One was like an inspirational journal. She wrote all
sorts of quotes by famous people."

"She was always doing that. Her grandfather encouraged
her to—" His voice caught.

Meredith rested a reassuring hand on his forearm. "Go
on, Charlotte."

"The other was a record of wines she tasted, with labels
and memos about flavors and aromas."

"Matthew does the same thing," Meredith said. "He's got
books and books of them. Pretty soon, we'll need a storage
unit to hold them all."

"I never want to forget a good wine I've tasted," he said.
"Noelle was the same. Man, she had a good palate."

"She had the finest palate ever," Boyd said, intruding a
second time into our conversation. I thought my hearing was
good; this guy had radio antennae for ears.

"Ignore him," I whispered.

Matthew said, "But he's right. She was a whiz at blind
taste testing."

"She shouldn't have lowered herself to come here." Boyd
beat his palm with his fist. "You made her do it, Bessette."

"I did not," Matthew said. "She created her own job; she
convinced Shelton to hire her."

"Yeah, make excuses, but you know as well as I do that
you're the one who lured her here. You." Boyd stabbed his

forefinger at Matthew then at his own eyes, as if signaling that he was keeping watch on Matthew. Without another word, he swung back to the counter and hunched forward. At the same time Delilah set the daily special in front of him, and he struck up a conversation.

"Odd guy," Meredith whispered. "Hot temper."

"He did it, Charlotte," Matthew said. "I can feel it."

Meredith clutched his hand. "Feelings aren't always right."

"Pages were torn out of the journals," I said.

"You think he"—Matthew motioned to Boyd—"might have ripped them out?"

"Or Noelle did."

"Why would she?"

"I don't know." I sighed. "Back to Ashley Yeats. What's your gut feeling about him?"

"He's cheap," Matthew said. "He came to the shop earlier looking to buy an expensive bottle of wine. He wound up buying an inexpensive one. 'What does it matter?' he said. 'All wines taste the same.' Like he knew the difference, the fraud."

"That's what I think he is." I tapped the table with my fingertip. "A huckster."

"Like Starbuck in *The Rainmaker*," Meredith said.

"Exactly. Or Harold Hill in *The Music Man*."

"Or Dracula," Matthew grinned. "Did you see that widow's peak he's got?"

I smirked. "Rebecca said the same thing. He reminds her of a vampire."

"I tried to educate him about the complexities of wine," Matthew continued, "but he wasn't interested."

Meredith nudged Matthew with her shoulder. "If you ask me, we have a whole slew of people who aren't interested in higher learning today." She nodded toward Boyd, who was suddenly all grins and smiles while chatting up Delilah. She played along; it was her job. "Oh my, look at the time." Meredith eyed her watch. "I've got to split."

"Remember, you can't keep one foot in both camps," Matthew said as Meredith slipped out of the booth. "Elementary school teacher or liberal arts college dean. Make a choice."

"They haven't offered the position yet." Meredith perched her knee on the booth seat, bent forward, and kissed him on the cheek. "See you later, handsome."

Matthew and I finished our meals in quiet. As a busboy removed our plates, Sylvie waltzed into the diner, dressed in something akin to a safari outfit—hound's-tooth jacket, jodh-pur trousers, stretch poplin shirt, riding boots, and a walking stick. The twins followed her, each looking normal in simple jeans, tee shirts, raincoats, and galoshes.

"Hi, Daddy," Amy and Clair called. They skipped toward us.

Sylvie peeped over her shoulder like she had lost something. When the door to the diner opened again, I realized she hadn't lost some*thing*; she had misplaced some*one*. Ashley Yeats, dressed in similar togs to Sylvie, pushed through the throng. With renewed confidence, Sylvie sashayed toward us. Apparently, she had lassoed a date with the journalist and couldn't wait to parade the man in front of her ex-husband.

The twins arrived at the booth and flung themselves at their father for a hug.

Matthew said, "Whoa, don't smother me. Back up." They obeyed, and he gestured for them to approach him, one at a time, for a hug; Amy first. "Where are you off to in this sluggish weather?"

"Kindred Creek." Clair flapped a brochure in Matthew's direction. Dutifully, he took it and browsed the pages.

Amy said, "We came here to show you our outfits."

More likely, Sylvie wanted to show off hers. That wasn't exactly fair of me. Sylvie was usually a good mother, and the twins seemed happy whenever they were with her, but I found it curious that she always had to make an appearance before she went somewhere with them, as if she wanted to flaunt what a good mother she was. To Matthew. To me. To the world.

Sylvie came to a stop, jutted a hip, and rested her forearm

on it. Had she memorized the pose from some glamour magazine? At any moment, I expected Ashley to swing around in front of her and fix her collar and makeup. With his striking visage, perhaps he had been a model in another life.

"Hello, love," Sylvie said. "We're going on the Best of Fall hike."

Best of Fall was an annual outing led by the Bird Watching Society of Providence.

"Doesn't it sound fun, Daddy?" Clair said. "We get to pick up leaves . . ."

". . . and put them in hiking journals that the park provides," Amy finished.

"And see birds . . ."

". . . and we can share them in school on Monday."

"Ashley suggested the idea," Sylvie said. "You've both met Ashley, haven't you?"

"Of course they have." Ashley elbowed Sylvie. "Fromagerie Bessette is where I bought the wine for you, love."

The *cheap* wine, I mused.

"Isn't it muddy at Kindred Creek?" Matthew said.

"We don't mind." Amy twirled in a circle. She was forever spinning. "It'll be fun. Mud washes off."

Sylvie wrinkled her nose. I got the distinct feeling she wasn't going to the creek out of a deep desire to commune with nature. "Let's go, my girlie-girls. Ta-ta, Matthew." She slipped her hand around Ashley's elbow and steered the girls toward the exit. Over her shoulder, she said, "I'll have them home by eight."

Matthew turned to me. "I'll believe that when it happens. The woman doesn't have a clue when it comes to time of day."

Whenever Sylvie entered and left a room, I felt depleted, as if she had taken a part of my soul or a smidgen of my life force with her. Matthew looked drained, too.

"It's always hard to keep up appearances, isn't it?" I said.

Matthew nodded. "What is she thinking taking the girls in this kind of cold weather to a wet park? And with him."

Delilah sidled up to the booth. "She has no filter," she

said. "So many in town don't. Take that guy at the counter, for instance."

I gazed at Boyd Hellman, who sat hunched over the daily special while shoveling food into his mouth.

"He speaks his mind"—Delilah nestled into the booth beside me—"without taking into account who is listening. At first he seemed keen on bending my ear about Ashley Yeats. Right after that, he launched into a rant about Harold Warfield. He doesn't have most of the facts straight, of course."

I wondered whether Boyd was spreading rumors simply to ward off Urso. "Do you know Harold?"

"Don't you remember him?" Delilah asked.

I shook my head.

"He was a few years ahead of us in high school. Class vice president. Co-captain of the debate team. Backup field goal kicker. He went off to college—I can't remember where— and one day, he returned married to that plain wife of his, which surprised many of us."

"Why?" Matthew asked.

"Because he had a second fiddle complex. He wanted to be number one so badly that he always made sure he dated pretty girls. When he came back to Providence, he had dreams of owning wineries, not managing them. I was off in New York when he moved back. A girlfriend called me and said she thought he must have gotten his new wife pregnant and that's why he married her, but they never had kids, so that theory was a bust. He went to work for the Bozzuto Winery for a couple of years, but when he was passed over for the job of manager, he lucked into a new position at Shelton Nelson's. He was in here the night Noelle Adams arrived in town," Delilah continued. "He didn't seem pleased. His wife kept saying, 'Don't worry.'"

"Maybe Rebecca was right to think Noelle was after his job."

"No way." Matthew slung an arm over the top of the banquette. "She was a people person, not a numbers person. She didn't want to manage that winery or any winery. She wanted the glitz, the glamour."

In Providence? That didn't add up.

"Whatever," Delilah said. "Harold was upset, and he threw down his napkin and stormed out."

I folded my hands on the table. "Delilah, do you think Harold, as misguided as his notion was, had it in him to kill Noelle to prevent her from rising in Shelton Nelson's company?"

From the counter, Boyd said, "Noelle didn't trust Shelton."

"Who asked you?" Delilah said.

"All I'm saying—"

Delilah scooted from the banquette and marched to Boyd. "Keep your nose out of our business, you hear?" She planted her hands on her hips. "Who are you anyway? You're always here, always inserting your opinion into everyone's business. You have no right. First, you're not smart enough. Second . . ."

I edged out of the booth and laid my hand on her shoulder as she was gearing up for another put-down. "Cool it. I want to hear what he knows."

Delilah muttered, "Whatever. He's your problem now. Don't get too close, though. His breath . . ." She fanned her nose.

I crowded Boyd on his stool. He avoided my gaze and hunched forward, both forearms on the counter as if he were protecting his food.

I gave his shoulder a gentle rap with my knuckles.

He whacked my hand away.

"Hey, buddy," Matthew jumped to his feet. "Lay off."

"No, you lay off," Boyd muttered.

I signaled Matthew to keep cool. "We only want to talk, Boyd. You said Noelle didn't trust Shelton Nelson. I didn't get that impression, and she was staying at my house."

"You don't know her like I do. Nobody does."

"Did," Matthew corrected.

Now, nobody would. My heart wrenched with sorrow.

Boyd shoveled a last bite of the cheese-stuffed chicken into his mouth. While chewing, he said, "She would come back from trips after she met with Nelson, and she would be hyped-up."

"Angry?" Matthew asked.

"No, excited. She said she was intrigued."

That sounded like a woman in love. I said, "Why do you think she didn't trust him?"

"She wrote notes." Boyd's voice rose with intensity. "Tons and tons of notes."

"In her journals."

He gave a perfunctory nod.

"How many journals did she keep?"

"Two at a time. When she didn't like a journal, she burned it. The nuns taught her to do that. Bury your past." Boyd spanked the counter. "Ashes to ashes, dust to dust. That's what she did with her folks. They burned her, so she burned them."

"Burned?"

"In here." He tapped his head. "In her mind. Poof."

Noelle had hesitated when I'd asked about her parents. I hadn't pressed. "Why—"

"Uh-uh. I'm not telling you anything else. That's personal." Boyd slapped a twenty-dollar bill on the counter and lumbered off his chair.

I said, "Wait. I've found the journals, Boyd. I gave them to Chief Urso. Noelle didn't destroy them."

"Whoop-dee-do. I hope he can make sense of them. I never could. Now, leave me alone." Without another word, he plodded out of the diner.

Matthew said, "Did you hear that? He read the journals. Maybe he killed her to get his hands on them. Maybe he tore out pages that mentioned him." His face lit up. "You know, whenever I make notes on my cell phone, I send them in an email to my computer. Maybe Noelle scanned her journals into her computer to make a record of them. A record is a kind of key, isn't it?"

CHAPTER

12

I returned to The Cheese Shop, retreated to the office for privacy, and called Urso to ask him about Noelle's journals. For a guy who had professed his love for me in the not-so-distant past, he sure could be curt.

"What don't you understand about butting out?" Urso yelled.

I held the telephone receiver away from my head. Even Rags, sitting in the office chair, perked up his ears. Resting a hip on the corner of the desk, I bent at the waist to pet Rags and cooed, "Calm down. It's simply our nasty chief of police getting all high and mighty."

"I heard that," Urso said.

"You were meant to." After drawing in a deep, calming breath, I said, "Look, all I want to know is whether you found any records on Noelle's computer. Maybe a digital journal. Or copies of her handwritten journals. Or sales accountings. Or client information. Or notes of her meetings with Shelton Nelson. Any records. A record could be a key."

"In whose thesaurus?" he snapped, then said, "I'm sorry,

but I need you to stop hypothesizing. You have no reason to get involved."

"Except Noelle was a guest in my house. And one of my cousin's best friends." A sob caught in my throat. I swallowed hard. "I liked her, U-ey. In a short time, I thought of her as family."

"Charlotte, I get it, I do, but—"

"U-ey, we seem to be the only ones thinking outside the box."

"*We* who?"

I hesitated. I was the object of Urso's wrath; Matthew didn't need to be as well. "Me. I meant *me*. Look, tell me yes or no. Have you scoured Noelle's computer?"

"Yes or no."

"Very funny."

He exhaled. "Yes."

"Did you find dated entries related to her work?"

"Yes."

Relief swept through me. "I told you that the journals were missing pages. In the diary journal, each was marked with a date. The last date was the day before she arrived in Providence. I saw her writing that night. There should have been a page with that date. Did you find scanned copies of her journal pages in her computer?"

"No."

I huffed. "That's it? 'No'?"

"Good-bye, Charlotte. I've got a meeting to attend."

"Wait. I wanted to talk to you more about Boyd Hellman. There's something fishy about the guy. He's hot-tempered and knows a ton about Noelle, but he won't tell."

"Good for him. That means he's honorable."

"You really don't think he's guilty?"

"Charlotte . . ."

"I also learned more about Harold Warfield. He—"

The phone clicked—dead—and my insides turned white-hot. If U-ey were standing in the room and I was a guy, I would punch him right in the kisser.

"*Chérie*." My grandfather scuttled through the door, out

of breath, his face shiny with perspiration. Had he run the entire way from his house to the shop?

I flung the receiver onto the cradle and hurried to him. "What's wrong? Is it Grandmère?"

"*Ce n'est rien.*" He waved for me to stop worrying. "I have come because you did not show up at the theater with the pizzas, and I thought there might be something amiss with you."

I slapped my forehead. I had promised to make kid-friendly turkey and mashed potato pizzas for the Thanksgiving play rehearsal. I grabbed his elbow and steered him to the kitchen. "Let's get cracking. I did the prep work already. The turkey is cooked, the potatoes mashed. All I need to do is grate the mozzarella cheese."

Rags peeped at me from his spot on the office chair and meowed.

I winked. "Yes, I'll bring you some turkey."

A second meow.

"And cheese."

* * *

While I stood at the cheese counter grating fist-sized rounds of Salted Lioni Mozzarella, a supple cheese from New Jersey, Tyanne Taylor breezed into the store.

"This way, y'all." Tyanne was a native Louisianan; she and her family had moved to Providence after Hurricane Katrina. A few years later, her husband—the skunk—left her for a lusty younger woman. She held the door open for Liberty Nelson, who ambled in looking uncomfortable in a frilly, high-necked ensemble suitable for a heroine in a Jane Austen novel. Tyanne let the door swing shut and finger-combed her bangs into place. "Honestly, sugar, I can't believe you haven't purchased anything here. In all these years? What you've been missing. You are going to be so pleased." She strolled toward the counter, the swirly hem of her burgundy dress swaying with a sultry vigor. "Charlotte, I have brought you a new and very eager client. Ooh, Liberty, look." She pointed at one of the cheeses in the display case and read: "*Lover Boy cheese.*" She laughed out loud. "That's precious. Charlotte, these tags are new, aren't they?"

I nodded.

"Get this, sugar," Tyanne continued reading: "*This is the cheese you would throw over your boyfriend for.* Love it."

Liberty tittered then smiled tightly. She squinted at me with a docility bordering on drug induced. What was going on with her? The overnight transformation from tiger to pussycat was downright eerie. I thought of Lois's comment that Liberty intended to change her ways. Had Liberty's religious boyfriend demanded the makeover, or was Liberty pretending she was the epitome of innocence so Urso would cross her off his suspect list? Did she think he was that naïve? "What kind of cheese is it, Miss Bessette?"

Miss Bessette? Heart be still. Okay, now I knew an alien had invaded her brain and removed her personality.

"It's Délice de Bourgogne," Tyanne chimed in. "A triple-cream cheese from France and perhaps the most luscious bloomy rind cheese ever. Read this cute flag."

Liberty recited: "*So smooth it makes Brad Pitt seem like a dullard.*" She fluttered her hand to cool her face.

I choked back a laugh as the term *phony* echoed in my head.

"That's double-cream Cremont, a scrumptious cheese from Vermont," Tyanne said.

"It's a blend of goat's cheese and cow's milk with notes of hazelnuts and a creamy texture," I added as I mounded the cheese I had grated and started on a second ball of the Salted Lioni.

"Hm-m-m." As quickly as Liberty's interest piqued, it fizzled. She moved toward the shelves holding honey and exotic vinegars.

I leaned into Tyanne. "We've missed having you around."

"Don't worry. I will be here bright and early tomorrow. I am never giving up my weekly commitment to tend the cheese counter, but whewie, am I ever busy. Who knew that brides love the holidays for weddings. And do not even start on the plethora of showers I've got on my agenda. In fact,

Liberty and I came in to design a cheese platter for her soi-ree, which is set for December 15th. Did I tell you she's get-ting married February 14th, Valentine's Day? How romantic is that?"

"Congratulations."

"She is marrying the sweetest guy in town," Tyanne said. "A devout Christian."

"So I heard."

From across the shop, Liberty said, "He's not devout. He's just, you know, dedicated."

Tyanne winked at me. "He is the nicest fellow you'd ever want to meet."

I whispered, "Is he the reason she's in that getup?" I glanced toward the street, wondering whether her fiancé was keeping an eye on her from the sidewalk to ensure she towed the line. If so, that would be no way to start a marriage.

"He likes her to look precious."

"But he fell in love with her before the change," I pro-tested.

"Some men say that, but in the end, they want what they want." Tyanne's mouth pulled into a frown. I imagined she was thinking about her ex. "No matter," she trilled and bat-ted my arm. "Whatever the concessions, our little Liberty is head over heels in love."

I couldn't imagine Liberty being a head-over-heels type of girl, especially when she possessed what I considered an unhealthy affection for her father. Desperate to know more about her and whether she was capable of murder, I said, "Confidentially, what kind of woman is she, Tyanne?"

Tyanne cut a look in Liberty's direction; Liberty was fully occupied with reading labels on jars. "A little exacting, but what bride isn't?"

"Meredith wasn't."

"Fine," Tyanne said. "Meredith was the exception. She's so levelheaded it's scary. So, yes, I was spoiled my first time out as a wedding planner. Ooh, look at this tag. *Smokin' sexy.* Too cute." She chuckled.

"Rebecca came up with that one."

"Of course she would, the imp."

"Are you talking about me?" Rebecca emerged from the kitchen while blotting her hands on a white towel. "Charlotte, Pépère needs more mozzarella."

"It's coming." I took the grated Salted Lioni, tossed it into a large white bowl, and started in on another round. A dozen pizzas required a lot of cheese.

"Hi, Tyanne," Rebecca said. "I haven't seen you in ages."

"I've been busier than a one-armed paperhanger. We have so much to catch up on, like the mur—" Tyanne blushed and tucked a lock of highlighted hair behind an ear. "Charlotte, I've been meaning to give Matthew my condolences. I know what good friends he and the deceased were. Do y'all have any idea who did it?"

I focused on Liberty, who was checking out price tags on cheese platters.

Tyanne followed my gaze. "You can't think Liberty had anything to do with it."

"There are rumors that Shelton and Noelle were romantically involved."

"If the rumors are true," Rebecca said, "then Liberty would not have been a happy camper. She loves her daddy."

"Heavens, no. Not like that. No." Tyanne slapped her chest with her palm. "I can't believe that she could ever . . ." She paused.

"What?" Rebecca and I said in unison.

"I heard about the murder weapon used and, well, Liberty has knowledge of it. She's been looking to use the same corkscrew as a table favor for her wedding. I have catalogues filled with other choices, but that's the one she's drawn to. You know how it is, with her association with the winery and all. Even so, no"—Tyanne peeked again at Liberty—"I don't think she's capable."

"Not many people in town knew Noelle," Rebecca said. "Who else would have motive?"

I flashed on my conversation with Lois about the car that had idled outside my house on the night of the murder. She had seemed certain that the driver was a woman. "What kind of car does Liberty drive?"

"A blue Camry," Tyanne said.

"A Camry looks like a Taurus, doesn't it?"

"Why are you asking?"

Because Lois was certain the car on the street had been a Taurus. What if she was wrong not only about the color of the car but also about the style?

"*Chérie.*" Pépère exited the kitchen carrying a bowl of ground turkey. With one latex-covered hand, he worked to break up the chunks of turkey.

"Almost done, Pépère." I assessed the amount of cheese in the bowl. I would need a cup more.

"Charlotte, spill," Tyanne said.

"What are we discussing?" my grandfather craned an ear.

"Lois Smith saw a dark-colored sedan near my house on the night of the murder."

Tyanne said, "And you think Liberty—"

Pépère cut in. "Miss Adams's ex-boyfriend drives a dark car."

I turned to him. "I know. A Chevy Malibu."

"He makes me uncomfortable," my grandfather said. "He is always hanging around the Country Kitchen. The past few days, I have seen him there every time I buy a cup of coffee."

"If he lived with Noelle," Rebecca said, "he might have been familiar with the murder weapon. Noelle attended the wedding, right?"

"*Oui,*" Pépère said. "I met her there. She was so charming and so happy for Matthew."

"But Noelle and Boyd had broken up before then," I said. "He wouldn't have seen the heart-shaped corkscrew."

"How can you be sure?" Pépère waggled his hand. "You should question him. He is in the wine annex."

Why was Boyd Hellman in our shop? Hadn't he made it clear in the diner that he didn't want anything to do with us? Matthew sauntered from the kitchen carrying a case of Carménère, a smoky red wine with hints of chocolate.

"Matthew, set down the wine and come with me." I wiped my hands on my apron and charged into the annex.

"Where's the fire?" Matthew said.

I raced toward a knot of people. Beyond them, Boyd loitered by the expensive wines that were slotted into cubbies on the wall. "Boyd Hellman," I said.

Boyd spun around. "What's the problem?" His words slurred together. His eyes were bloodshot; his breath, rancid. He stunk like a still.

"Did you know that Noelle owned a heart-shaped corkscrew?" I said.

"Huh?"

"A heart-shaped corkscrew." I mimed what it looked like.

"She had a whole collection of corkscrews. Why?"

"You drive a green Chevy."

His forehead creased. "Yeah, so?"

"Were you hanging outside my house the other night? The night Noelle died?"

"That depends. Where do you live?" He offered a shameless grin.

Matthew shoved past me. "Show some respect."

"Hey, it was a joke." Boyd jutted his arms; the move threw him off balance. He teetered.

Matthew reached to steady him. In a knee-jerk reaction, Boyd threw a punch. Matthew backed up; the jab fell short. Boyd stumbled. His shoulder rammed into the cubbies. Like a trained bouncer, Matthew grasped Boyd's wrist, flung him toward the wall, and pinned the guy's arm to his back. I raced to help.

Customers gasped. Above the horrified chatter that followed, I said, "What's your alibi for the night Noelle was killed?"

"I was w-w-walking," Boyd stammered.

"Where?"

"Just walking."

"At Kindred Creek?"

"What's that?"

"Noelle went hiking that night. I think she went to Kindred Creek."

"She wouldn't have. She's not a nature girl."

I leaned close. "Did you follow her?"

"Look, I'm telling you—"

Matthew twisted Boyd to face him. "Answer the question. Where did you go when you went walking? Who saw you?"

"I don't know." Boyd's gaze angled to the floor. "I . . . I don't remember."

"How is that possible?" Matthew demanded.

Boyd blew air out of his mouth. "I don't make eye contact with people. I—"

"Did you go into any stores?" I asked. Most were open until nine.

"I went into the diner. It was grilled cheese night."

"That doesn't prove anything," Matthew hissed. "Every night is grilled cheese night nowadays."

Delilah had finally gotten her wish and had organized a Grilled Cheese Cook-off. Chefs from all over the Midwest were coming to Providence in January to compete. She was constantly trying out new recipes.

"I didn't kill Noelle."

"Walking around town is a pretty weak alibi," I said.

"But it's true." Boyd reminded me of a rabbit pinned in a trap and in desperate need of an escape route. He was lying. Why did he need to keep his whereabouts a secret?

I recalled the first time I met him—a flush of red and rage. Noelle had warned him to back off *or else*. Though he didn't have any arrests as a petty thief, I wondered if he had been arrested for assault. Maybe that was why Noelle had threatened to turn him in to the police. Did he kill her before she could?

CHAPTER

13

Matthew and I let Boyd go, but neither of us was happy about it. The guy didn't have a strong alibi, but we had nothing of substance to take to Urso. Had he already heard Boyd's alibi? Had he found somebody who could confirm it? Man, I itched to get my fingers on Urso's list of suspects.

After apologizing to our customers—many said they understood our reaction to Boyd's presence because rumors about him were rampant in Providence—I returned to the main shop. Tyanne was chatting with Liberty by a display of gourmet crackers. She looked up and gave me a supportive smile. Liberty glanced up, too. Did I detect a hint of victory in her eyes? Maybe she was pleased that Matthew and I had lost control, or perhaps she was thrilled that Boyd Hellman had made such a spectacle. Did she think, when word got to Urso about the fracas, that it would make Urso redirect his suspicions to Boyd and divert him from suspecting her father or, better yet, herself of murder?

"Charlotte," Pépère said. "The pizzas."

"Yes, of course."

I washed my hands, gathered up the grated cheese, and retreated to the kitchen. In less than a half hour, my grandfather and I assembled and baked a dozen turkey–mashed potato pizzas. We boxed them to go and loaded them into his car. Before driving away, Pépère promised he would report back with the children's review.

When I returned to the cheese counter, Tyanne and Liberty were gone and Rebecca looked frazzled. "*Help*," she mouthed. More than a dozen new customers were begging for wedges of the daily special cheese: Bellwether Farms Carmody, a smooth cheese with a grassy finish, inspired by a Gorgonzola recipe that farmers discovered while traveling in Italy. I adored the cheese when served with olives, crusty bread, and a steely chardonnay.

When the crowd dispersed, Rebecca and I wiped down the knives on the counter and returned two wedges of Carmody cheese to the case.

"Are you ever going to tell me what you talked to Urso about earlier?" Rebecca asked. "He seemed really miffed when he snatched Deputy O'Shea out from under my umbrella."

"Deputy O'Shea. What a handsome hunk he is."

"And sweet. He asked me if I would like to meet for coffee sometime. I said yes, of course."

"What about Ipo?"

"What about him? He hasn't called to get back together or anything. We're through. Over. *Finis*." She huffed. "Don't sidetrack me. Back to Urso. What info did you pry out of him?"

"Nothing. Not an iota." I told her about the suspects I'd suggested to him.

"Whether Urso thinks Boyd Hellman is a suspect or not, you'd better watch out for him. That man seems unstable, and you and Matthew just stirred the pot."

I agreed.

The rest of the afternoon passed without altercation.

Around six P.M. I exited The Cheese Shop to lock up. Out of the corner of my eye I spotted a dark figure barreling toward the shop. Fifty feet, forty feet. Was it Boyd? I rushed to reopen the front door, but the key slipped out of my hand. Rags, picking up on my fear, snuggled by my ankles. I whispered, "It's okay, Ragsie," while a voice in my head yelled: *Hurry, hurry*, as I bent to retrieve the key. It stuck to the sidewalk as if it had been glued. I picked with my fingernail and finally flipped the key on its edge. Quickly, I lifted it and tried again to insert it into the lock.

The figure was gaining ground. I couldn't make out a face. Twenty feet, ten feet.

No one else was on the street. Where was everybody?

I tapped the windowpane. Rebecca was inside the shop but leaving through the back door. She didn't respond.

I swiveled around, fists raised, like that would do any good against a raging rhino. "Back off, Hellman," I yelled.

But I was wrong. I could see clearly, now. It wasn't Boyd; it was Harold Warfield. The tails of his gray jacket flew wide. His shoulder-length hair flapped.

Eight feet, six feet.

"You," he yelled.

I rapped on the doorframe. Hard. Rebecca spun around. I signaled that a crazy man was about to mow me down. I must have looked like a frantic kid singing "In a Cabin in a Wood".

Rebecca raced to the door and flung it open. In her zeal, she stumbled backward and landed on her rear end. If I weren't so scared, I would have laughed. Rags yowled. I scooped him into my arms, rushed inside, and tried to close the door. Too late.

Harold charged into the shop bellowing, "It's your fault."

"I don't know what you're talking about," I said, my voice tight with fear. "What's my fault?"

Rebecca scrambled to her feet and edged next to me. "Yeah, what's her fault?"

Rags echoed both of us in cat-speak; his heart chugged against my chest.

"Chief Urso ordered me to come to the precinct," Harold said.

Had Urso demanded a conference based on my shaky

theory that Noelle had taken compromising pictures to get Harold's job? Whether it was truth or fiction, I didn't care. Whatever it took to get the wheels of democracy in motion. *Hurrah, Urso.*

"Why do you think that's my fault?" I said.

"Because you have his ear. Everyone knows it. If he's after me, it's because of something you told him."

I kept silent.

Harold smirked. "Aha, I knew I was right. Don't deny it. You're a snoop. You're always sticking your nose into things."

"I am not," I said, though I was, of late. Tough. Some things needed to be investigated. My actions were paved with good intention. Feeling a tad bolder, I cocked a hip, adjusting Rags as I shifted. "What did he want to know?"

"My history from the day I was born."

"Which is . . . ?" Rebecca said, leading him.

"None of your business. Or yours, Miss Bessette." He stabbed my chest with an accusatory finger. "So watch it."

Bone on bone hurt. I winced and knocked his hand away. "Are you threatening me?"

"I'm telling you, keep your nose out of my life. It's private."

"It's not private when murder is involved."

"I did not kill Noelle Adams."

"You were worried that Shelton Nelson was thinking of replacing you with Noelle."

"I was not. What cockamamie jerk told you that? Liberty?" He grunted. "That girl has no idea what her father is planning. She thinks she does. She thinks she has a finger on his pulse, but she is screwy." He twirled a finger beside his head and spelled: "S-c-r-e-w-y."

"I heard that you wanted your own winery."

"That was years ago."

"You don't refute the notion?"

"The dream has faded. Besides, I would never kill to get a job or keep a job. Now, back off."

"Or what?" Rebecca raised her hands, like she wanted to flatten the guy. Really, her pluck worried me sometimes.

Soon, I would force her to take a good look in the mirror. She was wisp thin. A mosquito could topple her.

Harold turned to go.

I said, "Did Chief Urso ask you for your alibi on the night of the murder?"

He paused and cast a malicious look over his shoulder. "As a matter of fact, he did. I was at the library."

"Reading what?" Rebecca asked.

"A thriller."

"By whom?"

"Ludlum."

"Who was the co-author?" Rebecca persisted.

"Huh?"

"The Ludlum books now have co-authors." Rebecca smirked. "Was it Jamie Freveletti?"

"You're reading thrillers now, too?" I said.

"I can't get enough of them. Freveletti's a very good writer. Answer the question, Mr. Warfield."

"I don't know. Stop it." Harold straightened his tie and tucked strands of hair behind his ears. The motion made me think again of the driver that had idled across from my house. From a distance, Harold could have looked female.

"What kind of car do you drive?" I asked.

"A white Ford Taurus."

"White?" Shoot. A white car would not look blue, even in the dark of night. Had Lois's memory been affected by the hope to see her absent husband?

"You two are nuts." Harold sliced the air with the edge of his hand.

"Us?" I cried. "We're not the ones who just charged a helpless woman."

"You are far from helpless," he said. "We're through here." He pulled his lapel up, did a one-eighty, and marched off.

Reluctant to let me go home alone, for fear of a second run-in with Harold Warfield, Rebecca insisted on accompanying me. I tried to talk her out of it, but she wouldn't succumb. The promise of rain hadn't materialized, so we walked without umbrellas. By the time we reached Timothy O'Shea's Irish Pub, I was calm. By the time we turned onto my street, Rags was no longer chuffing with worry.

As we strolled past Lavender and Lace, Lois appeared on the porch and waved. "Hello, girls. Want some tea?"

What I wanted was a glass of wine and a chat with Jordan to settle my nerves, but Rebecca nudged me and whispered, "Say *yes*. Lois is a chatterbox."

I had heard enough gossip from Lois for the past couple of days, but Rebecca seemed so eager that I didn't turn down the invitation.

The kitchen at Lavender and Lace was huge. A large square island, fitted with antique stools, stood in the center. I let Rags play with Agatha, and Rebecca and I settled in for a spot of tea while Lois baked. The sweet aroma of chocolate, coconut, and mascarpone cheese–filled scones scented the air. My mouth started to water. I hadn't had a chance to taste-test the pizzas that Pépère took to the theater.

"I heard there was a little fracas outside your store a few minutes ago," Lois said.

"You already heard?" A guest must have beaten a path back to the B&B to share the news.

"Harold Warfield has anger issues, don't you know." Lois spooned healthy helpings of scone mixture from a bowl onto a baking tray. "Why, I've seen him throw cell phones and kick tires."

I've been known to kick a tire or two.

"Harold shouldn't be mad at Shelton, though," Lois went on.

"He wasn't," I admitted. "He was mad at me. He thinks I sicced Urso on him." And Liberty thought Harold had persuaded Urso to suspect her father.

"Humph." Lois set aside the scone mixture, donned a pair of oven mitts, and removed a tray of golden brown scones from the oven. "That man. If anyone should be angry, it's him."

"Who, Harold?" Rebecca said.

"No, Shelton. He has suffered so." Lois eyed me as she

slid the second tray of scones into the oven. "I told you about his ex-wife, Liberty's mother, skipping out, but did I tell you she was quite the hussy? She had multiple affairs." Using a spatula, Lois removed the scones from the baking tray and set them on metal racks to cool. "I don't think she ever embraced being a mother. The pregnancy might have been an accident." The teakettle began to whistle. Lois shuffled to the cabinet and returned with two sets of Victorian Farmhouse teacups and a selection of teas. As she filled the cups with steaming water, I chose an Earl Grey while Rebecca opted for a minty Tazo Zen tea.

"Why do people do such things?" Lois asked as she plated the scones and set them in front of us.

"Do what?" I asked.

"Cheat."

I ached for Lois. She hadn't gotten over the fact that her husband of over thirty years had strayed. She booted him out the night she learned of his betrayal. Once or twice since then she had acknowledged that she was lonely without him. Would she take him back if he came crawling? Time would tell.

"Lois, would you like to join me and my grandparents for Thanksgiving dinner?" I said. "It'll be a big group."

"I can't, dear. I have an inn full of guests. I'll be busier than ever, but thank you." She pushed the plate of scones closer so that we would each take one.

I obliged, choosing the closest, as my grandmother had taught me. The warm chocolate and coconut combination was heaven. The mascarpone added a lusciousness to the flaky pastry. "Delicious."

"Now, where was I?" Lois said. "Oh yes, Liberty's mother. Shelton was a saint about the whole kerfuffle. He didn't moon about. He went on as if he was destined to be a single father. You asked the other night whether he and Noelle could have been involved. I don't believe they were. I put on my thinking cap, and I remember hearing him a while back—I can't remember when—saying that he felt protective of Noelle. He seemed excited to be able to groom her."

So Shelton hadn't planned to make Noelle his new bride and Liberty's new mother? Perhaps Liberty had killed Noelle because she didn't want to share her father's love with a surrogate sister.

"Why, Shelton was interested in everything Noelle did," Lois went on. "I remember that time she was staying here, and she was reviewing pictures on her camera when Shelton arrived. He was very interested to see what she had been photographing, but faster than a magician, Noelle whisked that thingy, whatever it's called . . ." She mimed opening a camera and removing a disk.

"A memory card," I said.

"That's it. She pulled it out and pocketed it in her bra." Lois chuckled. "Shelton said, 'What are you up to, sneaky Pete?' That's what he called her. And Noelle said, 'You'll know soon enough.'" Lois settled onto a stool, quivering with giggles. "I had a good laugh over that. They didn't hear me, of course."

"I'll bet," I said, while my mind sped back to thoughts of Harold Warfield. Had Noelle taken compromising photos after all? Had he killed her to get his hands on them?

CHAPTER

14

The sky was dark with clouds. A light drizzle started to fall as Rebecca, Rags, and I headed home.

Rebecca, who had vowed to stick to me like glue until I was safely tucked inside my home, said, "You're pretty quiet."

Rags purred his agreement.

I didn't respond. I was too focused on Noelle and the many layers of her life. She wrote in journals. She took photographs. She had been raised in an orphanage where she had hidden things and kept secrets. Boyd Hellman had suggested that something untoward had happened between Noelle and her parents. He said they had burned her, and she had burned them. But he hadn't meant with fire. How had that shaped Noelle as an individual? How I wished I had known her better.

As we neared my house, my gaze was drawn to the garage. Masked by mist, it loomed like a ghostly monster. A shiver raced up my spine. I checked the area for idling cars but saw none. Still, an urgent need coursed through me.

I said, "I have to see the crime scene again."

"Why?"

"Remember, after our game of Bunco, when I raced home and felt like the killer had come back for something?"

"But you've gone through the garage twice now. The police, too."

"I missed seeing something. I'm sure of it."

"You sound like Sherlock Holmes. He had this uncanny ability to see things. Recently, I rented that movie with Robert Downey, Jr., *Sherlock Holmes: A Game of Shadows*. Did you see it? The camerawork was awesome, whipping the audience around the room so they could spot all the things he did. Birdseed. A piece of fabric. A picture."

"A picture." I snapped my fingers. Had Noelle hidden the camera's memory card—the key to whatever she was investigating, as Lois put it—in my workshop? Not in the desk but someplace else? Someplace the killer hadn't thought to look? "I've got to search the garage again."

Rebecca grabbed hold of my sleeve. "Wait. You said the police took items like Noelle's computer and her cell phone and other stuff. Whatever the killer wanted might be at the precinct. Maybe if you could see all those things, it would jog your memory."

"Maybe."

She swung me toward the sidewalk.

"What are you doing?" I said.

"We're going to the precinct."

I wrenched free. "Are you nuts?"

"Put Rags in the house, and then let's hotfoot it over there. The clerk that's on duty tonight will be a cinch to get past. And I happen to know the chief and his deputies are at a council meeting. Grandmère was in earlier and mentioned it. Let's go."

"No."

"You know you won't sleep until you settle this in your mind."

"But it's raining."

"This?" She held her arms out, palms up. "It's no worse

than morning dew. C'mon. I need an adventure. I'm single. So are you."

"I'm not single." I missed Jordan with a deep ache.

"Fine, you're lonely and bored. Don't deny you want to do this."

"We can't break into the precinct evidence room."

"We won't break in. We'll see if it's unlocked. If it is, it's public property."

I gasped. "It is not."

"On *Murder, She Wrote* or maybe it was *Buffy the Vampire Slayer*—whichever—the leading lady snuck past a sleeping police guard and did a search. Her defense was that anything in the police precinct is public property because the public pays for the police with its taxes. If we have to, we'll use that as our defense."

Great. Now, we were acting like imaginary characters from television shows. If caught, would Perry Mason take our case?

* * *

When Rebecca and I entered Providence Precinct, the silence stunned me. The reception area, which the precinct shared with the Tourist Information Center, was empty. I couldn't remember ever visiting the building after the TIC shut down for the night. It was deadly quiet.

The precinct clerk sat at her desk, toying with the gray strands of hair that cupped her heart-shaped face while gazing at something on her computer screen.

"We shouldn't be here," I whispered. A mouse on the hunt for cheese couldn't have looked guiltier than I did.

Rebecca shooed me with her hand and sidled up to the clerk. "Hey, Zelda."

The clerk startled, then fanned herself. "My, oh, my. You spooked me."

Was she deaf? As we approached, I had heard every footstep we made across the hardwood floor.

"Sorry. We were out for a stroll," Rebecca said, "and we thought you might like a little company. How's it going?"

"Fi-i-ine." The clerk shot Rebecca a knowing glance.

I wanted to retreat, but Rebecca must have suspected. She gripped the sleeve of my sweater and held fast.

"Zelda, I was in earlier today." Rebecca worked her toe coquettishly into the floor. "With Deputy O'Shea."

I shot her a glance. She hadn't mentioned a visit to the precinct.

"It was a little damp, and my hair was a mess, and"—Rebecca giggled—"I left my comb in the ladies' room, silly me."

I gaped, astounded that she could lie so easily and more stunned at her calm. Grandmère was going to do a cartwheel when she learned she had yet another actor to add to the Providence Playhouse roster.

"Mind if we go fetch it?" Rebecca gestured with her thumb to the door that led to the rest of the precinct. The clerk would have to press a button to clear the lock.

"You were here with O'Shea?" the clerk said.

"Yep. We came in before your shift."

The clerk cooed, "He sure is cute."

"And cavalier." Rebecca placed her hands on the clerk's desk and leaned forward. "He heard I was taking a walk in the rain, and he showed up out of the blue with an umbrella."

"Nice."

"Then he offered to give me a tour of his office. Of course, I jumped at the chance."

"Of course."

"Is he married, Zelda? You know everything about everybody."

I blinked, flabbergasted by my wily assistant's performance.

"He's not married," the clerk said. "But he was engaged once, and he's got at least three girls in town hankering for a date."

"Guess I'll have to get in line." Rebecca sighed like a veteran ham. "Um, my comb?"

"Sure. Go ahead." The clerk pressed a button beneath her desk. A buzz sounded.

With me firmly in tow, Rebecca nearly skipped to the door and pushed through. Once the door closed behind us, she broke into laughter. "How easy was that, huh?" And then she paused. "You don't think I'll go to hell for that, will I?"

"For telling a lie?"

"For deceiving a sweet old lady."

"I don't think so. You did no real harm."

"Phew. I really was here earlier. Deputy O'Shea is so darling. He has a dreamy smile." She fanned herself. "And he gave me the full tour. I saw his office and peeked into Urso's. I saw the coffee break room. It's all very male, with pictures of cowboys and Indians, all done in earth tones."

"Why didn't you tell me you came here earlier?"

"And spoil the fun? You should have seen your face as we tiptoed in."

"Ha-ha," I said with a bite. "Let's go."

"This way." She beckoned me to follow her.

I had visited Urso on numerous occasions, so I knew my way around the precinct. Urso's and the deputies' offices were down the hall to the right, the interrogation room and conference rooms to the left. We arrived at the evidence room in a matter of seconds.

Rebecca reached for the handle and grumbled. "Rats. It's locked. Think you can pick it?"

"Not a chance."

"Why not?"

"It's pretty obvious." On occasion, I had locked myself out of the house—when taking out the garbage or getting the mail—so I had learned to pick a simple lock with assorted tools. I actually kept a tool kit in my purse. But just in case I fumbled those, I had planted a spare key in a hideaway box tucked behind a drain spout. However, a double bolt like the one on the evidence room door was impossible for anyone but a pro.

Framing my face with my hands, I peered through the window, which was bulletproof glass laced with a wire underlay.

"See anything?" Rebecca said.

The room was small. The precinct had no reason to keep lots of evidence; crime in Providence was in short supply. A computer, a guest registry clipboard, and a jar of pens sat on the counter. Metal shelving stood behind the counter, against the wall. A variety of evidence was assembled on the shelves with tags attached to each piece.

I spied Noelle's bright pink iMac and cell phone on the second shelf from the top. In addition to the hardware, I noted a stack of clothes—the jeans, shirt, and hiking boots that Noelle wore the night she was killed. They were neatly folded; the boots appeared free of mud.

"O'Shea's office is down the hall," Rebecca said. "When I visited earlier, I saw a key ring hanging on the wall. I'll be right back."

I grabbed her. "No, wait. He's here."

"Who?"

I pointed. "O'Shea. Look."

The handsome deputy stepped out of the men's room and headed toward the water fountain, away from us.

"Why that Zelda," Rebecca muttered.

I would bet the clerk was having a good laugh right now.

Not one to give in without a fight, Rebecca squared her shoulders and fluffed her hair. "Don't worry. I'll handle this. I'll flirt a little and—"

"No, we're out of here."

"But—"

"No argument. I do not want him seeing us and reporting back to Urso."

"Zelda will tell the chief."

"She won't if she wants to keep her job. No, this was a prank. She skunked us. Let's go get some hot cocoa."

Rebecca resisted at first but finally submitted. As we hurried to the front, I rummaged through my purse and found a comb. I shoved it into Rebecca's hand. When we pushed through the doors, she waved it at the clerk, who looked disappointed that we hadn't been apprehended. "Got it. Thanks again."

Outside, relief burbled out of me. *He who laughs last, laughs best*, as the saying goes.

Minutes later, Rebecca and I entered Café au Lait, which was just around the corner.

"Wow, the place is packed," Rebecca said.

The fanciful French-themed shop bustled with talkative locals as well as joyful tourists showing each other their recent purchases. Providence was nothing if not a great place to find unique items. I spotted Shelton and Liberty Nelson, who were sitting at an antique iron bistro table with Tyanne and Liberty's studious-looking beau. They all appeared at ease and content. Light from the papier-mâché hot air balloon lamp that hung over their table cast a warm glow on their happy faces. Tyanne had spread a sampling of wedding paraphernalia—invitations, albums, and favors—on the table.

"Psst," Rebecca flicked my arm with her finger. "Look over there."

Urso and Delilah sat at a bistro table for two near the painting of the Arc de Triomphe.

I said, "I thought the chief was at a city council meeting. I guess it ended early."

"Are they on a date?"

"No way. Delilah has sworn off men for a while." Which begged the question, why had Urso brought her to the café?

"He's looking at someone," Rebecca said.

She was right. Urso was looking past Delilah at the man at the next table, Ashley Yeats, who was typing like a fiend on his cell phone. The guy looked remarkably spiffy after a day of hiking with Sylvie and the twins at Kindred Creek. In drizzling rain.

Rebecca curled up her nose. "I don't like that guy. What's he up to? If we could sit at a nearby table, I could peek over his shoulder."

But no nearby tables were to be had. I asked Rebecca to hold the table next to the exit while I fetched a couple of hot cocoas.

"Make mine peppermint stick with extra shavings of

white chocolate on top," she said, adding, "and get me a Chocko-Socko cheesecake, too. It's scrumptious. They use fresh cream cheese from Emerald Pastures Farm."

As I wound through the tables, purposely sweeping past Ashley Yeats, I glanced at his phone. He was either texting someone or doing email. As if sensing me spying on him, he clicked the application closed. His abrupt halt to his activities sent spirals of suspicion through me. I glanced at Urso, who frowned and hitched his head for me to skedaddle. I made a face back at him, giving him my best it's-a-free-world look, and moved to the counter.

After stating Rebecca's order and opting for a cheese plate with Camembert and apricot jam for myself—Lois's scone hadn't quite quenched my appetite—I pulled my cell phone from my purse, intent on finding out more about Ashley Yeats. I opened my browser and typed his name into the search line. A website page emerged that read: *UNDER CONSTRUCTION.* If Yeats was a legitimate journalist, shouldn't he have had an up-and-running website?

The legs of a chair scraped along the tile floor. Shelton Nelson rose from his table and sauntered to Ashley Yeats. The journalist gestured for Shelton to join him as he whipped out a tape recorder.

During the time I waited for our cocoas and treats, Rebecca had finagled a table near the twosome.

"How did you snare this?" I set a tray holding two cups of cocoa, our desserts, and silverware on the table.

"It's all about timing. I saw the couple packing up, so I dawdled until they left."

Rebecca picked up her cup of cocoa and licked off the whipped cream. I sat down and did the same, while peeking at Ashley and Shelton. The acoustics were great.

Ashley said, ". . . and that leads me to my next point. Your wine collection is famous."

Shelton chuckled. "It's not that renowned, except maybe to a few friends who like to drop in for a taste of Pétrus."

"Don't be modest. Tell me how you got started collecting."

"As you know, I began my career as a litigation attorney,

but I tired of that quickly. Don't get me wrong. I loved help-ing the destitute, but at the end of the day, I looked forward to a sip of the grape. On weekends, I would invite in friends. Many were collectors. Thanks to them, my thirst for knowl-edge grew. I was thirty when I had an epiphany and realized my destiny was wine. One must have passion to find joy in a career. That's the key to everything. I convinced my then-wife to move to Providence." He sat back in his chair. "The rest, as they say, is history. I began to invest. First with a single case, then two cases, then ten. I sold some of the wines I owned at a profit to obtain others. It's like gold, once you get the hang of it. Some people are willing to pay anything for an exquisite bottle."

"And yet you have so much in stock. When will you ever drink it all?"

Shelton chuckled. "My daughter hopes I won't be able to. Have I told you the story about the man who owned the French vineyard and feared his daughter wanted to take it over?"

The offhand comment made me sit taller. Did Liberty covet her father's wine cellar? Was that what her argument with her father had been about? Were Noelle's last words, *hell's key*, really *Shel's key* because he knew his daughter's intention and his testimony would be essential? If that were the case, wouldn't Liberty have done away with her father and not Noelle? I stiffened. Did I really believe Liberty, who was slated to marry a devout man, was capable of murder?

A wall of warm air closed in behind me; I swiveled in my chair.

"Are you two eavesdropping?" Urso said.

"No, we . . ." I straightened my back. "We're enjoying a cup of cocoa and a fabulous Old Chatham Hudson Valley Camembert from New York. Want a taste?"

He frowned.

"Oh, that's right. You're a hard cheese devotee," I teased. Boy, I could be semi-glib when I was on my game.

Taking the counteroffensive, Rebecca said, "What are you and Delilah doing, Chief? Spying on us?"

Urso said, "We were here first."

"Humph," Rebecca said. "Everyone knows that the best spy is the one who anticipates his enemy's actions."

"Where did you learn that, Miss Zook? By watching *The Bourne Identity*? And exactly when did I become your enemy?"

The door to the café flew open. "Nelson!" Boyd Hellman tramped in, his face a blaze of red. Drops of rain frosted his hair and clothes. He rushed toward Shelton.

Urso dodged me to thwart Boyd's advance, but Boyd was surprisingly fleet.

He skidded to a stop by Shelton Nelson's table. "You . . . You . . . You lured Noelle to this sty of a town."

Shelton rose to his feet. "I did no such—"

Boyd threw a punch and connected with Shelton's ear. The man fell sideways but gripped the edge of the table. Ashley steadied his side of the table, which kept Shelton from plunging to the floor.

Urso, who was bigger than Boyd by a head and a good fifty pounds heavier, grabbed Boyd from behind and held tight. "Enough, Hellman."

Boyd kicked at Shelton but missed.

In a split second, Urso whipped out a zip tie and secured Boyd's wrists. "Cool it, fella. You're going to jail to sober up."

As Urso muscled Boyd from the café, Rebecca said to me, "Did you get a whiff of Hellman? He was drunker than a sailor on shore leave."

Her remark made me refocus on Boyd Hellman. He had blamed Shelton for persuading Noelle to move to Providence for business and leaving him behind, but he had never accused Shelton of murdering her. Was that because he knew that he, and not Shelton, was the killer?

CHAPTER

15

All the way home, though I was exhausted and in dire need of a good night's sleep, I pondered Boyd's impetuous behavior. He had to have killed Noelle. He was hotheaded enough to have turned my workshop upside down. He seemed the type who would've plunged a corkscrew into her neck. With him in Urso's custody, I felt a whole lot safer walking up my front path.

When I reached the door, I was met with a huge surprise. Sitting beside the doormat was a vase filled with the most beautiful autumn-colored flowers: gerberas, mums, and fragrant lilies. Under the glow of the porch light, I read the note attached:

> *My love, I miss you more than life itself. I can't wait until this all ends and we can be together. J.*

My soul did a happy dance. I raced inside, gathered Rags in a celebratory hug, and called Jordan's handler. Of course, he didn't answer, so I left a syrupy message of thanks to the love of my life and hung up.

Hungrier than I could remember—thanks to Boyd's sudden appearance, I hadn't eaten my cheese or finished my hot chocolate—I hurried to the kitchen. I fixed Rags a quick treat then made myself an appetizer of melted Roquefort and mascarpone cheese on a whole wheat English muffin. I topped the concoction with slices of mango and poured myself a glass of Château Labégorce wine—a luscious red that Matthew said was subtle with alluring exotic notes.

Taking my feast and Rags up to my bedroom, I spread a blanket on the floor and pretended that Jordan and I were having one of our intimate picnics. He would have teased me about the simplicity of the outing; he preferred to do things a bit more elaborately in the culinary department, which made me fantasize about our future. Would he want to continue as a farmer, or would he return to the restaurant business, his first love, once this WITSEC nonsense was over? Maybe he would have an interest in buying La Bella Ristorante. A customer told me yesterday that Luigi Bozzuto was considering selling. I wondered if his breakup with Delilah had anything to do with the decision.

When I didn't hear back from Jordan or his handler and I was sufficiently blue to the point of distraction, I bussed my empty dishes back to the kitchen and prepared for bed. As I lay there, bathed in the heavenly scent coming from the flowers on the nightstand, a deep sense of longing overtook me. Tears streamed down my face. I wanted to talk to Jordan so badly. I wanted to kiss him and tell him I loved him and make mad passionate love. I wanted to spill everything about the murder—my concerns about who did it and my worry that I had misjudged Noelle in our brief encounter. Doubt pressed on my rib cage and made it hard to breathe. I anticipated having to post another flurry of positive-thinking sticky notes on my computer and around The Cheese Shop. Picturing the notes boomeranged my thoughts back to Noelle's diary—the one inscribed with inspirational sayings. The quote by Einstein had urged her to learn the rules of the game. The quote by Churchill had suggested she see the opportunity in difficulty. Another quote had reminded her to keep herself bolstered for action and focused on a task. What had that task been? Was it the investigation to which Lois had alluded?

In the gloom, I grew aware of how silent the house was. The heater kicked on with a moan. A shutter clacked against the exterior. When the wind gusted outside and tree branches scratched the windows, I couldn't lie still any longer. I leaped out of bed and paced the room. Rags vaulted to the floor and paced beside me. He yowled and head-butted my calf as if asking: *What's wrong?*

"I'm scared, Ragsie. Worried that I can't see the whole picture. Annoyed that I might have missed a vital clue. What if the killer thinks I'm onto him . . . or her . . . even though I'm not?"

The phone jingled. Pinpoints of angst zipped through me. I snatched up the receiver. My voice quavered as I said, "Hello?"

"Did I wake you?" Jordan said.

I felt so relieved I could barely speak.

"Charlotte? Can you hear me? Did I lose the connection?"

"I'm here. And I'm awake. I was . . ." I stopped short of blurting out that I had been conjuring up scenarios of a break-in or worse.

We talked for nearly fifteen minutes about nothing special—the weather, the latest cheese on the market, the twins' play.

And then Jordan said, "When are you going to fess up?"

"What are you talking about?"

"I'm not on a desert island. And I do have a sister and employees that reside in Providence. Talk to me. There was another murder. In your house."

"My workshop."

"Talk to me."

In one long stream, I told him about Noelle and how much I had liked her. I consolidated the list of suspects: her boss who might or might not have been in a relationship with her and might or might not be in financial straits, his jealous wardrobe-challenged daughter, the shady journalist who resembled a vampire, the hot-tempered winery overseer who had badgered me as I closed up shop, and Noelle's ex-boyfriend who had a serious drinking problem.

When I finished, he said, "You're missing your calling, sweetheart."

"How's that?"

"You shouldn't be running a cheese shop. You should be writing a novel. Add some steamy sex and you could conquer the romance market." His words sounded playful, but the concern in his voice was palpable. "Whatever you do, be careful. I want you in one piece and breathing the next time I see you."

"Heavily breathing?"

"Preferably."

"And when will that be?"

"Soon."

I made him promise.

When I hung up, I double-checked the windows and doors to make sure they were secure, then I crept back into bed, snuggled my cat, and fell asleep with a smile on my face.

* * *

The next morning at ten A.M., Matthew and I went to the Country Kitchen for coffee. The temperature outside was cold; a stiff wind had kicked up. Most often I loved autumn, but I didn't appreciate the bitter days.

"Boy, I needed this." I took a sip of my to-go coffee laced with vanilla syrup as I exited the diner. "Why is it that every day, midmorning, I need a sugar fix?"

"Because you've been going strong since six A.M.," my cousin said. "For most of the population, four hours after rising would be lunchtime. You know, you could sleep in occasionally, now that the girls and I have moved out."

"I've tried. My internal clock won't let me. Where are the twins, by the way?"

"Still with Sylvie. She called last night, long after their

trek to Kindred Creek, and asked to keep them. I heard them giggling hysterically in the background." He shrugged. "What could I say without sounding like a mean father? It was a weekend night, after all."

"Don't look now, but I think Sylvie is parking up the street. And I think Ashley Yeats is with her."

The moment Sylvie turned off her Mercedes, the twins bolted from the backseat. "Hi, Daddy. Hi, Aunt Charlotte. We went to church. Now, Mum is buying us breakfast." They darted past us and straight into the diner. The Country Kitchen always had a selection of donuts, pastries, and muffins on hand. Amy invariably chose a cheese croissant. Clair's latest favorite was the banana and chocolate chip gluten-free muffin.

"They look tired." Matthew groused. "Their mother lets them stay up until all hours. If I've told her once, I've told her a thousand times—"

"Relax. Their speed was supersonic."

From the car, Rocket barked. I turned.

Standing beside the rear seat with the door open wide, Sylvie, who had dressed in a low-cut sweater, swirly skirt, and spiky heels—hardly church-appropriate attire; hardly warm enough for the weather—struggled to get a leash around Rocket's neck while trying to keep her skirt from flying up in the wind. Rocket moved his massive head back and forth, which threw Sylvie off balance. She pitched forward, hitting her knees on the threshold of the car, and let out a yelp. Ashley Yeats hurried out of the car and inserted himself into the scuffle, but Rocket snarled, and the journalist heeded the warning.

Matthew muttered, "That Yeats guy had better not have spent the night. I don't want the girls exposed to . . . you know."

"He didn't. At least I don't think he did. I saw him last night at Café au Lait." I told Matthew about the interview that Ashley had conducted with Shelton and the ensuing brawl with Boyd Hellman.

"That doesn't mean Yeats didn't drop by Sylvie's place

afterward. I think it's time for a chat about parental rules."
He tramped toward Sylvie, yelling to me over his shoulder,
"Watch the girls when they exit the diner, would you?"

The girls would be dandy. I was more worried about Matthew hauling off and socking Ashley. When buying my coffee, I had spotted Urso in the diner. Given his current penchant for locking up disorderly guys, I sprinted after Matthew.

Before Matthew could reach the Mercedes, Ashley bussed Sylvie on the cheek and headed off in the opposite direction. At the same time, Rocket sprang from the car, his leash trailing behind him. Heading toward me, he nearly crashed into Matthew, who dodged right and kept marching. I grabbed hold of Rocket's collar and knelt on one knee. He licked my face and whimpered a merry hello.

"Yeah, I've missed you, too," I crooned while scrubbing his ears and muzzle.

Sylvie pivoted and, spying Matthew, pinned her skirt against her thighs and tugged up the top of her sweater. I smirked. No matter how hard she tried, she wouldn't be able to hide the deep cleavage. "Hello, love."

"What was that about?" Matthew demanded.

"What was what about?" Strands of acid white hair blew around Sylvie's cheeks. She tried to extract a piece that, thanks to the wind, had stuck to her lipstick, but to no avail.

"That guy Yeats," Matthew said. "Did he stay the night?"

"Why, Matthew, love, are you jealous?"

"Did he?" Matthew advanced on Sylvie. "I will take you back to court if I have to and prove you are an unfit mother."

She faltered. "No, he did not stay the night. I would never do that. Amy and Clair come first. Always."

"What do you know about him?" Matthew demanded.

"Whatever can you mean?"

"Don't play dumb. You and he went on a hike at Kindred Creek."

"We did and it was so pleasant. No mud. No slip and slide. The trees with their falling leaves smelled musty and—"

"Stop with the tour guide bit. Who is he? What did you find out about him on your outing?"

"You want his bio? Fine. He's from England." Sylvie ticked off the answers on her pointy fingernails. "He always wanted to be an on-camera journalist in the States, but he hasn't received an opportunity yet. He's a freelancer and needs stories—content, he calls it—so he's been scouring the globe for good ones."

Was that why he had been hounding Noelle? Did he know for a fact that she had some story to impart? Was it tawdry? Did it involve her parents? Maybe her refusal to give Yeats a scoop angered him enough to lash out.

"He has a luscious voice, don't you think, love? Like a radio announcer."

Matthew grimaced. "I think he looks like a bloodsucking creep."

"Matthew Bessette, those *are* the words of a jealous man. How delicious." Sylvie released her skirt. Maybe she thought a Marilyn Monroe moment of allowing the breeze to flute up her skirt and expose her legs would diminish Matthew's anger, but it didn't. A few tourists and parade volunteers got an eyeful, though.

"Does he have an alibi for the night of the murder?" Matthew asked.

"Tosh. Why would he need an alibi?"

"He knew Noelle."

"Says who?"

"Her ex. And Yeats came to town on the same day as Noelle."

"You are overreacting." Sylvie stroked Matthew's arm. He recoiled as if her hand were a blowtorch. "Ashley Yeats had nothing to do with Noelle Adams, I assure you."

"According to Noelle's ex," Matthew countered, "Ashley Yeats was calling Noelle on a regular basis and hounding her."

"What?" Sylvie shrieked as if she had been two-timed. "I have to go. I have business to attend to." She pushed past him and held out her hand for Rocket's leash. "If you don't mind, Charlotte."

At the same time that I relinquished control of the strap, Prudence rounded the corner. She was tilted forward to protect a pink-striped cake box from the wind. As she plowed past us, Rocket woofed. Prudence recoiled and bobbled the cake box. I lunged to help, but I wasn't quick enough. The box flew from her hands and landed with a thwack on the sidewalk. The box burst and the cake splattered. Prudence froze, her mouth agape. I hurried to clean up the mess before Rocket made it his breakfast. He loved sweets, and occasionally I had given him a bite of a sugar cookie, but chocolate was a no-no.

"Well, I never," Prudence growled. "Sylvie Bessette, now look what you've done."

"Me?" Sylvie squawked.

"If you don't get control of that darned dog, I'll have the dogcatcher after him."

"Don't threaten me, you ostrich."

Prudence sputtered. "What did you call me?"

"Ostrich." With a finger, Sylvie outlined a picture of the bird while continuing. "With your skinny neck and your beaky mouth and that ridiculous hairdo."

Two parade decorators stopped hanging a banner up the sidewalk. Behind us, a crowd formed, as well. Across the street, Rebecca popped from The Cheese Shop, wiping her hands on her apron. I gestured for her to stay put.

Prudence snarled at Sylvie. "You're the ostrich with its head in the sand. I warned you shops were going up for sale. Did you believe me? No, you did not. Well, for your information, I have jumped into the fray. That cake was intended for a celebratory hurrah with my Realtor."

"Your Realtor?"

"I have put a bid on The Silver Trader." That was the jewelry store to the east of Prudence's La Chic Boutique. "And I have also put a bid on The Spotted Giraffe."

Oh no. If she were to get one or both of those shops, she would be impossible to contain. Would she turn them all into dress shop annexes? Providence thrived on variety. The town didn't need more women's boutiques.

"But The Spotted Giraffe is right next to my shop," Sylvie cried. "How could they not have told me it was for sale? I want to expand."

"Because they don't like you." Prudence cackled. "If these deals go through, I intend to bury you and your shop, and then you and your supercilious attitude can go right to the devil, do you hear me?"

"Fiddle-dee-dee. You don't scare me, you bully." Sylvie raised her chin and gave the leash a jerk. "Let's go, Rocket. We have an appointment with *our* Realtor."

Though Sylvie's exit through the blossoming crowd packed a wallop, Prudence's exit was better. She snatched the box of cake remains from me, said, "Game, match, set," and after offering a grin worthy of the sorceress Maleficent, marched away. Thanks to her pronouncement, she knew Sylvie would yell at someone and make more enemies. What a witch.

The girls scampered from the diner carrying two bags of goodies. "Dad, where's Mum going?" Clair said.

"I have no clue." Matthew ran his hand along the side of his head.

"She's taking a walk to burn off a little steam," I said.

"What kind of steam?" Amy asked.

"Is she sick?" Clair said.

I reached for their hands. "Come with us to The Cheese Shop and we'll explain."

As we crossed the street, Rebecca dashed to me. "What was that all about?"

"It's a long story. I—"

"Rebecca!" Ipo Ho, the brawny Hawaiian honeybee farmer who was Rebecca's fiancé until recently, lumbered toward us. His massive chest heaved with exertion. "We need to talk. I—" He gaped at someone approaching from behind me. "Hi, Chief Urso."

Urso drew alongside me.

Ipo held up his hand as a gesture of peace. "Why do you look so angry? I'm not accosting Rebecca. Really."

I studied Urso. He did look mad. Super mad. The muscles in his jaw were twitching.

Ipo hurried to add, "I simply want to talk to her. See, we broke up, and it's my fault, and—"

"Sorry, Mr. Ho, but your conversation with Miss Zook will have to wait. I"—Urso growled out the word—"get first dibs."

CHAPTER

Without an explanation, Urso gripped Rebecca's elbow. He said, "Charlotte, you, too," and ushered us into Fromagerie Bessette.

"What's the problem?" I asked, although I was pretty sure I knew the answer. He was frowning so hard that his eyebrows nearly touched in the middle. My insides turned to jelly.

"Let's talk." He shepherded us around the cheese counter toward the office. The twins followed at a clip, crying in protest, but Urso didn't loosen his hold.

Tyanne, who was working the counter, peeked at me. Her forehead was creased with concern.

Putting on a brave face, I said, "Business good?"

"Booming." Tyanne gestured to all the customers.

"Why don't you slice up that wheel of Istara P'tit Basque and set it on the tasting counter."

"Good idea. It's one of our customers' favorites. So nutty and firm."

"Enough chatting, Charlotte. Keep walking." Urso allowed us to enter the office first, and then he shut the door with a bang. Rags, who must have been asleep on the desk chair before the intrusion, yowled his displeasure. Urso said, "I like you, cat, but you have no part in this, so keep it zipped."

"Don't call him *cat*," I said. "He's got feelings."

"Sorry. Rags."

Mollified, Rags paced in a circle and settled down. He liked Urso . . . usually.

I slipped behind the chair and gripped the upper rim to steady myself. Rebecca wove her hands together and played a nervous game of "Here's the church."

"You two"—Urso aimed a finger at me first, then Rebecca—"were snooping at the precinct."

Rebecca said, "No, we—"

"Don't deny it. I have the whole event on videotape. I assume you came to tell me something vital . . . or should I say *key* to the investigation."

Irked by his snarky tone, I rounded the chair and drew within inches of him. "Actually, we weren't coming to tell you anything. We have questions. Questions we need answered."

Urso folded his arms across his chest. "Is that really the defense you're going to take?"

Did he know that Rebecca and I had peeked into the evidence room, or was he hoping for a confession? Well, he wouldn't get one. "I repeat, we need answers."

"Like what?"

I inched closer. "I want to go through Noelle's computer."

"I already told you that we didn't find a thing."

"You've searched every file? Every single one? When did you find the time?" Why, oh, why couldn't I squelch sarcasm sometimes? "My computer has thousands of files. It would take me months. I can only imagine how many Noelle had on hers."

"Charlotte, be reasonable. We searched files that had been opened in the last week." Urso dropped his hands to his sides. "I assure you there's nothing on the computer that leads us to Miss Adams's killer. So why were you really at the precinct?"

I shifted feet. "Tell me who you suspect."

"We went through this already."

"And you revealed nothing."

Urso blew out a stream of air and swiped his hand down his neck.

"A killer is on the loose, Chief." Rebecca spanked the desk. "Why don't you have somebody in custody?"

"Because I need enough facts to convict."

"Boyd Hellman has a strong motive," Rebecca said, plowing ahead like a tugboat that refused to believe an iceberg could deter it. "He tracked his ex-girlfriend to Providence. When she rebuffed him, he lashed out the way he did last night at Café au Lait, except, luckily, you were there to stop him."

"He was drunk," Urso said. "That doesn't make him a killer."

"Maybe he was drunk on the night Noelle died," Rebecca suggested. "Maybe he doesn't remember killing her."

The two of them glowered at each other, and I was glad that neither had the superhero power of radiation.

"U-ey," I said, "Lois Smith saw someone lurking outside my place the night Noelle was killed. She said the car was a Taurus, but I think she was mistaken. A Taurus looks like a Chevy Malibu, and that's what Boyd Hellman drives."

"Those two cars look nothing alike."

"You're a car buff, so I'll concede you would know the difference. But to Lois's untrained eye they would appear similar. Both are sedans with four doors and no hard edges."

"Boyd Hellman doesn't look anything like a woman." Urso waited for his comment to sink in. "Yes, I've spoken to Mrs. Smith, and I've questioned Mr. Hellman. At length. He's unpredictable and edgy, but I'm not convinced he's the killer. He claims he was walking that night."

"Noelle went hiking," I said. "Coincidence?"

"We checked Mr. Hellman's hotel room for traces of mud to match the mud from Miss Adams's boots. We didn't find any."

"But there wasn't any mud in the guest room at my house, either. Maybe Boyd was smart enough to clean off his shoes or go barefoot."

Urso jammed his hands into his pockets. "Mr. Hellman gave me the route he traveled. My team is following up with everyone in town who was taking a stroll."

Providence had a number of regular walkers in town. Most would be reliable witnesses.

"Why is he acting so reckless, then?" Rebecca asked.

"He lost the love of his life," Urso replied.

"She wasn't the love of his life," I said. "Noelle broke up with him. She moved out."

"That doesn't mean he was over her." Urso's gaze softened. Given our history, I decided not to utter a word. "F.Y.I., last night, while Mr. Hellman was sobering up, he filled me in on Miss Adams's past. How much do you know?"

"That she lost her parents at the age of seven. She lived with her grandfather, but then he died. She was raised in a Catholic orphanage. She graduated high school and went to work as a bartender, where she met my cousin. Matthew taught her the art of being a sommelier."

"According to Boyd Hellman, Noelle's parents were grifters."

I gawked at him. "Really?" A grifter was a scam artist of the highest—or lowest—order. Had they involved Noelle in their scams when she was young? Was that why Boyd said Noelle had burned them from her memory? Why hadn't Matthew told me? Maybe he didn't know.

"I don't believe it for a second," Rebecca said. "Boyd Hellman is sending you on a wild-goose chase."

"Rebecca." I held up a hand.

"No, listen to me. I was watching this episode of *The Closer* or maybe it was *Body of Proof*. Anyway, the leading lady was onto the killer, but the killer kept giving her the runaround to keep her from digging too deeply into his past. He sent anonymous notes and planted all sorts of red herrings."

Urso snuffled.

"Don't mock me," Rebecca said. "Killers are wily."

"Rebecca, please," I said. "I'm sure Chief Urso has checked the validity of the statement."

"I have," he said. "They operated small-time cons. They died when a mark that got fed up shot them."

I gasped. No wonder Noelle hesitated when I asked about her folks. What kind of childhood had she lived? Losing my parents at the age of three had been sad, but my memories of them were sweet. I remembered reading with them and butterfly good night kisses at the end of the day and dancing with my father while perched on his feet. How had Noelle's traumatic childhood developed her as a person? Did scam artist talent pass down through genetic DNA? Had she been scamming someone in Providence? Had her deception made someone angry enough to kill her?

I gazed at Urso. "Have you considered that there might be people from her parents' lives who followed her here?"

"A lot of time has passed since then, but yes, I've taken that into account. I'm driving to Cleveland tomorrow to follow up on that angle. In the meantime, I want you and you"— he indicated Rebecca then me—"to promise you'll keep out of this while I'm gone." He turned to exit.

"Wait," I said. "What were you doing with Delilah at Café au Lait last night?"

"Why, Charlotte, are you concerned about my love life?" His mouth quirked up on one side and, for a second, I found myself awkwardly attracted to him. Dang. I was way lonelier than I realized.

I shifted feet, determined to be professional. "Was the date a ruse so you could observe Shelton and Liberty Nelson?"

"Or were you keeping an eye on Ashley Yeats?" Rebecca said.

Chuckling, Urso exited without answering either of us.

* * *

"I'm not promising Chief Urso anything." Rebecca smacked the wall in the hall as she stomped back to the main shop.

"And I'll tell you something else. I hate the way he laughs. Ho-ho-ho." She imitated him, heaving her shoulders and overexaggerating his head waggle. "Ooh, but he irks me."

He vexed me, too, but I wasn't about to fuel her fire.

Tyanne galloped to me, bubbling with curiosity. "Sugar, what was that about?"

"We'll talk later."

"Can I tell you my good news, then?"

I grinned. "Did we have a run on everything in the store? Are we rich beyond my wildest dreams?"

"Almost. Those tags you put in the cheese are a smash. We sold nearly all of the La Tur Goat Cheese." She recited: "*A cheese the angels created*. How yummy is that?" Beaming, she clutched my shoulders. "But that's not *my* news. Liberty Nelson just called. Mind you, I didn't talk on the telephone while anyone was in the store."

"Don't worry. You're a terrific employee. Go on."

For sure, Tyanne's news wasn't about the murder. She was smiling way too hard to say that Liberty had admitted to murder and Urso could wrap up the case.

"Liberty is doubling the amount I can spend on the entire wedding. Isn't that unbelievable? My fee will cover the mortgage for at least three months. I can't tell you how much that will help with finances."

"Great," I said, though her words made me flash on something Matthew had said about financial troubles brewing at the winery. Liberty's extravagance would challenge that theory. "Um, is she paying in cash?" Perhaps she intended to charge everything.

Tyanne tilted her head. "Why?"

"Just wondering, that's all."

"Should I ask her to pay in cash?"

"No, of course not." I fetched a pad and pencil and began to make a list. "So, does she want to double the amount of cheese platters? Perhaps some February specialties like Rivers Edge Chèvre. My personal favorite is Heart's Desire, a seductive goat cheese that's coated with a zippy paprika. And how about gift baskets of cheese to all of the guests or serving a cheese wedding cake, like we had at Matthew and Meredith's out-of-towners' dinner?"

Tyanne tittered. "You are too funny. Always thinking of business."

How wrong she was. For the last few days, all I had been thinking about was murder. If only Urso would nab somebody, maybe then I could start concentrating on life instead of death.

Tyanne wagged a finger. "By the way, speaking of cakes, I tasted the most glorious cake at Providence Pâtisserie this morning. It's white and dark chocolate with a mascarpone whipped cream filling. To die for. They call it Passionate Desire. Liberty is in lust with chocolate."

"Yoo-hoo, Tyanne," a woman called.

I said, "It looks like Mrs. Bell needs your assistance."

A woman, shaped like her name, stood beyond a group of mothers and their children—many who were in the Thanksgiving play. "Yoo-hoo," she repeated, waving like she had won a game show prize. A Cairn Terrier poked its head out of her tote bag.

Tyanne wiped her hands on a clean white towel then pitched the towel into a bin. "She probably wants me to suggest accoutrements. She purchased a pound of that mouthwatering Carr Valley Mobay."

It was one of my favorites, with ash made from grape vines separating the two kinds of milk.

As Tyanne dashed off to assist Mrs. Bell, Rebecca sidled to me. "I can see that brain of yours ticking away. What's with the questions about Liberty's finances?"

"Nothing."

"Liar."

Matthew strode from the wine annex carrying a bottle of Madrone Mountain Mundo Novo, a divine port-style wine that would go perfectly with the Mobay cheese. "Is everything okay between you and Urso?"

"Yes," Rebecca said, "except he wants us to nose out of the investigation. We said we would if he would arrest someone."

"You know, I can't get my mind off that Ashley Yeats guy." Matthew worked a corkscrew into the cork and pulled— *thwup.* "He acts guilty."

"Of what? Liking your ex-wife?" I teased.

"Something's off about that."

"You don't think Sylvie is loveable?"

"I'm serious."

Tyanne returned to the counter carrying a load of crackers and jams. "Mrs. Bell forgot to take a shopping basket. Sheesh." She rounded the register and set the items on the counter.

"I want to check him out," Matthew said as he twisted the cork off the corkscrew.

"Check who out?" Tyanne asked.

"Ashley Yeats."

"That journalist?" Tyanne sniffed. "I don't like him much. He's dating your ex, isn't he?"

"Yes." The snarl in Matthew's tone was unmistakable. "Where do I start, Charlotte? Should I poke around his garbage or something?"

"Matthew, please. I want you to keep your distance."

"Why shouldn't he get involved?" Rebecca said. "Matthew was Noelle's good friend, and he's officially part of the club now."

"What club?" Tyanne asked as she jotted prices for Mrs. Bell's items on a sales pad.

"The Snoop Club."

"There is no Snoop Club." I glared at Rebecca. "Cut it out. Don't stir up trouble."

"That Yeats fellow is the one that's trouble," Tyanne said. "Why just the other day, I caught him staring at my legs and every other woman's legs, too. He has no shame."

"He's a bum," Rebecca said.

"C'mon, Charlotte." Matthew jerked a thumb. "You're the pro. Tell me how I get the dirt on him."

Realizing my cousin would not be deterred, but mindful of the customers browsing the shop, I drew Matthew, Tyanne, and Rebecca into a huddle by the entry to the kitchen.

"Okay, first, Matthew, you have to drum up telephone records. Maybe you could call Ashley Yeats's employer and ask about his assignment and his travel schedule. See how other trips might have coincided with Noelle's."

Matthew said, "A former employee of mine in Cleveland left the restaurant business. He works at the telephone company."

"Perfect."

"I don't like that Harold Warfield," Rebecca said. "Especially after he attacked you last night."

Matthew shot me a look. "He did what?"

I waved for him to relax. "He didn't lay a finger on me. He harassed me as I was closing up shop. He said I was the one that made Urso interrogate him."

"He's got shifty eyes," Tyanne said.

Rebecca agreed. "I think he's having an affair. I'm going to tail him."

"No, you're not," I said. Where did she come up with these harebrained ideas? Her MINI Cooper would stick out like a sore thumb.

"Is it okay if I corroborate his alibi?" she asked.

I sighed. "Sure. Call the library."

"Better yet, I'll go there after work. What about you? What are you going to do?"

"I'm going to attend the twins' rehearsal."

"No, really. You've got to do something to solve this murder, with or without Chief Urso's approval. Something's got you bugged." She wiggled her pinky. "I can see it in your eyes."

"Honestly? I'm still miffed that I can't see everything Noelle stored on her computer."

Rebecca clapped her hands. "I knew it. We should go back and—"

"Not a chance." I did not want Urso locking us up and throwing away the key.

"Sugar, maybe I could help. I've learned a whole ton about the Internet." Tyanne gripped my wrist. "I bet I could hack into Noelle's emails. Maybe we could find out with whom she was communicating on a regular basis."

"Maybe that ex-boyfriend of hers," Rebecca said.

"Or Shelton Nelson." Matthew snapped his fingers. "Find out if he sent declarations of love."

I flashed on the Tupperware containers that held my parents' letters. One of the containers had been opened, the contents scattered. I didn't think the other had been disturbed. I remembered mentioning them to Noelle. Had she stored some kind of key in the second container? I hadn't thought to check. I would bet the police hadn't thought to, either.

CHAPTER

17

With everyone fixed on a plan of discovery, I hurried home. After settling Rags in the house and turning on Gershwin music to keep him company, I raced down the driveway to my makeshift workshop. I only had a few minutes to spare before I was due at the theater. Given what little time I had spent with the twins lately, I didn't want to disappoint them by showing up late to rehearsal. But I had to satisfy my curiosity first.

I switched on the garage light and scanned the area. The place appeared to be in order. I didn't suspect a recent intrusion. I strode to the shelf holding the containers of my parents' love letters. Would I find Noelle's elusive key inside? I removed both boxes from the shelf, and ignoring the topmost, knowing that I had replaced the letters inside it while Urso observed me, I peeled back the corner of the lower. It burped open. The scent of aging stationary wafted out. I removed the letters, untied the gold ribbon, and searched between each piece of paper. I wasn't sure what physical item I was seeking, but I didn't find a thing: no key or list or record of any kind.

Deflated, I hugged the letters to my chest. What was I missing?

When I had found Noelle, she was lying on her side beyond the secretary desk, her arms and legs at an angle. I recalled the first thing I had detected when entering—the smell of something metallic and marshy. Noelle's boots had been muddy. She had gone hiking. She had taken a flashlight with her. Where had it disappeared to? I swiveled and stared at the door leading to the backyard. What if Lois was wrong? What if the killer didn't wait in a car near my house? What if the killer arrived on foot? He might have taken the flashlight when he fled.

With renewed energy, I galloped to the kitchen, flipped on the exterior lights to illuminate the backyard, fetched the flashlight I kept in the drawer by the telephone, and dashed into the night. Arcing the flashlight's beam across the grass, I searched for signs of the killer's footprints. Not only had the police, my nieces, and Meredith trampled the area, but the weather hadn't cooperated, either. The grass was soaked. I flared the flashlight's beam at the pine needle mulch beneath a group of rose bushes, hoping to find footprints leading away from the garage, but I saw none. I swept the beam along the evergreen hedge and paused. A piece of what appeared to be material was flapping in the breeze. Was it a telltale shred of the killer's clothing? A swatch of Harold's tweed jacket or Ashley's natty plaid blazer? The hedges were so thick that someone trying to slip through would have gotten snagged.

I drew near, but all I spied was a piece of newspaper caught on the thorny leaves. In a huff, I wadded the paper into a miniscule ball and marched back to the house—none the wiser.

* * *

When I arrived at the theater, I noticed actors standing outside in pairs; they were preparing to audition for the winter play.

Using the front window of the theater like a mirror, one male actor swiveled his female partner to face the window. He held her firmly by the shoulders as he ordered her to look at his face and then her own. He was a bum, he told her. So was she.

Spying me, the actress broke apart from her audition buddy and giggled self-consciously.

"Don't stop on account of me," I said. "Sounds good. But why are you rehearsing outside?"

"There are so many others in the foyer, and it's almost dinner break for the kids," the actress said.

"Do you know about the rehearsal room at the rear of the theater?"

"Yeah, but it's under renovation."

My grandmother never failed to impress me with her ability to conjure up new funds for the Providence Playhouse.

"Well, *continuez* as my grandmother would say, and break a leg." I waved good-bye and moved into the foyer. To my surprise I found Amy chasing Clair with a fake roasted turkey leg.

"Run, scaredy cat." Amy cackled with glee.

Clair, laughing as hard as her sister, dropped to all fours and scrambled beneath the buffet table.

I nabbed Amy by the back of her sweater. She swung around, ready to wallop her attacker with the turkey leg, until she realized who it was. "Oops, sorry." She threw her arms around me. The turkey leg swatted my backside. "Clair," she yelled. "Aunt Charlotte's here."

Clair crawled from her hiding space and joined the group hug. "You made it."

I broke free and pointed at the roasted turkey leg. "Where did you get that monstrosity?"

"Mom's friend Ashley found it at a gag store in Cleveland." Amy waggled it. "He says pranks make life fun."

"Does he?"

"He's funny," Clair said.

"Funny, ha-ha?" I asked.

"Funny, different. He's sort of stuck-up. I don't think he likes us much, and he's always checking his telephone."

"It's like he's addicted to it." Amy mimed stabbing her finger on a cell phone keypad.

Hmm. It sounded like the girls were seeing more of Ashley Yeats than I had assumed. Was Sylvie aware they weren't fond of him?

A whistle blared. Like well-trained soldiers, the twins abandoned me and sped into the theater through the double doors.

"Put the turkey leg on the prop table," I called.

Delilah, who arrived to set napkins and plates on the buffet table, handed me a bundle of each. "Help me?"

"Sure."

The meal was potluck, with delicious items provided by the children's parents—platters filled with finger sandwiches, cold cuts, salads, and vegetables. In addition, there were juice boxes, bottled water, and cupcakes decorated with teensy plastic turkeys.

Delilah said, "By the way, the turkey pizzas you made yesterday were a huge hit. I had a slice. What was the cheese you used?"

"Salted Lioni Mozzarella."

She rolled her eyes. "*Très* exotic."

"I added lots of spices."

"Will you share the recipe? Those ingredients would make a fantastic grilled cheese."

"You bet."

She aligned the serving spoons. "Have you heard from Jordan lately?"

"He sent me flowers."

"Lucky you."

"And we talked last night."

"Any chance of seeing him?"

"He said we would meet soon, but you know . . ." My emotions caught in my throat. "Gosh, I miss him."

She petted my arm in understanding. "Men have no sense of timetables. You never know how soon *soon* might be." She grinned like the Cheshire Cat, but the smile quickly waffled and faded.

"Enough about me," I said. "How is the play turning out?"

"Excellently." Delilah drew me to the double doors and pointed. "Your grandmother is so playful with the kids, I barely have to do a thing. Most of them have their lines down. Our preteen duck is getting pretty good in the flying contraption, although he looks like his eyes might pop right out of his head with fear whenever we hook him into it."

I chuckled.

Grandmère sounded the whistle a second time, and the gaggle of children circled around her. Gripping her skirt in folds so that the children could see her ankles, she said, "Follow me. And a one, two, three." She marched in place. "Skip hop, skip hop. Do you understand?"

"*Oui*," the children shouted in unison.

"All right then, repeat the words with me."

Turkey trot music started to play through the speaker system. Children shouted, "And a one, two, three. Skip hop, skip hop."

"*De nouveau*," Grandmère said. "Again." They obeyed. "Now, follow me in a line." She clapped a rhythm and the line snaked downstage and then upstage, with a one, two, three, skip hop, skip hop. "*Exactement. Très bien.*"

I elbowed Delilah. "Who had a clue that the Indians and Pilgrims knew the turkey trot?"

She chuckled.

Suddenly the lights went out onstage. The children screamed.

"Lights," Grandmère yelled.

But no lights switched on. Where had the stage crew gone?

"Bernadette Bessette," a woman cried via a microphone. The speaker system popped. "You . . . You . . ." A toothpick-thin figure emerged from the wings. In the dim light provided by the twinkling lights surrounding the *Mayflower* and Plymouth Rock backdrop, I made out Prudence Hart in a knit dress, bolero cape, and high heels. She was holding the microphone so close to her mouth I thought she might consume it. "My Realtor said you are spreading lies about me."

I groaned. Prudence needed a good dose of therapy and perhaps some anti-paranoia drugs. First, she suspected Sylvie was set on destroying her, and now, my grandmother?

"I want it to stop, Bernadette. Do you hear me?"

"Loud and not so clear." Grandmère clapped her hands. "Children, calmly leave the stage and make your way to the foyer. Dinner."

"Delilah, follow me," I yelled. We jogged down the aisle. Over my shoulder, I said, "Prudence must have thrown the main light switch. Can you turn it back on? I'll corral the kids."

"I'm on it." Delilah charged past the children and up the stairs, then disappeared stage left.

"C'mon, kids," I said, directing the children like a crossing guard. "This way. Go to the foyer." They complied, but halfway up the aisle, they stopped in a cluster and pivoted to watch the drama unfold.

Prudence skulked toward my grandmother. "How dare you call me a land hog at last night's city council meeting, Bernadette."

A land hog? I couldn't possibly believe those were the words my grandmother used.

"Let us take this discussion to the theater office, Prudence," Grandmère said.

"No, I want to settle this now," she sputtered, which made her sound, with the help of the microphone, like a choking car. "First, I am not a land hog."

The lights on the stage flew on.

"Second, I have every right to purchase businesses in town."

"And drive them into the ground with your lack of know-how?" Grandmère said. "Not on my watch."

"I'll have you know I'm an excellent businesswoman. La Chic Boutique is thriving."

"It suffers, and you know it. You've driven off your best sales associates."

I cringed. Why was Grandmère inciting Prudence?

"Sylvie is wooing your clients away from you," Grandmère continued.

Prudence growled in frustration. "My Realtor told me that Councilwoman Bell"—the Cheese Shop customer who resembled her name—"is prying into my finances. Did you put her up to it?"

"I did no such thing."

"She is asking about my family. My brothers. My business practices."

"The town council has the right to investigate all hostile takeover activity."

"Hostile? I'll show you hostile."

Prudence sprinted off the stage, and I breathed easier thinking she was leaving the theater to regroup. Perhaps hire an attorney. Was I ever wrong. She returned, having fetched a prop from the prop table—Amy's fake turkey leg. Brandishing the prop like a medieval mace, she ran at my grandmother. The turkey leg made a goofy thwapping sound. The children mimicked it. Talk about theater of the absurd. Had Prudence lost complete hold of her senses?

Grandmère raised her arms to seize the rubber turkey leg. Her hands missed and caught the ties of Prudence's cape, unleashing it. The jacket flew backward like an out-of-control umbrella in a windstorm. Grandmère reached again for the turkey leg. She snared Prudence's pearl necklace. The strand snapped and beads scattered. A split second later, Prudence stepped on a bead. She lurched. Backpedaling while trying to keep her balance, she reeled toward the wings. In a last-ditch effort to save herself, she grabbed hold of a theater cord.

The effort triggered a sandbag overhead. The bag careened to the floor with a thud, and the cord, which happened to belong to the Peter Pan rigging, hoisted Prudence into the air. *Whoosh*. Prudence soared across the stage, kicking her bony legs and squealing with fear. Air caught her skirt; it billowed open. The children burst into laughter.

Grandmère yelled, "Hush," but the children couldn't help themselves. "*Chérie*." Grandmère beckoned me to help her rescue Prudence.

I have to admit that I hesitated for a brief moment. Watching Prudence literally get her comeuppance was deliciously fun.

CHAPTER

18

"*Chérie*," Grandmère commanded.

I saluted and dashed past the children. We caught hold of Prudence's ankles and pulled her back to earth.

Red-faced with embarrassment and angrier than I had ever seen her, Prudence stamped out of the theater yelling over her shoulder, "You'll get the lowdown on my finances, Bernadette, when hell freezes over."

Grandmère said, "Charlotte, let us keep quiet about all of this. There is no need to spread gossip about Prudence. She is obviously distraught."

"What about the children? They'll tell their folks."

"I will tend to them. Fetch Delilah and reset the rigging. *Merci.*"

While Delilah and I recoiled the rope and anchored it with the sandbag, something triggered in my mind.

Delilah gave me a sideways glance. "What's with the serious face? You look like you're trying to solve a crossword puzzle without writing down a letter."

"Prudence's words as she hurried away made me think

about something Shelton Nelson said when he and Liberty were talking with Matthew the other day. Liberty thought *hell's key* sounded religious. Shelton said that maybe Noelle's last breath was about needing some spiritual key to avoid going to hell. Noelle was raised in a Catholic orphanage."

"But why would she need a spiritual key? She seemed so nice. I sure hope I don't need one. I've certainly racked up my share of sins."

I told her about Noelle's parents being grifters.

"Aha. Do you think Noelle felt remorseful about being involved in her parents' scams?"

"Possibly. But I can't imagine why, after all these years, she would think that she needed to atone for what they made her do as a child, unless she was running a scam now." I mentioned the journal pages that were missing and Lois's account of Noelle hiding her camera's memory card.

Delilah said, "Do you think Noelle felt guilty about what she photographed?"

"Guilty enough to worry as she lay dying that she would go to hell? That seems unlikely." I felt like I was trying to make a complicated recipe and skipping a vital step.

"Find the missing pages and memory card, and I guarantee you'll find the killer." Delilah drew the rope around the sandbag into a knot. "Voilà. Problem solved."

But the problem wasn't solved. Not by a long shot.

* * *

As I drove home, taking a circuitous route so I could drink in the glow of the decorative window displays, the sparkling array of parade decorations, and the twinkling lights that had recently been added to the clock tower in the Village Green, I tried to create a list of motives for murder that made sense.

One: Liberty Nelson, despite her devout transformation, wanted Noelle out of the picture to clear a path to her father's love.

Two: Harold Warfield killed Noelle to keep an affair a secret or to protect his position at the winery.

Three: Boyd Hellman murdered her because she rejected him.

Four: Ashley Yeats—

I paused. He was a wild card, but he had a secret. What was it? I was determined to find out.

Five: Shelton Nelson—

I halted again. Other than Noelle discovering a possible financial shortfall that might predict SNW's future, I couldn't figure out a motive for Shelton. He seemed thrilled to have brought Noelle into the fold.

When I arrived home, the telephone was ringing. I snatched up the receiver.

Delilah said, "It took you long enough to get there. Where have you been?"

"Wandering the town. Were we having a race?" During high school, we often challenged each other. The first to class treated the other to a soda at the diner. The first to the parking lot after the last bell rang bought burgers.

"No, we weren't racing," she said.

"Then what? Oh no, don't tell me. Our quick fix on the theater's rigging didn't work. You need me to return."

"Nope. The rigging works. The duck will fly again. This call is all about me. I need a night on the town."

I glanced at my watch. Nearly nine. I loved my friend and I felt her pain about ending her relationship, but I was too tired to go to the pub. "I can't. I have a full day planned tomorrow at the shop. Vendors are coming in the morning, and in the afternoon I intend to catch up on back orders, not to mention I've got to tackle all the marketing stuff that has to get done online, which will take a long time. I am no Internet guru."

"C'mon. Just stop in next door at Lavender and Lace for a quick cup of tea. I'm already here. See me?"

I walked outside and around the side of the wraparound porch.

Delilah, with her cell phone pressed to her ear, waved to me from the B&B. "I'm wound up after the Prudence incident. Pretty please with a cherry on top? You can bring Rags."

I chuckled. "Okay." I hung up and rounded up my sweet pet.

As I headed toward Lavender and Lace, I spied a figure in a cloak racing along the gravel driveway. The figure disappeared behind the house. Was it the same woman I had seen the other day? A frisson of alarm coiled up my spine. Rags worked his head into my chest as if he sensed something was wrong, too. Who was she? Why was Lois hiding her? Did she have something to do with Noelle? The timing of the woman's arrival in town was too coincidental.

I jogged up the stairs and spotted Lois standing at the far end of the heated porch, chatting with a pair of guests at the inn. Agatha galloped circles around Lois's ankles.

Before I could draw near to say hello, Delilah flew through the screen door and whispered, "Psst." She hooked a finger to follow her inside. Something was up.

I edged past the screen door into the warmth of the inn's foyer and said, "Did you see that woman?"

"Shh."

"Did you see her, the one in the cloak?"

"Shh."

"What's with the hush-hush act? Who is she?"

"Who?"

"The woman in the cloak."

"What are you talking about?"

I told her my concern.

"I'll bet it's Lois's sister," Delilah said. "She left town under a cloud of suspicion. If I were her, I'd like to keep on the down-low, too." She clutched my elbow and dragged me toward the kitchen. "Let's go."

"Why are you acting so weirdly?"

"Me?"

"And why are we whispering?" Had the incident at the theater made Delilah loopy?

She didn't answer.

"Where are we going?" I demanded.

"I set up tea in the back. We have to talk. Well, you need to talk," she said, emphasizing the word *you*.

Something in my gut twisted. Did she think I was withholding information from her? Had Urso put her up to this charade? Was he sitting in the inn's kitchen ready to grill me? Would he cuff me in order to make me blab?

A few feet short of the kitchen, I dug in my heels. "Uh-uh. I'm not going into that kitchen until you tell me what's going on."

Rags yowled his agreement.

Delilah released my elbow. "Whatever do you mean?"

"Don't go all Scarlett O'Hara innocent on me. You're acting like a goof. Who's back there?"

The door to the kitchen opened. A man stood in the archway, backlit in a soft glow.

"Give me Rags," Delilah ordered.

I obeyed and raced into Jordan's arms. He swept me into the kitchen and closed the door. I heard Delilah coo to Rags, and then heard her footsteps retreat.

"This way," Jordan said, drawing me by the hand to the guest room at the rear of the inn. It used to be Lois and her husband's suite, but she had changed rooms the day she booted him out.

"What are you . . ." I stammered. "How— "

Jordan closed the guest room door, threw his arms around me, and lavished me with kisses. On my mouth, my cheeks, my neck, and back to my mouth. I could barely catch my breath and didn't want to.

"My handler drove me to town," Jordan whispered. "He'll return before dawn. We have the night." He drew me to the floral-covered queen-sized bed. We perched on the edge holding hands.

"I didn't dress for the occasion," I blurted. I had dreamed of the next time I would see him and how romantic it would be. I had set aside a lace peignoir, and I had purchased vanilla candles and new perfume.

"You look beautiful."

I plucked at strands of my hair. "I forgot to brush my teeth."

"Champagne washes away all sins." He nodded to the bottle and elegantly carved glasses sitting atop a silver tray on the bureau. Beside that was a simple cheese platter consisting of a large wedge of Jordan's Pace Hill Farm triple-cream Gouda, green grapes, and round crackers.

"How did you plan this?"

"My handler called my sister. Jacky called Delilah." Like me, Jordan's sister didn't know where he was being held during the trial. Jordan ran his fingers through my hair. "How I've missed you."

"Why now?" A panic cut through me. "You've come to see me because you'll never be able to come back. That's it, right? Oh no."

He put a finger to my lips. "I'm here because I missed you like crazy."

Phew. I hooked my finger with his and drew his hand to my chest. "How much longer will you be gone?"

"Four weeks. Six at the max."

I ran my tongue along my upper lip as I deliberated what I would say next. "I want to set a date now."

"We're on a date."

"No, silly. I know we talked about getting married and setting a date, and we almost did—on my parents' anniversary—but then the trial was moved up. I want to set a firm date. Let's make a vow."

"Valentine's Day."

"You romantic devil, you."

He grinned a smile that melted my heart then kissed my ears and murmured, "We'll follow that with a two-month trip to Europe."

"Two months?" My adrenaline kicked into overdrive. Yes, I wanted to see the world, but two months? "I can't. I'd need to plan. There's so much to do here."

"Keep calm. Breathe."

How well he knew me.

He traced a fingertip along my jaw. "You *can* do it. Matthew and your grandfather and all of your coworkers will manage Fromagerie Bessette, I promise you. Two months is a blink in the big scheme of things. We'll go to every cheese shop and cheese farm that you've ever wanted to visit."

A panoply of picture postcards shuffled through my brain. Where would we start? I would call all my cheese suppliers for recommendations. I would make cheese in France. Milk cows in the Pyrenees. Run my fingers through the *terroir* of Italy.

Suddenly, my breathing grew steady and my passion soared. The next few hours were magical. Jordan and I sipped champagne. We nibbled on cheese and fruit. And then we devoured each other. Inch by every glorious inch.

After we made love, we planned our honeymoon. And talked about having children. We agreed that I would have to be extra diligent with my health as I was approaching the delicate age of thirty-five.

Around three A.M., when the night cooled to a chilly temperature, we lay on our backs in bed with our faces pointed toward the ceiling, neither of us able or willing to sleep, and the conversation turned to darker fare. We discussed Jordan's trial and how his lawyer was reducing the opposing council to mush, and then we discussed Noelle's murder. Jordan asked me to replay the list of suspects. On the telephone the other night, we had only touched on the subject briefly. I included the nameless, faceless ones that might dwell in Cleveland. Jordan said he believed that money, jealousy, or revenge were the three primary motivators.

"Really, Mr. Detective?" I teased. "That's the best you can come up with? Those are Rebecca's top three, too."

He drew me closer. "I wish you wouldn't get involved."

"And I wish you never had." I was referring to the incident that had brought him to this point in his life. He had been a chef and owner of a fancy restaurant in upstate New York. One night, when he went outside for a smoke, he saw two thugs with knives attack a third man. Without hesitating, Jordan, a former military man, sprang to the third man's defense. The struggle turned bloody. Jordan stabbed and killed one of the two thugs; the other got away. The third man died. Jordan learned that the thugs were the lynchpins of a gambling ring, and days later, he entered the WITSEC Program to testify against the survivor.

Jordan rolled onto his back and laced his fingers behind his neck. "If you want me to be a sounding board, I will be. Let's start with Boyd Hellman. He's the impetuous, hot-tempered scorned lover, right?"

"Something like that, but there's something else at play with him. He knew so much about Noelle's past. He told Urso about her grifter parents, but he didn't tell me."

Jordan said, "That's because Urso is the official. You're not. Do you think her parents' shady past comes into play?"

"Maybe, but really, I can't see Noelle as a scam artist. She seemed so forthright and honest."

"Tell me about Shelton Nelson again."

"He has a pat alibi."

"That his daughter backs up. Daughters have been known to lie for fathers."

"You sound as cynical as Rebecca."

"Humor me."

"Shelton was either Noelle's lover or father figure. I'm not sure. Financial issues could be in the mix, none of which I can verify without breaking into the winery." I told him about the partial conversation that I had caught between Shelton and Liberty.

"You said Noelle was investigating something. Taking pictures."

"Of a man having an affair."

"Are you sure?"

"I'm not sure about anything. Rebecca's checking that angle. And then there's Liberty Nelson."

"The doting daughter."

"She's marrying a staunchly religious man." I paused. "I've got to admit that pairing doesn't make sense, but other than the uptight getups he wants her to wear, she looks happy."

"Uptight getups?"

"She usually likes wearing sexy, over-the-top kinds of clothes, like Sylvie, but ever since Noelle's death, Liberty has been donning Victorian dresses. I'm wondering if the trans-formation is because she's feeling guilty."

"She wants to divert Urso's suspicions."

"Yes."

"And you think she killed Noelle and lied about her father's alibi to create one for herself."

I tapped his nose. "You catch on quickly."

"I'm in trial mode. Continue, counselor." He pecked me on the cheek. His lips tracked down my neck to the hollow of my throat. I sighed. "You mentioned a journalist."

"Ashley Yeats," I said. "A con artist if ever I met one." I hummed a few bars of "Ya Got Trouble." Jordan joined me. Only recently did I discover he had a tremendous singing voice.

"So he's sort of like Noelle's parents. Do you think there's any connection between them?"

I hadn't considered the possibility.

"Who is looking into him?" Jordan asked.

"Matthew. He's scouring Yeats's phone records and travel plans to see if they coincide with Noelle's. And Tyanne is checking Noelle's emails."

"I'm impressed. You've become a delegator. It's a wonder your grandfather and grandmother aren't snooping on your behalf." Jordan rolled to his side and drew me into a tight embrace. "I assume you have revisited the crime scene and gone through Noelle's things again. You've reviewed every detail."

"Too many times to count."

"I want you to promise you'll be careful."

"I will be. I always am." Excluding, of course, when I was running headlong into a police precinct at Rebecca's insistence. I didn't reveal that tidbit to Jordan. "Did I mention there might be another woman in the equation? She's staying here at the inn."

"How does she fit in?"

"I'm not sure. I don't know who she is. I have yet to see her face. But I first caught sight of her the day after Noelle died. The timing bugs me. I wonder if she's someone from Noelle's past. You know, one of her parents' friends, or one of the nuns from the orphanage."

"You see mystery women everywhere." Jordan was referring to the moment when I first met his sister. I'd thought she was Jordan's lover, which only proved that the mind, if not kept in check, was like an ignored cheese that could become overripe and stinky.

"On the other hand, I get the feeling Lois knows her. If so, how could she have become acquainted with someone from Noelle's past?"

"Here's my two cents," Jordan said. "Set your mind at ease. In the morning, track down Lois and ask who the woman is. If she won't tell, I'm sure she has the woman's signature in a register."

"Is yours?"

"Tonight, my name is Delilah. Now, no more talking." Jordan gently pulled my face to his and kissed me.

He left before dawn.

* * *

At the sound of the crowing rooster that lived in a shed behind the bed-and-breakfast, I roused. Alone. Last night felt as if it had been a dream, and yet I awoke rested and at peace. Taking Jordan's admonition to heart, I dressed quickly and hurried to the kitchen to ambush Lois before she could sneak the cloaked woman from the premises.

"Lois," I called as I pushed through the swinging door. She wasn't there, but I swear I'd heard her humming right before I entered. The aroma of hazelnut coffee, tea, and freshly made chocolate-raspberry scones teased my nose and my appetite, but I didn't slow down. I heard footsteps retreating down the hall.

I raced to the foyer where more than a dozen guests chatted with a tour guide. "Lois?" I called up the stairs leading to guest rooms.

She didn't answer. None of the guests made eye contact with me.

As I rounded the newel post to head upstairs, I heard Delilah laugh outside. I peered through the screen door. Rain poured down and spilled from the eaves. Despite the chill in the air, Delilah sat nestled in one of the wicker chairs, warmed by a patio heater. She was playing chew toy tug-of-war with Agatha and Rags.

As I emerged from the house, she said, "Hey, sleepyhead." She tightened the cashmere scarf around her neck and leaped to her feet. "Please tell me you were surprised with your night visitor."

"Astounded and delighted. Thank you."

"It was Jordan's idea. When his sister called me, well, I can't tell you how hard it was for me to keep my trap shut at the theater last night. So, dish. Did you have fun?"

"More than fun. We connected. In the biblical sense."

"Heart be still." She swatted imaginary heat away from her face. "Want some breakfast?" She pointed to a Rosalinde pattern Haviland tea set and a plate of scones accompanied by a pot of mascarpone cheese, which were on the table beside her chair.

Although my stomach did a cha-cha, I said, "Not yet. I'm on the hunt for Lois."

"I saw her take a tray of food upstairs. Why do you need her?"

"That woman in the cloak." I told her what Jordan had advised me to do.

Delilah held up a hand to stop me. "Please assure me you did not spend the night with the love of your life theorizing about murder." She chafed a finger with the other. "If you did, shame, shame."

"No, I told you. We made mad, passionate love, but we did talk for a bit. He was concerned about me."

"What's the head-on rush to find this woman now?"

"Jordan said I should question—" Out of the corner of my eye, through the screen door, I spied movement inside the inn. The woman in the cloak, the hood pulled forward to obscure her face, was running down the stairs. "There she is."

I bounded to the front entrance. Delilah followed. As I whipped open the screen door, Delilah shrieked.

CHAPTER

"You." Delilah stamped her foot on the B&B porch and drilled her fists into her hips. Sunlight gleamed in at an angle and made her squint as she glowered at the woman in the cloak.

I squinted, too, and realized what I had missed before. The woman peering warily from beneath the hood was none other than Delilah's mother, Alexis, a free spirit who had moved to California.

"What are you doing here?" Delilah demanded.

"Better question," I said. "Why were you sneaking around in that hooded cape?"

"Sneaking?" Alexis pushed the hood off her face, fluffed her hair—hair that, other than a streak or two of gray, matched her daughter's unruly dark curls—and reached for her daughter's hands. "All right. Yes, I was sneaking. I didn't want Delilah to see me. We weren't supposed to meet. Not like this. I meant to call and give fair warning, but . . . Come here, darling. Give your mother a hug."

Delilah backed up a step. "Uh-uh, no way. The moment

we connect you'll begin to shake, then you'll throw your head back and your chin will quiver, and you'll announce you're *feeling something.*" Alexis did tarot card readings for a living. As girls, behind closed doors, Delilah and I had pretended to be Alexis. Donning wild costumes and howling like banshees, we would grab hold of each other's hands and predict the future.

Alexis held her arms wider. "Please."

Delilah didn't budge. "Why did you come here?"

"I missed you. It's been nearly five years." The same week that Delilah left home to try her luck on Broadway, Alexis deserted her husband of twenty-five years and moved to the West Coast. In the ensuing years, Alexis had never returned to Providence. Delilah had visited her mother once or twice in California, but they had never grown close. Delilah blamed her mother for breaking her father's heart.

"You can't simply appear and expect everything to be all cozy and nice," Delilah said.

Alexis dropped her arms to her sides and toyed with the folds of her cape. "That's what your brother said."

"You should have listened to him, Mother." I couldn't remember a time when Delilah had called her mother *Mom.* I wasn't sure if that was her choice or her mother's. "He might be messed up, but he is brilliant." Delilah's brother, an agoraphobic computer nerd, had moved to California with his mother. She babied him. Pops never had. He wasn't a callous father. He had truly believed that forcing his son to play outside was the way for him to overcome his fear; it hadn't been. "Do you want something? Is that why you came? Are you out of cash?"

"Quite the contrary. Your brother has made a killing in the computer world." Alexis released the cape and squared her shoulders. She had the same fine bone structure as Delilah, the same fiery eyes. "He saved up enough to invest in a bookstore, which I run with two of my friends. We sell candles and teas and such, too."

"And you do bogus readings."

"They're not bogus."

"They are phony as the day is long. You bilk people out of hard-earned money."

"Nonsense. I don't swindle a soul." Alexis raised her hands upward like an Egyptian queen. "The earth gods and goddesses speak to me, and I relay their guidance to my clients."

Were these the kinds of phrases Noelle's parents had used? I wished I knew what cons they had pulled and whether Noelle had been involved.

Delilah coughed into her hand and muttered, "Bull-puckey," then eyed me. "I'm heading to work. Coming? I have an umbrella."

Alexis snagged the sleeve of my sweater. "Charlotte, wait." She tugged me to her and, before I could break free, gripped my hands. "I have been meaning to speak to you. I had a vision."

"Mother, please," Delilah said. "You had a vision? What hoodoo. Did you use a crystal ball?" She curled her fingers around an imaginary circle and moaned, "Oo-o-oh."

"This had nothing to do with a crystal ball, Delilah, and it's not hoodoo."

"Hoodoo," Delilah hissed.

"I had a real vision. Charlotte"—Alexis gazed at me intently—"you have to believe me. It occurred the night I arrived."

I inhaled sharply. "The night my friend was murdered."

Alexis nodded.

"Did you see someone enter my garage?" I said.

"No, darling." She licked her ruby red lips. "But you came to see Lois that evening, and she spoke to me afterward. While I slept, I had a vision. It was clear and precise." She looked right and left, then lowered her voice. "Beware of a wolf in sheep's clothing."

Delilah scoffed. "Puh-leese, Mother. A wolf?"

"Hush." Alexis squeezed my hands and yanked them downward for effect. "Beware of a wolf in sheep's clothing, Charlotte."

My insides quivered. I knew the biblical phrase from the

book of Matthew: "Beware of false prophets, which come to you in sheep's clothing, but inwardly they are ravening wolves." In context, the phrase referred to the church having lost its ability to discern truth from error. So what did Alexis's vision mean? Was someone going to tell me a lie? Would someone come to me as a friend but turn out to be an enemy?

"Beware," Alexis repeated.

At this point in our childhood games, Delilah or I would pretend to faint. But Alexis held fast, as if she were one of those giant treelike creatures in *The Lord of the Rings* unwilling to let me escape. Ever.

* * *

Later that morning after meeting with vendors, I puttered around the shop by myself, checking on back orders and diddling with marketing ideas while replaying Alexis's warning about a wolf in sheep's clothing. At nine thirty A.M. I wondered whether the rainstorm—or a wolf—had caused some traffic mishap that was keeping the rest of the population from the shop. I telephoned Matthew, who supposedly was making deliveries, but the call glitched out. The same happened when I telephoned Rebecca. Where she was, was anyone's guess. I just hoped she wasn't prowling around the precinct.

Around ten A.M., right after I took a mini-break and downed a quick breakfast of toasted whole grain waffles topped with homemade ricotta, honey, and orange slices, my first customers arrived—Shelton and Liberty Nelson. While she slotted the pristine white umbrella that matched her raincoat into the stand by the door, Shelton batted water off his jacket. He did the same with his cowboy hat and tucked it beneath his arm.

"You're certainly hopping with business," Shelton quipped.

"It's the weather."

"Good for ducks." He pointed a thumb toward the wine annex. "Could I have a word?"

"Me first, Daddy, remember? Miss Bessette." Liberty shuffled toward me, her white rubber boots making squishing sounds. I dreaded the mopping up that I would need to do to the floor at the end of the day after a hundred customers came and went. "Have you seen Tyanne? She's not answering her cell phone. As of ten minutes ago, we have twenty more people to invite to the wedding, thanks to my future in-laws."

"Don't worry," I said. "That's easy to fix on all accounts, especially this far ahead." I offered a smile of reassurance as my mind flitted to my wedding. How many would I invite? Only friends and family? Would Tyanne be able to manage two weddings on the same day? I pushed my selfish thoughts aside and refocused on Liberty. "Now, if you were to add twenty the day of the wedding, you'd have one frazzled wedding planner."

Liberty hiccuped a laugh; it sounded cute but forced.

"However, with that many extras, you might consider more cheeses for your platters. Might I suggest—"

"Let Miss Zook help with that," Shelton said. "I need to speak with you, Charlotte."

"Rebecca is out," I said. "This won't take a minute. Liberty, try this." I shaved off a sliver of Villajos Artisan Manchego. "It's a raw milk cheese, very exclusive, made in small batches. It deserves to be treated with great respect. Present it on a cheese board with a little quince jam, but only a tad, otherwise the jam can overpower the cheese."

As Liberty deliberated and a pair of customers entered the shop, shimmying to shed the rainwater from their clothing, Shelton jerked his head toward the wine annex. Did he have a secret to impart? Was he going to confess to murder?

Feeling safe with the arrival of more people, I followed him.

As I neared, he said, "I would like to do something in Noelle's memory. Perhaps donate to the orphanage where she grew up."

So much for confessing. The guy was on a goodwill mission.

"But I don't know which orphanage it was," he added. "Do you?"

"I haven't a clue. Perhaps her ex-boyfriend would know."

"You mean Hellman, the hothead that blew up at Café au Lait? Like he would talk to me. If you ask me, he's the one that killed her. He doesn't seem like a good fit for her. Definitely beneath her."

The door to the shop opened and Urso entered. In much the same fashion as those that had come in moments before, he shook the rainwater from his clothes and hat then moved toward the display case to view sandwiches.

I whispered, "Shelton, Chief Urso might help you get in touch with Boyd Hellman."

"I don't think he'd be so inclined."

Liberty dashed to her father's side and clung to his elbow. "Daddy, let's get out of here."

"What's the rush?" I said.

"I told you before, Chief Urso suspects my father of killing Noelle." Liberty ogled me as if I were the stupidest woman on the planet. "Don't you see how he looks at us? His deputies have repeatedly come to the house and the winery. They're asking us all sorts of pointed questions like how often Noelle visited and why she would have taken a job in a small town."

The same questions that Boyd Hellman had asked. Had he encouraged Urso to take a longer look at Shelton Nelson?

"We've given answers," Shelton said, "but they don't seem to satisfy the chief."

I was pleased to hear how dogged Urso was acting and wondered if his persistence meant he had more on Shelton or Liberty Nelson than I did . . . which was nothing other than their weak alibis, their curious argument about Noelle and finances, and Liberty's Camry, which looked so much like a Taurus that it could place Liberty at the scene. Except she had an alibi that corroborated her father's.

"He even asked about my relationship with Noelle," Shelton continued, "which was aboveboard, believe me." He forced a laugh, but his neck had turned a stunning red, making me wonder how he defined *aboveboard*. "She wouldn't have wanted anything to do with an old codger like me."

Liberty whacked her father's arm. "You're not old."

"To someone as young and vibrant as Noelle I was. She had all sorts of suitors."

"Including that maniac Boyd Hellman," Liberty added. "And I wouldn't have put it past Harold to make a pass at her."

"Don't say something like that, darlin'," Shelton said. "Harold is a good man and wouldn't stray from that wife of his. He is devoted."

"Is he really?" Liberty smirked.

"Charlotte, got a sec? I'm ready to order," Urso said, looking totally disinterested in Shelton and Liberty.

I joined him at the counter. "Morning, U-ey. I thought you were going to Cleveland."

"Change of plans. You look rested."

My cheeks flared with heat. Did he know I'd had a visit from Jordan? "It's the weather," I said. "I love rain. It makes the air smell so fresh." Why was I babbling? For heaven's sake, a grown woman was allowed to have intimate relations with the man she loved, sans a wedding ring, in this day and age. "Do you want the usual?"

He nodded. "What's up with Shelton and his daughter? Why are they whispering?"

"Shelton wants to know—"

The door to the shop opened and Boyd Hellman stamped inside. Water matted his red hair and clung to his plaid coat. "Aha! Found you." He pointed at Shelton.

Not again, I thought. And not here.

"You did it," Boyd shouted. "You're not going to get away with it."

Shelton looked to Urso for support. He and Liberty had no hope of exiting the shop without bypassing Boyd Hellman and knocking over the display of large rounds of Kurtwood Farms' Francesca's Cheese.

"Excuse me, Charlotte." Urso rested his hand on the butt of his gun as he moved toward Shelton and Liberty.

I rounded the register to head off Boyd. "Hi, there." I smiled, trying to ease the tension. "I was wondering which

orphanage Noelle lived in. Some people want to make dona-
tions."

"St. Vincent's," Boyd said. "That's where we met."

I gaped. "You were an orphan, too?"

"We were seven at the time. We became best friends, and
I was the love of her life until—" Boyd jabbed a finger at
Shelton. "Then you came into the picture."

"Now, hold on," Shelton said. "I had nothing to do with
your breakup."

"You offered her peanuts to work for you, but she accepted. Why, huh?"

I thought Shelton had promised Noelle the moon and the
stars. If the job had paid less than her norm, why would Noelle have said yes? What was her endgame? Had she scammed
Shelton? About what? Had Liberty figured out Noelle's plan
and killed Noelle to protect her father?

"She was earning a fair salary," Shelton said.

"What did you have on her?" Boyd asked. "You had some
dirt. I know it."

I came up with another scenario. Perhaps Noelle had been
suffering financial hardship. Someone from her parents'
grifter-style past had resurfaced and demanded hush money.
Maybe that person had ended Noelle's career as a sommelier,
which had forced her to accept an out-of-town job well beneath her pay scale.

Liberty's face lit up. "Oh, look, there's Tyanne across the
street. Let's go, Daddy."

Like a child eager to meet Santa Claus, Liberty tugged
her father's hand, but Shelton broke free. The distraction
gave Boyd enough time to steal past Urso. He charged forward and, as quick as a prizefighter, shoved the heel of his
palm into Shelton's chest. Shelton punched back but missed.
Liberty screamed.

"Whoa, fellas." Urso inserted himself between the two to
keep them at arm's length. "I thought we'd worked this out
last night at the café, Boyd."

"He's lying about something," Boyd shouted. "To shield
himself or his precious winery."

"Look at him, Chief," Shelton said. "He's wasted."

Again? I thought. Boyd's eyes were glazed over. His words were slurring together.

"Okay, enough," Urso bellowed. "Let's all go to the precinct to settle this."

"I'll call the attorney, Daddy," Liberty said.

"You come along, too, Miss Nelson," Urso said. "Your father doesn't need an attorney . . . yet." He strong-armed Boyd. "Move it, Mr. Hellman." Urso was larger than both men, and he was all muscle. And he had a gun. They obeyed.

Liberty looked like she wanted to hide in a tornado shelter, but her father corralled her and ushered her toward the exit while whispering in her ear.

As Urso hustled the threesome outside, Rebecca shot in. She scurried behind the counter and clutched my arm. "What was that about?"

"Clan feud," I muttered. "Where have you been?"

Matthew slogged through the rear door and slammed it. "Whew, the weather is horrendous."

At the same time, Tyanne entered through the front door carrying a tray filled with four to-go coffees from the Country Kitchen. "Anybody need a little caffeine?"

Matthew said, "You bet."

"Me, too." I waved a hand. Because of the altercation with Delilah's mother, I had passed on tea. A cup of coffee would be a welcome pick-me-up.

Tyanne handed cups to both of us. "I added extra cream, the way you like it. I also brought brown sugar cream cheese muffins." She wagged a diner bag decorated with musical notes.

"You're a godsend," Matthew said as he set the cup by the register and removed his sopping wet jacket. "I'm chilled through."

I took a sip of the coffee, let the liquid stream down and warm my insides, then plucked a muffin from the Country Kitchen bag. I peeled the wrapping off and bit into brown sugar deliciousness. My stomach and brain thanked me.

"Are you ready to listen to what I learned?" Rebecca said,

hopping from foot to foot like a kid who had the answer to the hardest question on the test.

"Yes," Matthew and I said in unison.

Rebecca grinned. "I went to the library last night, but it was closed, so I tracked down Harold and I followed him."

I said, "I warned you not to."

"Shh." She waved me off. "It was easy. He had dinner with his wife at the Country Kitchen, but it was a lackluster affair. They ate across from each other, but they never talked. Not once." Rebecca strapped on an apron and withdrew a wedge of Mimolette, a rustic-looking orange cheese, originally created at the request of Louis XIV who wanted a competitor for Edam cheese. As she peeled off the wrapping so she could face the cheese with a sharp knife, she said, "Anyway, certain that I was right and there was something fishy going on with him, I went back to the library this morning, and I tracked down someone who knew the truth. Harold Warfield's alibi for the night Noelle was murdered was a lie."

"How can you be sure?" I said.

"The library hours have gotten screwy lately, with the town's budget cuts and all, and, well, it wasn't only closed last night. It's been closed every night this past week." Rebecca aimed the knife at me, then realized what she was doing and lowered it. "Harold lied. That means he's guilty."

I tossed aside my partially eaten muffin and headed for the telephone. "I should call Urso."

"Wait." Tyanne beckoned me back. "Harold's not the only one who might be guilty. I hacked into Noelle's email account."

"You did?"

"I told you, Charlotte, I have been well trained by our sweet Internet guru."

She was referring to Bozz, who had cancelled another work shift because of the demands of college. I missed seeing his goofy mug.

"Here's what I found." Tyanne placed the tray with the remaining coffees on the cheese counter, reached into her tote, and withdrew a sheaf of papers. "Most are copies of emails between Noelle and Shelton Nelson, all of which are pretty tame."

"Great," I groused.

"But"—Tyanne rifled through the pile and pulled out two sheets—"I was also able to uncover an email exchange between Noelle and Ashley Yeats."

"You're kidding. He couldn't reach her via the telephone, so he emailed her?" I snatched the pages from her. Ashley Yeats wrote that he knew Noelle had a story to tell. Was he referring to her parents' swindling history or to something that involved Noelle in the present?

"Look at her response," Tyanne said. "She ordered him to stop snooping. She said he was nuts."

Matthew peered over my shoulder. Ashley alleged that Noelle had high aspirations. Was he accusing her of going after Harold Warfield's job? Nothing in his email was specific; her response was cryptic.

"Doesn't prove much, does it?" Matthew said.

"No." I wadded up a napkin and tossed it into the garbage. "Were you able to make headway regarding Ashley Yeats's travel arrangements?"

"I couldn't track down an employer." Matthew rummaged in his pocket and pulled out a lined sheet of paper. Reading from his notes, he said, "But regarding his travel, he's paying for everything in cash. At Violet's Victoriana Inn. At the gas station. At the diner. I did a Google search, and all the hits referencing his name are written by some guy named Alcott Baldwin."

"I know that name," Rebecca said. "He's an Internet radio guy in South Carolina. He's pretty popular because he is a total gossip. He starts every show with a high-pitched, 'Oo-o-oh,' sort of girlie-like. He was a singer at one time."

"Well, whoever he is, Baldwin seems to be Yeats's biggest fan," Matthew said. "He put up articles on his website that were written by Yeats. They're not bad, though they do read a little thin. Weak verbs, trite themes."

"Maybe the radio guy is related to Yeats," I said. "Or maybe he's an old college roommate helping him network. What does he look like?"

"Can't tell," Matthew said. "He posted a photo of a bull-dog for his profile picture."

"What about phone records?" Tyanne asked.

"There aren't any for Yeats," Matthew answered. "The guy doesn't seem to have any accounts in his name."

"Curious," I said, feeling like Alice in Wonderland when she fell down the rabbit hole and telescoped to nine feet tall.

"On the other hand," Matthew said, "I was able to pull up cell phone records for Noelle, which showed dozens of phone calls received from the same out-of-town number, a number with a Holmes County prefix. All occurred after midnight and well into the wee hours of the morning. Someone was harassing her. And get this." Matthew's gaze gleamed with triumph. "Each call ended after three seconds."

I said, "That sounds like the caller waited to hear Noelle answer and then hung up."

"Exactly."

"Do you think it was a prank caller?" The other day, when I found the twins swatting each other with the rubber turkey leg, they said Ashley Yeats liked pranks. Had he slipped into Providence weeks ago and purchased a throwaway phone so he could badger Noelle into a confession about her past?

"I'm not sure. Do any of you recognize this number?" Matthew held out a piece of paper with a ten-digit telephone number scribbled on it.

"My word," Tyanne said. "That's Liberty's cell phone."

"Liberty?" I said. She was the one dogging Noelle? That sealed it. Liberty hated Noelle and didn't want Noelle in her father's life. I didn't know how the words *hell's key* related to her, but I didn't care. She was sneaky enough to have stolen into Noelle's room. She would have realized the journals were important. I'd bet dimes to dollars she was the one who had ripped out the pages. Had she intended to frighten Noelle or drive her crazy with multiple phone calls? When that didn't work, did she confront her and shove a corkscrew into her throat?

I raced to the telephone at the rear of the store and dialed the precinct. Urso hadn't arrived with his new wards yet, so I left a message. Perhaps Liberty, and not Shelton, was the one who needed an attorney.

CHAPTER

20

The remainder of the day flew by. Although I had anticipated
our typical swarm of customers, a tour bus arrived with an
additional fifty. By six P.M. I was ready for sleep, but my pals
talked me into a drink at Timothy O'Shea's Irish Pub. I sat
in our regular booth, twirling a paper turkey decoration
while half listening to Delilah, Tyanne, and Rebecca chatting as if they hadn't seen one another in weeks. Rebecca
was telling them about Harold and her fact-finding mission.
I tuned them out because I was too busy mentally berating
Urso. I don't know why I expected our illustrious chief of
police to return my call in lickety-split time. He had made it
perfectly clear that he didn't want me nosing around his investigation and, yet, would it have hurt him to thank me for
being a model citizen by reporting in?

"Charlotte, what's bothering you?" Delilah removed the
paper turkey from my hands. "Please tell me it's not that
prediction my mother made."

"No, of course it isn't," I replied, although I had replayed

Alexis's warning in my mind a couple of times during the late afternoon.

"Sugar, I suspect Charlotte is jumpy because she is getting thirsty like I am." Tyanne drummed the tabletop. "We have been waiting a mighty long time for service."

"Relax," Delilah said. "Someone will come over soon."

"I don't want to relax." Tyanne got up and flounced toward the bar.

"Who is she kidding?" Rebecca said. "She wants to flirt with our resident bartender."

"Why shouldn't she?" I said. "Timothy O'Shea is a good guy." I swiveled in my seat to watch Tyanne make her move and wasn't surprised to see how packed the pub had become in the past fifteen minutes. *Monday Night Football* was the draw. In Providence, when a major sports event was on the agenda at the pub, everyone showed up. Liberty and her fiancé sat at one of the round tables. The duo seemed content to hold hands and watch the many TVs that hung above the antique bar. Among the other pub patrons were Ashley Yeats and Sylvie, who were gazing into each other's eyes, and Harold Warfield, who was dining with his mousy, plumpish wife.

"Yoo-hoo," Rebecca said. "Back to our investigation."

"In a second. Harold's wife." I wiggled a finger in their direction. "What's her name? It's on the tip of my tongue." Usually I was good with names, but for some reason, hers escaped me.

"Velma," Delilah said.

"That's it."

Velma had a sweet face, but a light didn't glow in her eyes. Using her fork, she pushed around the food on her plate while talking to Harold. He wasn't listening; his gaze was fixed on the cell phone he held beneath the table. At Bunco night, Rebecca said Harold was texting sexy pictures to someone while standing outside The Cheese Shop. When Noelle said *hell's key*, could she have meant Harold's keypad? It was a stretch, sure, but if I could get my hands on his phone, maybe I could discover who he was texting.

I glanced at Tyanne, flirting with Tim at the bar. Given the right information, would she be able to hack into Harold's email or text messages? I didn't have a clue how to do either.

"Now?" Rebecca said, trying again to regain the floor.

"Whoa!" Delilah cut in. "What is Red Guy doing here? In the plaid jacket. Boyd." She jerked her chin at Boyd Hellman, who had taken up residence at a nearby table. He looked like a hungry hawk, his gazed focused on the three of us.

A shimmy of fear slithered up my spine. Any creep who stared unnerved me. He caught me looking and swung his gaze toward Harold Warfield . . . or was he glowering at Ashley Yeats?

Delilah said, "You know, it really irks me the way he's always craning an ear trying to listen in on conversations. It's not like he's a reporter or anything. Speaking of which, did you catch how buddy-buddy that Yeats guy is with Sylvie tonight? Is it possible the ice princess has captured a man's heart?"

"No way." Rebecca shook her head. "I think he's in love with the fact that someone is enamored with him."

We all laughed.

"Back to what I was saying about the investigation," Rebecca tried again.

"I don't want to hear any more about Harold's alibi," Delilah said. "Or Liberty's nasty phone calls."

"Aren't you the teensiest bit curious?" Rebecca said.

"Curious, yes. Enraptured? No."

Rebecca tossed a wadded-up napkin at Delilah, who swatted it like an expert baseball player.

"I'm back." Tyanne returned to the table with a pitcher of beer and four glasses. "Sorry, Rebecca. No matter how hard I tried, I couldn't get Tim to make a Cosmo."

"Liar. You're trying to convert me."

"Not me, sugar. Tim. He loves his beer." The pub had a list of over one hundred and fifty beers. "I also ordered appetizers. Some turkey sliders made with melted Salemville Amish Gorgonzola—they're new. And supersized meatballs in a mozzarella red sauce—they're messy." She plunked down in her seat, grinning from ear to ear. "Tim is the sweetest man, isn't he? He cares about everyone. Why, he even told me he's concerned about that guy in the red jacket."

"Boyd?" I said. "Why?"

"Tim said he's been drinking heavily. He's worried the guy's spirit is broken."

"Oh, please."

"He's on his fourth drink," Tyanne said.

Rebecca waggled her eyebrows. "Maybe he's feeling guilty about something, like murder."

"He doesn't look drunk," I said.

"Tim says Boyd has a hollow leg," Tyanne went on. "He also told me that Boyd was in AA for a stint, but he fell off the wagon right after Noelle was killed. I guess he's been here a couple of hours pouring out his soul to anyone who will listen."

"Which appears to be no one," Delilah said.

I recalled a passage from *Days of Wine and Roses.* The female lead believed the world, without the haze created by alcohol, looked dirty. Was that how Boyd felt? Did Noelle leave him because of his drinking problem? Did he go through recovery just to win her back? After she rebuffed him at The Cheese Shop, did he lose his resolve? I imagined the scenario. With liquor as his fortification, Boyd approached Noelle at my house. He begged her forgiveness. Sadly, she rejected him again. That's when blind fury took over and Boyd lashed out. Did he forget that he killed Noelle? Did he remember later? Was that why he was drowning his sorrows, day in and day out?

The door to the bar swung open and Ipo Ho, Rebecca's former fiancé, entered.

"Twelve o'clock." I nudged Rebecca. She looked in that direction. "Did you ever find out why Ipo wanted to talk to you outside the shop?"

"No, and I don't care. We're through."

"He looks lonely. Throw him a bone."

"For heaven's sake, Charlotte, he's not a dog."

I bit back a smile. For a smart girl on a steady path to educating herself, she didn't grasp some typical idioms.

She brushed her ponytail over her shoulder and rose from the table. "I think I'll go chat with that cute Deputy O'Shea."

The deputy, who resembled his uncle Tim with his broad smile and gleaming eyes, stood at the far end of the bar. Ipo watched as Rebecca sashayed to the deputy, and then like an injured puppy, he lumbered to a stool, sat down, and hunched forward. I caught him glancing over at Rebecca, and I had to fight the urge to go to him and calm his fears. I knew Rebecca loved him, but as my grandmother often reminded me, I couldn't fix everything—Rebecca's love life included.

Movement across the room drew my attention. Boyd was on his feet, stamping toward Harold Warfield's table.

What now? I wondered.

Boyd said something. Velma gaped. Harold responded. Boyd smacked the table. Glasses and plates bounced.

"Liar," Boyd shouted.

None of the bar patrons' reacted because the excitement of a touchdown had grabbed their attention, not even Deputy O'Shea, who appeared captivated by Rebecca.

I bounded from my seat.

Delilah hurried after me. "Where are you going?"

"To help."

As I reached their table, Harold said, "Stay away, Miss Bessette. I can handle drunks."

"I'm not drunk," Boyd said, but clearly he was. "He lied about his alibi for the night Noelle died."

"I did no such thing," Harold said.

"I heard those women talking." Boyd swung around, almost clapping me in the face with his arm as he pointed at our table. "They know."

"Know what?" Harold demanded.

"You weren't at the library the night Noelle was killed, that's what."

Aha. Delilah had been right. Boyd had listened in on our conversation and heard Rebecca talking about her fact-finding mission.

"He's telling the truth, Harold," I said. "Rebecca asked around. The library was closed."

"He made a mistake is all," Velma said, her voice whiny and thin. "My husband was home with me. His memory isn't what it used to be."

Memory-schmemory. The man couldn't be more than forty. Unless he had been afflicted with early-onset Alzheimer's, his memory was still sharp.

Boyd lurched and swung at Harold. Harold grabbed a knife from the table, hopped to his feet, and jabbed at Boyd. Velma screamed.

I yelled, "Deputy."

That got his attention. O'Shea whipped around. Thanks to his long limbs, he was at our table in a few strides. With one quick motion, he wrenched the knife out of Harold's hand. As if given an opening, Boyd pitched forward, fingers ready to grab Harold's neck, but Deputy O'Shea clouted him in the throat with his forearm. Boyd gagged and staggered backward.

Harold smacked his chair, toppling it to the ground, and shouted, "This is nonsense. I'm out of here." He fled toward the rear exit. Velma sat frozen.

"Hold it, Mr. Warfield," Deputy O'Shea said. "I've got a few questions."

But Harold didn't pause; he rushed out of the pub.

"Aren't you going to stop him?" Boyd said.

"The way I see it, pal, you started the fight." Deputy O'Shea eyed Velma. "Ma'am, are you all right?"

"I . . . I . . ." Velma scrambled to her feet and raced after her husband, forgetting to take her raincoat with her.

I grabbed it and followed. I hoped my goodwill would get Velma to open up and give me the straight scoop. Had Harold been with her on the night of the murder, or was she covering for him? If so, why?

* * *

Rain poured down in sheets. The parking lot lights cast an eerie glow across the pavement. I caught sight of Velma climbing into a blue sedan—a car that looked suspiciously like a Taurus. Theories turned topsy-turvy in my mind. Was Velma the woman Lois had seen lurking outside my house? Did she think her husband was having an affair with Noelle? Had Velma killed Noelle in a jealous rage?

Shielding myself with Velma's raincoat, I zipped across the lot and rapped on the driver's door. Velma gawked at me. She shook her head. I knocked again. "Open up." I dangled her raincoat. "You forgot this." I put on my best *trust me* face.

Cautiously, Velma opened the door.

As I handed over the coat, I wedged myself between the door and the car. "We need to talk."

"No." She tugged on the door handle, but it was slippery with rainwater.

"What were you doing outside my house the night Noelle Adams died?"

"I don't know what you're talking about."

"Lois Smith saw your car. A blue Taurus."

"Lots of people own similar cars."

"Lois said a woman was driving. She memorized half of the license plate," I lied.

Velma leaned back in the driver's seat and closed her eyes, a clear admission that she had been present that night.

"Did you kill Noelle?"

Velma's eyes widened. "No."

"Velma, talk to me. We're friends." Another lie. Strike me dumb. "I make sure you taste all the new hard cheeses. You like that Hook's Five Year Sharp Cheddar and the Cabot Clothbound Cheddar that I suggested." Swell. I could remember the cheeses she ate but not her name. "Remember? Both are buttery. The Cabot Clothbound has notes of caramel." When trying to win friends and influence enemies, my grandfather said to appeal to a person's taste buds.

Velma's shoulders rolled forward, and she burst into tears. "Oh, Charlotte, I wasn't watching your house. I swear. I was"—she hiccupped—"keeping an eye on Lavender and Lace. I thought . . ." She bit her lip. "I thought Harold was having—"

"An affair."

She smacked the steering wheel. "He's been acting strangely. Aloof. Out lots of nights during the week." She shuddered. "He wasn't there. At the inn. I waited all night."

"That's not true. Lois said you left."

"I drove off to peek at the parking lot behind the inn. His car wasn't there. So I returned to the street, but I parked on the other side of the inn. Far away from your house. And . . ." She tapped the steering wheel with her thumb, as if deliberating.

"What?"

She stopped the rhythm. "I did see a person head up your driveway. All I remember is he was big and broad and wearing a red jacket."

She was describing Boyd Hellman. "Are you sure? It was dark."

"The light from your garage helped."

"Were you still there when the police arrived?"

She hesitated. "Yes, but I drove away. A car lurking near a murder scene would look suspicious."

"How did you know it was a murder scene?"

"In retrospect," she blurted out. "I knew something bad had happened. Why else would the police come? I didn't hang around." Was she lying about seeing a man in red? To implicate Boyd and protect her husband?

"Velma . . ."

"I'm done talking. My coat, please." She held out her hand and jammed her lips together.

I recognized that look; I would get nothing more out of her. Reluctantly, I removed myself as a human wedge. The moment I closed her door, she ground the car into gear and tore out of the parking lot.

When I headed back toward the pub, a figure—a man— emerged from the shadows, hat pitched forward to keep rain off his face. As he drew near, I gasped. It was Shelton Nelson and he was wearing his shearling jacket, the one he had worn the day we toured the winery. Was he the wolf in sheep's clothing that Alexis had foreseen? Fear zipped through me.

"Charlotte, what do you think you're doing?"

"Getting drenched," I said with all the pluck I could muster. I started to move past him, but he caught my upper arm and spun me to face him.

"I don't need your sass, young lady. I repeat, what do you think you're doing? Why are you getting involved?"

"I don't know what you mean. I was simply chatting with Velma."

"I'm not referring to your attempt to play marriage counselor. I'm asking why you and that little gal who works for you are checking my daughter's phone records."

I tensed. Where did he learn that? Did Liberty overhear Rebecca getting a word in edgewise to Delilah? Did Liberty alert Daddy? Shoot. "I—"

"I heard you sneaked into the precinct, as well. Don't you think Chief Urso is competent?"

"I—"

"What did you expect to find?"

"I—" A motorboat with a flooded engine could crank into gear faster than I could.

"Yoo-hoo, Charlotte," Tyanne called from just outside the pub's door. "Our turkey sliders are ready, and you're getting soaked."

As she jogged to me holding an umbrella overhead, Shelton released me. He grumbled something that I couldn't make out. *Back off? Barking up a wrong tree? Behave?* Why was I suddenly hearing impaired? Had he pursued me in the parking lot because he was protecting his daughter? Maybe he knew her alibi was bogus.

Tyanne gripped my hand. "Really, sugar, you'd think a businesswoman as smart as you would have more sense than to stand in the rain. You must be dotty." She winked at Shelton. "Don't tell a soul, Mr. Nelson, or her business could suffer, you hear?"

As we returned to the warmth of the pub, I couldn't stop shaking and I couldn't stop picturing Shelton in his shearling coat. Delilah would say her mother's vision was hogwash, but was it?

CHAPTER

21

While I had been sparring with Velma and Shelton in the parking lot, Urso must have entered the pub through the front door. He stood at the bar with Deputy O'Shea, grilling Boyd, who was perched on a stool. The moment Urso spotted me, he made a beeline for me.

He caught up with me before I could reach the safety of my pals, and he gripped my shoulders. Heat spiraled off of him. "Where have you been, Charlotte? My deputy said you raced outside." His gaze radiated concern. "You're cold and wet."

"I needed to talk to Velma Warfield. Her husband lied about his alibi. He wasn't at the library."

"How do you know?"

"I . . . I just do." I wrested free. "Also, Velma told me that she saw Boyd Hellman outside my house on the night of the murder. And on my way back inside, seconds ago, Shelton Nelson—" I hesitated. "Hey, I left a message for you. Why didn't you call me back?"

Urso blew out an exasperated breath. "My cell provider

has been giving me trouble. Your message only came through in bits and pieces. Go on about Shelton."

I told him about Shelton's threat. "I want you to take a good look at Liberty Nelson. I think she might have lied about her whereabouts on the night of the murder, and Shelton is covering for her."

Urso ran a hand through his hair. "First, you think Harold is the killer, then Boyd, now Liberty? Look, how many times do I have to tell you that I don't want you involved? I don't want you hurt. This killer grabbed a wine opener and shoved it into Noelle Adams's throat. He—"

"Or she—"

"Won't hesitate to kill again."

"You don't know that."

"I'm pretty darned positive. You poke your nose into a nest of hornets, they get feisty and sting."

"You sound like Tyanne."

"Don't make light of my warning. You think you're invincible. You're not. Nobody is."

The concern in his eyes made me back off but not back down. "I can't promise anything, U-ey. I'm sorry. You hate to see an injustice. I hate it, too. It gnaws at me. It gnaws at you."

"Then get a badge."

I sighed. "I won't do anything crazy."

"That's a relative term."

I patted his arm. "I know."

Exhausted and in need of a good night's sleep, I returned to the booth, ate two quick appetizers with my friends while sharing my encounters outside, and then bid them good night.

I had dropped off Rags at home before heading to the pub. When I returned, he greeted me with a rousing yowl. He wasn't scared. He was communicating that someone friendly was in the house. Silly cat didn't realize that I had already spied my cousin's car in the driveway.

"Matthew?"

"In here," he called.

I strode to the office; Rags followed. Before I reached the doorway, the strong odor of fresh paint hit me like a rousing tonic. My fatigue vanished. I peeked in. "What are you doing?"

"What does it look like?" Matthew crawled atop carpet padding while smoothing the padding with his hands to unfurl it. "I've painted the walls and resealed the cans." A stack of paint cans stood in the far corner. All of the furniture that I hadn't moved to the garage, including the antique file cabinet, a pair of Queen Anne's chairs, and a floor lamp, were pushed to the side and covered with tarps. My sweet cousin had draped the mahogany bookshelves with tarps, as well. "I promised to help you with this project," he said, huffing. "It's the least I could do."

"Urso put you up to this."

"Did not."

"He wants you to watch over me."

"Haven't spoken word one to him."

"Then Jordan or Meredith."

Matthew frowned. His eyebrows merged. "This was my very own idea. I have a few, you know."

"I didn't mean . . ." I grinned. "What can I do to help?"

Rags circled my ankles; his tail batted my trousers.

"Grab the cat and stand to the side to watch my next magic trick."

I picked up Rags, who chugged his satisfaction. Matthew unrolled the newly dry-cleaned Persian carpet. I couldn't believe how gorgeous and rich the blue central medallion had turned out. Amazing when dust was removed how a color could shine.

"It's stunning," I said.

"Now," Matthew said as he removed the tarps from the furniture, "let's put this stuff in place, and then we'll fetch the desk. It's okay to disassemble the crime scene, right?"

I nodded.

Ten minutes later, after rearranging what was already in the room, I set Rags into a Queen Anne chair and told him to stay. "Back soon."

As Matthew and I traipsed across the yard to the garage, I noticed his shoulders were tense and his neck rigid. I assumed he was tamping down the feelings that would boil up once he reentered the crime scene. I had visited the garage a number of times. I wasn't inured, but I could breathe normally.

When Matthew crossed the threshold of the garage, he halted and his back stiffened.

"Are you okay?" I asked.

"I will be." He strode to the secretary's desk and ran his hand along the edge. "It's beautiful. You and Noelle . . ." His voice caught. "You did good work."

"She said her paps—her grandfather—was a master builder."

"I didn't know that." Matthew moved to the far end of the desk and lifted. "I'll walk backward." As we carried the desk to the office, he said, "I keep thinking about the night she died, Charlotte. It haunts me. Her death was so brutal. And I can't help thinking about those missing journal pages. They have to hold the key that she referred to. She was steadfast when it came to making notes. What if a Shelton Nelson Winery wine she tasted was bad? What if she wrote that in her notes?"

"And that would be worth killing over because . . . "

"Subpar wines might be predictive of the winery's future. That happened to Beaulieu Vineyards back in the 1990s when they released a batch of wine that tested positive for TCA, which is usually attributed to bad corks. It created a lot of bad press and consumer backlash."

"You're suggesting that Shelton removed the journal pages to keep a tainted batch of wine a secret."

He nodded. "Or Liberty or Harold could have."

We positioned the desk on the carpet where it had stood before, then fetched the other office furniture and the Tupperware boxes filled with my parents' love letters. After we set everything in place, I took in the room.

"It looks beautiful, Matthew. Thank you. I couldn't have done it without you."

He turned to me, his eyes filled with moisture. "Charlotte, may I see Noelle's room? Maybe something will jog my memory."

"Jordan encouraged me to do the same. Review every detail."

"When did you talk to him?"

I paused. Heat rushed up my neck and cheeks. "Actually I *saw* him. He sneaked into town last night. He left before dawn."

"The devil he did."

Jordan's clandestine visit made me think of Noelle and Shelton. "Matthew, the other day at your house, when you and Pépère were repairing the plumbing, you seemed surprised to hear Pépère say that Noelle and Shelton appeared *intime*."

Matthew grunted. "For all we know, Pépère misinterpreted the gesture. You know what I mean; either Noelle patted Shelton's hand or whispered in his ear. Innocent, except to the observer."

"That's not why I'm bringing up the subject. It bothered you that you didn't know about her visit."

"Yes, of course it did." He sighed. "But you know how it is. When you go to a town where you know a lot of people, you can't always see everyone. And, honestly, wouldn't you agree that people are an enigma? There are all sorts of things we don't know about someone else's life. You don't know everything about Jordan's. I don't know everything about Meredith's. But I intend to learn. That's an investment of a lifetime."

He was right. I let the matter go.

We climbed the stairs to the second floor. I swung open the door to the guest room. Matthew edged past me and stood in the middle of the room, pivoting as he scanned the space. I hadn't found the wherewithal to pack up Noelle's things yet. I didn't have a clue where I would send them.

"Where did you find the journals?" Matthew asked.

"The diary was slotted into the cubbies of the desk. The wine journal was tucked between the mattresses."

"And both were missing pages?"

I nodded. "Urso claims his guys have reviewed them and found nothing. Do you see anything I might have missed?"

Matthew shook his head then pinched his lips together to prevent tears from falling from his eyes. The sight made my heart wrench.

I said, "Let's get something to eat. How does a smoked trout and Gouda sandwich on pumpernickel with sliced apples sound?"

"Fine. In Noelle's honor, I'll open a bottle of the Maison Champy Bourgogne. She loved that wine."

After our meal, we adjourned to the office for an after-dinner drink. Matthew sat behind the desk; I nestled into one of the armchairs with Rags curled on the floor beside my feet. Over a tiny glass of port, we rehashed what Noelle could have written in her journals.

"So many pages of her personal diary were dedicated to inspirational quotes," I said. "Telling her not to quit and never give up. That might have been her way of exorcising her past."

"Her past?"

"If she was a scam artist—"

"A what? No way," he said with force. "She was as honest as all get-out."

"Not even as a child? If coerced by her parents?"

"What are you talking about?"

"You really don't know." I filled him in about Noelle's parents being grifters.

"Wow." Matthew rubbed his neck. "I had no clue. Maybe that's why she was so rules-oriented as an adult. I remember once, when a customer used a counterfeit credit card, Noelle chased the guy for blocks to apprehend him." He sank into himself, looking even more discouraged than before. The woman he thought he knew had so many secrets. "Talk to me about the journals again. Describe them."

"On the last page of the wine-related journal, she had jotted the usual notes around the edges, as she was inclined to do. She wrote about the nose and aromas. A word was cut off: *short*. I guess she could have been hinting that the wine was short on flavor. The label was gone, but there was a stick figure drawing of a guy in a noose. Maybe the word *short* was part of a hangman game. A doodle."

"Or she was suggesting that whoever made an insubstantial wine was going to hang for what he or she did."

"That's a hefty penalty, don't you think?"

Matthew set down his empty snifter and rose from the chair. He paced in front of the desk. "I keep thinking about the mud on her boots. Would she really have gone on a hike to Kindred Creek at night?"

"I've been thinking about that, too. Boyd said she wasn't a nature girl."

Matthew stopped pacing mid-carpet. "What if she went somewhere else? The day we toured the winery, Shelton told us to be careful because the path was slippery. What if Noelle went there?"

"Lois believed Noelle was investigating something. What if, on an earlier visit to town—the visit you didn't know about—Noelle saw Harold meeting a lover clandestinely in Shelton's tasting room?"

"Harold has a lover?"

"Boy, I thought you were up to date on all the gossip. Yes, he might. I'm not sure. But what if he does, and on the night Noelle died, she went to the tasting room to take compromising photos of Harold and his paramour?" I took a sip of port. "On the other hand, I remember Noelle saying that going on a hike would be like going on a quest. Taking photos of an affair doesn't seem to fall into that category. What if she went to find something else, like evidence of the subpar wine you mentioned?"

Matthew snapped his fingers. "The day we toured the place, Shelton was acting strangely. You know, showing off, as if trying to impress Noelle. I had expected some swagger—he's a peacock of a guy—but his behavior was beyond normal for him."

"He was flirting with her."

"No, it was more like he was taunting her. You know, by revealing the secret passage and bragging about his extensive wine collection."

I sprang to my feet. "The key."

"What key?"

"The four-inch-long one that Shelton used to open his wine vault." I did a mental forehead smack. "How could we have forgotten that?"

Matthew shook his head. "Noelle can't have meant that key. Shelton wouldn't have stored any subpar wines in with his private collection." He resumed pacing. "No, the key has to be something else. Let's go back to my previous assumption. Noelle stole into the cellar that night and found written evidence that SNW was making inferior batches of wine. Evidence could be *key*. Somehow Shelton, Liberty, or Harold found out she had been there."

"We're onto something. Let's call Urso." I reached for the telephone on the desk.

"No, wait." Matthew restrained me. "We have to see for ourselves. We'll sneak inside. We'll make certain."

"But we don't know what we're looking for. The police can—"

"Charlotte, I owe her."

"You *owe*—" My insides tensed. I had glided over Matthew's past with Noelle. He was happily married now. What did it matter? Whatever his relationship had been with Noelle was no longer possible, and yet something nagged at me. I wrenched free of him. "Matthew, talk to me. The truth this time. What was your relationship with Noelle?"

"I was her boss. She was my assistant."

"C'mon. It's me you're talking to. Did you lie to me before? Were you two romantically involved?"

He drew in a deep breath and let it out. His face flushed crimson.

"Did you date?" I asked.

"Yes."

"Were you in love?"

He nodded.

"When? For how long?"

He glanced over his shoulder as if he thought a tabloid reporter might pop into the room. Ashley Yeats was nowhere near.

I crossed to the door and closed it, and then I returned to

the desk and sat down. "No matter what you say, I will not tell Meredith." I eyed the Tupperware boxes. "I swear on the memory of my parents' love."

Matthew's shoulders sagged. "It was thirteen years ago, before I met Sylvie. Noelle and I were together for about eight months."

"Boyd was out of the picture?"

"Definitely. Their teen romance was over. They were history."

"Did you and Noelle move in together?"

"No, which is why I never mentioned her to anyone." Matthew hesitated. "To you or Meredith. We talked about marriage, but in the end, she pushed me away. She couldn't commit to me. She was so . . . private. She wouldn't open up. The thought occurred to me that she might have been abused as a child, but she was very demonstrative and loving. We never talked about her parents. If only I'd known." He bowed his head. "A month after we broke up, I met Sylvie and you know the rest."

A whirlwind romance, a hasty wedding, a marriage that lasted less than twenty-four months. Sylvie walked out on him and the twins, and a few years later, he moved back to Providence to make a fresh start.

"You kept in touch with Noelle because you were still in love with her."

He nodded. "I followed her career. I introduced her to Shelton Nelson."

"You knew she got back together with Boyd."

"I told you, I warned her to stay away from him, but she wouldn't listen to me."

A restless silence fell between us.

Matthew ran his palm down the front of his face. I could only imagine what was zipping through his mind. Finally, he dropped his hands to his sides and said, "I should have been a better friend. I should have pried the truth out of her. I'm going to the winery, Charlotte. I've got to find out what she was investigating."

CHAPTER

22

I couldn't very well let my cousin run off on a clandestine adventure by himself. He needed a flashlight, a dark-colored rain slicker, and someone who was thinking clearly—namely, me. So much for my halfhearted promise to Urso. I grabbed my purse and slipped into the Jeep's passenger seat seconds before Matthew tore out of the driveway.

The rain hadn't let up. Water teemed in sheets across the windshield of the Jeep. Working at top speed, the wipers couldn't keep the glass free of moisture.

"How will we get inside?" Matthew whipped around a corner.

"Aha," I teased. "You didn't think about that before we left the house, did you? Don't worry. I can pick a lock."

His eyes widened.

I hurried to add, "I've been locked out of my house once too often, and I carry the requisite tools with me." I patted my purse.

"We can't go through the front door."

"I was thinking we'd go through the cellar. It's remote

and, if I recall, it's secured with a simple lock. Whoa, swerve right. Parade stand at the northwest corner." I shot a finger in that direction. "See it?"

Matthew veered; the Jeep skidded. Matthew countered and regained control. "When the heck did those show up?"

"Volunteers have been busy all week. Where have you been?"

"You could've warned me."

"Don't shout."

"I'm not shouting."

"And don't speed. We don't want Urso and his deputies pulling us over for a traffic violation."

Matthew snarled. "Aren't you Miss Bossy?"

"Sorry." Nervous energy pulsed inside me and made me feel like I was a live wire flailing in an electrical storm. If only Matthew would be more rational. If only I felt he was on the wrong track. But he wasn't. The mud on Noelle's boots mattered. The missing pages in the journal were significant.

Matthew drummed the steering wheel. As if hearing the questions cycling in my brain, he said, "Whatever she was after must have had something to do with that conversation you overheard between Liberty and Shelton Nelson."

"Why do you think that?"

"Shelton and Liberty argued while we were on the premises. They couldn't hold off. That means their emotions were running hot. Noelle's presence triggered something. C'mon, humor me. Review what you heard."

"They were simply words. Phrases."

"Tell me again."

"Liberty said, 'lover,' then 'phony,' then 'financial mess.' It sounded like she was talking about a relationship that might cost Shelton a pretty penny. Right after that, she said, '. . . charted for disaster.'"

Matthew turned right and headed north of town. "Go on."

As we passed roadside stores and the many farms we visited on a weekly basis, I continued. "Shelton said it was always about money for Liberty. She's spoiled."

"Absolutely."

"Except now, she appears to be changing for her fiancé. Perhaps to the extreme. It could be an act."

"Keep talking."

"The next thing I heard didn't follow. Liberty said, 'What label would you put on it?' It sounded as if she needed to pigeonhole something."

"She could have been referring to the winery's artwork. Labels are a big deal in sales nowadays."

"True, if they were talking about wine. But if they were talking about Noelle, perhaps Shelton didn't want Liberty to label her a phony."

"Except you didn't hear the two phrases together."

I swiveled in my seat. "You know, maybe Liberty was referring to Ashley Yeats. Where did he come from? Why did he arrive in town on the same day as Noelle? Why did he come to the winery? He bugs me."

"Me, too. Talk about a fake. Even his accent sounds bogus, not that I'm an expert on British accents."

"Yeats had some hold over Noelle. He emailed her. She ordered him to back off. Maybe his arrival in Providence triggered the argument between Liberty and Shelton."

As we passed the Bozzuto Winery, Matthew said, "You mentioned that Shelton said the word *nose*."

"I think he wanted Liberty to keep her nose out of his affairs, or maybe Liberty thought Noelle was acting snooty, you know, with her nose in the air."

"Don't forget nose is a wine term, too."

"What if you're right, and this is about poor wine quality, and Harold was the one responsible? He is the manager, after all. Maybe Yeats had an inkling. There's the winery." I pointed. "Slow down."

"I see it," he barked. "Do you think I'm blind?"

"Don't shoot the messenger."

The entrance to the Shelton Nelson Winery abutted the main road. The two-story Victorian home, painted with winery colors of moss green and burgundy, stood to the left of the visitors' room. Lights were turned off in the lower portion of the house. Two lights shone in windows on the second floor. Liberty's Camry was parked in the semi-circular driveway. I didn't see Shelton's Lexus.

"Ready?" Matthew's shoulders heaved with anticipation.

I laid a hand on his forearm. "Breaking and entering isn't as easy as it looks. Why don't we return to town and talk to Urso?"

"And tell him what? We have nothing except suppositions about the missing journal pages and about Noelle running an investigation." Matthew squeezed the steering wheel like he wanted to wring the life out of it. "No, we're going in. If the winery was suffering financially or producing inferior wines and Noelle knew and threatened to reveal it to somebody—"

"To whom?"

"The press, a competitor, anybody. Charlotte, she wrote something in that danged journal."

"We're not certain of that. We can't build a case on *if*."

"You said Shelton said to Liberty, '. . . only when I die,' which could have meant his daughter demanded an immediate partnership in the winery or she would blab to authorities."

"Except right after, Shelton said, 'Noelle is here to stay. Live with it,' which takes us right back to the lover angle."

"I don't buy it. Shelton was not her type."

I shook my head. Matthew was wearing blinders.

After a moment of silence, I said, "If Shelton and Liberty were arguing about ownership of the winery, then that would provide all the more reason for Liberty to kill *him*, not Noelle."

"I hear you. I do." Matthew's voice grew thin. "If something illegal is going on, I'm going to find out. You're either with me or you're not." He drove a hundred yards beyond the winery, parked beside a stand of evergreen bushes, and hurried out of the car. Reluctantly, I joined him. I loved him too much to let him take this next step alone.

Both of us pulled the hoods of our rain slickers over our heads and stole up the driveway.

Matthew darted between the house and the winery's visitors' room. I followed. Halfway along the building, he threw out an arm to stop me. We scanned the area to see if anyone had detected our arrival. No additional lights switched on in the house.

"Follow me," Matthew said. Aiming the beam of his flashlight at the ground, he stole beneath the arbor of leafless vines toward the path that led to what Shelton called his hideout. Any remnants of Noelle's footprints—if this was where she had gone the night she died—had been washed away by the heavy rains.

When we reached the pair of ironwork-studded oak doors, I said, "Are you sure you're ready to break the law?"

Matthew craned an ear. "I think I hear someone screaming inside, don't you? It's our civic duty to offer assistance."

I moaned. "Rebecca is a bad influence."

He gestured toward the lock. "Do your magic."

As I had remembered, the lock was simple. Perhaps Shelton thought the cellar's hidden entrance was enough to keep thieves at bay.

Using a hook pick and a tension tool, I was able to unlock the door in a matter of seconds. We entered and paused. A string of low-level lights illuminated the casing around the ceiling. Elegant for a dinner. Perfect for reconnaissance.

We tiptoed down the hall, through the brick archway. We passed the wooden cubbies holding bottles of wine and halted outside the iron gates that protected Shelton's most expensive wines.

Matthew shook his head. "I repeat, Shelton would not have stored his subpar wine in there. It would be mixed in with the large lots of wine. This is not the key Noelle was talking about."

"Stubborn," I muttered.

"But right, and you know it." He focused his flashlight beam at the floor ahead. "Hey, is that the remnant of a muddy footprint near the bookcase?"

"I think it is." Behind the bookcase was the secret passage leading to the main house. Excitement coursed through me. "It looks small enough to be Noelle's."

Matthew bolted to the bookcase and pressed the handle that Shelton had used. The wall opened and revealed the secret passage. "Look, there's another muddy print on the stairs, heading in the opposite direction." He bent to double-check his findings. "Shelton's office is where he keeps his financial information. Maybe Noelle stole inside. Using a key, she unlocked his desk or possibly a safe—"

"That's what Rebecca guessed."

"Then Noelle made notes about his finances in her journals."

"She carried her journals with her?"

"She always did."

"Except the night she died."

"How do you know?"

"Because I found them hidden in the guest room," I said. "There was no trace of mud inside my house. Noelle must have stashed the journals there before she soiled her boots."

"You're wrong. She could have returned to your house, taken off her boots, concealed the journals, and then put her boots back on. She went to the garage to work on the desk so it would seem like she'd never left."

Except for the telltale mud.

"The missing journal pages," I said. "What if the torn-out pages are the *key*?"

Matthew moved ahead. "That makes sense. Imagine this. Noelle was in Shelton's office when she heard someone coming. She thought she was going to get caught." He did a one-eighty and sped back down the stairs. "She escaped, tore out the pages, and found someplace here to hide them. She would come back later to retrieve them."

Swept up in his enthusiasm, I added, "If anyone nabbed her, they would merely find her journals with normal labels and notes."

"Exactly. Same goes for if someone found the journals back at your place." Matthew scanned the wine cave. "Oh my gosh." He pointed to the heavy wrought iron gate that we had bypassed minutes before. "What if we're both right? What if *key* has a dual meaning? What if Noelle took the vault key from Shelton's office, and she hid the missing pages beneath a fine bottle of wine? Can you pick that lock?"

"Not a chance."

Matthew raced to the gates and aimed his flashlight beam inside. "We've got to get in there."

"And do what? Search under three thousand bottles?" The wines looked undisturbed.

"Noelle would have chosen the most expensive, believing Shelton wouldn't drink them," Matthew reasoned. "Either the Pétrus or the wines from Pauillac. C'mon." He waved for me to follow him. "Shelton must keep this key in his office."

"Wait." I grabbed his arm. "Shelton had the key on him when we visited, and even if Noelle found it, wouldn't she—"

Something made a scraping sound, whether outside or overhead, I couldn't be sure.

"Shh," I whispered.

Matthew didn't heed the warning. He broke free and hurried up the secret passage.

Safety in numbers, I heard an inner voice insist, and I darted after him.

No one attacked us as we slipped into the hallway. No one appeared as we crept into Shelton's office. Perhaps all I had heard was a squirrel crawling in the space between the cellar ceiling and the floor above.

Matthew dashed to Shelton's desk. "The key to the vault has got to be here."

"No, it doesn't."

"Why not?" He pulled on a drawer. It didn't open.

"I tried to tell you a minute ago, even if Noelle did find the key, she was on the run. She would have taken the key with her."

"You're right. Shoot." He spanked the desk. "Hey, I remember seeing an object gleaming outside the cellar, under the vines. Maybe she tossed it there so she could retrieve it later. Find those financials while I search." He hurried out of the office.

"Come back," I rasped.

But he didn't. His footsteps echoed down the hall. Dang.

All the drawers on Shelton's desk were locked, which made me snicker. Why have security on some of the doors but not all the doors? But then I quieted. I couldn't point a finger. At Fromagerie Bessette I only had locks on the front and back doors and a combination lock for the safe that held the day's returns. There were no locks on my cheese cases, refrigerators, cellar door, or office door.

I worked my lock-picking magic on the center drawer and drew it open. Inside were pencils, erasers, fine writing implements, iron stamps that resembled mini branding irons, fresh corks, bottles of ink, and blank labels. Nothing looked like financial data.

I jimmied the lowest drawer on the right. As it clicked open, Matthew howled at the top of his lungs. From the cellar.

"Matthew?" I sprinted from the office, down the stairs, and into the wine cave. I found him lying on his side, arms at an odd angle, legs sprawled. Blood seeped from beneath his head. "Oh no." I knelt beside him. "Matthew, are you okay?"

He was breathing. His eyes fluttered open. "Catch . . . him."

The door to Shelton's hideout stood ajar. Grabbing a bottle of Shelton Nelson chardonnay from a cubby and wielding it like a cudgel, I flew to the door and arced my flashlight into the gloom outside. Rain pelted the area, obscuring my view; I couldn't see a soul. An engine sputtered to life and tires screeched. Whoever had hit Matthew was fleeing. Dang.

I rushed back to him. He had raised himself to a sitting position; he was rubbing the back of his head. I said, "I'm calling 911."

"No. And have Urso find us here? Uh-uh. I can stand."

I replaced the bottle of chardonnay and helped Matthew to his feet. "Did you see who hit you?"

"No."

"You said, 'Catch him.' Was it a man?"

"I can't be sure."

Well, I was sure of one thing. Meredith was going to kill me.

CHAPTER

23

Meredith didn't want to kill me, but she sure wanted to throttle me. Sitting next to Matthew on the bench outside the hospital emergency room near the reception desk, she—and he—held an ice pack to his head. From where I stood a safe distance away, I could swear I saw angry fumes rising from her scalp.

"What were you thinking?" she hissed. Not at him. At me. I couldn't remember ever hearing her hiss. It wasn't pretty. Her sun-kissed nose was scrunched; her eyes blazed with fury. "Why didn't you call U-ey?"

"Because . . ." What could I say without getting my cousin in trouble?

"You investigated on your own," she continued. "And you dragged my husband along."

My husband. What happened to *We're best friends for-ever; no man will ever come between us*? So much for an eight-year-old's vows.

"It's my fault." Matthew offered a weak smile. "I dragged Charlotte."

"Are you nuts?" Meredith responded.

Certifiable, I wanted to say, but I wasn't a licensed therapist. I muttered, "Meredith, I'm sorry."

"Sorry isn't good enough."

A nurse, who looked like she swallowed a daily dose of starch, rushed from the reception desk. "Hush, all of you. We have real patients who need quiet."

"I won't hush," Meredith roared like a tigress protecting her cub. "This woman—my best friend—endangered my husband. Her cousin. And he's a real patient, too."

"Meredith, honey, relax. I'm going to be fine." Matthew patted her thigh. "It's nothing that a couple of aspirin won't fix."

"How can you be sure? How do you know there isn't bleeding on the brain? What was the weapon, a brick?"

"Whoa, honey, slow down. I'm fine. Really. I figure it was a wine bottle," he said.

"A wine bottle?" Her voice skated up an octave.

"One that didn't shatter." He kissed her forehead then rapped his knuckles on his own. "Hard head."

On the way to the hospital, I had kept Matthew talking so I could make sure he was all right. We discussed the weapon and decided that a wine bottle made the most sense. It also suggested that the assailant had come unarmed and had chosen a weapon on the spur of the moment. Even though Matthew had said *Chase him*, and my first suspicions had flown to Boyd, Harold, Ashley, and Shelton—even though Shelton didn't seem the kind that would get his hands dirty by using blunt force; he'd carry a gun—we had determined that Liberty Nelson was the one that attacked him. She had been at home; she would have been justified as a woman protecting her property. On the other hand, would Liberty have run from the scene? I had heard an engine start. Whoever hit Matthew had fled. Flustered and anxious to race Matthew to the hospital, I had failed to check whether Liberty's Camry was still in the driveway or not.

"*Chérie.*" Grandmère sat nestled on the bench beside Meredith. While driving, I had called her and asked her to fetch Meredith and the girls and meet us at the hospital. "*Crois-moi.*" She slung an arm around Meredith's shoulders. "*Il va guérir cent pour cent.*" The fact that my grandmother spoke French to Meredith meant she was as nervous as my best friend.

I hurried to translate. "What Grandmère said—"

"I know what she said," Meredith cut me off. "'Believe me, he'll heal one hundred percent.' Have you forgotten I took French and aced it?"

"Ouch." I raised my arms and backed up a space. "I'm not the enemy."

"I'm sorry. It's only . . ." Meredith released her hold on the ice pack and threw herself into Grandmère's embrace.

Pépère, who was standing to the side holding hands with the twins, said, "Charlotte, *mon amie*, tend to the young ones."

"Yes, of course." I reached for the girls. "I'm so sorry, Amy and Clair, but don't worry. Your daddy is going to be fine." My words did not do the trick. They squinted skeptically at their father, who appeared about as healthy as a zombie in a horror movie. "Really," I assured them. "Grandmère is right. Your dad is going to heal one hundred percent."

"Can we kiss him?" Clair asked.

"Yes," Matthew said. "I won't break."

He bent forward and moaned slightly as the girls pressed their lips against either cheek. I ached at the sound. His injury was my fault. I should have talked him out of breaking into Shelton's cellar and office. I knew the risks. How could I have let him browbeat me into being a follower?

"We brought you a sandwich, Daddy," Amy said. "Your favorite. Turkey and Swiss cheese with pesto sauce." She pulled a sandwich wrapped in foil from her backpack and offered it to him. "It's a little squished."

Matthew cradled it in his lap. "I'm sure it's delicious."

Meredith edged away from my grandmother. "Matthew, if something horrible had happened . . ."

Grandmère said, "*Chérie*, as King Lear would say, 'The worst is not, so long as we can say, "This is the worst."' *Non?*"

Meredith sobbed some more.

But not nearly as loudly as Sylvie. She tore into the hospital looking and bleating like a fire engine. "Matthew," she cried, arms outstretched, her blazing red raincoat flying open, the soles of her Dalmatian faux fur boots slapping the linoleum. "Matthew, sweet, sweet Matthew."

Matthew put up a hand to block her. "Don't touch me." His ex-wife's distress might have been real, but he didn't need a hug from her to add to the headache with his bride. "I'm fine, Sylvie."

"But you're so pale."

"Who called you?"

"Why, Nurse Nenette, love." She glanced over her shoulder at the starched nurse. "She's been so wonderful with the girls, and she adores me."

Matthew cut a look at the nurse and back to Sylvie. "How does Nurse Nenette know the girls?"

Sylvie bit her lip. "There have been a few scrapes and bruises I haven't told you about."

"What?" Meredith yelped.

Amy fudged her foot. "Don't blame Mum. It was me. I'm the klutz. I ran too fast on our outing the other day. I was showing off to Clair."

"To Mr. Yeats, you mean," Clair said.

"I slid down the hill and scraped my arms." Amy's tone was so plaintive I wanted to scoop her up. "I didn't want to tell you—"

"You have to tell us," Meredith said. "You—"

Matthew grabbed her arm to rein her in. "It's okay, girls," he said gently. "You're not to blame. But from now on your mother and you have to agree to full disclosure."

"Yes, sir," Amy and Clair chimed.

Sylvie held up a hand as if on the witness stand. "I promise, too. Oh, love, I'm so glad you've got your tough guy demeanor back. That relieves me."

Meredith rolled her eyes. I smirked. Yeah, Matthew was a tough guy, all right. Mr. Pussycat.

"Whatever were you doing at Shelton Nelson's place, anyway?" Sylvie asked.

"How did you—"

"Nurse Nenette has ears, love."

Meredith shot another if-looks-could-kill glare at the nurse. So did Matthew. "I ought to report her for eavesdropping." The prim nurse wisely ducked out of sight.

Sylvie hitched her Dalmatian faux fur purse higher on her shoulder. "So, what were you doing there?"

"We were checking out Shelton's wine collection," Matthew lied.

My grandparents exchanged a look. Neither said a word.

"Ooh, I've heard it's quite extensive," Sylvie said in an animated voice that indicated she'd forgotten all about Matthew's pain. "Ashley showed me the article he's writing about Shelton Nelson. He has an incredible stash of wine. Did you know I've tasted one of them? A French wine. The Château Haut-Brion Blanc." She flourished a hand. "Back in the days when Mumsie and Dad were flush, they entertained so much." Her parents had invested poorly in the past few years. Both had needed to return to work. "My father hobnobbed with some of the most vigorous investors in Europe. We had lavish dinners and wine tastings like you throw, love. I remember the wine had the flavor of ambrosia and pineapple with hints of honey and melon. It was so sweet."

"You're lying, Sylvie," Matthew said. "You've never tasted that wine. It's a dry white wine."

"No, no, I tasted it."

"What color was it?"

"Deep amber."

"Wrong. It's the color of pale yellow straw."

Sylvie blanched. "I'm sure I drank it. I believe it was a 1985 vintage. Somewhere in the range of a thousand dollars a bottle at the time. Maybe it had turned color."

Matthew sneered. "Bottles like that don't turn."

The door to the emergency room swung open and Urso marched in, rainwater dripping off his overcoat and hat. "Well, well, well. Here we are again, except this time it's Matthew that's bruised. I thought you had more brains."

"Apparently, I don't," he joked.

Urso faced me. "What in the heck were you thinking, Charlotte?"

"How . . . What . . ." I stammered. I knew for a fact that neither Meredith nor my grandparents had called him. Nurse Nenette, who had reappeared and was hovering in the archway by the check-in counter, thumbed her chest and vehemently shook her head. I didn't believe her for a second.

"Liberty Nelson is quite upset." Urso removed his hat and ran a finger around the brim slowly. Ever so slowly. Not good. The move was a clear sign he was reining in his temper. "It seems Miss Nelson has video footage of a pair of upstanding Providence citizens breaking into her wine cellar."

His words clanged in my head: *her* cellar, not her *father's*.

I peeked at Matthew, who winced. We had been so concentrated on searching for Noelle's footprints that we hadn't searched for surveillance cameras. How stupid were we?

Urso clicked his tongue. "Miss Nelson asked me to arrest you two."

"Liberty?" I said. "Not her father?"

"She hasn't told him."

Why not? I wondered. Did she have something to hide?

Adhering to the belief that a good offense was better than a good defense, I said, "How about you arrest her, instead? She attacked Matthew."

Urso scoffed. "That's it? That's all you've got?"

"Did she admit to assaulting my cousin?"

"Quite the contrary. She was home reading *The Last Time I Saw Paris* when she heard wheels squealing on the pavement."

How much did the woman read? With my schedule, I could barely manage to get in a couple of chapters of a good mystery each night.

"She told me she heard something, ran to the security room, and on the screen, saw two people sprinting from her place."

More like hobbling from her place, but I didn't correct him.

"Look, Charlotte, let's talk straight. You broke into the

Nelsons' property. Care to tell me why, after our recent conversation at the pub?" Urso flattened a palm. "No, don't bother. I'm taking you in."

"But—"

"You broke into someone's home."

"Cellar."

"A man's castle," he argued.

"U-ey, we think either Liberty or her father is hiding something. We think Noelle went there to investigate. The mud on her shoes"—I pointed to the gunk clinging to mine—"might have come from there. Possibly, she gleaned evidence and threatened to reveal the problem."

"Did Miss Adams seem like a blackmailer to you?" he asked.

No, actually she didn't, but she had said: *So much is at stake*.

"Chief Urso, please don't arrest our aunt," Clair said.

"Or our daddy," Amy cried.

Urso released the tension in his shoulders. "It's all right, girls. I'm not going to. Miss Nelson withdrew the request. She said these two"—he waggled a finger at Matthew and me—"were under such duress and not thinking straight, seeing as Miss Adams had been staying with your aunt and was a close friend of your father's."

I glowered at Urso. Why had he baited me? Better yet, why had Liberty Nelson forgiven us? Was she entirely innocent, or had she withdrawn charges to divert suspicion from herself? Or, more to the point, to keep her father from finding out the truth about her blind ambition?

"Is she claiming she didn't hit Matthew?" I said.

"She never mentioned it."

If she didn't hit Matthew, who did?

Urso hitched up his belt, squared the holster holding his gun, and left his hand poised above the butt of his weapon. "In the meantime, I don't want to have any more of your interference, or I will slap you with obstruction. Are we clear?"

CHAPTER

24

Sleep did not come easily. For hours I paced my bedroom asking out loud: *who, what, where, when,* and *why.* I knew the *how.* In between my deliberations, I berated Urso. Why was he so bullheaded? Thunder and lightning helped enhance my tirade. Rags hid beneath a chair.

At eight A.M. the storm had passed, but my foul mood hadn't. I stood in The Cheese Shop kitchen and pounded balls of dough as if each were Urso's thick skull. We had been friends for a long time. Why couldn't he see that I had done everything I could to aid his investigation? Why didn't he appreciate my efforts? Granted, I had said *no* to his marriage proposal way back when, but he didn't have to treat me like a numbskull.

Rebecca, who loved to assist when baking the morning quiches, said, "Go ahead and beat those suckers into submission, but if you do, know that you'll have to make a whole new batch because the pastry won't be flaky."

My cheeks reddened. I pushed the dough aside and slumped onto a stool. Assembling the bacon, Havarti, and

quince quiches would have to wait. Thankfully, I had already
cooked the bacon to a crisp and stewed the quinces.

"Don't worry about Urso," Rebecca said. "You'll patch
things up. Promise."

"Yoo-hoo, Charlotte, love." Sylvie, dressed in a cherry red
Chinese sarong—one of her go-to outfits whenever she was
feeling under the weather—appeared in the archway. "Have
you seen Matthew?"

"He's in the annex."

"No, he's not."

Matthew had arrived at the shop a half hour after me. As
a result of the attack, he had a bump on his head, but his eyes
were bright, and he had assured me that after another hour of
explaining his complicity in our mission, Meredith didn't
want my head on a platter—although he had confided that she
wasn't likely to chat with me for a day or two. *Swell.* He was
putting together the educational wine tasting he had sched-
uled for the evening, an event where students would receive
a check-off list and a glass of wine, and they would go around
to snifters filled with a variety of fruits, nuts, and candies to
compare which aromas matched the wine.

"Yes, he is, Sylvie. You didn't look hard enough."

"Show me. I'm worried about him." She clutched my
elbow and, despite my doughy fingers, dragged me through
the shop to the annex. I tried to put on the brakes, but the
fight had leaked out of me.

I peered into the annex. It was empty. I called, "Matthew,"
but he didn't answer. The glasses for the event were set on the
bar, the snifters prepared. "Matt—"

Behind the wine bar, I spied ankles and shoes. The toes
were pointing toward the floor. Had Matthew fainted? Face-
down? Panicked, I raced to the bar and peered over.

Perched on his hands and knees, Matthew peeked over his
shoulder at me and whispered, "Shh."

I gaped. The scamp was hiding from his ex? "Get up,
coward. If I can see you, so can Sylvie. She's concerned. She
wants to know how you are."

Grumbling, he scrambled to a stand, edged from behind

the bar, and skirted past Sylvie. Without offering a word, he tore down the hall, into the office, and slammed the door.

Sylvie darted after him. "Matthew Bessette, unlock this door. How dare you."

"I need to rest," he shouted. "Go away."

Sylvie stomped her foot. "Open up."

I heard a howl. From Rags. I didn't think he needed rescuing. Matthew had probably grabbed him for emotional support. Refusing to be an intermediary, I returned to the shop.

At the same time, Ipo marched in looking like a mighty Hawaiian warrior ready to subdue a raging volcano. "Rebecca," he bellowed, "I'd like a word with you, please."

At least, though he was loud, he was polite.

My sassy assistant emerged from the kitchen, her apron dusted in flour. "What are you doing here?"

He pulled alongside the cash register. "I don't like you flirting with that deputy."

Rebecca flipped her ponytail with defiance. "What are you talking about?"

"I saw you last night. At the pub. I don't like it. You and I are not finished."

"Yes, we are. You're moving back to Hawaii."

"No, I'm not. I told my parents that I make my own decisions. I choose my life. And it's here. With you." Ipo planted his fists against his hips. "Now, are we going on a date Friday or not?"

Rebecca fought a smile with all her might, but her eyes twinkled with humor. "Where would we go?"

"To the movies."

"Do I get to pick the movie?"

"Yes."

"Do we get to eat cheddar popcorn?"

"If that's what you want." He swiveled on his heel. "I'll pick you up at six thirty. Aloha."

When he exited the shop, Rebecca did a fist pump. "The movies. He never wants to go to the movies. Exploring nature has always been his thing. Oh, yay, he's a changed man." She danced a jig.

"Not so fast, my little leprechaun," I said. "He's changed for the moment and only the moment. Permanent change takes time. And don't forget that Deputy O'Shea has his eye on you."

"Oh, gosh. You're right. Did I tell you that he asked me to dinner on Saturday?" She clapped. "Can you believe it? I'm actually dating more than one man at a time. For real." When she first moved to town, she had never dated. She hop-skipped around the store but came to a halt as my grandmother scuttled inside. "Bernadette, are you okay?"

Grandmère hurried to the cheese counter. "Hide me, Charlotte."

"From whom?"

She darted around the cheese counter and ducked behind me. "Prudence is on the warpath."

I spun to face her. "What did you do?"

"Nothing."

"You didn't tell everyone about Prudence's meltdown at the theater, did you?"

"No. I would never." She crossed her heart. "I am a caring person; I have taught you to be the same."

"Then what is this about?"

"I fear she might have lost her marbles for good this time."

Prudence Hart charged into the shop, her face as beet red as her suit. "Where is she?" She stomped forward and shot a finger at me—well, really, at my grandmother. "I see you, Bernadette. How dare you use your mayoral powers to slap an injunction on me."

"What?" Grandmère gasped. "I did no such thing." Finding her courage, she squared her shoulders and moved around the register. Though she was barely five-feet-two and shrinking by the month, in her black coat, swirly skirt, and boots, she appeared as feisty as a toreador. "Is that what you believe?"

"Who else could have done it?"

"It is a lie. In fact, I stood in favor of your right to invest.

Some declared you unstable, but I assured them of your mental acuity."

"Unstable?"

Sylvie, who apparently had given up on seeing Matthew, waltzed down the hall and stopped by my side. "What's going on?"

Rebecca whizzed in from the opposite direction and clutched my arm. "Uh-oh. Should I call the police?"

"I have every right to own more than three shops," Prudence said.

"No, you don't." Sylvie sprinted around the cash register and faced Prudence. "This city requires financial transparency."

Where had she come up with that phrase? Was Ashley Yeats filling her with this lingo?

"If one person owns everything," Sylvie continued, "it becomes a monopoly. You might pull the wool over buyers' eyes." I'd bet her parents had done that multiple times. They weren't too different from Noelle's parents.

Prudence snarled. "Oh, hush, Sylvie. You're just jealous because I have the means and wherewithal to change how business is done around here."

"You take shortcuts," Sylvie said, "hurting the customers in the process."

"I have every right to buy up businesses."

"Not if you're cuckoo."

Oh, heavens, had the twins told their mother about the fiasco? I would have to . . . No, I wouldn't. Matthew or Meredith would have to talk to them about spreading gossip.

Prudence lasered Sylvie with a glare. "It was you. You brought the injunction."

"What if I did?" Sylvie smirked. "Bring your records before the city council. Let them vote."

"Bernadette." Prudence pleaded with my grandmother. "Help me."

"No, Bernadette, help me," Sylvie cried. That was a first.

Each of the women grabbed one of Grandmère's arms. As

they did, a pair of customers entered the shop. Prudence, Grandmère, and Sylvie quieted and watched them as if they were fish in an aquarium.

"Okay," I said. I'd endured enough. "You three. Out. Grandmère, Prudence, and Sylvie, leave or I'll make each of you purchase a fair share of today's special Cambazola to make up for any loss you cause the shop." I aimed a finger at the exit to make my point. "Settle your differences outside."

Grandmère broke free and hurried to me. "*Chérie*, I am sorry."

"I know." I kissed her and whispered, "Maybe suggest to Prudence, in private, that she get some professional help."

"*Oui*. A sound idea."

"And I don't mean a lawyer."

When they left and I returned to my spot behind the cheese counter, Rebecca slung an arm around my shoulder. "You threatened them with buying Cambazola? Like that would be punishment?" Cambazola was a delicious combination of a French soft-ripened triple-cream cheese and Italian Gorgonzola. "It's time for you to take a breather." She released me and pressed my lower back. "Go find Meredith and have a chat."

"Oh yeah, like she'll spare two words for me."

"Visit Delilah, then, at the diner. A cup of hot chocolate with extra whipped cream would do you wonders."

CHAPTER

When I entered the Country Kitchen, Delilah and the other waitstaff were sashaying down the aisle between the counter and booths singing Elvis's "A Big Hunk O' Love." From a booth at the far end, Delilah's mother Alexis waved and beckoned me to sit with her. Pops, Delilah's father, hovered behind the pass-through counter to the kitchen and gawked at me as if I were a traitor. As I made my way along the aisle, I blew him a kiss and patted my heart with the tips of my fingers. I hoped he would understand the gesture—I adored him and would never throw him over for Delilah's flighty mother.

"Charlotte." The roomy sleeves of Alexis's quilted jacket billowed as she patted the banquette indicating I should sit. "Delilah and I are having an early lunch and talking about life's grand issues."

I glanced at Delilah who seemed more than happy to be dancing for the patrons and not chatting with her mother. On the other hand, two places were set at the table. One held a bowl of soup, the other a sandwich.

"What are you eating?" Alexis said. "I'm having vegetarian soup smothered in Parmesan. Delilah made it especially for me, knowing my dietary restraints. No meat has touched these lips since I left Ohio." She tapped her burgundy-tinged mouth. "Delilah is having yet another grilled cheese. I think she said it was rosemary-crusted cheese and scallions."

"It's a rosemary Manchego-like cheese, though because of the rosemary it can't be an official Manchego."

"Whatever. It's getting cold. She should sit down. All this dancing and singing. I don't know why the customers put up with it."

Any time a patron chose an Elvis song on one of the tabletop jukeboxes, the waitstaff stopped what they were doing and sang.

Alexis's aversion to the performances had to do with the fact that Delilah had been swept up in the allure of singing and dancing onstage and had moved to New York. Years ago, Alexis claimed her world had ended that day. Talk about putting a guilt trip on a daughter.

"Why don't you eat the sandwich?" Alexis said. "And, meanwhile, tell me what's going on in your life. There's a man, I assume."

In the nick of time, the music ended and Delilah slid into the booth beside me. "Uh-uh, Mother. No grilling my friends."

"But you grill . . . grilled cheese." Pleased with her joke, Alexis cackled and wiggled her colorful hand, each nail painted with a different sign of the zodiac. "Fine, fine. No questions, except I would like to know why you're upset with Umberto Urso, Charlotte. That's why you came into the diner, isn't it, dear? He was harsh with you, and that hurt your feelings."

My mouth fell open.

Delilah gaped at me. "Lord, tell me she's wrong."

"I divine, darling," Alexis said. "In fact, I *am* divine." She chuckled again.

I had to admit it was hard not to like Alexis. "I need a cup of hot chocolate, first."

Delilah fetched a luscious mug of cocoa topped with swirls of whipped cream and chocolate sprinkles and set it in front of me. She slid back in her seat and said, "Tell me—"

"Us," Alexis corrected.

Delilah ground her teeth. "Tell us what's going on. Why is U-ey annoyed with you now?"

"U-ey," Alexis sniffed. "For heaven's sake, girls, can't you stop calling him that? He's a grown man. His name is Umberto."

"But he likes U-ey, Mother. Go on, Charlotte."

I didn't tell them about Matthew's and my foray into the winery or U-ey lambasting us. I merely said, "I suggested he take a harder look at all suspects."

"Like Boyd Hellman," Delilah said.

"Yes, for one."

"The man with the red hair who wears the plaid coat?" Alexis asked.

I nodded. "That's the one. Velma Warfield said she saw him idling outside my house the night Noelle was killed."

Alexis shook her head. "But she couldn't have."

Delilah shot her mother a look. "How would you know? And don't tell me you saw that in your crystal ball."

"No, darling. I left my ball at home," Alexis teased. "But I have been a little concerned about that man. He looks at you in such a way."

"What way?"

"With googly eyes. He's very interested in you."

Delilah groaned. "Mother, you think every man is interested in me."

"Not every man, but this one is smitten in the worst way, so I've been keeping a watch on him ever since I arrived."

"You've what?" Delilah's voice glided upward.

"Keep your voice down." Alexis petted her daughter's hand. "He hasn't made any overt moves."

Delilah sputtered. "You think he's a stalker?"

"I wouldn't go that far, but he was hanging outside the diner the night Charlotte's houseguest was killed. Peeking in through the window."

I'd seen him doing the same thing the other day. At the time, I thought he was spying on Urso. Pépère mentioned that he had seen Boyd loitering, too.

"Why, last night, Delilah," Alexis continued, "I tailed him when he followed you to your gym class."

"Why on earth would you do that, Mother?"

"Because I was curious and concerned. But then he did something strange. While you were working out, he popped into his car and drove north of town to the Shelton Nelson Winery. Why he wanted to go there, of all places, was beyond me. It wasn't like they were open for wine tastings."

"So he was the one," I muttered.

Delilah raised an eyebrow. "The one that what?"

I recounted the entire evening.

"He hit Matthew?" Alexis clucked her tongue. "Poor dear."

"I can't believe you, Charlotte Erin Bessette," Delilah said, sounding as irritated as our chief of police. "You could've been killed."

I didn't remind her that we had gone on a similar *extra-curricular* excursion months ago. She didn't need the grief from her mother. "What else could I do?" I said. "Matthew was adamant about going. I couldn't let him run off half-cocked. Putting that aside, let's return to the topic of Boyd Hellman." I rested my forearms on the table. "If he had a verifiable alibi for the night of Noelle's murder, like keeping an eye on you, why did he tell Urso, Matthew, and me that he was walking? That's so darned vague."

"Let's ask him," Alexis said. "He's right outside."

* * *

Leading the way, Alexis sneaked ahead of Delilah and me to the alley behind the diner. Her cape fluttered behind her like wings. At the corner, she halted and pointed. "There he is. Beside your car, Delilah. He's been there all morning."

Delilah said, "Why that—"

I hindered her from hurtling at Boyd and scaring the be-jeebers out of him. "Let's be reasonable."

"He's a creep."

"He's besotted," Alexis said. "Look at him."

Boyd was buffing the hood of Delilah's car with a chamois cloth. He spit on a particular spot and went at it again.

As stealthily as if I were trying to capture a stray cat, I slinked forward. Delilah and Alexis followed. When I drew within a few feet of the car, I said, "Hi, Boyd."

He jolted and searched right and left for an escape route. The far end of the alley was blocked by a garbage truck. Other than fleeing past us, there was no exit. He backed up a pace.

"You're doing a nice job on Delilah's car," I said. "She's not angry."

Under her breath she rasped, "Oh yes, I am."

"His aura is good," her mother said. "He's harmless."

"Mother, please. You can't see auras."

"I can so."

"Shh, you two." I crept closer. "Boyd, do you mind if I ask you a question?"

"What kind of question?" His voice had an edge but he seemed sober. His eyes were clear.

"Why were you at the Shelton Nelson Winery last night?"

"Who says I was?"

Alexis joined ranks with me. The aroma of lavender accompanied her and brought back all sorts of childhood memories. My mother had worn a lavender-scented fragrance. "I do," she said.

Boyd squinted. "What's it to you?"

I cocked my head. "Boyd, you throttled my cousin."

"No, I didn't."

"I don't know who you thought you knocked down with that wine bottle, but it was my cousin Matthew. Don't worry. He's fine. He will not press charges. What I want to know is why you were at the winery."

"I wasn't—"

Alexis clucked.

"Okay, fine. I was." Boyd wiped his hands with the chamois. "See, back in Cleveland, Noelle was acting sort of strange."

"How would you know that?" I said. "You two had broken up."

"That doesn't mean I didn't keep an eye out."

"Did you stalk her, too?" Delilah said.

"No, I don't stalk, I—" Boyd fixed his gaze on her for a long moment. It took a lot of effort for him to refocus on me. "Look, I asked Noelle why she was acting weird, and she said she had big plans. She said a lot was at stake."

The same words she had said to me. I shuddered.

"But I didn't buy it," Boyd said. "I mean, the job she got from Shelton Nelson . . . It was stupid. He was paying her chicken feed." He stuffed the chamois into his pocket. "I kept wondering why she would shoot down her career that way."

"Maybe she wanted to con him," I said.

"Nah, Noelle wouldn't do that. Ever. She was as honest as the day is long."

Alexis tweaked my elbow. "He's telling the truth. I can feel waves of good vibrations from him."

"Puh-lease." Delilah knuckled her mother in the shoulder. Alexis countered with a swat to Delilah's leg.

I said, "Did you tell your suspicions to Chief Urso, Boyd?"

"Sure, but I had nothing to back them up. Face it, I was a suspect in Noelle's murder. When he interrogated me, he wanted to know if I'd gone hiking at Kindred Creek and asked to see my boots. He went to my place to check them out. There wasn't any mud on them, but I figured he was asking because Noelle had mud on her shoes, so I got to thinking. Noelle never would have gone down to that creek place."

"Because she wasn't a nature girl," I said.

"That's right. Want to know why?" He didn't wait for a response. "When we were in the orphanage, one of the bad girls led Noelle to this brook down the road, then she ran off and left Noelle there." He muttered a curse beneath his breath. "Night came on fast, and Noelle became disoriented. Around ten P.M., I found her huddled in a ball, covered with scrapes and mud."

Poor Noelle. What a traumatic life she had lived.

"See, it was the mud that got me thinking," Boyd continued. "I work in construction."

Which explained the brawn. I could see him digging ditches or lifting a slug of two-by-fours on his shoulder.

"I know soil," he said. "So I went back to the precinct, and I asked Chief Urso to show me the boots. He obliged."

That was more courtesy than Urso would have afforded me.

"I noticed grape leaves in Noelle's shoes and pointed them out, but the chief dismissed my findings saying Noelle had been to the winery a couple of times. Later on, I thought some more."

"You're a real pensive guy," Delilah said.

"Actually, I am," he answered. "I'm even better when I'm sober. Anyway, because of what her folks did, Noelle didn't abide people scamming other people, so she took it upon herself to investigate. You know, she'd really delve into a person's past. I thought maybe she'd found some dirt on Shelton Nelson."

Like his troubled financial status, I mused.

"So I drove to the winery. If Nelson had anything to hide, I intended to find it. I saw a door open, so I sneaked in that way."

"Through the wine cellar."

"Yeah. But before I could get ten feet, I ran into someone. It was dark. I thought it was Nelson. Panicked, I grabbed the first thing I could"—he mimed grabbing hold of a bottle—"and swung, then I hightailed it out of there."

"You left Charlotte's cousin lying there," Delilah said. "What kind of jerk are you?"

"I was scared."

"A big guy like you?"

Alexis put one hand on Delilah's arm and the other on mine and squeezed to make us stay put, then she moved closer to Boyd.

"Mother, stop."

"I know what I'm doing, darling." Alexis reached for Boyd. "Young man, take hold of my hands."

As if mesmerized, he obeyed.

Alexis lowered her voice. "On the night your ex-girlfriend was killed, I caught you spying on my daughter."

Boyd kicked a pebble. His eyes flickered.

"Uh-uh, Boyd," Alexis said. "Reconnect with me." Magically, Boyd did. Whatever technique or magic Alexis was using was working. In a soothing tone, she said, "Why did you make up that story about going walking when you had an alibi?"

"Because."

"Because why?"

I flashed on Noelle's rebuke when Boyd had shown up at The Cheese Shop. She had warned him to stop harassing her, *or else*. I said, "You lied because Noelle put a restraining order on you, didn't she? You scared her. Did you abuse her?"

"No." Boyd released Alexis's hands as if he'd been singed and raised his arms in the air. "I never laid a hand on her. I swear."

"You can swear all you want," I said, "but it's true. You scared her."

"Tell the truth, Boyd," Alexis coaxed. She didn't reach for him again.

"I . . ." He licked his teeth. "When I drink, I have a temper. One night, I threw things around the apartment and drove my fist into a wall. That was the last straw for Noelle. I got into AA and anger management, but she wouldn't take me back. I was good with the liquor until she died. I've fallen off the wagon since then, but I'm already back on track." He gazed at Delilah. "I am. But I'm not supposed to hang around anybody for a long time."

"You mean you're not supposed to *stalk* someone," Delilah muttered.

I nudged Alexis aside and, channeling her, grabbed Boyd's hands. "Look at me, Boyd."

Delilah said, "Mumbo jumbo."

I ignored her and searched his eyes. His gaze didn't waver.

Tears pooled in the corners. After a long moment, I said, "You're telling the truth."

He nodded vigorously. "I'm a changed man."

"Does Chief Urso know about your past, Boyd?" I asked.

"It's not like I have a record or anything. I never violated the order."

"You showed up here, you creep," Delilah said. "You watched her."

"From afar."

Delilah strode to me and swatted my arm. "Hold on. He said Noelle told him there was a lot at stake. How would he know that unless he spoke to her?"

I kept a firm grip on Boyd's hands and felt a tremor shimmy through his palms. "Boyd," I said, drawing out his name. "The truth."

"I called her once. Only once. That's when she told me she was moving." Boyd curled his chin into his chest like a boxer needing to protect his core. He tried to free himself from my grip, but I wouldn't let go. "I followed her here to make sure she was going to be okay."

I understood. Ever since they had met at the orphanage, he had assigned himself her protector.

"At The Cheese Shop, she warned me off, and I'll admit I was upset, but then I saw Delilah and"—his eyes turned glossy with enchantment—"I fell hard."

"For me?" Delilah squawked. "Swell."

CHAPTER

26

Back at Fromagerie Bessette, I found Rebecca at the cheese counter assembling a cheese basket for the city council-woman.

When I sidled up to her, she begged me to tell her where I had been. I started to speak but Matthew said, "Hold it. I want to listen in." He stopped bustling around the wine annex and joined us.

"How's your head?" I asked.

"Sore, but my hearing seems to have improved tenfold." He grinned. "Go on."

I glanced at the councilwoman and the other customers. None seemed to be listening in, so I told Rebecca and Matthew about how Alexis, Delilah, and I trapped Boyd behind the diner and how he admitted his affection for—obsession with—Delilah, which established his alibi.

"When you held his hands, did you really feel hoodoo energy like Delilah's mother?" Rebecca asked, her eyes widening in awe.

"I'm not sure what I felt. I only know that Boyd was telling the truth. And thanks to Alexis's eyewitness account, he is innocent of killing Noelle. He watched Delilah for over two hours. He knew absolutely every move she had made."

"Hand me a jar of that California honey, would you?" Rebecca tucked a round of Cowgirl Creamery Mt Tam cheese—a rich, earthy triple cream—into the basket in front of a box of garlic potato thins. The California-themed array already held a wedge of Vella Dry Monterey Jack and Cypress Grove Truffle Tremor—a luscious union of truffles and goat cheese—and a bottle of Silver Horse Albariño wine. With its flavors of apricots and peaches, it would complement all three cheeses.

I said, "Why the West Coast flair?"

"The councilwoman's daughter is in town. You know the one, the actress in Los Angeles. They're celebrating. She just got a leading role on a new murder mystery series." As Rebecca gathered the cellophane around the basket and secured it with burgundy raffia, she said, "If Boyd is innocent, we only have four suspects."

"More," Matthew said, "if you include people who were bilked by Noelle's parents and want revenge."

"But Urso didn't come up with any names on that front, right?" Rebecca said.

"He hasn't gone to Cleveland yet," I said. "He got delayed."

Rebecca shook her head. "I'd rule them out anyway, wouldn't you? This seems personal. The weapon, the missing journal pages."

"The picture of the stick figure in the noose," Matthew added.

"What stick figure?" Rebecca said.

I explained and I agreed. I believed Noelle had known her killer.

Rebecca ticked off suspects on her fingertips. "We've got Shelton Nelson, who had two reasons to kill her, either to hide some secret that Noelle was investigating or because of some snag in their relationship. And then there's Harold Warfield, who might have been jealous that Noelle was hired."

"Or he was having an affair, and Noelle had compromising photos."

Rebecca brandished a finger. "You know, I saw him looking pretty intimate with Liberty Nelson yesterday. I hadn't thought anything about it until now."

I gawked. "What? Where? They're enemies."

"They didn't look like it to me. Liberty was leaving the grocery store, and Harold offered to carry her bags. He walked her to her car."

"Big deal," I said. "They didn't kiss or anything, did they?"

"No, but it was a public place."

"Uh-uh." I shook my head. "They're not a couple. She's engaged."

"And he's married," Rebecca sniggered. "That doesn't keep people apart."

What if she was right? I remembered Liberty smirking when her father said how devoted Harold was to his wife. Maybe they acted like they hated each other to keep the secret.

"That's a perfect scenario for murder," Rebecca went on. "Like in that Hitchcock movie *Strangers on the Train*. You kill mine and I'll kill yours."

I slugged her. "You've been watching way too many movies. They're corrupting you. And let's be clear: neither Harold's wife nor Liberty's fiancé is dead."

"What if Liberty's father learned of the affair?" Rebecca persisted. "What if Noelle told him? I bet if Shelton found out that his manager and daughter were, ahem, *involved*, he might have killed Noelle to keep it all hush-hush."

I said, "Why, for heaven's sake?"

"To protect his reputation as well as his daughter's."

"I'm sorry, but that's a little far-fetched. He'd more likely punish Harold, put Liberty on probation, and give Noelle a bonus."

Matthew formed a T with his hands. "Time out. Let's go back to Harold. He lied about his alibi."

"To cover up his affair."

"His wife lied, too," I said. "She told me she saw Boyd

walking up my driveway that night." The encounter with Velma in the parking lot outside the pub still perplexed me. What did she know and when did she know it?

The door chimes jingled. A handful of female customers wearing matching tour tee shirts entered the shop and headed for the display of new cheese platters that had come in last week—beautiful ones that resembled stained glass. The women's *oohs*, all in different keys, made them sound like choir members warming up.

"Don't forget Ashley Yeats," Rebecca continued. "He pestered Noelle, saying he knew she had a story to tell. She told him to bug off. Did that drive him to kill her? Of course, there's Liberty Nelson, too. She might have wanted to kill the competition in order to keep her father's affection or kill the person who knew about her affair with Harold."

"Alleged affair," I said.

"Alleged." Rebecca inserted sprigs of pine beneath the raffia, fanned them out, and hooked a tiny silver bell as a final touch. "If only I could wheedle something out of Deputy O'Shea. He—"

"Hold that thought," I said, then took the basket from her and carried it to the register where the councilwoman was waiting.

"It's beautiful," the councilwoman said. "I love how you take care of me."

"We aim to please. Congratulations to your daughter."

"Thank you, dear. How's Matthew?" she asked as she paid. "He looks okay, but I heard he bumped his head."

At least she hadn't heard how the injury had occurred. Throwing a gag order at Nurse Nenette had been a stroke of genius. I had Urso to thank for that.

"He's fine, ma'am. Though between you and me, I think he believes he is made of steel and only Kryptonite will harm him."

"I heard that," Matthew said. "I now have supersonic hearing."

The councilwoman tittered. "I'm looking forward to the wine tasting later, Matthew."

"Me, too," he said. "Have your palate ready."

As she exited, I rejoined Rebecca and Matthew. "Now, what did you learn from Deputy O'Shea?"

"That's just it. Nothing." Rebecca growled. "He slipped into the store for a small wedge of cheese while you were at the diner. I talked him into trying something new, that Somerdale Red Dragon with mustard seed, but boy, he's tight-lipped. I'm wondering if that's the way he kisses, too. If so, I'm not interested in him."

"You're tough." I laughed.

"My, my, how you have grown up over the past few months," Matthew said.

"Sorry, Matthew. I didn't mean to make you blush." Rebecca twirled her ponytail around a finger.

"You couldn't. I have a house full of girls."

"Wait until they're teens," I said.

"And wanting to talk to you about the birds and the bees," Rebecca added.

Matthew moaned. "Back to our investigation. What do we need to do?"

"You heard U-ey at the hospital." I grabbed a towel and mopped up the cheese counter, plucking bits of the pine bough off the wood. "We've been ordered to back off."

Matthew smirked. "Yeah, like we'll obey."

Rebecca clapped Matthew on the shoulder. "He's right. We're the Snoop Club."

"Cut that out," I said. "If U-ey learns about your silly nickname for us, we're doomed."

"Shh," Matthew said. "Look who just walked in."

Liberty Nelson flounced toward the cheese counter with Tyanne in tow. Once again, Liberty was dressed in buttons and bows, her hair swished into a tidy twist at the nape of her neck, her makeup understated. What a transformation. She appeared the epitome of Miss Elizabeth Bennet in *Pride and Prejudice*. I think I preferred the former Liberty and her feline-style garb.

I whispered, "Why is she here? You would think she wouldn't want to be within a thousand yards of us."

Tyanne waved. "Hello, all." She prodded Liberty at the arch of her back. "Go on, sugar, they don't bite."

No. We break into people's homes—cellars—and have scrapes with strangers. Honestly, lately, my ability to judge when to act and when not to act was impaired. Could I chalk up my more-than-usual impetuousness to being frazzled because Jordan was out of town? How I missed him. The memory of our night together made me shiver with delight.

Liberty transferred her ecru Hermes handbag to the other arm, raised her pretty chin, and drew near. "Charlotte and Matthew, I have come to apologize."

"You don't have to," I said.

Matthew muttered, "She's right."

"I do, indeed. I am trying to mend all fences before my impending nuptials." She turned to Tyanne for support. "Isn't that right, Miss Tyanne?"

As Liberty looked away, Rebecca kicked my foot and whispered, "If you ask me, she's been reading too many Jane Austen novels. She not only looks like the heroines, she's beginning to talk like them. *Miss* Tyanne. Give me a break."

A flurry of giggles gushed up my throat. I bit them back and said, "Hush."

"Go on, Liberty," Tyanne said. Obviously she was acting as more than wedding planner; she was nearly a companion therapist.

"Charlotte, I know how deeply you and your cousin cared for Noelle." Liberty didn't look at me. She fidgeted with the clasp on her purse. "And I know you invaded my home to find answers—answers that you simply won't find there, I'm afraid—but I shouldn't have called the police and reported you. I don't want you to think I'm a bully."

I swallowed hard. This much humility was hard to bear. "Liberty, you had every right—"

She held up a dainty hand. "Stop, Charlotte. I was in the wrong, and I want you to forgive me. To make amends, I came in to buys lots of cheese for whoever was in the shop, but my boyfriend has put the brakes on that. I need to curb my spending habits." She glanced over her shoulder at her fiancé who stood, arms folded, on the sidewalk. Had he in-stigated this apology? Was there some truth to Liberty hav-ing an affair with Harold? Had the fiancé found out? Was he now keeping her on a short leash?

I said, "How about I make it up to you by giving you some cheese, and we'll call us square."

"No, please don't. I do not wish to be a bother. I only want . . ." She fluttered a hand. "I want to do what is right from now on. Full disclosure."

Itching to take advantage of her vulnerability, I said, "Okay, Liberty, in that case, could you tell me what you and your father were arguing about the day we toured the win-ery?"

"Arguing?" Her hand flew to her chest. "Whatever can you mean?"

Puh-leese, as Delilah would say. I smiled. "I believe you were arguing about Noelle."

Liberty's face turned as red as winterberries. "Why, I never. Were you eavesdropping? How dare you. You had no right. What goes on behind closed doors is secret, do you understand me?" Her hands turned into claws. She looked like she wanted to rip my heart out.

Ha! I knew her virtuous act had been too good to be true. I pressed on. "You were talking about Noelle coming to work at the winery."

She jammed her lips together in a thin line.

"Maybe the argument started because your father found out from Noelle that you and Harold were involved."

"What?" she cried. "Harold and me? My father and I were not talking about—" She shook her head. "It's none of your business."

"Why did you telephone Noelle repeatedly and hang up?" To tell her to mind her own beeswax was my guess.

"I did no such thing."

"Don't bother denying it. There are phone records. Ty-anne confirmed the calls were made from your telephone number."

"I never called Noelle, not once, and that is all you need

to know. We're done here. Tyanne, cancel all orders." With dramatic flair, Liberty pivoted on her heel and stormed out of the shop.

Tyanne sputtered, "Charlotte . . . Sugar, I don't know what to say. Liberty's hormones . . . Brides can be mighty emotional . . . I . . ." She tore after her charge, yelling over her shoulder to me, "Don't cancel anything yet."

I watched Tyanne catch up to Liberty and her fiancé on the street. Liberty's arms flew every which way, then she pulled her cell phone from her purse and flaunted it. Hadn't she called Noelle? Who else could have done so without Liberty having a clue? I said as much out loud.

Matthew said, "Yeah, who?"

Rebecca sniffed. "May I refresh your memory as to her supposed alibi? Liberty claimed she was reading in the room next to her father's and heard him singing. I think she lied about that." She swung her gaze from Matthew to me. "Oh, sure, she was pulling off a good act until you pinned her to the wall, Charlotte. If I might refer you back to the movie *Legally Blonde*. Remember how the victim's daughter reacted when Elle grilled her on the witness stand? Her mouth puckered. Her eyes went wide. Well, Liberty did the same right now." Rebecca stabbed her palm with her index finger. "That conversation you overheard matters to this case."

I said, "The question is, is she protecting her father or herself?"

Rebecca removed her apron and slung it on a hook on the wall. "Let's find out."

I grabbed her shoulder. "What are you doing?"

"I'm going to slip into the Nelson house and see how thick those walls really are."

"Are you nuts? U-ey's got eyes on Matthew and me, and I'll bet that he's put Deputy O'Shea on your tail."

"Oh my gosh, do you think?"

I retrieved her apron and shoved it into her chest. "Back to work. We have customers."

"But—"

"No argument."

For the next couple of hours, Rebecca and I served customers while Matthew continued to prepare his wine-tasting event. None of us discussed what we could do to solve Noelle's murder. The respite for my beleaguered brain felt good. I offered tastings of cheese to customers, I drank in strength from the nurturing aromas, and I listened to local gossip. At one point, I noticed Deputy O'Shea swing by the front of the store and peek in, but he kept moving. Whether he was spying on Rebecca or hoping to catch a moment with her, I wasn't sure.

After the noon rush was over, my grandfather arrived. He suggested I take a stroll around town and drink in the sunshine. I knew his real intention. With me gone, he could sneak a morsel of imported French Brie.

"I'll go with you," Rebecca said. "My legs could use a stretch." Truth be known, she didn't want to be the one who saw Pépère divert from his diet. She might accidentally blab to my grandmother, the diet taskmaster.

As we rounded the corner to walk up Cherry Orchard Street, I spied Sylvie walking hand in hand with Ashley Yeats. Surprisingly, she wore a tasteful blue dress that seemed specifically chosen to compliment his blue pin-striped suit. Their heads were tilted inward, as if the two were engaged in an enthralling conversation, and I wondered if she had found her soul mate, after all.

A flare of orange caught my eye. Prudence exited Café au Lait at a clip. She was carrying a bag of goodies while nibbling on a donut doused in powdered sugar. Why was she eating sweets? She rarely did. Was the city council's injunction stressing her out?

From across the street, Sylvie sniggered loudly enough for everyone to hear.

Prudence looked up. Her face puckered with rage.

"Uh-oh," Rebecca said.

"Uh-oh is right," I muttered. All thoughts of a pleasant stroll went bye-bye.

Prudence dropped the pastry in the street and made a mad dash for Sylvie. En route, she sideswiped a ladder, on top of which balanced a volunteer who was hoisting a holiday flag on a lamppost. The ladder joggled; the volunteer shrieked. Rebecca and I raced to stabilize the ladder. Just in time. The volunteer, who was pasty with fright, thanked us.

On the other hand, Prudence didn't break stride. "Sylvie Bessette." She darted in front of Sylvie and Ashley, forcing them to a halt. "What was that sound you just made?"

"I don't have a clue what you're talking about," Sylvie said.

"You snorted. Were you inferring that I am a pig?"

"Tosh."

Prudence reeled around and glared at me. "Charlotte, you heard her."

Dang. There was nowhere for me to run.

"You did," Prudence said. "I know you heard her. She was making fun of me."

Despite the subdued outfit, Sylvie was still a minx. She winked at me, then said, "You do look like you have put on a little weight, Pru."

"Why, you!" Prudence lunged for Sylvie.

Ashley darted in front of Sylvie and batted the bag of goodies from Prudence's hands. Powdered sugar billowed in clouds as the bag opened and the sweet contents tumbled to the ground.

Prudence lashed out.

"Oo-o-oh." Ashley raised his arms to defend himself. "She didn't mean any harm, love. Take a load off."

Rebecca thwacked me on the back. "Did you hear that?"

"What?"

"Ashley Yeats. His accent wavered."

"Wavered?"

"He sounded . . . Southern. Remember when I told you about that gossipy Internet radio guy, Alcott Baldwin? The one that touts Ashley's writing? He's from the South—Alabama, I think. He starts his show every time with this high-pitched, 'Oo-o-oh,' just like Yeats did. He's him. Ashley is Alcott."

"Are you sure?"

"Ninety-nine percent positive. I told you there was something about the guy that bothered me from the get-go."

I trotted toward Prudence. "May I have a word?"

"No, you may not." Prudence thwacked Ashley. "Let me at her."

"Prudence, stop hitting him," I said. "Just for a sec. Humor me."

"Oh, for heaven's sake," she said. "None of you—not one—is worth the effort. You're all crazy." She was one to talk. Apparently my grandmother hadn't made any headway regarding Prudence finding professional help. She kicked her busted bag of goodies and marched off.

I whirled on Ashley Yeats. "Where are you from?"

He gulped. "Huh?"

"Alabama?"

Sylvie ducked from behind Ashley. "What's going on?"

"He's not from England, Sylvie," I said. "He's putting on an act."

"For heaven's sake, Charlotte," Sylvie said. "Are you trying to ruin my love life? I won't have it. Matthew put you up to this, didn't he?"

"Sylvie, listen to me. I believe Ashley Yeats is none other than that gossip Alcott Baldwin from—"

"South Carolina," Rebecca blurted. "Not Alabama. I was wrong. It's South Carolina. Charleston, to be exact."

Sylvie's eyes sparked with indignity. "Is it true, Ashley?"

The guy stretched his neck. "No . . . she . . . they . . . are making this all up," he said, his proper British accent restored.

"The heck we are," I said. I trusted Rebecca's savvy Internet ear.

Sylvie planted her hands on her hips. "Where were you raised in England, Ashley?"

"Hampshire."

"With that accent?" Sylvie arched a brow.

"Somerset," he revised. "Uh, I mean, Sussex. The North."

"Those are all counties in the south, you buffoon." Sylvie withered. "Cripes, Charlotte, you're right." She scowled at

Ashley a.k.a. Alcott. "How could I have ever believed you? And you said you adored me."

"But, love, I do."

"Don't *love* me, you no good, lying fraud." She thrust out her lower lip. Now I knew where the twins got the move. I had to admit the ploy was impressive.

Ashley looked ready to bolt.

"Not so fast, Mr. Yeats," I said, "or shall we call you Mr. Baldwin?"

"Aw, heck," he said in a Southern drawl as he scuffed the soul of his shoe against the pavement. "I guess the cat's out of the bag. It was a risk, but I needed a leg up as a journalist. I needed someone to plug my career. I needed buzz. Who better to do it than myself?"

"Noelle knew, didn't she?" I said.

"No."

"You killed her to keep your secret safe."

"No."

"You exchanged emails."

"Yes, but that doesn't make me a murderer. I'd been following her career for years. I met her in Cleveland when she was a sommelier. She suggested a wine that I'll remember to this day. A Haut-Brion that was to die for."

"I drank a Haut-Brion," Sylvie said.

"Quiet." I speared her with a glance and returned my focus to Ashley a.k.a. Alcott. "Go on."

He ran a finger under the collar of his shirt as if he were roasting under the impromptu interrogation. "When I learned Noelle was giving up her career to move here, I had to know why. I thought her story could be a life changer for me. She was amazing. She could have been working in any of the most elite restaurants in New York. Aw, heck, in the world. She was a big fish moving to a little pond. There had to be something behind that, right? She wasn't pregnant. I checked. It cost me a pretty penny to get that insider info, I've got to tell you. And she wasn't on the lam from the law. I sensed corruption." He tapped his nose. "So I called her. We talked once. After that, she snubbed me."

A thought occurred to me, one that would answer the question that had plagued me since Liberty Nelson had come into The Cheese Shop earlier. "You followed Noelle here weeks ago. You scoped out the winery."

"No, I—"

I held up a hand. "Don't deny it. You saw Liberty Nelson talking on her cell phone, and you realized an opportunity."

"I'm not following."

"You got close enough to Liberty to clone her cell phone."

Rebecca knuckled my arm. "Omigosh. You're right. That's exactly what he did. I saw a perp do that in an episode of *Law and Order*."

"You used that number to call Noelle repeatedly after midnight," I continued. "She answered because Liberty's name appeared on the readout, but soon Noelle got wise and hung up on you every time."

Ashley—I couldn't get used to referring to him as Alcott—looked down and away.

"Answer her, you phony," Sylvie demanded.

"Okay, yes, you guessed right. I know how to hack into all sorts of things. I'm all about shortcuts. If I can find a way to scoop a story the easy way, I do it. I wanted one of my features to be good." He grimaced. "No, not just good. Great. Noelle had left a big-time job to work at little old Shelton Nelson Winery. Something bad was going on. I researched her. I found out about her folks. Her past."

"You blackmailed her."

"I wanted her to confide in me. I believed, with her insider information, I could go wide with the story, and maybe I would be taken seriously as a journalist."

But Noelle, believing the only reason he wanted to interview her was so he could expose her parents' dicey past, shunned him.

Sylvie huffed. "No one will take you seriously ever again, Ashley, not if I have anything to do with it, you two-bit—"

He raised his hand, as if about to strike Sylvie, but quickly diverted his hand to the back of his neck and rubbed hard. "No matter what you think, I didn't kill Noelle Adams."

"Grab hold of him, Charlotte," Rebecca said. "Do what Delilah's mom does. Divine the truth."

"I can't," I whispered. The moment in the alley with Boyd was a fluke.

"Try."

"I'm telling the truth," Ashley said, his face bleak with resignation. He spread his arms, palms up. "Look, I couldn't have killed Noelle. I have a tight alibi. I was live on my Internet radio program the night Noelle was killed. I took calls. There's no way to fake that."

"Why didn't you say that before?" I asked.

"Because Chief Urso didn't consider me a suspect. He never asked for an alibi. If he did, I guess I would have told the truth. It's better to be a fraud than a killer, right?" He attempted a smile, but his lips quivered.

"I'll say this, Mr. Yeats . . . I mean, Baldwin," Rebecca said. "You do have a nice voice. Whenever you sing on the show, that seems to get the most call-ins."

Sylvie groaned. "You've got to be kidding. He has a horrible voice."

"Me?" he wailed. "You're the one who can't sing a lick. You're always singing in the wrong key." He demonstrated.

Sylvie stamped her foot and told Ashley to keep his opinion to himself.

As they mocked each other, I sank into a quiet funk and returned to the real matter at hand: Noelle. Who had killed her and why?

CHAPTER

27

Later that afternoon, while straightening shelves at Fromagerie Bessette, the words *hell's key* kept blinking like a neon sign in my brain. Had Noelle given me other clues to determine the meaning? She had gone out of her way to make sure Matthew put her in touch with Shelton so she could get the job. The night she died, she was going on a quest. So much was *at stake*, she had said.

Suddenly the imaginary neon sign burst into a kaleidoscope of color. "That's it," I said out loud to no one. Matthew had left the shop to deliver an order, Rebecca had gone to the hothouse behind the shop to fetch some basil, and the last customer had exited the shop minutes ago. I stopped realigning jars of jam and focused on the incident on the street between Sylvie and Ashley a.k.a. Alcott. *I'm all about shortcuts*, he had said, and then he accused Sylvie of singing in the *wrong key*. The two phrases wouldn't mean anything to anyone else but, for me, they conjured up a very distinct memory. I recalled the night after the winery tour and coming upon Noelle in the guest room. She had been humming.

On key. It wasn't the singing that mattered. It was what else she had been doing—writing in her journal. We shared a brief exchange. She said Shelton Nelson wasn't into short-cuts, and then her mouth quirked up. Had she been cuing me in on the fact that Shelton *was* into shortcuts? If so, why hadn't she come right out and said so?

Next, Noelle slid off the bed and removed a blue thumb drive from her computer. As she did, her journal fell open. Had she intended for me to glimpse one of the pages? There were wine labels and notes.

I closed my eyes and tried to envision her notes. She had written the word *shortcuts* in the margin. In the journal that I found tucked between the mattress and box spring, I had seen only the word *short*. Was the word *cuts* missing? Had Noelle torn out the specific page that she had accidentally on purpose let me see? Did the picture of the man in a noose signify something, or was Noelle just doodling, sort of hint-ing that when the truth was discovered the man would want to hang himself? What if Shelton was being truthful, and he wasn't into shortcuts? Did he joke about that at the winery to imply that someone else, like Liberty or Harold, was?

"*Chérie*," my grandmother called from the doorway. The twins scampered in behind her, their faces flushed from the cold. They let the door slam shut. "Girls," Grandmère chided.

"Sorry," they sang in unison.

"We have good news." Grandmère scuttled to the cheese counter. "The Thanksgiving Extravaganza is ready. It is *parfait*."

"Perfect," the girls chimed.

"The duck flies like a dream."

"And we all know our lines."

"It is all about repetition, is it not? *Répétér. Répétér. Ré-pétér.*" Grandmère clapped in rhythm.

"No shortcuts for you," I said, the word emblazoned on my brain.

"*Mais oui.*"

What might shortcuts cause? I wondered. Inferior wine, Matthew had suggested. Anything else?

Grandmère said, "Amy and Clair, you may play with Rags for fifteen minutes, then it is time for homework." When Grandmère learned that Noelle was coming to town and staying with me, she offered to take over my responsibility of shuttling the children from school to rehearsals. I think she relished the extra time with the twins. As the girls flew to the office, Grandmère settled onto a ladder-back stool by the tasting bar and slipped a morsel of Rogue Creamery Tou-Velle into her mouth. "I love the smoky goodness." She purred with contentment and took another slice. Nibbling the corners, she said, "Charlotte, what is puzzling you? Your forehead. It is creased."

"Nothing," I said, not wishing to worry her. All I had to go on were words that I'd overheard and suppositions and tidbits of evidence gleaned when Matthew and I had stolen into the winery—footprints, expensive wines stored behind a locked gate, and a cursory view of the insides of a few drawers in Shelton's office. My thoughts scudded back to the expensive wines. How might Noelle's note about shortcuts fit that scenario?

The rear door of the shop opened, and Rebecca waltzed in with two fists full of basil and other herbs that she had collected from the town's communal hothouse located in the alley behind the shop. "*Bonjour*. Aren't these gorgeous?" She stopped short of the kitchen and gave me a hard look. "What's up? Charlotte, your face is all scrunched up."

"You see?" Grandmère spread her hands.

I grabbed a towel and started cleaning the cutting surface.

"You're thinking about that skirmish on the street, aren't you?" Rebecca said.

Grandmère's gaze swung between us.

I told her about Sylvie and Prudence's free-for-all.

"Poor Prudence," Grandmère muttered.

Rebecca recounted the clash between Sylvie and Ashley Yeats, a.k.a. Alcott Baldwin, right through to the final words that I was replaying in my head.

Grandmère said, "Our upcoming play, *Days of Wine and Roses*, will not have as much drama."

I said, "Battling alcoholism"—the theme of the play—
"can be pretty dramatic."

"*Oui.*"

I flashed on Boyd Hellman, who would battle alcohol the
rest of his life, but I put him from my mind. He had an alibi
for the night Noelle died. Though it was quirky, it was solid.
Alexis confirmed it.

"But life. That is the real drama," my grandmother said.

Rebecca flaunted the herbs. "If you ask me, that Ashley-
Alcott guy is lucky he has an alibi, because he has the best
motive to kill Noelle so far. Keeping his secret hidden."

"Except Noelle didn't know his secret," I said. "I think
she was avoiding him to keep her parents' illegal activities
buried."

Grandmère held up a finger. "Seneca said, 'If you wish
another to keep your secret, first keep it to yourself.'"

"Wait, wait, I know the book that came from," Rebecca
said. "*Hippolytus.*"

"*Oui. Bravo.* You are becoming a true student." Grandmère glanced at her watch. "Oh my, we must go." After giving Rebecca and me kisses, she collected the girls.

The remainder of the afternoon sped past. With the arrival of a passel of tour bus customers as well as a pair of
women frantic to put together a cheese plate for their evening
game of mahjong, I didn't give my musings another thought.

However, as Rags and I headed home, leaving Matthew to
attend to his wine tasting alone, the notion of secrets swelled
again in my mind. Who had the best secret to keep? Was
Ashley's alternate identity a secret worth killing for? Hardly.
I focused on the father/daughter argument that I had overheard at the winery. Had I fabricated a soap opera from Liberty and Shelton's words when really they were talking
business? If so, then why had Liberty seemed so upset that I
had listened in? I strung the words together in no particular
order: *label, lover, nose, charted for disaster.* As Matthew
and I had discussed, a few were words that could apply to the
wine business—the label on a bottle; a lover or connoisseur
of wine; the nose or bouquet of the wine. If the winery was

strapped financially, it could be charted for disaster. How did the word *phony* fit in?

"Here you go, Ragsie." I entered the kitchen and released him from his leash. He galloped to his bed and retrieved a jingle bell. While he batted it, I threw together dinner. Cooking for one could make a girl feel lonely, but I was dead set against dining on leftovers. I wanted fresh. My brain needed energy as well as flavor. A chopped Italian salad with homemade dressing, sweetened ever so slightly with sugar, would do the trick. I sliced mozzarella into cubes, diced Genoa salami, and opened a can of garbanzo beans.

As I stood at the sink chopping cherry tomatoes that I had collected from the hothouse before leaving the shop, I peered through the kitchen window at the garage and thought again about Noelle's final words: *hell's key* or *Shel's key*. Which was it? The day we toured Shelton Nelson's cellar, Noelle had cleared her throat before asking him whether he kept a log of his precious wines. A log, or register, could be a kind of key, essential to keeping things organized, like a color code for a painter. Had she cleared her throat to clue in Matthew or me to her plan to expose Shelton? Expose him for what?

The word *phony* popped into my mind again. What if Noelle discovered the winery was intentionally creating a counterfeit wine? *Phony, label, nose.*

I recalled Matthew telling me about a wine scam where a vintner duplicated a very expensive wine. The vintner sold it at auction, and a few wine snobs, not willing to reveal that they couldn't tell the difference between the wines, lost a lot of money. The story made the wine journals.

Boyd said that, thanks to her parents' lifestyle, Noelle didn't take kindly to scam artists. If my theory was correct, when Noelle realized someone at SNW was swindling the public, she made it her mission to blow the whistle.

I flashed on the brief moment I had spent in Shelton's office rummaging through his top desk drawer, which held a collection of items: blank labels, ink, specialized pens, corks, and what had resembled a branding tool. Were those the tools that could help perpetrate a fraud?

Noelle had devised the job for herself. She had begged Matthew to introduce her to Shelton. She had given up a cushy job to work for SNW. Had she discovered the winery's scam while working as a sommelier? If I was correct, was Shelton, Liberty, or Harold the culprit? After Matthew and I had raided the winery, Liberty had come to The Cheese Shop to find out what we had discovered. She hadn't told her father about our foray. Was she afraid of what he might do to her if he found out that she and/or her possible lover Harold were bastardizing his wine?

Noelle went to investigate something the night she died. Did she find evidence that would convict someone? Maybe she made notes and took photographs, crafting her own kind of key. Maybe she taunted the killer and told him or her that she had the evidence. Or did the killer figure it out on his or her own? Matthew and I found traces of Noelle's muddy footprints. The killer could have, as well. Would Noelle have risked leaving her evidence at the winery? I didn't think so. She returned to my house. She must have hidden it here.

Zinging with pent-up energy, I placed the knife on the counter, wiped my hands on a towel and tossed it beside the knife, then sprinted to the garage, which was cleaner now that Matthew had helped move the furniture back to the office. I stood in what could once again be used as a garage and tried to picture that night. Noelle lying beside the reassembled desk. A screwdriver nearby. No flashlight. Boxes strewn.

I thought again of the desk and flashed on a comment made at the pub the other night. Tyanne said Boyd Hellman had a hollow leg. When I left the garage on the night Noelle died, the legs of the secretary desk were lying on the floor. They were hollow. Had Noelle stuffed whatever evidence she had collected into those hollow legs and attached the legs before the killer found her? Other than me, no one would have known the legs had been off the desk.

CHAPTER

I fetched my cordless power screwdriver and raced back to the house. I bolted through the kitchen door and was heading for the office when I felt a presence. I whirled to my right. Harold Warfield charged me. Light glinted off the sharp knife in his hand—the knife I had used to slice tomatoes.

"Don't kill me," I shouted. Not clever. Not even scary. I raised the power tool, which was heavy but no match for the blade. It would work better as a shield. Where had he come from? Had he broken in through a window? I had locked the front door after Rags and I entered. "I don't know where it is."

"Where what is?"

"The key."

"What key?"

"The key Noelle stole . . . copied . . . whatever." My mouth felt as dry as sawdust; my heart drummed my rib cage. I edged to my left, but I couldn't evade Harold. The kitchen table was in my way. Ducking and scrambling on my knees would do no good. "I don't know where she hid it." I was lying. I felt certain that I did know.

"Hid what?"

"The key." *Hell's key. Harold's key.* "Isn't that why you're here? To retrieve the key?"

"You've been talking to my wife."

"Velma didn't tell me about the key."

"What key?"

"*The* key." I felt like I was performing a bizarre routine of "Who's on First?".

He said, "I'm not here for a key."

"You're not?"

"You're digging around my life." His voice rasped with anger. "You interrogated my wife."

"No, I didn't." Okay, yes, I had. Yet again I was lying. But the guy was pointing a knife at my chest, and he was twisting and turning it like he wanted to cut out my heart. I clutched the power drill tighter.

"How dare you," he hissed.

He slinked toward me, his hand shaking, and I thought maybe I had the advantage, after all. If I threw the power tool at him, I could knock away the knife. But I would need to run away and the kitchen door had slammed closed. And Harold was bigger than I was and probably faster. I wouldn't get far.

"Velma put a GPS in my car."

I swallowed hard. "That's great. She wants to make sure you won't get lost."

He snarled. "Very funny."

"It wasn't meant to be." If I dropped the power tool and tried to get control of the knife, he would slice my hands to ribbons.

"Velma followed me to Wooster."

"What's in Wooster?"

"Exactly."

"Exactly what?" I asked, returning to our "Who's on First?" routine. When would the scary merry-go-round ride end? My head was spinning.

"She found out I was having an affair."

Uh-oh. Not good. He had wanted to keep the affair secret, and I had incited his wife to action. What kind of key fit that scenario? A key to the woman's apartment. Would Noelle have hidden something that small in the leg of the desk? Except Harold said he wasn't here for a key.

Shut up, brain. Concentrate. Lunatic, straight ahead.

I said, "I'm sure you can patch things up. End it with Liberty."

"Liberty?"

"Aren't you involved with Shelton Nelson's daughter?"

"Are you crazy? She's a nutcase."

Talk about a pot calling a kettle black. "Well, whoever the woman is, end it, and go to marriage counseling with Velma."

"I can't."

"Why not?" I could be such a Pollyanna at times.

"I'm having an affair with a man."

With a man. Even worse. Well, not worse, just different, but that scenario had to really upset Velma. How could she compete with a man? She had a chance at winning her husband back from a woman, but from a man? I remembered Velma saying during a visit to The Cheese Shop that Harold spent a lot of time with his college buddies. At the time, I hadn't thought anything about it. How dense could I be?

"Does the man own a dog?" I said, thinking back to when Meredith had seen Harold acting strangely at the pet store.

"Who cares?"

"Nobody. Not me. Maybe the man . . . Maybe the dog." I couldn't believe the babble blathering out of my mouth. Having a case of the jitters while trying to defend oneself against a man with a knife was not smart.

"That's where I was on the night of Noelle's murder," Harold said.

"You weren't at the library."

He frowned. "You already established that."

"That's great," I said. "You have an alibi." He wasn't the killer. He hadn't come to my house to do me in. He was angry, outed, and desperate to vent.

I eyed the towel that I had discarded on the counter. Maybe I could swap it for the power tool. If I could wrap the towel around my hand, I could go for the knife, and—

No, Rebecca would tell me she had seen it work in a movie, but I would wager the knife would pierce right through the fabric. Only last week, I had sharpened the entire collection of knives.

Reason with the guy would be Jordan's suggestion. But it would be hard to convince Harold I was levelheaded with an anvil-sized power tool in my hands. Perhaps a melding of both Rebecca and Jordan's ideas would work.

In the gentlest voice I could muster, I said, "Harold, let's talk civilly. I'm going to put down the power tool." I twisted to my right and placed it on the counter and picked up the towel, pretending to wipe off my hands, while wrapping it around my fingertips and palm. "I'm sorry about your marriage woes. I am. Velma must be distraught, and I never meant to hurt her. But you should be happy that you have an alibi. Only minutes ago, I was wondering if you were Noelle Adams's killer. When you showed up and lunged at me, well . . ." I chuckled. A nervous cockatoo couldn't have sounded wackier. "Please put down the knife. I won't tell anyone what you told me. As for you and Velma, well, that's up to you guys to sort out. Counseling might be a good idea. Do you want me to drive you home so you can talk to her? You look pretty upset."

Drive him home? Was I loco?

Harold muttered, "I can drive."

"Promise you won't take out your anger on Velma." I eyed the knife.

"On Velma? I would never . . ." His gaze zipped from the knife, to me, and back to the knife. He seemed to be wondering where he had found the darned thing. He hurled it to the floor, then stormed out of the kitchen toward the front of the house. When the door slammed, I picked up the knife and reinserted it into the knife block.

Seconds later, Rags scooted from the pantry and sprang into my arms. He mewled his fear and support. His throbbing heart matched mine.

CHAPTER

With Rags in my arms, I jogged to the front of the house and peeked through the window that flanked the door. A car peeled away from the house, tires screeching with venom. As my pulse returned to normal, I retrieved the power screwdriver and hurried to the office. What had Noelle hidden?

The room appeared the same as when Matthew and I had left it—the secretary desk on the carpet, the Queen Anne chairs in their places, and the floor lamp in the corner. Piles of used tarps and paint cans were shoved to one side. I would clean up tomorrow. Right now, I craved a peek inside the desk's legs.

I set Rags on the Queen Anne chair and scruffed his head behind the ears to calm him. He was no watchdog, but he was a wonderful companion. The sound of his steady breathing calmed me. "Maybe I should call U-ey first." I pulled my cell phone from my pocket and started to punch in Urso's number but stopped after hitting the third button, wondering whether I should call him before I had concrete—or *paper*—

proof of something. Hearing from me otherwise might irritate him.

"Of course, I should," I whispered. I had information to impart. At the very least, I should alert him to Harold's distressed state of mind.

I continued inputting the number while working through the conversation in my head. I would start by saying, "Don't get mad," though, of course, Urso would. How could he not? He had asked me to keep my nose out of his investigation, and yet Harold had invaded my house. And I had learned Boyd was hounding Delilah. And Ashley had out-and-out lied about who and what he was. And now I was in search of evidence to prove that the Shelton Nelson Winery was trying to dupe the public.

The phone rang once and Urso answered. "I'm on it, Charlotte," he carped. Apparently my name had appeared in his caller I.D. "Truly, I am. I went to Cleveland today. I followed up on Noelle's past. I spoke to the nuns at the orphanage where she grew up. I tracked down a few of her parents' dissatisfied customers. Happy?" He sighed. "You know what? I don't care if you're happy. I'm tired. I'm heading to my folks for a plate of Mama's lasagna. If it's not important, can it wait until tomorrow?"

Heat flooded my chest, neck, and cheeks. Honestly, if I'd had hackles at the back of my neck, they would have risen. I had never felt so dismissed in my life. I muttered, "Never mind," and hung up. If I was wrong about Noelle's hiding place, Urso would never let me hear the end of it. For all I knew, the desk's legs were empty. I mean, after the killer's second foray into my garage/workshop, he or she must have found what Noelle had hidden, right? That's why there wasn't a third incursion. Or maybe the killer had given up the search.

Holding on to that hope, I dialed Matthew and filled him in. He sounded as excited as a schoolboy. "I'm just wrapping up the wine tasting, then I'll be right over," he said.

"Great." However, I wasn't in the mood to wait.

Tipping over the desk without help was going to be a challenge, but I could do it. First, I removed all the items from the top: the pen set, the blotter, the lamp, and the picture frames of my parents, my grandparents, and a wedding picture of Matthew, Meredith, and the twins. Next, I moved the other Queen Anne chair to the far side of the desk and anchored the arms beneath the ledge of the desk. Then I plucked a couple of books from the mahogany shelves and set them on the carpet where I thought the edge of the desk would come to rest.

Returning to the drawer side, I pushed the edge. The secretary desk tilted and balanced against the chair; the desk's front legs rose off the floor, exactly as I'd planned.

Rags sat up on his perch and eyeballed me.

"I've got it," I assured him as I skirted around the desk and gripped the desk's edge on the other side. After nudging the chair out of the way with my hip and heel, I guided the desk to the array of books I'd rested on the floor. Carefully, I slid the books out from under. The desk landed with a soft thud, its legs free. "Done, Ragsie. You can relax."

Rags settled back down.

I grabbed the power screwdriver, set it in reverse, and removed the screws of the uppermost left leg. I pulled the leg free and inspected the inside. Empty. I did the same with the uppermost right and lowermost right legs. All were empty. Frustration gripped me as I lit into the screws on the fourth leg. Had I been wrong? As the leg came off, I drew in a deep breath and peered inside. Something was in the leg, all right—stuffed way at the bottom. I turned the leg upside down and a shiny blue object about two inches long fell out. Elation swept through me. It had to be the thumb drive that I had seen Noelle pull from her computer. A thumb drive was a type of key. You slotted it into a hole; it opened up a set of files. Was there anything else in the leg? I fetched a flashlight and trained the beam down the inside. Papers clung to the sides. I turned the leg upside down again and shook. The papers didn't budge. I needed long—super-long—tweezers. I sprinted to the kitchen. Cooking tongs were too short, but a barbecue fork might be long enough. I grabbed it and raced back to the office.

I dropped to my knees and, carefully, so as not to poke holes in the paper, ran the fork along the inside of the leg. I twisted. I toyed. The papers loosened.

The front door squeaked opened, and I said, "In here," to Matthew.

I turned the leg on its end a second time, and papers spilled to the carpet. I stared at wine labels affixed to torn pages from Noelle's journals. I snatched them up and peered at the notes along the edges. On one she had written, *Phony, fresh, soft, no complexity.* On a second note she wrote: *Same as HBB at Le Parq.* Le Parq was one of the restaurants where she had worked as a sommelier. HBB? Haut-Brion Blanc, perhaps. And yet the label was a Shelton Nelson white Burgundy. Excitement jetted through me. Was I right? Had Shelton Nelson substituted his wine for a Haut-Brion Blanc? Was he counterfeiting wine? Had he made other switches? The labels, coupled with the information on the thumb drive, had to be what Noelle had referred to as *hell's* or *Shel's key,* a log or code breaker, if you will, of all his swaps.

"Hand those over," a woman said. Not a man. Not Matthew.

Rags leaped to the ground and ran to my side. Still perched on my knees, I gazed at Liberty Nelson, clad in an ecru turtleneck, jeans, and a caramel-colored leather coat. She stood beneath the arch, her arms limp at her sides, her face sallow and drawn. I thought of Alexis's warning to keep away from a person in sheep's clothing. Was Liberty the one Alexis had envisioned and not Shelton? Without her typical strut, Liberty appeared about as forbidding as a lamb.

"Give them to me." Liberty moved into the room, her hand extended.

"Do you know what they are?"

"Of course I do." She shook her hand. "I want them now."

"Why should I give them to you?"

"Because."

"Because you want to destroy them. If the police see

them, your winery will be ruined. Noelle knew what was
going on. You were pretending you had all the expensive
wines, but you had drunk them and put your own wines in
the bottles. You were selling counterfeited Haut-Brion Blanc
at auction."

Liberty didn't have a weapon that I could see. Maybe if I
acted reasonably, she would do the same. I set the barbecue
fork on the carpet and scrambled to my feet. "Your father's
treasure trove of wine is phony. Noelle found out. You saw
her sneaking around. You saw her writing notes in a journal.
You followed her to my house."

"That's not true."

"You killed her to keep the secret. Whether to protect the
winery's reputation or your inheritance, it doesn't matter.
You can't claim it was self-defense."

"It wasn't self-defense," a man said from the foyer.

Relief swept through me. Matthew had arrived. My calm
was short-lived.

Shelton Nelson strode through the doorway. In his shearling coat, jeans, boots, and cowboy hat, he appeared formi-
dable. "Don't say anything more, Liberty."

"Daddy." Liberty gulped. "What are you—"

"You were about to confess, weren't you? I knew it. That's
why I followed you."

"I can't keep the secret any longer, Daddy." Liberty sobbed.
"I told you if your lover found out about the phony wine, then
the vineyard would be ruined."

Lover, phony, charted for disaster.

"So it was true?" I said. "You and Noelle were lovers,
Shelton?"

"No." He grabbed Liberty's arm. "I've told you a dozen
times, you fool. Noelle and I were never involved."

"You wanted her," Liberty cried. "Everyone saw you
fawning over her. It made you blind to her plan."

Did Noelle play up the lover angle? Did she scam Shelton,
letting him think he had a chance with her so she could get
closer to the truth about his wines?

Liberty twisted free with a fierceness I hadn't expected

and dashed to me. "It wasn't my fault, Charlotte." She clutched my hands. "You've got to believe me."

Shelton growled. "Damn that darned fiancé of yours, Liberty. He's hypnotized you. He put you up to this. He wants you to cleanse your soul. He probably convinced you that Charlotte has pull with the police, and she'll be your advocate. Think again. You're as guilty as I am."

Liberty glanced over her shoulder. "I didn't kill Noelle, Daddy. You did." She turned back to me. "You're right. For years, Daddy has been filling empty rare French bottles with our wine and auctioning them at extravagant prices."

"Hush," Shelton ordered.

"Noelle figured it out. That's why she wanted the job. She needed evidence. I begged Daddy not to hire her, but he was in it for the game. He said if he could fool her, he could fool everyone. He got a kick out of hiding our wine in plain sight."

"I told you to stop talking, Liberty." Shelton took a menacing step toward his daughter, his hands balled into fists.

But Liberty continued, her words streaming together. "Mainly he sold the wines in China. It's a huge international scam."

"Shut your trap, girl."

"Bottles of Haut-Brion Blanc could go for thousands of dollars. We didn't try selling reds, only whites. The really savvy wine guys know the difference, but the general public doesn't. When the price of goods is expensive"—she wiggled her hand—"the buyer pretends to take more time to contemplate the purchase, but really they don't. Daddy collected Haut-Brion Blanc bottles for years. When those ran out, he found a talented glassblower who could duplicate the bottles with the crest. We put aged labels on them and sealed them with corks that we branded."

"We," Shelton brayed. "She said, 'We.' Did you hear her? She's in this as much as I am."

Liberty spun around; her curls whipped her face. "You killed Noelle, Daddy, to keep her from revealing your scheme."

Shelton's jaw twitched. "Charlotte, Liberty isn't right in the head. She's been under a lot of stress with the wedding."

"I'm fine, Daddy."

"Darlin', you seem to have forgotten that I have an alibi. You heard me singing in the shower. Maybe you lied because you were the one who was out of the house. Did you kill Noelle?"

I gaped. Would he turn the table on his own daughter? What kind of monster was he?

Liberty sputtered. "What? No, I don't lie. Never again. I made a vow to Leonard." Her fiancé. "You're the one that's lying." She shot a finger at her father. "I was home reading. And yes, I heard you singing, but . . ." She swung around to me. "It could have been a soundtrack."

I knew her guess was right. Shelton had built a recording studio in his office to make commercials. Why hadn't I considered that his alibi could be a recording? Or why hadn't Rebecca thought of the possibility? She always came up with off-the-wall theories like that.

Shelton scowled. "Liberty, darlin', think about what you're saying."

"I have. I am." She turned to me. "At first, I wasn't sure Daddy did it. I thought maybe that reporter or Noelle's ex-boyfriend killed her, so I kept quiet. But my fiancé"—she hiccupped—"told me I needed to face the truth, the whole truth . . ."

And nothing but the truth, so help you God.

I said, "The day we were at the winery, you argued with your father. You were trying to convince him to stop."

"Yes, yes, yes." Liberty whirled on her father. "Please stop, Daddy. Turn yourself in."

"Don't be an idiot," he said. "I won't throw away my business or ruin my reputation because you have a flash of conscience. Go out to my car and wait for me." He lasered me with an ominous gaze. What did he have in mind? Why, in heaven's name, had I set down the barbecue fork?

"No, Daddy." Liberty stamped her foot. "I'm not leaving Charlotte."

"What has gotten into you, girl? You are as guilty as I am. You are every bit a part of this operation."

"No-o-o-o." Liberty ran at her father.

He swung out, smashing her across the head with his forearm. She stumbled backward and crashed against the wall. She slumped to the floor.

"Liberty." I raced to her. Her chest was moving, but her head and neck were fixed at an awful angle and her eyes were closed; she seemed unconscious.

At the same time, footsteps pounded the foyer floor. "Charlotte," Matthew called as he charged into the office. "I heard a—"

Shelton wheeled backward and pulled a gun from his pocket. He aimed it at Matthew. "I didn't want to have to use this, but it seems I'm outnumbered."

I had assumed right the other day. Shelton was the kind of man to pack a pistol. He was, as Tyanne would say, all hat with no cattle.

Matthew held up his hands. "Whoa, Shelton, take a deep breath. What's going on?"

I quickly explained. Matthew whistled. "Noelle had documented evidence." I gestured to the thumb drive and the labels lying beside the secretary desk.

Shelton said, "Pick them up, Charlotte, and give them to me."

"No."

He brandished the gun. "Do it."

"I've called Chief Urso," Matthew said.

"Liar," Shelton said. "You had no reason to call him. You didn't know Liberty or I were coming here. You have nothing. I was trying to avoid any confrontation, but I can see that's impossible. This ends. Right here. Right now. The goods, Charlotte."

I inched across the room, trying to figure out what I could do to quash Shelton. Rags poked his head out from behind the desk. I gave him an eye signal to keep hidden. As I spied the detached legs near him, the memory of the twins racing around the theater's foyer, attacking each other with the fake roasted turkey leg, flickered through my mind, and an idea came to me.

"Matthew," I said. "Tell Shelton about all the pictures we took at the cellar when we stole in the other night."

"The pictures? Ah, the pictures," Matthew said, vamping. "Yes, we have dozens of photographs. Of documents. And wine bottles and your secret passage."

"Pictures won't prove anything."

"Sure they will."

I drew near to the desk. I crouched down, as if to pick up the thumb drive and labels. Instead, I grabbed the desk leg. Before Shelton realized what I'd done, I charged him, swinging the desk leg like a sledgehammer. He fired. Luckily for me he wasn't a crack shot. A bullet whizzed past me and spit into the wall.

I swung out and connected with Shelton's forearm. He yelped with pain. The gun flew out of his hand. Wielding the desk leg like a baseball bat, I hit his torso. He caved in on himself and dropped to his knees.

At the same time, Matthew crawled across the carpet and retrieved the gun. While he trained the weapon on Shelton, his hand trembling as much as mine would have, I dialed Urso.

For the first time in an eon, the man was happy to hear from me.

CHAPTER

Standing with my grandmother, Delilah, and Alexis in the doorway connecting the foyer and the theater of the Providence Playhouse, we watched the children take their bows onstage. What a difference ten days could make. The play was a smash hit. The flying duck had soared across the stage to wild applause.

"You look *très bonne, mon amie*," Grandmère said to me. "Rested."

"*Merci*."

"It's nice what you did for Noelle," Delilah said.

"Yes, putting together a funeral and burying her properly," Alexis said. "It helps the spirit move onward and upward." She clutched my forearm, and I felt a tingling of something shimmy all the way to the roots of my hair. "Good things are coming for you, too, Charlotte. You'll see."

"Mother, stop." Delilah peeled her mother's hand off of me. "Charlotte's fine."

I knew, now, that I couldn't have saved Noelle. She had set her own drama in action, but at least she could rest in peace;

her sacrifice was not in vain. She had stopped a scam, one that could have damaged the reputation of so many of Providence's vintners. I had to admit that, because of my involvement in the resolution, I felt stronger than I ever had. Surviving a confrontation with Shelton Nelson that had turned from verbal to physical in a matter of seconds made me a little giddy, almost jubilant. When I arrived at The Cheese Shop the next morning, Rebecca smacked my shoulder with pride. I was growing into a smart sleuth, she told me. What she didn't add, and didn't realize, was that something in me had changed. I didn't feel like my impulses controlled me any longer; I felt clearheaded and discerning. I liked the transformation.

As for Shelton Nelson, he was officially charged with Noelle's murder. Liberty, although she had been aware of her father's deception, would be released from the hospital, once she was given the doctor's okay, and would serve two hundred hours of community service. Her fiancé had enlisted the swift help of a powerful lawyer. The Shelton Nelson Winery, according to rumors, was already up for sale. Supposedly, Harold's paramour had put in the first bid. Harold's wife, Velma, had filed for divorce.

"Delilah! Bernadette! Delilah! Bernadette!" the audience chanted.

I nudged them. "Go. Get onstage with the children. Your fans await you."

Both glowed with pride as they hurried down the aisle toward the stage.

"Oh, there's Lois," Alexis said, breaking away from me. "I have a man I want her to meet." She trotted away.

"*Chérie.*" Pépère appeared and steered me toward the banquet table set up in the foyer. "Let us prepare for the *charge.*"

"It will not be an onslaught," I said. "The children know the rules."

"*Oui,* but the adults do not." He chuckled. "And the food smells so good."

Grandmère had arranged for a pre-Thanksgiving banquet

that included appetizers galore, turkey potpie, sweet potato tartlets, cornbread, and a veggie platter complete with a turkey-shaped centerpiece made of fresh vegetables.

The applause inside the theater died down, and attendees started to file into the foyer.

"Oh no," Pépère said as he fiddled with a cheese platter.

"What?" I asked. "Didn't I bring enough cheese?" I had sliced an assortment thinly, laid the choices in two S-curves down a white oval platter, and added mounds of gluten-free crackers, green grapes, almonds, and a pot of apricot preserves.

"There is never enough cheese, but that is not my concern." He pointed. "What is she doing here?"

Outside the theater, Prudence Hart, wearing a DayGlo red suit, marched in front of the theater while pumping a protest sign that read: *Do Not Support Sylvie Bessette. She is evil!!!!*

"Don't worry." I petted his cheek. "Prudence won't attack anyone. She is simply utilizing her freedom of speech rights. Many would applaud her."

He ogled me.

"One voice will not ruin this evening," I continued. "I promise. Ignore her. Prudence will tire of her protest and retreat. She's merely upset because Sylvie was able to convince the town council to vote against Prudence's expansion plans."

"But I heard that she was able to seal the deal on two shops."

I giggled. *Seal the deal.* My grandparents loved what they liked to call Americanisms. "No, I don't think so."

"Charlotte, love." Sylvie broke from the pack of theatergoers, and I bit back a smile. Where did she find her clothes? I mean, really. She was wearing a floor-length, Dracula-style black cape with a pointy red collar. If she opened her mouth and I spotted fangs, I might scream. "Weren't my girlie-girls fabulous?"

"Everyone was," I said. "Um, where's your date?"

"Date?" She waved a hand that sported long bloodred nails. Had she missed Halloween? "Who needs a date when I've got my talented girlie-girls?"

"No date?"

"I've sworn off men. They are lying, cheating—"

"Not all," I said.

"Oh, but of course. I forgot you have snared the dream man of the century. Except he is in absentia, isn't he?"

Her potshot zinged me right where she had intended. Given my newfound confidence, however, I refused to give her that kind of power. I smiled.

Sylvie looked past me and gasped. "Is that Prudence protesting outside? No, no, no. She will not ruin my daughters' night." With the swiftness of a raptor, she collected her cape and flew through the foyer and into the cold after her prey.

The drama that ensued, with both women finger pointing, reminded me of two fierce beasts having at it. If I could have gotten away with it, I would have sold tickets and donated the proceeds to the theater fund.

"Charlotte." Rebecca sashayed to me looking as pretty as I had ever seen her, with her long hair loose and her slim figure dressed in a maroon sweater dress. Over her shoulder, I spied both the deputy and the honeybee farmer ogling her with interest. She hadn't attended the play with either of them, but I had no doubt that the remainder of the night would include some heavy-duty flirting. "I've been thinking about the shop. There are some changes we should make to draw in new customers."

"Not tonight, Rebecca." Meredith wedged in between us. "No business talk."

"Just a little," Rebecca said.

"Uh-uh." Meredith clutched my hand and squeezed. I returned the gesture. We could never be mad at each other for long. Thankfully, Matthew had no lingering side effects from the beating he had taken at the winery. The fact that he had aided me in the capture of Shelton Nelson and was fast becoming a local hero didn't hurt, either. "I'm here on a mission," Meredith continued. "The chief wants a word with you." She tilted her head.

Urso stood across the foyer looking slightly uncomfortable in his brown suit.

I sauntered to him, my shoulders back, my chin held high. When he had arrived at my house after Matthew and I captured Shelton Nelson, he was terse. Yet again, he protested my involvement in the case, but when I explained that I did not deliberately summon Liberty or Shelton to my doorstep— I was merely trying to find the evidence that Noelle had hidden so I could hand it over to the police—he cut me a little slack. I hadn't seen him since he put Liberty into an ambulance and hauled Shelton to the precinct.

"Hi, Chief," I said.

"No more U-ey?"

"I should show you more respect."

His eyes sparkled with humor. "Yes, you should, but you won't."

"I've changed."

"Ha! How about calling me Chief Urso whenever we're involved in an investigation, which I hope is never again."

I heard the slip. He had said *we*. I ignored it. "Any word on your brother's running for election?"

"He's still considering."

"And you? Will you help with the campaign?"

"Other than the job, there's not much that holds me here in Providence."

I felt a pang in my stomach; I was pretty sure it was hunger.

He slipped his hands into his pockets. "But enough about me. Right now, I think you have a visitor."

I pivoted and delight whooped out of me. Jordan was strolling through the front door looking as handsome as I had ever seen him. Crisp white shirt. Slim blue jeans. A relaxed smile. He strode forward, arms outstretched, and drew me into an embrace. The scent of him was delicious, like honey and pine all mixed into one. He kissed my hair, my forehead, my mouth. When we came up for air, he whispered into my ear, "I'm free."

I pressed apart, keeping hold of his arms, and gazed into his eyes. "What are you saying?"

"The trial is over. Weeks sooner than expected. We won.

The man I testified against is going away for life, with no possibility of parole."

"Is there an enforcer he might send after you?"

"They don't know my name. They don't know where I live."

"But the tentacles of all of those inmates." My stomach panged again, this time with fear.

"It's over, Charlotte. Trust me." He hugged me and twirled me around so fast my feet flew off the ground. "Now, let's plan that wedding."

RECIPES

Chopped Salad

(MAKES 2 ENTRÉE-SIZE OR 4 DINNER-SIZE SALADS)

Salad:

¼ pound salami, cubed or sliced
¼ pound mozzarella cheese, cubed
6–12 baby tomatoes
6–12 pitted green olives
4–8 artichoke quarters (in their own oil or water)
4 tablespoons red onion, shredded
¼ cup garbanzo beans (may use kidney beans)
2 cups chopped Romaine lettuce

Dressing:

1 teaspoon sugar
⅛ teaspoon salt
¼ cup white wine vinegar
⅛ cup extra virgin olive oil
Cracked black pepper (3–6 grinds of the peppermill)
2 teaspoons fresh basil (or 1 teaspoon dried basil)

For the salad, arrange lettuce, cheese, salami, tomatoes, olives, onion, beans, and artichokes on a plate.

For the dressing, mix sugar, salt, vinegar, olive oil, and

pepper. Snip the basil using kitchen shears. Add the basil to the mixture. Drizzle the dressing over the salad mixture.

Serve cold.

[Note from Charlotte: This is so easy, Clair and Amy were able to make it without any supervision. Enjoy the combo of flavors. Divine.]

* * *

Delilah's Grilled Cheese with Bacon & Fig Jam

(SERVES 2)

4 slices bread
3–4 tablespoons butter
3–4 tablespoons cream cheese
2 tablespoons fig jam or preserves
4 ounces (4 slices) Swiss cheese
4 slices bacon, cooked crisply and crumbled
2 tablespoons scallions, diced

For each sandwich, butter two slices of bread on one side. Flip the bread over and spread cream cheese on the other side of the bread. Now, spread the cream cheese side of the bread with fig jam. Place a slice of Swiss cheese on top of the jam.

On two of the cheese-bread combos, add the cooked bacon, dividing equally, and then the chopped scallions. Top with the other cheese-bread combo.

Heat up a flat grilling pan or a panini grill. Place the sandwiches on the grill. [If using a grilling pan, grill the sandwich on low to medium for 4 minutes. Flip the sandwich and grill for another 4, until the bread is a nice golden brown and cheese is oozing. If using a panini grill, cook the sandwich for a total of 4 minutes, until the bread is a nice golden brown.]

Remove from heat and serve immediately.

[**Note from Delilah:** *This can be made on gluten-free bread; it is still amazing. Also, if you prefer another jam, feel free to use it. It's the combination of the salty with the sweet that matters.]*

* * *

Turkey Chèvre Pizza à la Pépère

1 10–12 inch round pizza crust
½ pound ground turkey
2 shallots, peeled and sliced
2–3 tablespoons olive oil
2–3 ounces chèvre cheese
1 teaspoon salt
1 tablespoon dried rosemary
1 tablespoon dried oregano
Dash of paprika

Bake pizza crust at 450 degrees F for 10 minutes. *If you prefer to make the pizza crust from a mix rather than use a pre-made crust, follow the instructions given by maker.*

While pizza is baking, in a sauté pan over medium heat, cook the ground turkey and sliced shallots. Stir occasionally so the turkey doesn't overcook, about 4–5 minutes. Drain on paper towels.

Remove pizza from oven and drizzle with the 2–3 tablespoons of olive oil. Sprinkle with salt.

Arrange the turkey and shallots on the pizza. Crumble the chèvre cheese and scatter on top of the turkey. Sprinkle with rosemary, oregano, and paprika.

Bake in oven for 10 minutes until cheese melts and turns golden.

Serve immediately.

[Note from Pépère: Feel free to use more chèvre. When it comes to a pizza, it is all about the flavors that the chef prefers.]

* * *

Chocolate Cherry Mascarpone Bars

(MAKES 12–16)

1½ cups all-purpose flour
¾ cup good-quality cocoa powder
1 teaspoon salt
1 teaspoon baking soda
1 stick butter, softened
¾ cup granulated sugar
¾ cup packed brown sugar
1 large egg
1 teaspoon vanilla extract
½ cup mascarpone cheese
10 ounces dark chocolate chips
1 cup tart pitted cherries (canned in water; water drained)

Preheat oven to 375 degrees F.

Combine flour, cocoa powder, salt, and baking soda in a small bowl and set aside.

In a medium bowl, using a mixer, combine butter and sugars. Add egg, vanilla, and mascarpone cheese, and combine. Slowly, in batches, add the flour mixture until just combined.

Chop the cherries in a food processor. One cup of cherries

will reduce in size to approximately ½ cup. Drain off excess liquid.

Stir the chocolate and cherries into the flour mixture. It is a stiff dough.

Press the mixture into a greased 13" x 9" pan.

Bake 25–30 minutes, or until top is still soft looking. Rotate the pan halfway through the baking process.

Remove the pan from the oven and let the bars cool completely before slicing. [The texture is like a gooey, chewy brownie.]

[*Note from Charlotte: You might not be able to see the cherries once these are baked, but you can sure taste them!*]

* * *

Chocko-Socko Cheesecake

SERVES 8–12

1 pound (16 ounces) ricotta cheese
¼ cup rice flour
½ teaspoon xanthan gum
4 egg yolks
½ cup sugar
1 tablespoon lemon juice
½ teaspoon vanilla
½ teaspoon salt
1 pound (16 ounces) cream cheese
½ cup sour cream
4 egg whites (no yolks!)
½ cup MORE sugar
½ cup crushed chocolate cream cookies
2 tablespoons butter

Topping:

> *4 extra tablespoons sour cream*
> *1–2 tablespoons cocoa powder*
> *½ cup chocolate chips*

Preheat oven to 300 degrees F.

Line a springform pan with parchment paper. You might want to rub a little butter on the bottom of the pan to hold the paper.

In a large bowl, mix ricotta cheese, rice flour, xanthan gum, egg yolks, ½ cup sugar, lemon juice, vanilla, and salt until well blended.

Add cream cheese and sour cream and mix well.

In a small bowl, mix separately: egg whites (with no egg yolks in them) and ½ cup MORE sugar until the egg whites form a soft peak (about 6–8 minutes).

Fold the egg white mixture gently into the cheese mixture.

In a springform pan, lay out the crushed chocolate cream cookies on top of the parchment paper. Drizzle with 2 tablespoons butter and press with your fingertips to create a "crust." Pour cheese mixture on top of cookie crust.

Bake at 300 degrees F for 1–1¼ hour. Let STAND IN OVEN, with the oven turned off, for 2 hours so the cheesecake will set. This will prevent drooping in the middle of the cake.

Remove cake from the oven. Let cool another hour. Run a knife around the cake and remove the springform pan. Then run a knife between the parchment paper and the bottom of the springform pan. Slide the cake onto a cake plate.

To decorate the cake, spread the extra 4 tablespoons of sour cream onto the top of the cake. Sprinkle cocoa on the sour cream and dot with chocolate chips. Store the cake in the refrigerator. Serve cold.

[Note from Rebecca: *This is the cheesecake I always order when I go to Café au Lait coffee shop. It is packed with choco-*

laty goodness. Also, I found out the shop occasionally makes this using gluten-free chocolate cream cookies for the crust so people with celiac disease can eat it. Matthew's daughter Clair told me. How nice is that!]

* * *

Roquefort Bosc Pear Quiche

(SERVES 6)

> 1 pie shell (homemade or frozen)
> 2–3 ounces (about ⅓ cup) Roquefort cheese (or good blue cheese)
> ½ cup whipping cream
> 3 eggs
> ¼ cup sour cream
> 1½ cups milk
> Pinch: nutmeg, cinnamon, and ginger
> Pinch: salt and pepper
> 1 Bosc pear, peeled, sliced
> 1 teaspoon honey

Remove the Roquefort cheese from the refrigerator and bring to room temperature.

Preheat the oven to 425 degrees F.

Bake the pie shell for 12–14 minutes until lightly golden. Remove from oven. Let cool. Reduce the oven to 375 degrees F.

Meanwhile, in a medium-sized bowl, mush the Roquefort cheese with 2 tablespoons of the whipping cream. Add the rest of the cream and beat for 1 minute.

Add the eggs and beat until the mixture is blended, but not whipped to a froth. Add the sour cream, milk, and spices, and mix until blended.

Peel, core, and slice the Bosc pear into 6–8 slices. Arrange the slices on the bottom of the baked pie shell. Drizzle with honey. Put the pan on a baking sheet. Stir the egg and cream mixture once, then pour the mixture on top of the pears. Carefully move the baking sheet to the oven.

Bake the quiche in a 375 degree F oven for 30–35 minutes or until it is puffy and lightly browned on top.

Remove from oven and cool slightly for about 10 minutes. Serve warm.

*[**Note from Charlotte:** I simply had to make this quiche. There's almost nothing better than a pairing of blue cheese or Roquefort and pears.]*

Dear Reader,

Do you love books? Do you love to eat? I adore both, which is why I write culinary mysteries. My latest dip into the tasty world of food is the Cookbook Nook Mysteries, which I am writing under my real name, Daryl Wood Gerber. The series has debuted to rave reviews. In Final Sentence, *the first book in the Cookbook Nook Mysteries, Jenna Hart, a successful advertising executive, leaves the high-pressure corporate world to help her aunt open a culinary bookshop and café in Crystal Cove, California, which is a lovely seaside town south of San Francisco and north of Monterey.*

Turn the page for a special preview of the second installment, Inherit the Word, *which debuts in March 2014. It's hard for Jenna to follow a simple recipe for relaxation when murder gets thrown in the mix.*

I hope you will join Jenna, her family, and friends, as Jenna figures out whodunnit. Perhaps you'll even find the title of a new cookbook or a great recipe to share with friends.

For those of you who love the Cheese Shop Mysteries, don't dismay. I will be continuing that series, too. The next installment is titled As Gouda as Dead, *coming soon from Berkley Prime Crime.*

Say Cheese!

Avery aka Daryl

I clambered down the ladder in the storeroom of The Cookbook Nook, carrying a stack of cookie cookbooks in my arms. My foot hit something soft. I shrieked. Tigger, a stray kitten that had scampered into my life and won my heart a month ago, yowled. His claws skittered beneath him as he dashed from my path.

"Shh, Tigger. Hush, baby." I had barely touched him with my toe. I knew he wasn't hurt. "C'mere, little guy." I arrived at the floor, knelt down, and spied him hunkering beneath the ladder, staring at me with his wide eyes. "It's okay," I cooed. As I scooped him up, one-armed, and nuzzled his neck, I felt a cool stream of the unknowable course its way up my spine. Tigger was a ginger-striped tabby, not a black cat. Passing beneath a ladder wasn't a bad omen, was it? Why did I suddenly feel like seven years of bad luck was lurking in the shadows?

"Miss Jenna, yoo-hoo," a girl squealed. "Miss Jenna, come quick!"

Fear ticked inside me. We had invited children to The

Cookbook Nook for a cookie-decorating event—my Aunt Vera's idea. She was a master cookie baker herself, with an extensive personal collection of cookie cookbooks. Did one of the children get hurt? Was that the dark cloud I'd sensed in the storeroom? I raced into the shop and skidded to a slippery halt in my flip-flops.

"Look at my killer shark." The girl with frothy orange hair was standing beside the tot-height table in the children's corner, brandishing a deep blue, shark-shaped cookie.

Nothing amiss. Kids being kids. No one hurt. *Thank the breezes*, as my mother used to say.

I steadied my racing heart and said, "Cool cookie." I set the cookbooks on the sales counter, then put Tigger on the floor and gave his bottom a push. Brave feline, he meandered beneath the children's table, probably hoping to score a crumb. "But please, kids, call me Jenna. Not Miss Jenna. I'm not a teacher."

The girl's father frowned. Guess he preferred decorum. I wasn't so hot on it. I liked to live fast and loose . . . sort of.

"But you're so tall," the girl said.

I grinned. I wasn't an Amazon, but at five-eight, I was slightly taller than her doughy father. "Just because I'm tall doesn't make me a teacher."

"If you say so."

The first Friday of September was a perfect time in Crystal Cove to invite children to a cookie-decorating class. The weather hovered in the low seventies. Nearly every day by midmorning, the sun shone brightly. And school and homework hadn't taken over the kids' total concentration quite yet. For the class, in addition to ordering a fresh batch of cookie cookbooks like *The All-American Cookie Book*, *Betty Crocker The Big Book of Cookies*, and *Simply Sensational Cookies*, we had stocked up on fun cookie-decorating sets complete with squeezable icing bottles and interchangeable design tips. Our theme for today's class was creatures of the deep.

"Did you bake the cookies, Jenna?" one of the parents asked.

"Me? What a laugh." I was barely adept at making cookie batter—my limit of ingredients for recipes was a *daring* total of seven—but as an occasional artist, I embraced piping icing out of a squeeze bottle.

"Miss Jenna, look at my octopus." A boy with gigantic freckles wiggled his green, gooey octopus cookie in the air, and then shoved his gruesome creation toward the face of the frothy-haired girl. She squeaked.

Aunt Vera, a flamboyant sixty-something and co-owner of The Cookbook Nook, moved to my side, the fabric of her exotic caftan billowing and falling. "Don't you love kids?"

Me? I adored them. Except for the time I did an ad campaign at Taylor & Squibb, my previous employer, for Dabble Doodles. A few prankster boys squeezed the contents of their glue and glitter pens onto the girls' clothing and—*gag me*—hair. Parents were livid.

"Yoo-hoo, Jenna. Kids?" my aunt repeated.

"Uh, sure. Love 'em." I didn't want any of my own. Not yet. I wasn't quite thirty. And a widow. Timing was everything. I said, "Absolutely. How about you?"

She chuckled while adjusting the silver bejeweled turban on her head—my aunt would prefer giving tarot card readings to figuring out how to market our joint enterprise. "I would have loved to have a dozen. Just like you."

"Aw. I love you, too." My aunt, on my father's side, had doted on me from the day I was born. When I moved back to Crystal Cove to help her open the cookbook shop, she offered me the cottage beside her beach house. I felt blessed to have her in my life, especially with my mother gone.

"While the kiddies finish up," Aunt Vera said, "let's discuss the town's other ventures for this month."

"As far as I know, the mayor has planned a dozen new events for September, including a Frisbee contest, a paddle boarding race, and Movie Night on the Strand." Crystal Cove was a lovely seaside town on the coast of California with beautiful rolling hills to the east and a glorious stretch of ocean running the length of the town to the west. The mayor of our fair city was always on the lookout for events that would lure tourists. "To pay tribute to the events the mayor has fashioned, I've ordered dozens of new cookbooks with beach and/or movie themes."

"Ooh, lovely. You've included *The Beach House Cookbook*, I assume?"

"I have." *The Beach House Cookbook* had beautiful photographs of food and the seaside. In our business, cookbooks with enticing pictures were guaranteed sales. I still couldn't believe it, but some people bought cookbooks merely to peruse. Prior to my new enterprise, I was a function and use person. If it didn't have a function, I didn't use it. "I've also brought in *At Blanchard's Table: A Trip to the Beach Cookbook*." This particular cookbook included recipes that were as delicious as they were simple. Prosciutto bundles? Balsamic goat cheese? They sounded easy enough that even I could make them. "Also, I ordered *Good Fish: Sustainable Seafood Recipes from the Pacific Coast*." The Seattle-based author of *Good Fish* was a seafood advocate who really educated her readers. I especially loved that she had brought in another knowledgeable source to pair the fish with wine.

"That title's a mouthful."

"Between you, me, and the lamppost," I said, "some titles on cookbooks go on forever."

"They do, but competition is fierce and specificity matters. An unpretentious title like *Good Food* won't light a fire under the audience intended."

My aunt was right. She was always right. She knew cookbooks backward and forward. Me? I was just getting the hang of how popular they were. At my aunt's behest, a couple of months ago I returned to Crystal Cove to run The Cookbook Nook and café because, well, my life in San Francisco, as I'd dreamed it, was over. I needed a new beginning. My aunt needed a marketing whiz.

"I love what you've done in the bay window," Aunt Vera said.

Our store was one of many in the Fisherman's Village complex. The bay window faced the parking lot and was our first calling card to passersby. In keeping with the town's monthly events, I had set out a seaside-themed display, complete with bright yellow oars, aqua blue Frisbees, and coral and white sand toys. Near the decorative kitchen items that we carried, I had set up our movie-themed display, which included the women's fiction books *Chocolat* and *Like Water for Chocolate,* both of which had been made into movies, and a mystery series about a cheese shop, which I heard might become a television show à la *Murder, She Wrote.*

"Jenna." My best friend and new assistant in the store, Bailey Bird—Minnie Mouse in size and Mighty Mouse in energy—hurried into the shop. "Whee. You'll never guess."

"What's with you?" I grinned.

"No caffeine. For twenty-four hours. I feel so-o-o good."

I liked a cup of coffee each morning, something with a little zip, but I didn't drink it throughout the day. Bailey, on the other hand, nursed a coffee or cola about every two hours. She was off the stuff? When would she crash? My aunt gave me a worried look and began to rub the phoenix amulet she wore around her neck.

"Listen. Listen." Bailey spun in a circle. The skirt of her silky halter dress fluted around her well-formed calves. Sun streaming in the big plate-glass windows highlighted her short copper hair. "I just spoke with the mayor, and she wants us."

"For what?"

"To hold the Grill Fest."

"But Brick's always hosts the Grill Fest." Brick's was a barbecue restaurant about a half mile from Fisherman's Village.

"Brick's is going under. It just declared bankruptcy."

"How horrible."

"It is, isn't it? Tragic. However, the mayor doesn't want to delay the four-day fest. She's afraid that could hurt the town's economy," Bailey rushed on. "Tourism—"

"Can't afford any setbacks," I finished, quoting the mayor.

"It takes money to run this place, she says. The squeaky wheel gets the biggest piece of the pie."

"Excuse me?"

"The mayor messed up the wording, not I."

Our mayor, a frizzy bundle of raw energy, was nothing if not Crystal Cove proactive. Without tourists and the taxes they paid, how else could we finance our infrastructure? Only a few thousand people, including part-timers, lived here. Though many residents had incomes well above normal, the town couldn't manage to maintain the elaborate maze of windy roads, the parks, the aquarium, the junior college that offered a specialized degree in the study of grapes, and The Pier, which was a major go-to spot, complete with a boardwalk, restaurants, stores, and more.

"I suggested we have the Grill Fest at the shop," Bailey said, polishing her fingernails on her silky bodice. "I said, 'Jenna and Vera will think it's a fabulous idea.' You do, don't you? Think it's a good idea?" She slurped in an excited breath.

The contest consisted of four rounds, eight contestants. All contestants would participate in the opening round. After each round, judges would make their determinations, and two contestants would be eliminated, until only two contestants remained. They would vie for the grand prize—a medal and boasting rights.

"Well?" Bailey said.

My aunt and I nodded. How could we disappoint her?

"We can set up portable cooking stations, like we do for cooking classes," Bailey continued. "We'll ask the kitchen shop down the way to provide the tools and grills or sauté pans, depending on a contestant's preference. Think of the traffic. The cross-promotion. The conflict. The press."

Last year's Grill Fest had garnered all sorts of media coverage thanks to one contestant—the winner for eight straight years—who lambasted the runner-up for her grilled steak recipe. They ended up in a spatula fight. Someone had filmed the spectacle, which went viral on YouTube.

"And think of all the grilling cookbooks we can stock, like *Simply Grilling: 105 Recipes for Quick and Casual Grilling*," Bailey said, the title tripping easily off her tongue.

See what I mean about long book titles?

"The author not only gives a clear account of the types of grilling and the utensils needed," Bailey continued, "but she also includes a recipe for one of my all-time favorite foods, Buffalo Sliders with Blue Cheese Slaw. And the pictures? Family-style adorable." Bailey had a mind like a steel trap. She could probably recite the contents of every book in the shop.

"What's this year's challenge?" I asked.

"Grilled cheese."

Aunt Vera applauded. "Yum. We'll serve delectable sandwiches at the Nook Café." The café was an adjunct to The Cookbook Nook. During the opening month, we hadn't landed on a name for the café, and then we settled on the obvious. "Folks will flock to us for lunch and dinner. Ka-ching." My aunt was not interested in money. She had plenty because, years ago, she had invested wisely in the stock market. But she was all about bragging rights. She took great pride in our tasty enterprise.

"Ka-ching is right," Bailey said. She was all about dollar signs. Back at Taylor & Squibb, Bailey, who had been in charge of monitoring on-air, magazine, and Internet campaigns, would visit my office daily and give me a rundown of our earnings. Not our, as in Taylor & Squibb, but *our*, as in ours. Hers and mine. Every Christmas she found out early, down to the penny, what we were earning for our holiday bonuses. She needed to because she had to budget for her monthly clothes-buying sprees.

"Meow!" Tigger raced from beneath the cookie preparation table and leaped onto the counter by the register.

"I didn't do it." The freckle-faced boy threw his hands in the air, which of course meant he had done whatever *it* was.

I hurried to the counter and scooped up Tigger, a new wave of anxiety gushing through me. "Shh, fella. You're okay. Why are you so jumpy today?" I checked him out, making sure he didn't have icing in his eyes or ears—he didn't—and breathed a sigh of relief. I frowned at the boy, whose mother was giving him a quiet talking-to. I imagined pulling a cat's tail had been one of his crimes. He nodded obediently to her, but I could see he was holding back giggles.

As I set Tigger on the ground and encouraged him to be brave and mingle with the public again, I heard a jingle.

"Phone's ringing," Bailey said as she sidled behind me to set down her things.

I rummaged through my purse, which I had stowed on a shelf beneath the antique National cash register, and retrieved my cell phone. The readout said: *Whitney*. Wholesome, wondrous Whitney. My sister was brilliant at most things, but being a home business entrepreneur, she was a little dim when it came to knowing the hours other people kept at work. I asked Bailey to mind the shop, then sneaked to the storage room with my cell phone and pressed Send. "Hey, Sis. I can't talk right now. We have a kids' soiree going on." Not to mention a café to run and more cookbooks to inventory.

"Jenna Starrett Hart, listen up."

I was single when I had established myself in my advertising career. After David and I got married, I decided not to change my surname to his, Harris. Hart . . . Harris. People would get confused.

"Jenna," my sister barked.

"Don't have a tizzy." I laughed. I loved pushing my sister's buttons. "What's up?"

"You know I'm here in Crystal Cove."

"No." If she was checking up on me after my encounter with a murderer last month, I was going to clock her. I didn't need a reminder. I had put the past behind me. And I could clock her. I had six inches on her and a lot more hard-earned muscle, especially since I'd returned to a daily routine of running on the beach.

"Well, I am. I'm at the Seaside Bakery on The Pier getting the cake for Dad's surprise party tonight. You know it's tonight, right?"

I would if she would clue me in. To anything. Ever. Well-meaning, warped Whitney. All my life I'd slung *W* adjectives together for my sister. She did the same for me. Jazzy, jittery Jenna. Luckily I didn't have plans.

"Anyway," my sister continued. "I need you to pick up—"
She halted then screeched. "Omigosh!"

"What?

"Get down here. Right. Now."

"No need to shout. Where are you?"

"The Seaside Bakery. Aren't you listening? I mean it.
Come right now. And bring Bailey. Her mom, Lola. I think
she's going to throw a punch."

Ellery Adams serves up another
mystery that's a real peach...

FROM
ELLERY ADAMS

Peach Pies and Alibis
A Charmed Pie Shoppe Mystery

Ella Mae LeFaye's Charmed Pie Shoppe is wildly popular.
Not surprising since Ella Mae can lace her baked goods with
enchantments. But when she's asked to handle the dessert
buffet at a wedding, and a guest becomes seriously ill, she'll
have to use all of her skills to prove her pies didn't contain
a killer ingredient.

Includes pie recipes!

PRAISE FOR THE CHARMED PIE SHOPPE MYSTERIES

"[A] delicious, delightful, and deadly new series."
—Jenn McKinlay, *New York Times* bestselling author

"Enchanting! The Charmed Pie Shoppe
has cast its spell on me!"
—Krista Davis, national bestselling author of
the Domestic Diva Mysteries

elleryadamsmysteries.com
facebook.com/ellery.adams
facebook.com/TheCrimeSceneBooks
penguin.com

M1361T0813